ECHOES

OF

TREASON

DEREK BIRKS

PRAISE FOR THE CRAFT OF KINGS SERIES

'Derek Birks has taken his usual high standard of storytelling to a whole new level. **Scars From the Past** is impossible to put down... I defy you to enjoy this book and not want to go back to **Feud**, where it all started.'
The Review

'As with all good historical fiction, the reader learns fascinating period detail, while being entertained by an experienced author who knows his trade.'
Historical Novels Review

'I have to say, Derek Birks has done it again! **The Blood of Princes** is a masterpiece of adventure and intrigue.' *Sharon Bennett Connolly*

PRAISE FOR THE REBELS AND BROTHERS SERIES

'From the eye-catching cover to the last page, **Feud** is an exciting story of survival through personal upheaval during a vicious war, where the outcome is not always certain.' *Historical Novel Society*

'It is well written, full of action and the picture of fifteenth century life is skilfully woven by the author. Thoroughly recommended.' *Historical Novel Society on* **Kingdom of Rebels**

'This magnificent story captures life in the 15th Century with wonderful skill.' *Helen Hollick*

'It is impossible not to feel invested in the characters - they are flawed and damaged, but trying their best to survive and you find yourself willing them on.' *The Review*

Also by Derek Birks:

Rebels and Brothers Series

Feud

A Traitor's Fate

Kingdom of Rebels

The Last Shroud

The Craft of Kings Series

Scars from the Past

The Blood of Princes

5

For my sister-in-law, Yvonne Thompson, who has always been an interested and enthusiastic supporter.

DEREK BIRKS

Acknowledgements

I would like to acknowledge the debt owed to my creative team for their constructive suggestions, astute observations and all round support. I am fortunate to have a talented graphic designer, Katie, to produce such a stunning cover design. Many thanks also to Sharon Bennett Connolly for joining my small, but perfectly formed, team.

I am grateful to the staff of Poole Museum and nearby Scaplen's Court for their help in my research.

Finally, as always, I must thank Janet for her long-suffering support – and for joining me, with several other members of the family, in exploring what little remains of fifteenth century Poole and Studland.

DEREK BIRKS

CONTENTS

DEREK BIRKS

The Players in Echoes of Treason

For those readers who like a handy checklist of characters, this is for you.

The Elders

Lord John Elder, outlawed and exiled head of the family

Lady Margaret (Meg) Elder, John's young stepsister

Lady Eleanor Elder, John's aunt

Will Coster, Eleanor's son and John's cousin

Lady Katharine (Kate) Elder, Eleanor's daughter

Lady Emma Radcliffe, Eleanor's sister, also John's aunt

Alice Radcliffe, aka Isabel of Coverham, Lady Emma's bastard daughter

Master Hooper, trusted man of Lady Emma Radcliffe

Master Grim, trusted man of Lady Emma Radcliffe

John Elder's household

Hal, an archer and loyal retainer of the Elders

Thomas Skirett, a London youth beloved of Meg Elder

Conal, an Irish ex-mercenary

Alain, a Breton archer in John's service

Monk, a former priest, now a man at arms

Lady Eleanor's household

Augustine Grave, a former agent of Edward IV who is Lady Eleanor's lover

Mary, servant to Lady Eleanor

Peter, aka 'Spindle', Londoner, servant to Lady Eleanor

Sarah, aka 'Jug', a former London whore, now servant to Lady Eleanor

The agents of King Richard III
    William Catesby, an ambitious lawyer and one of the king's chief advisers
    Geoffrey Fisher, agent of William Catesby
    Elizabeth [Bess] Fisher, agent of William Catesby
    Walter Nevil, agent of William Catesby
    Seth & Tom Snagg, agents of William Catesby

Leading Nobles & Gentry
    Henry Tudor, Earl of Richmond, Lancastrian heir, exiled in Brittany
    Lady Margaret Stanley, wife of Lord Thomas Stanley; mother of Henry Tudor
    Jasper Tudor, Earl of Pembroke, Henry's uncle, also in Brittany
Others
    James Finch, ship's master of the Catherine
    Matthew Finch, his son, ship's master of the Margaret
    René de Merckes, Breton pirate, trader and mercenary
    Elias Slade, smuggler, thief and former enemy of the Elders
    Diggory Clynt, smuggler and trader sailing out of Poole
    Sir Simon Cayne, keeper of Handfast Castle on Studland
    Roger Cayne, Simon's younger brother, the Mayor of Poole
    Richard Morton, Thomas Audley, John Cheverell & William Twynho, leading Dorset rebels
    George Palmer, Sir Simon's servant
    Cradoc, a Welsh captain of the Earl of Pembroke

Maps

Poole
in 1483
WEST STREET
FIELDS
MARKET STREET
FIELDS
St. James
CHURCH STREET
Priests' House
HIGH STREET
WETLANDS
GATE
Mayor Cayne's
Town House
Docks
THAMES STREET
BAITER
Wool House
Water Gate
QUAY
POOLE HARBOUR
KEY
MUD AT LOW TIDE
TOWN WALL & DITCH
WATER LINE

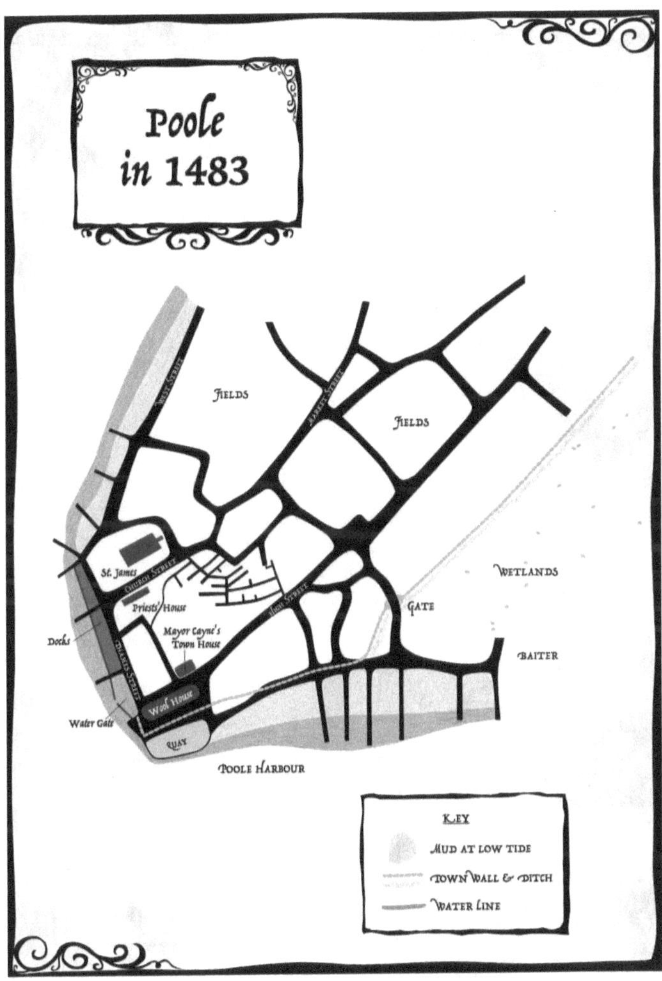

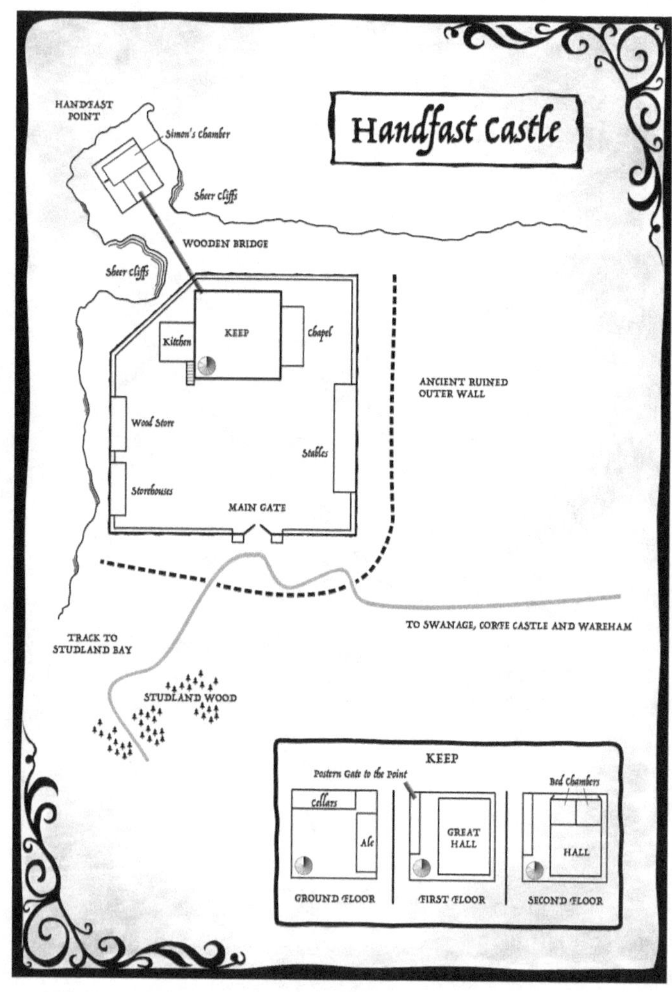
HANDFAST POINT
Simon's Chamber
Sheer cliffs
Handfast Castle
WOODEN BRIDGE
Sheer cliffs
Kitchen
KEEP
Chapel
ANCIENT RUINED OUTER WALL
Wood Store
Stables
Storehouses
MAIN GATE
TO SWANAGE, CORFE CASTLE AND WAREHAM
TRACK TO STUDLAND BAY
STUDLAND WOOD
KEEP
Postern Gate to the Point
Bed Chambers
Cellars
Ale
GREAT HALL
HALL
GROUND FLOOR
FIRST FLOOR
SECOND FLOOR

Part One: New Lives for Old

1

23rd September 1483, in Grasche Street in London

All the way back from the church, Emma Radcliffe clung to Master Hooper's arm. But though the presence of her late husband's captain gave her much reassurance, what she really craved now was the peace and solitude of her own house – there to succumb in private to her grief. Yet, with the house only a few yards away, Hooper came to an abrupt halt and gently, but firmly, prised her hand from his arm.

"Stay here, my lady," he said softly.

"Hooper?" she murmured, bewildered.

"Wait here, my lady, if you please…"

"But I don't please, Hooper…" Brim full of heartache, her fragile resolve crumbled. "In God's name, must I stand in the wretched street for every man to gawp at?"

"Stay here, my lady," he insisted, "for your own safety."

Seizing one of his men by the shoulder, he told him: "Stay close by your lady, Master Worth!"

Though Emma recognised the gruff voice that Hooper reserved only for times of trouble, she could see no actual threat and watched in disbelief as Hooper's hand reached for the hilt of his sword. When he led the remainder of the Radcliffe men across the street, she took several faltering steps after him, despite his warning. Then she looked at the house and stopped, open-mouthed.

"Best wait here, my lady," advised Master Worth.

But, brushing aside his protesting arm, Emma ran to the open doorway of her house. There she cried out in dismay, to discover two of her servants lying beaten and bloodied. Dropping to her knees beside them, she could find no signs of life. Only a few yards away, in the torch-lit passage to her hall, Hooper was grappling with a man she did not know. While she looked on, the two men, as if yoked together, crashed along the passage into the hall.

"My lady!" warned Master Worth, who now had his sword unsheathed.

Desperate to discover what was happening, Emma ignored him again, stepping across the threshold to run along the passage. In her richly-decorated hall, she found chaos: tapestries pulled down, furniture pushed aside and assorted plate tossed into several wooden crates. A bloody skirmish was spiralling around piles of looted goods, as her men at arms laboured to expel the intruders. Hooper and his adversary rolled around the great chamber like wild men, cursing as they clattered against walls and tripped over benches.

Emma recoiled in shock, swaying a little as she reached out to Master Worth beside her.

"Sweet Christ, stay with me!" she pleaded, gasping with relief when he took her by the arm – until she saw the stranger at his back. Before she could cry out, Worth took a dagger thrust under his ribs. For a moment he still gripped her hand, attempting to drag her to safety. But then, letting the hand fall, he crumpled against her. Her mouth opened to scream, but no sound emerged as Worth, with a gentle cough, sent a spatter of blood into her face and fell at her feet.

Swiftly pinning Emma's arms behind her back, Worth's killer dragged her from the hall to the rear of the house where he tossed her outside onto the cobbled yard.

"Wait there!" he growled and, pausing only to spit down upon her, he turned to re-enter the hall. But on the threshold, he encountered Hooper who, with a streak of wet blood scarring his face, looked more murderous than Emma had ever seen him.

"Lay hands upon my lady, would you?" he roared and, with only the briefest glance at her, Hooper hacked his opponent down with two brutal blows. Then, kicking the still-twitching corpse in disgust, he took a step towards her.

"Stay out here, my lady," he ordered. "And this time, if you want to live, do as I ask!"

With a grim, unforgiving stare upon his face, he returned inside and she, terrified, remained exactly where she was in the certain knowledge that Hooper, her husband's most loyal retainer, was most likely all that stood between her and death. Hardly daring even to rise from the blood-spattered cobbles, she continued to lie there, peering into the cold eyes of the mangled corpse beside her. Why had this man and his fellows decided to ransack her house? Why, in the very pit of her bereavement, did they come to steal her goods and assault her person? Had someone set them to it? She could see no badge upon the corpse before her, nor livery...

In the ensuing few minutes, Emma strove to determine the likely outcome of the struggle from what she could hear. Thus, when the sounds of strife began to fade, she knew that - one way or the other - the fight was almost over. But what if it was not Hooper who emerged into the yard?

Unnerved by doubt and fear, she retreated from the bloodied body, crawling further into the kitchen garden to hide under a timber bench and pray in silence. There, lying on the moss-covered cobbles, she beseeched the Holy Virgin to save her from a bloody end to her life. Had she not already seen a mountain of woe heaped upon her? Was it not misery enough that her eldest, brave Richard, was killed defending his prince; nor that his young brother, sweet Ralph, should fall victim to a summer fever; nor that her daughter, Alice, should be lost to her forever? Was all that not penance enough, that now, on the very day that she laid her poor, dear Robert to rest, she must come to the end of her days in such a barbarous manner?

Her flood of self-pity was only stemmed when a wounded man lurched out into the yard and stepped over the corpse. As he staggered towards the bench – her bench, and last place of refuge - she could only stare, dry-mouthed. Her eyes were drawn to a trickle of blood which dripped down from his arm, but the wound was slight. Here was the wounded victor, not one of her men, who was coming to claim his prize. And, since there was no other way out of the walled garden, he would have her.

When he grinned, she knew he had seen her, but he came on unhurried, as if savouring the moment. Even if she could summon the will to resist, she had no weapon. In desperation, she explored the ground nearby with her hands until she discovered several pieces of stone. Just wrapping her fingers around one gave her a little more belief, feeling its rough edges sharp against her soft hand. It was perfect: heavy, but not too heavy. Hope flickered in her breast. She could do this; she could fight back.

"Well, well," he said, as he drew nearer. "Lady Radcliffe, I reckon. Lady Radcliffe, crawling around, like a dog…"

"Aye, Lady Radcliffe!" she cried, leaping up to swing the stone-charged hand at his head with all her strength. He burst out laughing as he swayed to avoid the blow and then slapped her so hard on the cheek, she fell back down again and the primitive weapon tumbled from her grasp. Lying there on her back, she could see that all vestiges of hope were gone.

"Why are you here?" she whimpered.

A crooked smile crept across his face.

"Sir Robert Radcliffe is stiff and grey now, so what need would he have of rich tapestries, or silver plate, or even this fine town house? Your dead husband, lady, is attainted and all his lands forfeit-"

"That's a lie!" Emma dared to protest.

"That's what my master told me, lady... and what did he say about you? Yeh, that was it: 'Toss the lying bitch out onto the street like the common whore she is.'"

A shudder went through her – who hated her that much? "Who is your master?" she whispered, but even as she said the words, she already knew the answer.

"Master... William... Catesby," announced the injured man, a gleam of triumph in his eye.

"Catesby..." murmured Emma, but of course, when the fatal blow came, it had to be Catesby.

Taking a step forward, he stood leering over her. "I've always fancied having a lady!" he said, with a chuckle. But his laughter stopped with a grunt as he contemplated the bloody tip of the sword which had just emerged from his chest.

When Hooper withdrew his weapon, her captor gave only a final gasp and dropped down upon Emma who thrashed her angry fists against his torn chest to push him aside.

"Come, my lady," said Hooper, holding out a bloody hand to help her up.

Ceasing her wild battering of the body, she spat in the dead man's lifeless eyes. Then she took Hooper's outstretched hand and allowed him to haul her up. But when she gazed down at her tormentor, her trembling legs refused to hold her up and Hooper had to carry her out of the yard. He sat her down in the middle of her ravaged hall.

"They've paid a high price for their bloody work, my lady," he told her, "but, I fear, so have we. God damn me! I should have seen it coming!"

"No-one could have foreseen this, Hooper," she breathed, distracted by the devastation.

"Pah! I should have known, my lady!" he replied. "Sir Robert's burial is the first time in months that the household's been so deserted." Then, as if suddenly seeing her despair, he bore her swiftly out of the hall past several more bodies.

"God bless you, Master Hooper, for your loyalty today," murmured Emma.

"It's no less than I owe you, my lady, but please don't think you're safe now."

"Aye, I know. Now that Robert's gone and, it appears, is attainted, I understand… Catesby will allow me no peace…" Her words faltered, seeing again the servants who lay by the door. "Put me down please, Hooper."

She knelt beside the bludgeoned gatekeeper, a man she had known for twenty years. Resting a gentle hand upon the dead man's head, she asked: "Where are the other servants?"

"The first ones here, my lady - after the burial - came to prepare the house. I fear they were… most harshly dealt with… though your maid still lives."

Unwilling to look at him, Emma had to ask. "And your own men?"

"Sold their lives dearly, my lady; only two remain but, be assured, they'll not let you down."

"I'm sorry."

"I've set your maid to look out what you must take with you, my lady."

"But… where can I go? If our lands are being taken… where is there left to go?" she cried. "What am I to do, Hooper? If Catesby has poisoned folk against me, who would risk helping me?"

"Someone with no love at all for Master Catesby, my lady?"

But there was no-one. God had stripped all her family from her - and even the rest of her kin were scattered like forsaken leaves in autumn. There was no-one left who could possibly stand against Catesby.

"Help me, Hooper," she whispered. "Help me, I beg you."

2

1ˢᵗ October 1483, in the Port of Sluys in Flanders

"God's blood," muttered John Elder, turning away from the dockside in disgust.

After another long day, it was a weary outlaw who set off from the wharf to return to his lodgings. Trudging along in his wake were his few remaining comrades, who were also only too pleased to be leaving their wretched place of work behind them. Decay pervaded the warehouses and rundown premises that bordered the harbour, corrupting the disconsolate folk who still attempted to scrape out a living there. Now that its lifeblood, sea trade, was steadily seeping away to rival ports, Sluys was a sombre shithole of a town.

For the best part of two and half months, John's small company of banished souls had languished there. Arriving almost penniless, they had only the stinking clothes they wore and their weapons, still black with dried blood. Without some swiftly-earned coin, they would likely have starved to death. Fortunately, wherever goods were still traded, there were also thieves; and, where there were thieves, there was always a need for men who would risk injury to thwart them. Thus John, and his household men - though they still bore a few of the wounds sustained in London - hired themselves out as watchmen to the merchants who traded in the port. Using their dark skills — acquired in tavern brawls and pitched battles alike, they managed to survive those first weeks of exile.

For the time being at least, they were lodged in several modest chambers at the Black Ship, one of many shabby inns that Sluys boasted. Though John's first intention had been to move on up the river Zwin to Bruges, hoping to lose himself and his comrades in the large city, somehow he could not quite summon up the will to leave the port. Nor, despite the failings of Sluys, did any of his companions seem especially eager to venture further into Flanders. When they were not employed, most were just grateful to rest in peace and allow their wounds to heal.

That was all well and good, thought John, as he led them into the inn, but how long could he linger here in Flanders when his Aunt Eleanor and her daughter, Kate, were awaiting him in Spain? And how safe was he here in any case? Then there was the small matter of trying to reverse his exile, not to mention the attainder which had brought it about… and then there was Isabel…

"Fellow asking for you," Nicholas told him, the moment he entered.

Nicholas, the proprietor of the Black Ship, was a Yorkshireman like John – at least he had been once. Though his accent told of a long absence from the dales, the two men got on well.

John looked up with interest. "Name of?" he enquired.

"Didn't give a name."

Since Nicholas had refined brevity to a fine art, John knew he would have to prise out of the man anything worth knowing. Mind you, not much they said was ever worth knowing, so it had become something of a game between them.

"Did he say anything else?" asked John.

"Aye, said he'd see you at the docks…"

Along with hundreds of other folk, thought John, but this was the first time a prospective employer had ever called at the inn to leave a message for him.

"And where, exactly, does he expect to see me?"

"Said he'd be on his ship..." added the landlord, with a sly grin.

"And," continued John, "did he happen to mention which ship?"

"Aye, he gave me the ship's name!"

"Which… was?"

Nicholas frowned. "Ah, now, it was a woman's name…"

"Any idea which one?" prompted John.

"Now don't be so hasty, Lord John."

"As if…" muttered John.

"Let me think - it was a few hours ago now."

"Had a lot of ship names to remember today have you, Nick?"

"The Margaret!" announced Nicholas, with a broad grin. "Aye, that was it! The Margaret. He said you could find him there."

John's expression must have betrayed his first thought, for the innkeeper's smile faded swiftly. "Is 'owt wrong, John?"

"No, nothing," replied John, a little too sharply. "Thank you, Nick."

"It has to be some ruse!" declared Will, John's cousin and closest companion.

"Not here," warned John and led the men up the stairs to the larger of the chambers he rented on the first floor.

"Where are the ladies?" he asked his cousin.

"Not back from the town yet, I expect," said Will.

And, John hoped, not spending every last coin he had so far scraped together. Their mysterious caller worried him. If he was a potential employer, why come to the inn? Surely a ship's master could have found him easily enough at the port?

There was, of course, a less likely, and much less welcome, possibility. Though he had escaped England, there was always the chance that the new king, Richard III, might choose to pursue him for what he had dared to do. If the king did so, then they would be far from safe in Sluys – or indeed any other port – for the presence of a renegade group of Englishmen would be common knowledge.

"This fellow has to be a king's agent," declared Will. "No-one knows where we are!"

"The king's not supposed to know where we are either, Will!" said John. "And a king's man would hardly saunter in to hand me a warning, would he?"

"And, lord, a ship called the Margaret? Do you know of it?" asked Hal, his oldest and most loyal, man at arms whose advice was invariably sound.

"I don't believe I do, Hal."

"Perhaps, lord," said Hal, "he wants to lure you aboard his ship, where he can take you as he pleases and there's not a damned thing we can do about it!"

"He's right," agreed Will and all the rest nodded their accord.

"Aye, perhaps Hal is right," acknowledged John, "but I won't know what this stranger is, unless I meet him, will I?"

"Then wait for the others to come back and we'll all go," suggested Will. "Aye, and go well-armed!"

Until Meg and Isabel returned, John was two men short for he never let the ladies walk out without at least two guards. But that still left him with Will, Monk and the two archers, Hal and Alain.

"So Will," he said, "your advice is that the outlaw trying to avoid being noticed should plough through the docks with as strong a show of arms as he can muster?"

"No, coz, but–"

"Good, because just you and I are going," said John. "Hal and Alain can keep an eye on us from a safe distance, leaving Monk here to explain to the ladies where we've gone."

"I don't like it, lord," grumbled Hal, "'Cos once you're on board…"

"I know, Hal, once we're on board anything could happen! But isn't that why I have you watching over me?"

⌂⌂⌂⌂⌂⌂

It took only a few brief enquiries on the docks to find out where the Margaret was moored and the moment they reached it, to their surprise, they were cheerily hailed from the stern deck. Even so, despite his earlier expression of confidence, John could not help feeling a little uneasy as he stepped aboard the vessel. Much blood and toil had been expended in fleeing from London; if his fate was to be hauled back there in chains then he should certainly not make it too easy.

The stocky young fellow who had called them aboard hurried down onto the main deck to greet them.

"Matthew Finch," he announced, "master of the Margaret."

"Finch? Kin of James Finch, the master of the Catherine?" enquired John.

"Yes, indeed! James Finch is my father."

"Well, I know Finch," said John, "and I can't say you look much like him."

Matthew gave him a disarming grin. "I'll admit that, in my looks, I favour my mother, but fortunately, I've inherited a little of my father's seamanship too. Now, please, come to my cabin —it's small, but a lot more private."

John exchanged a warning glance with Will, for if there was to be any treachery, it would surely come when they descended below deck.

"If you're in the king's service," warned Will, "you'll have a devil of a task dragging us back to England!"

"Give the man a chance, Will," admonished John, "But you've been watching us, Master Finch?"

"For a few days," admitted Matthew, as they squeezed into his tiny cabin beneath the stern deck. "Long enough to be sure I had found the right man."

"Let's say for the moment that you are Master Matthew Finch," said John, "and that I am the man you seek, what do you want with me?"

"There's no mystery, my lord, I bring you some news."

"Go on," said John warily.

"In August, news reached London of your old friend, Felix of Bordeaux, the vintner-"

"I know what he is," said John, unable to keep the tension from his voice.

"Well, it seems… dear old Felix passed away a month or so ago in Ludlow. It was a peaceful end, I'm told."

Whatever John had been expecting to hear, it certainly wasn't that. Felix the vintner, the great friend of his father, Ned, had been around as long as John could remember. In truth, he had been almost a second father to John and had ever been a source of wise counsel. The shock he felt must have been all too evident, because Finch said no more for a moment.

"How do you know this?" asked Will, also visibly chastened by the news.

"Felix's factor in London, Master Jack Goldwell, your bro-"

"Aye, my half-brother," said Will.

"Indeed, your brother Jack – it was he that told me."

"But, hold fast a little, Master Finch," said John. "How did Jack know where to find me at all? He had no part in our leaving – and I certainly didn't tell him what ship we were taking!"

"Indeed you did not, my lord; and Jack made no attempt to find out until a few weeks ago when he received news of the death of Felix. At first he could find no trace of your leaving-"

"That was rather the point!" snapped John.

"But Master Goldwell, unlike the king's agents, has a very good understanding with many of those who trade through the port of London - even the Hanse merchants. It did not take him long to work out which ships you could have taken, though I have to tell you that Sluys was not my first port of call! But, never mind, here I am and better late than not at all."

"Allow me to judge that for myself," said John. "So, tell me: why all this trouble to inform me of a man's death? Aye, he was a dear friend, but you risked a great deal - for all of us - in seeking me out. Why?"

"Be calm, my lord," said Matthew. "It has to do with Master Felix's last will. As you know, he had no children, so he bestowed much of his estate on his honest and hardworking factor, Jack Goldwell. Jack has inherited the vintner's business and warehouses in London as well as the London house and a half share in each of the three ships Felix owned."

"Felix owned three ships?" cried John. "By Christ! I'd no idea he was that wealthy but, though I'm glad to hear of Jack's reward for his loyal service, how does all that concern me?"

"I'm getting to that," said Matthew.

"Well, get to it quicker!" urged John.

"Jack was not the only one to benefit, my lord. Felix left you the other half share in the three ships: the Catherine, the Margaret and the Elizabeth. He also left his Ludlow house to your aunt, Lady Eleanor Elder – for as long as she doesn't marry..."

For a moment John was stunned into silence by Matthew's revelations until it dawned upon him that he would receive nothing.

"You do know I'm an outlaw?" he said.

"Of course," replied Matthew, "but Jack felt honour bound to tell you as he thought you might not be an outlaw forever. Besides that, he reckoned that, given your present circumstances, even one ship might be of great value to you… so, here I am… with the Margaret."

"… which would be half mine, if only I wasn't an outlaw…"

"Well yes… so there you have it. What do you wish me to do?"

"Do?" asked John.

"As far as Jack Goldwell's concerned, the Margaret is yours to use – if you want it. In name, she will be Jack's, but in practice she's at your disposal. So, you'll need to decide what you want to do with her."

Rarely had John felt so completely out of his depth. "What to do with her? Doesn't she have goods to carry somewhere?" he asked, acutely aware of just how ignorant he sounded.

"The Margaret came here laden with wool which has since been unloaded," Finch told him. "Jack arranged for a valuable cargo of Swedish furs and Flemish pottery to be brought up the Zwin from Bruges in flat-bottomed barges three days ago. So, if you've no use for the ship, I need to get it loaded."

Did he have a use for the ship? By Christ, thought John, a ship changed everything! But yet, it was all so sudden. He needed to think matters through for there were several paths he might take if he had a ship…

"I'll need to seek counsel from others in my household," he told Matthew.

"Of course, my lord," said Matthew, "but I can't stayed moored here empty for long – especially since the goods are sitting there on the wharf beside the ship! Why, I've to mount a guard on it overnight!"

"Very good. I understand, Master Finch."

"Already there are suspicions in the port," continued Matthew. "And not just whispers among the seamen. Official enquiries have been made about what in God's name the Margaret is waiting for? I can only find so many excuses – and it's costing me too, or rather you and Jack!"

John laid a reassuring hand upon his arm. "I'll send word to you on the morrow, Matthew."

All sorts of possibilities flew through his head until a darker thought emerged to smother them all.

"Master Finch," he said softly, "who else knows I'm here?"

"Only three of my crew know who you are – and I trust them all."

"So, apart from those three, you and Jack – no-one else knows where I am?"

"No-one; you have my word!"

"And you carried no passengers from London?"

"Only a married couple – a merchant, Master Geoffrey Fisher, and his wife."

"And how did they come to be on your ship?"

"I believe they approached Jack and he sent them along – they were desperate to get to Bruges, you see. I imagine they'll be there by now - a quiet, inoffensive pair and certainly no threat to you!"

"But they were on this ship..."

"Yes, but they left it when we docked!" insisted Matthew. "Why would they even be interested in you? He was just a merchant - and no mention was made of you in their hearing. I swear it, my lord!"

"But what if their business was simply to go wherever you were going?" asked John. "What if they were set to watch where you went – and who you met?"

Matthew laughed. "I assure you, my lord, they were decent folk - not royal agents!"

"Do you know what a royal agent looks like then?" asked John.

"Perhaps they were indeed innocent merchants, Master Finch," said Will, his voice icy cold, "but if – like us – you've been hunted, and your ladies demeaned, beaten or tortured, you might not think quite so lightly on such a matter."

"But-"

"We're still alive, Matthew, because we're careful," said John. "Very careful... now, describe the passengers."

"I don't know: both quite tall, both dark-haired..."

"Voices?"

"They didn't say much – London folk, I should think. But they were going on to Bruges, I tell you!"

"Did you see them take a boat up the river?" asked Will.

"Of course not!" replied Matthew. "Why would I want to? Now, enough my lord. You are quite safe!"

"Safe?" scoffed John. "By God, man, I'm John Elder - I've not been safe since the day I was born!"

With a dismissive gesture, he left the matter there and walked up the small, narrow stair back to the main deck where he surveyed the vessel with a wholly changed perspective. The Margaret indeed! No doubt his presumptuous little sister, Meg, would get the idea into her head that old Felix had named the ship for her. But God help them all if the ship was as brash as his sister!

At the bow, one or two crewmen sat in quiet conversation whilst a few others gambled more noisily amidships. With a sudden insight, it occurred to him that an idle crew was not helpful either to him, or the ship's master. A swift decision was needed: should he take the ship? He'd be a damned fool not to! He could sail at once to Spain to join his aunt! But, of course... if he really wanted to cease being an outlaw and return to England, there was really only one place to go and it was not Spain.

"Matthew," he said, "this load on the wharf – is it to go to London?"

"Yes, London, my lord."

"And how long would it take to deliver your goods and return here?"

"If we started loading today and caught the early tide tomorrow, depending on the wind -which can sometimes be a devil here - we could reach the Thames Estuary sometime the day after tomorrow."

John looked across to the ship's rail, where Hal waited, though John had ordered him to keep out of sight.

"Very well," he said. "It would be foolish to keep you idly here, so you go back to London. Will there be more wool to bring back here?"

"There usually is, but it will cost us another day or two at least. Still, we could be back here fully laden in under a week."

John nodded. "As swift as you can then – and, after that, make no firm arrangements with Jack for the Margaret – and, in God's name, carry no more passengers!"

"So you'll take the ship then?" said Matthew.

"Aye, I will, but there's more," replied John, lowering his voice. "I need to get word to my aunt that I'm taking us all to Brittany."

"Brittany?" echoed Matthew. "Where in Brittany?"

"I've no idea - choose a port."

"What? Oh, I don't know," mused Matthew. "Brest, perhaps?"

"Since I've no idea where any Breton ports are, I suppose that'll do for now."

"But what's in Brittany, my lord?"

"That's my business, Matthew. Is it possible for the Catherine to take my aunt to meet us in Brest, or not?"

"My father was on his way to Genoa when he saw your aunt safely to northern Spain; he could be back in London by now. Perhaps - if Jack can spare the Catherine – my father might take her."

"'Perhaps' and 'ifs' are not very reassuring, Matthew," grumbled John. "Can it be done or not?"

"Yes, it can," said Matthew, "but I can't possibly say how soon."

"Good enough," nodded John. "And no-one else must know where I'm going - you understand that?"

"Of course, my lord, I think we all understand that!"

"Very good then, I'll see you in a week or so," agreed John, shaking Matthew's outstretched hand before leaving to join Will and Hal on the dockside.

"All well, coz?" enquired Will.

"I don't know yet, Will," John replied, deep in thought. "I fear we'll just have to wait and see about that – and let's not worry the ladies by mentioning anything about the Fishers, eh?"

3

2nd October 1483, at midday in St Laurence's Church, London

All Emma had left was her faith; but, by all the saints, in the past week it had been sorely tested. In the gloomy mausoleum where she knelt, the cool air evoked only the chill of death – for which she needed no reminder. Without Hooper, she would have followed the rest of her family to the grave. After they fled from Grasche Street, it was he that found safe lodgings for Emma, her one remaining servant and the three men at arms. In return, he asked only for her trust - which was just as well for she had nothing else left to give.

Yet Hooper had been tight-lipped about this meeting, perhaps, in view of recent events, for good reason, but it worried her nonetheless. The sound of the outer door being opened told her that whatever Hooper had arranged was about to begin.

A light patter of footsteps approached her across the tiles - a woman then… But the unknown woman did not join Emma upon her knees, preferring instead to stand over her. With a flicker of disquiet, Emma rose to her feet. She would keep this brief, for though Hooper meant well, she could not see how anyone had the power to save her now. She had no hope of survival, unless she could go into hiding somewhere – but where?

"Perhaps we should sit down, my dear," said the veiled woman, her voice barely a whisper. "We've much to discuss, you and I."

"My lady?" Emma gave a start, for she had come to know that voice – and the lady – quite well over the past ten years. But what possible help could she be now? She surely had enough troubles of her own and… in any case, she was a dangerous woman to know.

Without a word, Lady Margaret Stanley, Countess of Richmond, slid her arm through Emma's and guided her to the nearest bench. It was as well that Emma had an arm to lean on for with every step, her legs seemed to weaken further.

"Sit," invited Lady Stanley.

"Do you want to pray?" asked Emma, feeling as if she had just fallen into the deepest possible abyss.

"I suspect we've both prayed enough for now," replied Lady Stanley, lifting her veil.

"We should not be seen here together, my lady," whispered Emma, "for I am marked now by Catesby."

"Marked are you?" said Lady Stanley, with a bitter smile. "I was marked when I was born – and after forty years you almost get used to it … Did you know I was forty this year?"

"Why did you come, my lady?" asked Emma.

"I wanted to… express my regret," said Lady Stanley, "at your loss, your losses – severe, heart-rending losses…"

"Aye, but you wrote to me about…"

"But, in person…"

"I thank you, my lady," said Emma, "but what did Master Hooper tell you?"

"Only that you needed my help…"

"It was not his place to ask," murmured Emma.

"But… you do… need help, don't you?"

"Your help will come, I fear, at a high price for us both, my lady…"

"Do you have so many offers of support, Emma, that you can reject mine so freely?" said Lady Stanley. "I think

God sent Master Hooper to me. Your man was simply His servant – as are we all…"

Shame and humiliation sharpened Emma's tongue. "Hooper should not have called upon you, my lady, for my parlous circumstances are, I fear, beyond mending!"

Lady Stanley smiled at her. "My dear Emma, life has taught me that few matters are beyond mending."

"Your husband is still King Richard's chamberlain?" asked Emma pointedly.

"Indeed, and that's where he intends to stay."

"He is committed to the new king then?"

"Lord Thomas is committed, as ever, to the good health and good fortune of… his family, my dear."

"Then you are fortunate, my lady, for my family has been swept aside!"

"But you have a wider family, Emma: a sister - and nephews, nieces?"

"My lady, I'm sure you are well enough informed to know that my family is shattered beyond any hope of restoration."

"What I know, Emma Radcliffe, is that nothing is beyond hope."

Emma shook her head. "I don't even know where any of them are…"

"What about your nephew, John?"

"Of all the members of my family, Why do you choose him?" replied Emma, standing up. "I don't want to speak about my nephew – now, or ever! It was he that brought Catesby down upon our heads! He that caused Robert to be mortally wounded! I swear if Catesby had a shred of proof, he'd have hanged every one of us back in July! And all that is the fault of my nephew, John!"

Perhaps taken aback by her sudden vehemence, Lady Stanley reached out a hand.

"But Catesby can prove nothing against you – which is why he resorts to attainder."

"Aye, he has only to declare my husband a traitor and his friends in parliament will make him one!"

"But, my dear, there will be no parliament for many months," said Lady Stanley, "and you have a staunch ally in my husband, Lord Thomas. Robert was very dear to him. While your connection to your outlawed nephew may place you under suspicion, time can change any path."

"You can do nothing for me, my lady – except perhaps pray for the souls of my dead."

After a moment's silence, Lady Stanley said: "I saw your nephew before he left London."

Fighting to control her rage, Emma made no reply, not trusting herself to speak of John. Though Robert had said nothing about what occurred in those last hours before her nephew escaped, all her instincts told her what had happened.

"I asked him about his… visit to the Tower," said Lady Stanley.

"What do you want from me, my lady?" demanded Emma.

"A careful youth; he hinted at much, but said little."

"Aye, that's how he always was: secretive - and deadly to friend and foe alike. My nephew is a dangerous, haunted, young man."

"Your bitterness will destroy you, Emma…"

"Well, how would you see a man who tempts all those you love into a plot and then, when most of them lie dead, he flees, stealing away with him the very last scrap of your heart."

An awkward silence ensued punctuated only by a cough from Hooper, still waiting for her in the shadows. With a sigh, she slumped back down onto the seat, understanding at last the reason for Lady Stanley's sudden interest in her woes.

"What a fool I am!" she murmured. "You didn't come here to help me, my lady. You just want to know whether the princes are still alive!"

"I wanted to know in July, when I spoke to your nephew," affirmed Lady Stanley, "and I still do."

"Because of your own son!" hissed Emma. "Your offer of help was never about me; it was always about your son!"

"No, Emma, I do want to help you, if I can, but yes, I want to see my son again too. I thought you, as a mother, would understand that. You want to see your daughter again, don't you?"

"Oh, aye I want to see my daughter again, but the difference between us is that your son claims the throne of England!"

"When I saw your nephew, he was grieving…" said Lady Stanley.

"Aye, well he had plenty to grieve about," snarled Emma, "for all those killed because of his selfish folly!"

"But for the late king's sons too, I thought," mused Lady Stanley. "But he would tell me only that 'he came too late.'"

"Then he failed," said Emma. Whether the princes were killed or taken elsewhere, she no longer cared. She would have done once, but now all she knew was that her own son was dead because of them.

"He said he knew not where they were…" continued Lady Stanley.

"There you are then," said Emma, "they were already taken away."

"But… if the king had them taken to a more privy place, someone would know – someone always knows… And if anyone did know, I would have discovered it by now."

Emma moved to stand once more, but Lady Stanley caught her arm and pulled her back down.

"You are in trouble, Emma, and I offer you my support. You want your daughter back – and I want my son. I believe we can help each other to bring them both home..."

"Then you do dream, lady," retorted Emma. "Sweet Christ! What madness are we dancing around here?"

Lady Stanley's voice fell to a whisper. "Treason, Emma, that's what we're dancing around: treason. And this much I know: there are many who would join us, but we need a man around whom our friends will rally."

"Your son, Henry of Richmond, I suppose."

"That day back in July, when I saw your nephew, I gave him a letter of introduction to my son. Unless I am a very poor judge of men, I believe that John Elder will go to Henry in Brittany and swear his allegiance."

"Well, you're wrong! John swore an oath to the young king, Edward. Don't you see: that's the very cause of all the misery he wrought upon his family! He would never, ever break that oath!"

"No, he would not," agreed Lady Stanley, "unless, of course, he knew that the young King Edward and his brother were already dead..."

For the first time, Emma actually stopped to think what the lady was saying. "So... you think... that if he goes to your son in Brittany then the princes of York must truly be dead..."

"Yes, I believe so."

Though she followed Lady Stanley's reasoning well enough, Emma still could not see how it could possibly help her.

"Why should I care whether my nephew goes to your son, or not? Why should I care whether the princes are dead. or not? We have a king, an anointed king… there can be no other."

"Your daughter is with John Elder, is she not?"

"You cannot know that," breathed Emma. "How do you know that? No-one knows that…"

"As I told you, someone always knows…"

"I warned Alice against it but she ignored my advice and escaped with him anyway. Sweet Christ! She changed her name to Isabel." Emma gave a harsh laugh. "As if that mattered!"

Her daughter was truly lost - body and soul; seduced by her own cousin into a life where she would drown in her own sin.

"So, wherever your nephew goes, your daughter Alice will go too, won't she?"

"Aye, I suppose, until he tires of her, discards her – or gets her killed – because, believe me, he's very good at that!"

Lady Margaret offered a thin smile. "When I met your nephew, I did not see the man you describe."

Emma's response was swift and savage. "Aye, but you saw him for a few minutes… I know that youth! He drew my Alice into his treason, into his world of blood…"

"Did he?" mused Lady Stanley. "I wonder who took the first step?"

"What?" snapped Emma.

"Which of them took the first step?" repeated Lady Stanley. "Did he seek her out, or she him?"

Emma hesitated. "She was bound to be curious about an outlawed cousin – hardly surprising, was it? She hadn't seen him in many years."

"He must have seduced her very quickly then," remarked Lady Margaret.

"Aye - as some men will!"

Lady Margaret looked away when she spoke again. "I used to think as you do... by God, I did! I held men to blame for all my ills."

"It was his doing, I tell you!" insisted Emma. "He bought her with his wild, deceitful promises..."

"Perhaps, Emma, but I've seen ladies - without a blemish in their lives – abandon everything, do anything, for a man they loved..."

"That's not how it was with Alice!"

"Well, of course, you know your daughter better than anyone... but, however she went, I can help you to see her again."

"By all the saints, lady, I weary of your games! Just tell me the price for your help, or I shall leave at once."

"I want you to go to Brittany."

There it was then, out in the open; and Emma was too stunned to reply, for it was not at all what she expected.

"Our interests align perfectly, my dear," continued Lady Stanley. "You need a safe haven and I need to send a messenger I can trust to my son."

"You must have legions of messengers!" retorted Emma.

Lady Stanley gave her a grim smile. "Hardly legions, but yes, there are one or two others I could send, but none of them could persuade John Elder to come back to England."

"But I don't want him back!"

"But I need him back!" said Lady Stanley. "And for what it's worth, let me tell you that if you drive your daughter from the man she loves, you will lose her forever."

"What, so I should abandon my daughter to him just so that he can serve your interests? As you well know, God does not smile upon the union of first cousins, my lady. She will fritter her soul away on that youth..."

"For your sake, and your daughter's sake, make your peace with him," advised Lady Stanley. "Better to be closer to both, than neither. Slow, gentle steps, Emma."

"Why in God's name do you want him back here anyway? He didn't do so well before, did he?"

"We need leaders who can inspire, Emma – we have few enough of them. And he brings the Elder name – a name that many who fought for the old king, Edward IV, will remember fondly…"

"Aye, well, perhaps if you had his father, Ned, then you would have such a man – but not John. He has all his father's faults and none of his virtues!"

"We've lost a vital man in Dorset and I believe John Elder could take his place."

"But he can't be trusted! He brought us all down!"

"Are you so sure?" asked Lady Stanley, lowering her voice. "Why don't you ask your man, Hooper?"

Emma glanced into the dark corner where Hooper stood. "Hooper?" she whispered. "Why Hooper?"

"Because in the summer he was much closer to what happened than you were – and because you trust him."

"Hooper keeps matters close," she said.

"But you trust him," repeated Lady Stanley.

"Aye, with my life."

"Then why not ask him if he would fight for John Elder."

"But…" Emma was discomfited by the sudden inclusion of the one man upon whom she relied utterly.

"Take Hooper with you to Brittany and wring the truth out of him. I think you'll know it when you hear it."

"Brittany…" sighed Emma, "in the vain hope that I might see my daughter? And what if you're wrong and my nephew doesn't go there at all?"

"You'll be safer there than here, Emma and - let's be honest, that one vain hope is the only hope you have. And, if I am wrong and John does not go to Brittany, then at least you will be safe there under my son's protection."

43

4

5th October 1483 in the late morning, in Sluys in Flanders

"Oh, do drop further back, Thomas!" complained Meg Elder. "How are we two ladies to share our most privy secrets when you and Conal loiter but a short yard away?"

Had her words not been hotly pursued by the most mischievous of grins, Thomas Skirett might have looked more aggrieved. As it was, he slowed to allow the two young ladies to drift ahead a little and she rewarded him with a sly wink, which of course made him blush. Poor Thomas, he was blushing quite a lot these days, she thought.

The previous evening she had asked her brother, John, if she and Thomas could share the smallest of the three chambers which he had rented for his household at the Black Ship. Since John had never denied her any request, she was most put out when he refused. In fact, she was livid and, since she felt awkward discussing it with Thomas, it was Isabel to whom she turned for advice.

"Of course he refused you, Meg," declared Isabel. "What sensible brother wouldn't? You're just too young."

"Too young? I'm almost thirteen years old!" said Meg. "And Thomas is at least fifteen – as far as anyone knows... Lasses marry at thirteen all the time – why not me?"

Of course Isabel would argue John's point of view – and it was rich for her to argue against her since she lay in John's bed every night. And Meg did understand her brother's reluctance since she had, quite literally, found Thomas in the gutter. John was trying to protect her – a lady, at least by birth - from an ill-advised union. Ill-matched by birth she and Thomas might be, but the pair had formed a very close bond.

Several times in London, Thomas had held her very life in his broad hands and even her brother had to concede that she would never have survived without him. Once safe aboard the ship leaving England, the pair had said the words to each other and within days of their arrival in Sluys, they had sealed their union. Meg flushed now at the thought of the clumsy kisses and frantic few moments of love-making. But then, of course, they both wanted more…

Though her proposal to share a bed every night with Thomas might seem shocking for a child, it was not so outrageous for Meg, whose childhood had been so savagely cut short. By her wits and courage, she had survived a grim ordeal of captivity, but her survival was bought at a cost. Never again would Meg Elder see the world through the eyes of a child. The months of imprisonment toughened her resolve, forging a spirit of tempered steel that few women of any age possessed, let alone thirteen years.

"Meg?"

Meg stared blankly at Isabel.

"You went quiet…"

"I should've thought you'd be relieved," grumbled Meg, "since everyone complains that I talk too much!"

"Oh, the smell!" protested Isabel, wrinkling her nose, for they had reached their destination: the fish market. "Do we really have to buy fish?"

"We most certainly do," said Meg, glad to talk about something else. "We should make the most of it too, coz, for soon we'll be back aboard ship and our meals will be a lot worse!

"Aye, I dread it, coz. I suppose we should treasure these times on dry land, but somehow I don't think I'll miss the fish market!"

"Don't worry," laughed Meg, "Thomas will carry it home; you won't reek of it when you lie with my brother tonight."

"Hush Meg Elder, you wicked lass! I don't know where you get such thoughts!"

"Alas, coz, I always have such thoughts…"

"And alas, always give voice to them!" groaned Isabel, steering her cousin towards several more stalls.

"It's late in the day," lamented Meg.

"Aye, whatever's left is either too expensive, or slowly rotting before our eyes," said Isabel. "Some turbot would be nice."

"Not at that price!" observed Meg.

"You'll have us all eating salted whale!" complained Isabel.

"Salted herring perhaps," said Meg, surveying the dwindling array of fish.

With her attention on the stall, Meg barely noticed the young woman until she lurched forward and stumbled heavily into Isabel, knocking her to the ground. Torn between helping Isabel up and berating the clumsy woman who had come to rest at the feet of Thomas, Meg hesitated. Her eyes were drawn to the poor woman's bloodstained kirtle and shift which had been torn open at the front to reveal more than a glimpse of two full, bare breasts.

Before Meg could move, a firm hand was clamped over her mouth and she was lifted off her feet. Cursing her own folly, Meg was borne away, squirming, into one of the many small alleys leading away from the market. Too much time talking and not enough watching those around her! God's teeth, she was usually so careful! She should have seen her attacker coming, love-besotted fool that she was!

Her captor slammed her against a wall which ran alongside the alley, his hand still over her mouth. First things first, thought Meg, biting one of his fingers as hard as she could. While he was yelping with pain, she twisted half out of his grasp and reached down to her boot. But he recovered swiftly and they grappled with each other in a whirling flurry of arms until his greater strength enabled him to pin her to the wall once more with his hand around her neck. With his other hand he held a knife at her breast but she simply glared back at him, two sapphire eyes boring into his.

To her surprise, he sought to reassure her. "Don't be alarmed, girl; you've no need to be frightened; I'll not hurt you."

But, far from being afraid, Meg was just warming to her work. "Put up your blade," she warned.

He gave a shake of the head until she pressed the point of her knife against his neck – the knife she had retrieved from her boot. Now, for the first time, she had his full attention.

"By Christ, little girl!" he cried. "Have a care with that knife!"

Being called 'little girl' vexed her even more than the attack itself, so she pricked the skin of his throat with her knife point. "I said, put up your blade," she repeated.

"But I won't hurt you," he insisted.

"But I shall certainly hurt you…"

Her manner was cool, bleak; Meg meant what she said, but to her annoyance, she realised that the body leaning upon her was not exactly quaking with fear.

"You won't," he told her, with infuriating calm. "You might think you can, girl, but it takes a lot to kill a man… close up."

Straining to move her face ever nearer to his, she whispered: "Aye, that was true for my first, but then you… get used to it."

"Fine talk, girl; now give up the blade and I'll forget all this happened."

"If you don't drop that weapon," breathed Meg, "you'll find out what a year in the company of thieves and whores taught me."

By way of persuasion, she began to carve a fine, hairline groove across his flesh and soon felt the sweat upon his skin. "And I swear you'll bleed to death here in this wretched alley."

A few moments later he let fall the knife and loosened his hold upon her. Keeping her eyes fixed upon his face, she left the steel blade an inch from his neck, confident that her so-called escort would arrive in a few moments.

"Now, who are you?" she demanded, moving away from the wall. "And what do you want with me?"

In response he gave a sudden grin and, too late, she heard the steps behind her. A hammer blow to the side of her head sent her reeling to the ground. Though stunned, she managed to roll onto her knees and looked up to see the owner of the bloodied kirtle, standing beside her assailant. And where in God's name were Thomas and Conal?

5

5ᵗʰ October 1483, in Sluys

Geoffrey Fisher watched his sister take a swift pace towards the staggering girl and strike her hard again. This time he was relieved to see that the little bitch stayed down.

"You misjudged her," Bess told him. "Women can fight back, you know."

"Pah! She's just a child," he murmured, as he bundled the girl up into his arms and tossed her over his shoulder.

"Well, that child gave you enough trouble, didn't she?" replied Bess. "You were fortunate – I was able to send her escort in the wrong direction."

As ever, she could not resist a sly smirk at his expense. Later, he would have to remind her just who was in command of their venture.

"She's heavier than she looks too," he grumbled. "You'd best go on ahead and clean yourself up at the lodgings – you look as if you've bled to death."

"'Tis pig's blood, dear brother, just pig's blood…" she laughed, "but, if you're sure you can manage her on your own…"

"I'll meet you at the warehouse," he said.

With a curt nod, she was gone and he was glad to see her leave – somehow she made him nervous and he could do without that. All had gone so well up to now. They had easily found the Elders – indeed a small child could have followed them from Matthew Finch's ship. The Fishers' plan was simple: capture the sister; hold her at the rented warehouse and a paid messenger would deliver their terms to the Black Ship where John Elder was lodged. Simple, but effective, for Lord Elder would surrender himself at once to prevent the threatened execution of his precious sister. The only weakness was that the young outlaw might doubt their resolve, might not believe the threat. But, for the girl's sake, Geoffrey hoped he would; for Bess, he thought, might actually carry out the threat.

By God, the girl might look small, but she was a dead weight! Suddenly two elderly women blocked his path so that he was obliged to come to halt or knock them aside.

They were speaking to him in Flemish and though he understood not a word of what was said, he noted that their eyes were fixed upon the girl slumped over his shoulder.

"She's quite well, goodwives," he said, with a smile, but his words did not seem to allay their concerns.

"I thank you kindly for your trouble," he told them, attempting to walk on.

Still they held their ground and talked... and talked! Never had words seemed such a barrier to understanding!

Geoffrey continued to force a smile. "Yes, yes," he replied. "The poor girl's ill and, with your leave, kind goodwives, I need to get her home."

One of the women thrust an evil-smelling pot of herbs at him, while her cunning confederate slipped behind him to inspect Meg Elder's face resting against his back. She might see some bruising and he guessed that such a discovery would prompt even more pointless questions.

Sure enough the second witch cried out and caused other folk to start gathering around. By Christ! Attention was the very last thing he needed.

"Does anyone speak English?" he called out, desperate to put an end to the inquisition.

"A little," said a short, stocky fellow who had joined the half dozen or so milling around him.

"My daughter is ill," he explained. "I'm just trying to get her home."

There was a brief exchange between his interpreter and the two Flemish women.

"She's got a bruised head," reported the man.

"I know she's got a bruised head!" Geoffrey ground out the response, desperate to keep his temper.

"And there's blood in her hair…"

"Yes, yes, she fell," agreed Geoffrey, "so, if you'll just allow me to pass-"

"You just said she was ill," the man pointed out.

"Ill… fell – what does it matter?" declared Geoffrey, beginning to think he might be better off without someone who spoke his own language.

"Well, which is it?" continued the man. "Let the women look at her head."

When the aged pair began pawing at the girl's hair to examine the wound, the shallow residue of Geoffrey's patience evaporated completely.

"That's enough, by God!" he shouted. "Now stand aside, you interfering old hags!"

Pushing his way through, he elbowed aside one of the women and was greeted by a chorus of outrage as she tumbled down onto the cobbles. In a breath, the street seemed crammed with people; where, in the name of Christ, had all these inquisitive locals come from? Rough hands plucked at his cloak and he roared at them in protest. It was all so unfair!

◊◊◊◊◊◊

Meg awoke to the sound of warring voices and what seemed like a hundred hands pulling at her. When she opened her eyes, she was falling from her captor's grasp but somehow she was caught before she landed upon the street. Close by, a woman bleeding from the mouth sat propped up against a low wall. Meg watched her erstwhile assailant, raging at those around him, until he was punched and pushed away. It served him right, thought Meg. While a

51

kind-faced woman tended to her cuts and scrapes, Meg scanned the crowd for a sight of the woman who had struck her, but without success.

Allowing her rescuers to tend to her trifling wounds, Meg said nothing until one man addressed her directly in English.

"You live here in Sluys?" he asked.

"Yes," she said, wondering how much she dared reveal, for it would surely be ill-advised to admit that she was lodging with an outlaw. "I live with my brother and his… wife… in the west of the town."

"It's getting late," said her helpful new friend.

"Aye, but I can find my own way back," she told him.

The fellow nodded, picking up on her hesitation, if she had secrets so, no doubt, did he. Everyone had their secrets.

The throng of well-wishers and casual observers had thinned by the time Meg gave a final hug to the two women who had come to her aid – one of whom now wore a darkening bruise of her own.

When Meg set off, there was still a steady trickle of folk, treading a weary path homeward at the end of their working day. But Meg was not yet finished for the day. She did not walk westward, nor did she head for the area behind the docks where her lodgings actually were. Instead, she set off in the direction taken by the man who had abducted her because, though it was late – and it would be curfew soon – she thought he might still be lingering close by. It was foolhardy, of course, but when did Meg Elder ever take the safe option?

She reckoned it was worth the risk, because if she could find him, she might follow him back to where he lodged. After that, she could leave the rest to her brother. Keeping close to the houses, she hurried along the road – one of the narrower thoroughfares in the small town, In the gloomy evening she paused at the entrance to every lane and alley but, as the light began to fade, so did her hopes of finding him. Nevertheless, she was loathe to abandon her quest and stalked on a little further, until a hand gripped her by the shoulder.

"Oh, shit," murmured Meg.

Fists clenched, she made a sudden turn about and pounded her hands into her attacker's body like a she-devil. Her anger roused, she was ready to face anyone – even unarmed – for her nails could rake like claws if need be.

"Meg!" hissed Thomas. "It's me!"

She blinked at him, fists faltering, as she drank in his familiar face, rugged features, broad shoulders....

"Thomas?" she murmured. "However did you find me?"

"I didn't," he said. "You sorta found me…"

She flew into his arms and rejoiced as he pressed her to him.

"Thank the lord, you're alright, my love?" he whispered into her hair.

She pulled away, fixing him with an aggrieved stare. "Aye!" she said. "But no thanks to you and Conal!" And to make sure he understood, she aimed one last punch at his shoulder. "How did you not see someone dragging me away?"

"Well… we were 'witched, Meg," said Thomas. "'Witched by a woman with blood on her…"

"Hah! I'd say a couple of turnips hanging round a woman's neck would be enough to distract you and Conal – blood or no blood!"

"But I knew you could look arter yerself," said Thomas, with a sheepish grin.

"Aye, Thomas, but it might be nice if, occasionally, you cared to defend me instead!"

But Meg's wrath lasted no more than a few heartbeats.

"Yer 'ed's cut," observed Thomas.

"Aye, I know that," said Meg, rubbing her sore skull. "That woman with the breasts you couldn't take your eyes off knocked me down!"

"Did she? Sorry, Meg. What did they want, d' ya' fink? They take anyfin?'"

"Hah, as if I have anything worth stealing!"

"Come on," urged Thomas, "let's get ya back to the Ship – they'll be worried!"

"Wait," said Meg, taking his hand. "We're not going back yet. I'm trying to track him down."

"What? Arter curfew, Meg? An' the light's goin'!"

"It's light enough yet."

"Give it up, Meg. Give it up now."

"I'll go on alone then, Thomas, shall I?" she asked, dropping his hand.

With a heavy sigh, he acquiesced and she threaded her arm through his.

"It can't be far," she said. "Just you keep your sharp eyes open!"

They wandered around the increasingly deserted streets until all except the criminal and the destitute had retired indoors. Several times they almost encountered watchmen, but the custodians of the peace, of course, preferred to avoid trouble and Thomas was an imposing youth. It was the same all over Christendom with watchmen; they saw nothing, knew nothing and did nothing. But, in this case, Meg was glad of their indolence.

Nevertheless, despite all her initial enthusiasm, they saw no trace of the fellow who had abducted her and, in the end, when darkness descended, even she lost heart.

"Come, Thomas," she conceded in a quiet voice, "let's return to the inn…"

Thomas gave her arm a squeeze but, when they turned about, he froze mid-stride, staring up the lane where a woman was walking briskly away from them.

"Shit, it's 'er!" he murmured, pulling Meg along after him.

Careful not to scrape their boots on the occasional cobbled stretch of lane, they drew closer. Thomas stopped abruptly and hauled Meg into a doorway. They peered out together, faces touching.

"You're sure it was her?" breathed Meg, more than a little distracted by the warmth of his cheek against hers.

"Oh, yeh…" he replied, pulling her back behind the wall.

"Know her shape well from behind then, do you?" she teased.

"Not like I know yours, Meg Elder," he replied, planting a kiss upon her nose. "But she's the one, alright."

"By the Virgin!" whispered Meg.

"I don't fink she's that, Meg…"

6

5th October 1483 in the early evening, at the Black Ship in Sluys

Ever since his conversation with Matthew Finch, John had a persistent gnawing in his belly – a vague, but nagging unease that only a fugitive could understand… Returning to the Black Ship after a long and arduous day, he found Isabel waiting upstairs with two of his men at arms: Conal and Monk. The sight of Isabel's bruised, forlorn face told him that his worst fears had been realised.

"Where have you been?" she shrieked, flying into his arms.

Holding her in a close embrace, her hot tears spilling onto his cheek, he glared at Conal. Having met John when the pair were mercenaries, Conal now served as one of his lord's half-dozen household men. A ferocious Irish warrior, he was equally at home in a street brawl or a pitched battle. He was not, however, very comfortable now.

"Well?" asked John.

While Conal stumbled through his sorry tale in a string of short, guilt-ridden phrases, John resisted the urge to rail at the Irishman. Where was the sense in chastising a comrade who had rarely, if ever, let him down? By God, the fellow had already saved Meg's life a time or two.

"So," said John, when Conal's story was finished, "Thomas is still out there searching for her."

"Wouldn't come back without her, lord," groaned Conal.

Since it was already past curfew, John knew from experience that any search through the town in the darkness would be futile. Such adventures never ended well, but this was different. This was his half-sister, Meg - the closest kin he had. When, as a child, she was abducted before, it had changed all their lives. To find Meg, he would reduce the port of Sluys to rubble - no matter whether it was day or night.

"Arm yourselves!" he said. "For we will scour every house, lane, ditch and alley in this Godless town until we find her!"

"No need!" chirped a voice from the doorway.

"Meg?" cried John, opening his arms to hug her small frame to his breast with Isabel.

"God's truth! The two lasses I love best!" he cried, his voice cracking with relief.

"Thomas rescued you, thank the Lord!" said Isabel.

"Aye," agreed Meg, with a smirk. "Well, he found me at least…"

John broke from their embrace to shake Thomas by the hand. "Once again, I'm in your debt, young man."

Meg gave a weary shake of the head. "There's more," she said, "because we know where they're lodged."

"You followed them?" John's tersely put question was followed by a flash of displeasure directed at Thomas.

"It wasn't his doing, brother," said Meg. "But whatever the fault; you must post watchers – at once! There's two of them, a man-"

"-and a woman," said John. "Aye, and their names are Geoffrey and Bess Fisher."

Meg, pulled away from him, mouth gaping. "How do you…"

"Never mind, Meg, but they're most likely agents of the king."

"Aye! Well, if you knew of them, you might have warned us!" grumbled Meg.

"I knew nothing for certain, but you're right: I should have told you about them. Thanks to you, we can keep an eye on them – at least until we're ready to leave. Conal and Alain, that's your task tonight - Monk and Hal will relieve you at dawn. Thomas, show them the place then come back here."

"They're really a little pitiful," said Meg, with a laugh. "If I could disarm the man, I don't think we have too much to fear from either of them!"

"Peace, sister!" John scolded. "We've everything to fear from them – because they've found us. And if they can, others will and we've still a few more days to survive here!"

"Then why don't we just take them out now?" suggested Will.

"No, this pair can't be working alone – and they didn't just decide to visit Sluys on the chance that I might be here. Someone sent them to look – and, if they just disappear, that someone will send others. At least we know who we're dealing with now."

"So what do we do then?" asked Will.

"Simple," said John. "We watch them closely and keep ourselves safe for the next few days and then we leave the moment the Margaret returns."

"But what if the Fishers make another attempt before the ship arrives?" asked Will.

"If we're keeping a close watch on their lodgings we'll have fair warning; so, we'll meet that threat if it happens. But for now, get some rest; we'll need to be at our best."

⌂⌂⌂⌂⌂⌂

Later, after sending Meg to the tiny garret room, he made certain that Thomas accompanied the other men to the chamber next to his. When he retired to his own chamber, he listened at the door for a few moments for,

58

though he trusted Thomas, he knew that it was not beyond his headstrong sister to entice the lad up to the garret.

The fact that Isabel was already waiting in his own bed did cause him a small pang of guilt, but only for an instant.

"Perhaps you should lock her in?" suggested Isabel. "Though I doubt our union is any less damnable than theirs."

"It's not the same at all!" he scoffed.

"No, coz, when the church would allow those two to live as man and wife, but not us?"

"What's brought this on?" he said, uncertain whether her concern was genuine or not. Indeed he never could tell if a woman was mocking him. "I've told you: we'll get a dispensation – we'll hardly be the first pair of cousins to marry!"

"Oh aye, and tell me: when was the last time an outlaw was granted a papal dispensation to marry his first cousin, I wonder?"

"I won't be an outlaw forever."

"But, what if you are?" said Isabel. "Am I to live in sinful union with you forever?

"Even now," he retorted, "tell me you want to leave and I'll send you back to England the moment the Margaret docks! If that's what you want..."

"Want?" she smiled. "I want to keep what we discovered one night in a most disreputable room in the Southwark stews - unless you don't..."

That night they had seen each other at their very worst and yet emerged with the fire of their love undimmed. He thought that had to count for something... Now he felt her closeness again, the touch of her, the curve of her hips, the intense blue of her eyes and her beguiling smile – how could he ever have considered leaving her behind in London? Cupping her breast in his hand, he kissed her – a mere taste of her lips, but with the promise of more to come.

For a time at least, the passion of their love-making distracted him from the other, more relentless, concerns that dogged his waking hours. Afterwards, while Isabel slept at peace in his arms, the doubts returned. Haunted by his past mistakes and fearful of what the future might bring, John's role of leader weighed ever more heavily upon him.

He had encouraged them all to believe that when Finch returned they would be sailing to join his aunt Eleanor in Spain, but of course the sudden windfall of a ship had opened up another possibility. The sealed letter he carried from Lady Margaret Stanley was, she had told him, a letter of introduction to her son, Henry Tudor. But why was she so keen for him to go to Henry in Brittany? He knew almost nothing of the lady, so for all he knew, the letter could contain his own death warrant.

Since his arrival in Sluys he had put the matter to the back of his mind, but Matthew Finch's arrival forced him to make a choice and so he had. Without thinking it through at all, he had chosen the path to Brittany, though he struggled to explain his sudden decision, even to himself. Could Henry Tudor, a penniless exile, really offer him hope of redemption and a chance to return home to England?

Though the Tudor lad was now pretty much the only Lancastrian heir to the English throne, his claim was so weak that few men would even know of him, let alone support him. Clearly, he had little to offer England – even the fractured England of 1483. He might have dismissed the wretched fellow out of hand, yet what he witnessed that night in July at the Tower meant that he could not do so. Though it was many weeks ago now, those events would scar his memory for as long as he lived. He also had a duty – not simply for revenge - but more than that, a duty to somehow help to put things right. But whether Henry Tudor would be willing to help him do that, he knew not.

Isabel, stirring from her sleep, leaned over to rest her head upon his shoulder. She knew about the letter but they had not discussed it.

"Is that it?" she asked.

"Aye," he said, handing to her.

"Letters always look important," she said, turning over the grubby letter in her hands.

"Aye, well I think this one actually might be."

Deliver it or burn it, as you please, Lady Stanley had told him. When he boarded the ship in London in July, he had every intention of burning it and hurling the ashes into the sea. Yet, by the time he arrived in Sluys, he had not done so – nor had he during the ensuing months spent in Flanders. Instead the letter remained at his breast, goading, prodding and gnawing away at him like some festering sore.

Handing the letter back to him, Isabel asked: "Have you decided what to do with it?"

"Aye, I believe I have..."

"Will you tell me then... please?"

So he did. He laid it all out for her – only her - explaining both his fondest dreams and bleakest fears, leaving out nothing.

"So, there it is," he concluded. "Either we hide ourselves away and live some sort of life together in exile; or we brazen it out and risk all on the very slimmest of hopes."

Isabel gave a wan smile and rested her head against his. "You do know, don't you, that Isabel of Coverham doesn't care at all. She's pledged herself to you and, wherever you are, she will be with you, or waiting for you."

"What about Lady Alice Radcliffe – what does she say?"

"Alice Radcliffe died in London; she doesn't have a say..."

"But-"

"Your cousin Alice is dead, John," whispered Isabel. "Let her lie…"

"But I want to call you wife-"

"Then call me wife - you can call Isabel wife …"

"Isabel isn't real..."

"Isn't she?" she breathed. "You're touching her now, your cheek pressed against hers; your thigh beside her hip. Doesn't she feel real to you?"

"But could you be content, living a lie and breaking God's law?"

"I'm content that God will know and, in the end, will judge us both – as doth ever happen."

"So, what shall we do?" he asked.

She took his fingers in hers. "Well, I think, you should ask Isabel to marry you…"

"Well, will you marry me?"

"Aye, I will, but I come from a very poor family and sadly will bring nothing to this marriage… save only my body."

"That is sad," he observed, "but it is an exceptional body…"

"Mmm, perhaps you should make sure this body meets all your needs, before committing yourself," she murmured, pulling his hand down to stroke her upper leg.

7

5th October 1483 in the early evening, at Sluys

Bess Fisher found her brother standing by the window of their small chamber, which was a relief, because she had missed him at the warehouse. It was a tawdry little room they shared, posing as man and wife, and hardly worth the rent demanded for it. But Catesby's paltry provision for their expenses meant they could afford nothing better.

"You were followed," Geoffrey said at once.

"No I wasn't!" She was always careful.

"You were," he insisted.

"Who could possibly have followed me?"

"Margaret Elder…"

"But you had her!"

"There was a problem," he said, "and she managed to… get away."

She glared at him. "Get away? How? I knocked the little cow senseless!" Bess could scarcely believe it.

"Fortune turned against me-"

"Spare me cruel fortune, Geoffrey, I beg you," she groaned.

Seething, she nonetheless suppressed her anger, for it would serve no purpose now. Her foolish brother had let Margaret Elder slip through his fingers and then - either by luck or skill - the girl had stumbled upon her.

"The bitch was lucky," she told him. "She must have picked me up on my way from the warehouse – a wasted journey, of course, since you weren't there!"

Bess was not a girl to dwell upon the past; once she might have, but not now. Bitter experience had taught her that much. Chained in a brutal, loveless marriage at a very young age – about the age of John Elder's sister – she had endured the ordeal for several years, believing it to be her lot in life. Then, one bright Sunday morning, finding herself lying, battered and bruised, beside her drunken husband - as she often was - something changed.

It was as if, somewhere in her head, a door was flung open which had always been kept securely locked. She got up, walked from their chamber into the hall and picked up a discarded knife from the long table. She would never forget that knife: a strong, narrow blade with tiny strips of dried meat still adhering to it. As if entranced, she walked back to the chamber and plunged that knife through her husband's right eye. It was so easy; when the knife struck, his body just gave a sudden jerk and it was done. And, in that moment, Bess freed herself.

A little later, after giving the matter some thought, she screamed. She screamed many more times and, for good measure, cut her own arm. The local sergeant could see how badly beaten and cut she was but, though many folk scoured the neighbourhood, they never found the culprit. If you never looked back, she told herself, there could be no regrets.

"It's over, Bess," lamented Geoffrey. "We can't exchange her for John Elder – by Christ, we'll never get near him now!"

Resisting the strong temptation to slap her brother across the cheek, Bess softened her tone a little. "We just need to think again, that's all."

"But at any moment he'll know exactly where we are!" cried Geoffrey. "He'll come crashing through that door!"

"Listen to me," said Bess, struggling to maintain her calm. "It's no use brooding on today's failure."

"But we'll have to use the rest of our purse just to buy passage back to England!" he cried. "And by Christ, we'll have to hope we can keep well clear of Catesby!" He stared at her for a moment, frowning. "Please don't tell me you've just bought new clothing!"

"Did you expect to find me scrubbing the pig's blood out of my kirtle like some common washerwoman?"

"But our purse is almost empty! We've not got enough coin for you to scatter it around the town at will!"

In his hands, she observed, he cradled a pot of wine – no expense spared in that respect then.

"I didn't buy these clothes," she told him. "I exchanged them for mine."

"And who in Christ's name would want your bloodstained kirtle?" he cried.

"I didn't ask her if she wanted it," said Bess, "I just asked her if she wanted to see the sun rise on the morrow – and… it turned out, she did."

"By God, you take such risks!" said Geoffrey, hugging the pot of wine closer to his chest.

"By the Virgin's hair!" cried Bess, snatching the vessel from him. Stalking across the chamber, she finished the rest of the flagon and tossed it back to him, licking the wine from her lips.

Geoffrey got up and looked about the room.

"Oh sweet Mary," she moaned, as he acquired another jug of wine. In a short while, there would be no reasoning with him at all.

"Now's the time to act, Geoffrey! We must strike again this very night."

In response Geoffrey raised his pot of wine in a mock toast to her. "Whatever few wits you once possessed, Bess, you've clearly lost them now."

With a swipe of her hand she dashed the flagon from his lips and, seizing him by the throat, thrust him back against the wall.

"Hear me out, you shit-headed drunk!" she said, nails digging into his throat and eyes scouring his until he was forced to look away.

"Hear me," she said more gently, relaxing her grip a little. "On the morrow – most likely – a ship will arrive with Catesby's agent aboard and he'll expect to take us back to London – with John Elder as our prisoner-"

"But Bess-" Her fingers pressed hard into his throat again.

"Though we may have lost the chance of an exchange," she continued, "we can still capture the outlaw!"

"Just the two of us, Bess?" he croaked.

"That's what we came here for, isn't it?" she insisted, releasing him. "We just have to get him to the warehouse!"

"Oh, is that all?" he cried. "Well, that's alright then – for a moment I was worried. We just have to take on a notorious outlaw and his half dozen murderous men at arms? By Christ, sis, today I let one small girl escape me! How in God's name could I possibly overcome so many men at arms?"

"But, this evening, they won't all be there, will they?" she said, with a cunning grin. "If John Elder knows we're here, you can be sure that he'll post at least two of his men outside our lodgings this very night! He'll be desperate not to lose us, but he'll do nothing more tonight. And, as long as those two men are here, they're not protecting him, are they? So, while he thinks we're safely boxed up in this little chamber, we slip out. We leave a candle burning here, so they'll have to stay and watch."

Geoffrey shook his head. "Even if we had fewer opponents, Bess, we'd still be overmatched by them. Elder's men are former mercenaries, now fiercely loyal to him - if Catesby's to be believed."

"Catesby! Oh please, spare me the wittering of that odious little man!" cried Bess. "If he knows so much, how is it that we've found John Elder where he could not?"

"Whatever you may think, Bess, if it comes down to brute force, we shall fail."

"You're as good with a blade as any man," she declared, pressing her hand to his arm.

"Perhaps once I was, but – after that night – I fear I lost my nerve…"

She shuddered just to think of it; the business in July at the Tower, with James Tyrell, had almost killed him. When he fled to her in the small hours of the night, her brother was a wretched creature - shorn of the easy assurance that made him the man he once was. It was she who calmed him, washed the blood from his hands, took him into her bed and held him. That night and the days that followed changed them both, forever.

"I'll be with you, as always," she told him softly. "You know well enough I can hold my own in a fight."

Retrieving the wine pot from the floor, he examined its interior and sighed with disappointment.

"You've had more than enough already," she chided. "If we're going to do this, either we act now, or risk losing our chance forever – a chance to clear the debts that weigh us down so. Catesby's agent will be here tomorrow – so it must be tonight!"

Bess went to him and wrapped her arms around him in a close embrace, leaning her body into his, pressing the shape of her against him and feeling his response. Because, however much he tried to resist, she knew she had her brother, and his eternal soul, firmly in her hands, always…

"Very well, Bess," he conceded, "tonight then…"

Emboldened by her embrace, he touched his lips to hers. One pair of lips brushing briefly against another; well, there was no harm in that between husband and wife was there?

8

6th October 1483 just past midnight, at the Fishers' lodgings in Sluys

"Is one candle enough?" asked Geoffrey, in a hoarse voice.

"No, better light another, my dear," Bess murmured. "We must be sure they think we are still here."

"Such expense," he grumbled, as he tried to put a lighted rush to another candle.

Whether he was shaking from fear, or simply from a little too much of the liquid courage he had consumed earlier, she could not tell. Taking his trembling hand in hers, she steadied the glowing rush until the candle flared.

"That should give more than enough light," she said, when the candle began to burn up more brightly.

"Is it time?" he asked.

"Yes," she said, still clasping his hand in hers. "We shall do this, Geoffrey. Blood of the Virgin, we'll drag this outlaw back to his fate!"

Hand in hand, they crept from the chamber and down the creaking stairs to ease the bolts on the outer door. This was the worst moment because for two short yards they would be visible as they passed through into the gloomy yard. Once outside, Bess still kept a tight grip upon her brother's hand as they hugged the shadows. Passing a small stable, they reached the dilapidated wooden fence that backed onto several warehouses. The fence presented no obstacle at all since there were gaping holes in it where the wood had rotted away.

Fifty yards or so beyond the fence, they waited, pressed against a warehouse wall, to see if they were being followed. Then, hearing no sounds of pursuit, they set off once more, confident that their departure had not been observed. By a swift, direct route they made their way down to the docks. In theory of course, there was a curfew in Sluys – and the church bells had sounded many hours earlier – but, in practice, the wharves were alive with folk well into the night. While whores plied their trade along the waterfront and thieves sold on some newly-acquired wares, any goods left unguarded were pilfered at will. Clandestine meetings were held and illicit bargains struck. Thus, no-one paid the slightest attention to the darkly-dressed couple as they wove a devious path from the docks and into a warehouse, where they deposited their few belongings before continuing into the town.

If they were to succeed, Bess knew that stealth must be their ally. Since they had watched the Black Ship over the past two days, they knew that most of Lord Elder's men were lodged on the first floor of the house. The lord and his whore would be in the chamber opposite. Bess suppressed a sharp pang of jealousy: lucky cow, rutting every night with that broad-shouldered wedge of manhood! But those two could safely be ignored for the time being. First they would have to deal with the men at arms in the larger room. Since two of them would already be engaged fruitlessly watching the Fishers' lodgings, that left four more to overcome before they could capture Lord Elder.

Four men at arms? Perhaps Geoffrey was right: it was utter madness! Just thinking about it now terrified her; yet, it also excited her beyond anything she had felt before. One of the four was usually loitering by the outside door, so he could be taken first – indeed he would have to be! After that… they would need to draw one or two down and then… well, she would worry about that if they got that far…

As she guided Geoffrey past a tavern, now in darkness, the anonymity of the docks seemed more than just a few hundred yards away. They passed house after house, all now dark or dimly lit and silent, until they reached the Black Ship. It could all end here, thought Bess. But, if it did, it would end in blood – and she would have it no other way…

"Wish me good fortune," whispered Bess, giving Geoffrey's hand a final squeeze before she released it. From now on every touch might be the last.

Gulping in a deep draught of air, she began walking towards the murky building. After a swift glance behind to confirm that Geoffrey was following, she peered into the gloom to locate the man on watch – for he would certainly be there. Almost at once a large figure ghosted out of a dark alley to stand beside her.

Knife in the hand by her side, she stopped.

"Keep walking," advised the stranger.

It was a strangely gentle voice for such a large man, she thought.

"I can make your night pass more pleasantly," she offered, her tone soft, enticing.

But the fellow was clearly not enticed, for he gripped her arm with sudden menace. "I told you to move on, girl."

"You did," she agreed, smiling. "But you can't blame a working girl, can you?"

She was still smiling as she considered where she could strike most easily. He was a little tall for her, so it would not be so easy.

"Are you going?" he asked. "Or do I need to persuade you?"

"Don't trouble yourself," she replied, placing one hand upon his leather jerkin, high up on his chest. "I'm leaving, but how about a kiss?"

He opened his mouth to reply and she saw the word 'no' forming on his lips when she thrust her knife up through his throat. It was hard, forcing the blade through the tough muscle below his jaw. Terrified he would cry out, she carved the knife across his windpipe. For a moment, a dull rumble of outrage sounded in his throat, but after that the brute uttered not a word.

By the Virgin's blood, he was heavy though! She was forced to let his limp and bleeding body slide down onto the cobbles. Wiping the blood from her hands, she waited, breathless, for Geoffrey to join her.

"You were right," he told her. "He would never have let me get that close."

Together they laboured to drag the body a few yards off the street to the entrance of a nearby alley. Panting from the exertion, Bess leant against her brother for a moment.

"So, now," she breathed, her forehead resting against his, "it's your turn, brother."

"Yes, the door," he replied, without moving away. No doubt still intoxicated by the wine, he let his fingers brush against her cap and kissed her lightly on the cheek.

"My dear," she said, turning her head away. "Remember our plan… we must strike fast."

He jerked away from her, as if she had slapped him hard.

"Yes, yes, I know," he muttered and moved off along the alley beside the inn wall, to the rear of the property.

According to Geoffrey, it was always easier to break through a poorly-maintained fence than a bolted door. And it seemed he was right for in a short time, and with very little effort, he located a damaged section of the high wattle fence. As they crawled through the gap into the yard, she wrinkled her nose in disgust.

"This is a foul place!" she whispered, scrambling through the layer of rotten detritus that covered the ground.

"Don't disturb the pigs!" he warned.

"As if I'd want to!" she replied, but he was already striding away across the yard to the door.

Worried that he might lose his nerve as the effects of the wine wore off, she was much encouraged by his confident manner. With ease he snapped the rusting latch on the door and stepped inside.

Following him in, she laid a hand upon his arm. "There will be others in the house, servants…"

She cast her eyes around the large, unlit chamber, knowing that somewhere close by servants would be sleeping on the floor. By the Virgin's hair, it was black; and, almost at once, her brother tripped over a large, slumbering body. Before the fellow could do more than grunt in surprise, Geoffrey struck him hard on the head and then crept over to the stairs.

In the meantime, Bess located two serving girls lying together and shook them awake. When they looked up at her in shock, she cracked their heads together before they could even cry out. One lay still but the other moaned in protest. Clamping both hands around the wretched girl's throat, Bess squeezed with all her strength until the last gasp of life shuddered from the young body.

Before she released her hold on the girl, there was a low groan from the fellow her brother had subdued. With a sigh, Bess went to him and took out her knife. When she was wiping the blade, she found Geoffrey standing over her, his face a mask of shock.

"Had to be done," she hissed. How each kill seemed easier than the last… "Come on, upstairs!"

This time she led the way, but before she could set foot upon the stair, a door creaked open on the landing above. Virgin's breath! Was every plan they made to be wrecked by ill-fortune?

While Geoffrey stood rooted to the spot, Bess scanned the dim chamber for somewhere to hide. Snatching up a flagon from a nearby table, she seized her brother's hand and dragged him under the stair. There they would at least be concealed from anyone descending from the floor above.

For the first time that evening, as she stood there holding her breath, doubts began to undermine her confidence. Whoever was coming down the stairs – man or maid – would have to be silenced before they could raise the alarm. Yet another death…

Her brother was close beside her, half-bent under the timber frame of the stairs. Would he have the stomach for it? Were his lips, his mouth, as dry as hers, she wondered? She took a large swig from the pewter flagon, not caring that the excess of sweet wine dribbled down her chin.

When a boot scraped on the treads above them, the siblings exchanged a nervous glance. Half-way down the stairs, a shadowy figure paused to glance to left and right. Bess cursed the sluggard for they could do nothing until he reached them – and if he saw them first, it would be a bloody night for them all.

At last the stranger made up his mind, moved on down the stair and headed for the main door. But of course they could not allow him outside for he would discover the murdered guard – perhaps he was even on his way to relieve the dead man.

Darting forward, Bess swung the flagon hard to crack it against his bare head. He dropped like a stone, but the sound seemed to echo around the chamber. Surely the whole household must have heard.

"It's him!" hissed Geoffrey, after a swift examination of the body.

"No! Are you sure?" whispered Bess.

"I'm not likely to forget what he looks like," growled Geoffrey.

"Is he dead?"

"No, he's out cold."

While they listened, anticipating voices of alarm from upstairs, Bess swallowed down the last dregs of wine from the dented pewter flagon. From the chambers above, came only silence and she grinned in triumph at her brother. At last, some good fortune: their prey delivered straight into their hands! They had him – and there would be no-one else to subdue! All they had to do now was make a clean escape with their captive.

Geoffrey quickly bound John Elder's hands with the leather cords they had brought for the task and then stuffed a wad of linen into the outlaw's mouth.

While he worked, Bess discovered another half empty flagon; she took another drink and passed it to her brother, who drank heavily from it. Well, this time he had earned it, she reckoned.

"Best not forget our friend," said Bess, pouring the remains of the wine onto John Elder's chest and shoulders. Any watchman who bothered to challenge them might just be persuaded that they were helping a drunken friend to safety.

"Are you ready?" asked Geoffrey, "because he'll be a weight to carry."

She nodded and together they raised up their prize, supporting his weight between them – and, Virgin's blood, he was heavy! Staggering out of the house, they almost stumbled over the corpse in the alley but managed to reach the street without falling.

Bess thought this would be the easiest part of their night's work; but it wasn't. By the time they conveyed their man to the warehouse on the docks, they were bone-weary. Yet they still had to haul him up the stairs to one of the two small, rented storage rooms which were theirs for one more day. When they had finished, leaving him gagged and with a sack over his head, they flopped down together on the bare floor boards of the adjacent chamber.

Breathless and exhilarated, Bess clung to her brother. Far from sober, she felt her skin tingle as elation overwhelmed her.

"We did it… my love," she whispered into his hair. "By the Virgin, we actually did it!"

"Sweet victory," he said, nuzzling against her neck.

And the sweetest victory could only be celebrated by satisfying the raging passion that coursed through her; for once you tasted forbidden fruit, nothing else could assuage that hunger…

Geoffrey kissed her neck and she laughed, pressing her body against his.

"I'm so hot," she breathed. "Unlace my kirtle…"

While his nervous fingers started to work at the ties down her back, she kissed him full upon the mouth, tasting the wine on his lips. Then easing out of her kirtle, she steered his hands to massage the thin linen which was all that covered her breasts.

"Sister," he moaned.

"Husband," she murmured, undressing him as he lifted up her shift.

9

6th October 1483 in the early morning, in Sluys

With a shake of the head, Will Coster brought himself fully awake. His first thought was that the dawn light alone had disturbed him, until he heard a sound from below – a voice singing perhaps, but quiet, almost melancholy. Then it occurred to him that if it was close to dawn then Monk should have woken him hours before. That raised two possibilities: either Monk was asleep, or he was dead. Neither prospect seemed very likely, so he got up and kicked Hal awake too.

"What?" mumbled Hal, aggrieved at his sudden awakening.

"Wake Lord Elder," Will told him. "Something's amiss. Thomas! Go and wake Lady Margaret up!"

Leaving a bemused Hal and Thomas, Will hurried two treads at a time to the bottom of the stairs but then came to a dead stop. Before him sat one of the innkeeper's daughters, Eva, who Will knew very well – indeed, as well as any man could know any lass. At once he saw that he was mistaken, for it was not singing that he had heard but Eva, sitting on the floor, wailing and weeping as she cradled the still form of her sister. A yard or two away, lay their father, Nicholas, with a ragged gouge in his neck.

When Hal thundered down the stairs to join him, Will struggled for a moment to find his voice. "Find Monk," he murmured finally.

"But-" Hal did not move.

"But what?" said Will, as he went to comfort the girl.

"I've waked Lady Isabel and now she's shaking all over, Will, because your cousin's not there. Lord Elder isn't there!"

Will, his arms around the grieving girl, struggled to think what to do next.

"Shall I fetch Lady Margaret down?" asked Hal.

"Aye, fetch Meg," muttered Will, "and then find Monk!"

Taking Eva's hand, Will persuaded her from her sister's corpse to sit up at a table. Her head was cut and bruised, but that would wait. He tapped out a jug of her father's best strong beer and sat down with her, clasping her hand in his.

"What happened, Eva?" he asked, but her English was halting at the best of times and this was not such a time. With a gentle squeeze of her hands, he said: "Tell me what you remember; anything at all."

For an instant her eyes opened wider, glaring at him. "A woman," she said, "such a strong..." She fell silent, staring across the room to her sister. "Such a strong... most terrible, woman."

Seeing Thomas come down the stairs with Hal, Will left Eva to her grief.

"Where's Meg?" he enquired.

"With Lady Isabel," explained Thomas. "She'll be down. What's 'appened?"

Will shrugged. "Someone's been in... murder's been done... and our lord... well, we don't know where he is..."

When Hal stepped out of the inn door, he was greeted by Conal, struggling to carry Monk's pale corpse inside.

"God's truth!" raged Will. "What next?"

Hal helped the Irishman to lay down Monk's corpse on the floor, near the bodies of the landlord, Nicholas and his younger daughter.

"What's going on?" demanded Conal.

"We thought you could tell us!" replied Will, a waspish tone to his voice. "Weren't you supposed to be watching the Fishers last night?"

"Yeh, we were there all night – Alain's still there now!"

"Then by God you must have fallen asleep and let them creep out!" accused Will.

"No, we didn't!" retorted Conal. "They were there all night - with a candle burning!"

"Who burns a candle all night, Conal?" asked Hal.

"Well, look around you!" cried Will. "It's bloody enough here – and we know who the culprits must be! Take Hal back with you and root the Fishers out! Break in, if you have to."

Conal did not move. "What's Lord Elder say?"

"Not much!" shouted Will. "Because he's not here, is he? Now get going!"

Conal looked first to Hal who gave a nod of agreement.

As soon as they left, Will sent Thomas up again to fetch Meg and then sat down again beside the mourning girl.

Dark thoughts assailed him: if John had been taken, how had they gotten him out of his chamber without rousing the whole household – not least, Isabel, who appeared to have slept on, oblivious? Perhaps John had disturbed the intruders, but surely then he would have alerted them all? Will could not think straight, worried that every moment he delayed might be the moment John died.

He offered a silent prayer that John had set off in pursuit and would at any moment come through the door, safe and well. Because, if he did not then, wherever his cousin was, Will would feel the weight of responsibility fall squarely upon him. John was the star Will followed; without him, he would be utterly lost.

◌◌◌◌◌◌

As she made a slow, thoughtful, descent of the stairs, Meg observing the three corpses upon the floor, took a deep breath. At the table sat the hunched and downcast figure of Will comforting young Eva. Studying her cousin's face, Meg gave a little sigh. He would need more than a little help, she decided.

"Coz," she said, "surely poor Nicholas, his daughter and our friend, Master Monk, should be covered."

Will gave her a blank look before mumbling: "Aye, do you want me to…"

"No," replied Meg. "Eva will do it, won't you Eva?"

Eva looked up at her, brushed away her tears and, without a word, got up from the table. Crossing the chamber, she went to the small back room to find some cloths to serve as shrouds for the dead.

"That was harsh, coz," whispered Will. "Her father and sister are both killed!"

Meg gave a dismissive shake of the head. "And, at such times, Will, a young girl needs something simple and useful to do," she told him.

Memories of her own childhood abduction flooded into Meg's head - savage echoes of the worst day of her life. "Believe me, Will," she said, "no-one in Christendom knows that better than me."

"As you please," he muttered.

"So, what do we know?" she asked him.

"Nothing!" he cried. "We know nothing - except what you see before you!"

"My brother?"

"We don't know!"

"Well," persisted Meg, with a hard edge to her voice, "are we finding out?"

"Aye, of course we are!"

"When the others return - if John's not with them - we've a search to make."

"I know that Meg. I'm not a fool, but where in God's name do we start?"

"If he's not at their lodgings – which I doubt he will be – we should look in the port first. If they have him, they'll need to get him to a ship – it's their only way out of Sluys. So they must keep him close to the docks."

"But all those warehouses," lamented Will. "He could be anywhere…"

"Aye."

"Unless… what, if he's… already dead?" breathed Will.

"We must assume that he's not!" declared Meg. But she had little time to dwell upon that dread thought before Hal returned with Conal and Alain; and her brother was not with them.

"The Fishers are gone," reported Hal.

Will stood up, glaring at Conal. "Right then, Meg," he said, "I'll leave Hal and Thomas with you and Isabel."

"We should all search for my brother," insisted Meg.

"I can't risk you and Lady Isabel-"

"They're hardly going to want me or Isabel if they've already got John, are they?" growled Meg. "But, never mind, because it's not your decision; it's mine. Thomas will stay with us and the rest of you will search – except Hal. Hal, while the others search, you must watch the docks. We don't want to miss the Fishers."

"But Thomas is still not fully recovered," protested Will. "You'll be at risk."

"We'll be safe enough here, coz; now please, delay no longer. John's surely taken and we have little time to track him down. A few more hours and we may lose him forever."

"Aye, Meg, but what about all this?" he said, waving a hand at the corpses. "I can't just leave poor Eva to…"

"Go!" ordered Meg. "I'll deal with this. Thomas can fetch the watch and I'll speak to the sergeant with Eva."

"But…" Will broke off as Isabel trudged downstairs, her eyes red with tears.

Meg glared at Will until he acquiesced and led the others out of the inn. Then she helped Eva to unfold a linen cloth over the last victim, hiding at last the angry, purple bruises that encircled her dead sister's neck.

With one arm wrapped around Eva, Meg grasped Isabel's hand and pulled them all together in a comforting embrace.

"How would men endure," she murmured, "without us to flush away their blood with our tears?"

10

6th October 1483 at dawn, at the docks in Sluys

Bess could feel his wild eyes upon her as she lay, half-naked, on the floor. The crumpled linen of her shift was twisted up around her waist - like a dockside whore, she thought. Aroused by the idea, she opened her eyes but saw only revulsion etched upon his face.

"Oh, Bess," he moaned. "It's a mortal sin..."

If he was so consumed with guilt, she wondered, why did the sight of her rose nipples appear to stir his slumbering loins?

"I trust you're not going to rattle on about illicit fornication all day," she grumbled. "Be of good cheer, brother, because in case you've forgotten, we have John Elder…"

"We're damned," he muttered. "Our wretched union…"

"Well, I didn't think it was that bad," She reached out a hand. "Come here, my love and I'll banish all your doubts…"

"You've no shame!" he cried, turning away from her to fumble with his clothes. "Have you no ounce of remorse? By God, the church teaches true about women! You beguiled me, seduced me!"

"I'm not sure, Geoffrey, was it you or me who was seduced?"

"You've utterly undone me!" he wailed.

"Well… lover… I think, if you recall, it was you undid me first..."

"It's all a jest to you! But what of your immortal soul?" he railed at her. "Or, is there truly nothing you care about?"

"Oh, I care, brother," she replied, impaling him with her dark, keen eyes. "I care about me. I care about what I want. I care about having my considerable debts paid off – and yes, I care about who I take into my bed!"

"Even your own…"

"Where were your hollow cries of protest last night?" she snarled at him.

"I was drunk!"

"Yes, you were! You were drunk with desire and you knew exactly what you were doing!"

"Women are such evil vessels!"

"Are we?" cried Bess, standing up, to allow her shift to fall to the floor. "Last night, you couldn't wait to paw at me with your sweating hands!"

"For God's sake, cover your nakedness!" he shouted.

"Even now, as you beseech God for forgiveness, the swelling in your loins tells a different tale," said Bess. "And the loins never lie…"

Geoffrey fell silent; his storm of protest played out.

"We should make haste," he murmured, "for we still have work to do…"

"As you wish," she conceded.

"I'll go and watch for the ship."

"You do that, brother," she said, with a smile, as she retrieved her discarded clothing. "And watch out for evil women, for the docks are full of them. I wouldn't want you to be seduced again…"

"God curse you, woman," he said, as he slammed the door.

"Oh Bess," she muttered to herself. "Why do you do these things? Were those few moments of pleasure really worth all the shit he's going to give you?"

Once dressed to her satisfaction, she packed the few items she owned in a leather bag, by which time she heard Geoffrey's tread upon the steps.

"The ship's already docked!" he called out from the stairs. "We'd better get him out before it gets too crowded down there."

By the time her brother reached the top of the steps, Bess was already kicking John Elder awake. He looked up at her with his brooding grey eyes, but there was little sign of recognition.

"He looks as if he's still out of it," said Geoffrey.

"Good! It'll go easier at the ship if he's not screaming 'murder', won't it?"

Between them they raised their prisoner from the floor and Bess groaned with the effort of it.

"He should be wide awake by now," said Geoffrey. "That blow of yours must have rattled his wits!"

"Better his wits than ours!" snapped Bess.

"Perhaps he's feigning though…" suggested Geoffrey.

Without warning, Bess prodded her knife blade twice at John's shoulder but got no reaction.

"No, it seems not," she declared.

"Take care," warned her brother. "I doubt the ship's master will let us bring him aboard if he's covered in blood!"

"Oh, stop fussing!" scolded Bess.

As they struggled to manoeuvre their charge down the steps, they stumbled several times and almost fell. Bess cursed both men roundly throughout. Only when they reached the bottom of the flight, did John Elder give a groan – the first sign that he might be regaining consciousness.

"Come on!" urged Geoffrey. "Let's get him aboard before he's awake enough to raise the alarm."

Bess drew her knife again and held it at John's back. "Just in case he gets too lively," she explained. "Now, how far is it to the ship?"

"Far enough," replied Geoffrey. "So keep your eyes open for any of the outlaw's comrades."

11

6th October 1483 in the morning, at the docks in Sluys

Hal had been reassured by young Lady Margaret's resolve, though anyone who had served the Elders as long as he had should not have been surprised. Apart from Lady Eleanor, Lady Meg had more fire in her belly than all the rest of her family put together. Though her cousin, Will, was a capable lad, he lacked the grit to make tough decisions. Lady Meg did not and, knowing her brother's mind, she quickly grasped what needed to be done.

When she set him to the task, it sounded simple enough: watch the wharves for any trace of Lord Elder, or the Fishers, while his comrades scoured every warehouse and store along the docks. But that was two hours ago; dawn had come and gone and still he had found nothing. He had already walked twice along the docks and was on his third pass towards the far end of the port. He was looking for a group of three, for both the Fishers would be needed to get John Elder onto a ship. Three folk, as tight together as if they were bound, was an unusual sight. But, with the docks growing ever more crowded, picking out anyone amid the throng was becoming close to impossible.

He was obliged to weave a more tortuous path as all along the dockside the gantry cranes were shifting their heavy cargoes. Passing one, his eye was drawn to the men sweating on the treadwheels and the sight reminded him that there were worse ways to spend his day than being a man at arms. As he stared along the ragged line of cranes, he came to a sudden halt. Three distant figures traversed one of the wharves furthest from him and something about the crab-like way in which they moved attracted his attention. It was pure luck though; they had just separated from the crowd near one of the cranes, or he would never have noticed them.

Stepping forward again, he tried to keep his eyes fixed upon them but, with men constantly shuttling goods across his path, it was a difficult task. They were still too far away to recognise any individual but, the nearer he came, the more certain he was that there were two of them supporting a captive John Elder. But, having found them, should he just follow or fetch assistance?

Worried that he might lose them in the crowd, he decided to pursue them. He hoped he might encounter one or two of his comrades along the way. However, the small group was already close to the far end of the wharf where several ships were berthed. Fear gripped him as he realised that any one of the vessels could be the Fishers' escape route. Once they managed to load his master aboard a ship, that would be it; even Lord Elder's men at arms would never get him off again. Quickening his pace, Hal continued to dodge expertly between the port labourers and the countless pedlars of God knew what.

Another worrying thought crossed his mind – what about the tide? Hal knew nothing about tides but, since several other ships had only just berthed, he wondered if it was just as likely that the tide might be suitable for a ship to leave. If he did not hurry, his lord could soon be lost altogether. A few moments later, he saw where the fugitives were heading and his heart sank; he would not overtake them in time.

With a heavy sigh, he knew he must abandon all pretence of stealth. Breaking into a trot, he slipped the bow from his shoulder, swiftly strung it and drew out an arrow from his bag. Using such a weapon here, on the docks, was surely an offence of some sort and, in the open, he could hardly escape notice. Since he might only get time for one attempt, he prayed that one, well-aimed shaft would be enough.

"Pray God, I do not kill my lord," he breathed, "but… if I do, please God make it a swift death…"

He was close enough now to pick out Lord Elder, but only a fool would try to make such a shot over the heads of the crowd – a fool, or someone who had once been a master archer. Hal stopped and, in an instant, he took aim and let fly. The range was so short that when the arrow struck Geoffrey Fisher in the small of the back, the slender shaft sped through the man leaving scarcely a wisp of goose feather to mark its point of entry. All three stumbling figures were knocked sideways by the impact and Hal sprinted towards the thrashing heap of bodies. But, as he feared, his actions had not gone unobserved and cries of outrage were hurled at him by folk as he darted between them. People on the wharves were well used to fights and brawls where men wielded knives and cudgels – sometimes on a colossal scale – but this was different; it looked like murder. It looked like murder because, Hal supposed, that was exactly what it was.

Desperate to cover the distance quickly, he jostled aside the rough hands that grabbed at him. Someone aimed a fist at his head but he ducked and, though forced to weave a less direct path, he managed to break away. Looking up, he saw Bess Fisher try to haul both her prisoner and her wounded confederate to the ship. By God, the woman was stronger than she looked, but he reckoned it was too far. Cursing, he saw that two men were hurrying down the ship's gangplank to help her.

"God forgive me," he muttered. More murder, he thought, as he stopped to despatch another arrow which plucked the leading rescuer off the gangway and pinned him to the ship's hull. At once the three staggering figures changed direction and Hal, still fifty yards away, lost them as a hostile crowd closed in on him once again. Peering towards the warehouses, he caught a glimpse of them hobbling towards an alley but, before he could follow, he was tripped and almost fell. Despite the stumble, he pressed on until he was struck down from behind.

⌂⌂⌂⌂⌂⌂

"The three of us should've split up," grumbled Conal.

"No, we agreed," said Will, "if we found them, one of us alone wouldn't be enough."

"You might not," retorted the Irishman.

Though they were well-known on the docks, their search had been savage and uncompromising. At least twice they were forced to draw their weapons to insist on gaining entry to some of the premises. They had found neither the Fishers, nor their missing lord and, with so many places still to search, time was against them.

"This is all taking too long," said Will, beginning to despair. "We must search faster!"

"But what if we miss him in our haste?" asked Alain.

"We'll have to risk it – there's still a dozen or more warehouses we've not searched at all! It's just too many, my friend."

"What's going on over there?" asked Conal, pointing to a huddle of folk. "Let's get a closer look."

"Wait!" yelled Will, exasperated by the crowds and the sense of failure he felt so keenly. "It's only a fight, you mad Irish dog!"

But Conal was already moving.

"God's truth, man!" yelled Will. "You don't have to join in every damned scrap on the docks!"

"Look closer!" roared Conal, breaking into a run.

"Oh, shit!" breathed Will and sped off after him.

Conal's arrival scattered the horde of wrestling men to reveal Hal lying on the cobbles in the midst of them.

Alain, the Breton archer, did not follow but instead moved across to stand in the cover of a flight of steps beside one of the warehouses. There, in his usual, careful manner, he laid a shaft against his bow and waited, still as stone.

By the time Will ran up, Conal had bludgeoned several of Hal's attackers aside with the hilt of his scian. Helping the older man up, Will escorted him away, followed by the Irishman who glared at any who dared to block their path. Few did, for though many were willing to set upon the lone archer, they were rather less keen to take on both the Irishman and Will, for the pair had gained a fearsome reputation in the port.

"Bess Fisher!" gasped Hal.

"Where?" demanded Will.

"I had them! I think I took down her husband, but I lost her," sobbed Hal. "She was making for an alley – near the end of the wharf! But go careful, lads, for she'll not hesitate to kill him."

12

6th October 1483, in the morning on the dockside at Sluys

Only when John was dragged across the cobbles did he begin to stir from his stupor. Firm hands gripped his arms as he was hauled along and slowly the idea sank into his throbbing head: the Fishers! That instant, he planted both feet and struggled to free himself.

"Don't!" Bess warned, digging her knife into his back. "You make a fight of it, brave boy, and I swear I'll pluck out your heart with this blade!"

Allowing them to push him forward once more, he concentrated instead on working out exactly where he was. His familiarity with the docks made it easy enough and he saw that they were making for a ship moored at the far end of the port. Crewmen crawled across her deck, busy releasing the ropes which secured some of her deck cargo. Since the vessel was preparing to unload it must have just arrived but, if they took him up that gangplank, he reckoned he would not leave the ship before it sailed.

If he could attract a little attention, perhaps he might raise a few suspicions amongst those nearby on the wharves. But, just as he opened his mouth to shout, both he and the Fishers were knocked off their feet. The arrow lodged deep into Geoffrey Fisher's back had only just missed him. The three of them ended up in a tangle on the wharf. Bess, though she must have been shocked, was swift to react.

Pressing her blade to his throat, she hissed: "I swear, John Elder, if I fall… so will you! I swear it! So, help me get my husband to the ship."

Though he considered trying to wrest the blade from her, the cool menace in her eyes told him she would kill him rather than let him escape. With a bitter smile at his captor, he examined Geoffrey's wound. Rarely had he seen one that looked more fatal, but he snapped off the protruding arrow shaft; the rest he could do nothing about.

"He won't live," he told her, "not with that wound!"

"Well, you'd better pray he does!" spat Bess.

Fisher whimpered with pain when John lifted him and the three shambled unsteadily towards the ship's gangway. When they were still thirty yards short, a cloaked figure appeared astride the gangplank. "Is that him?" he called out.

"Of course it's him, you fool!" shouted Bess.

John opened his mouth to speak but felt her knife prick him.

"Help me get him aboard, you coward!" Bess screamed at the waiting man. "My husband's wounded!"

Her desperate words seemed to goad the fellow into action but the moment he moved a well-aimed shaft punched into him, persuading a companion nearby to dive back onto the deck seeking cover.

With a wretched torrent of blaspheming oaths, Bess stopped, her desolate eyes seeking another way out. With a final gasp of frustrated rage, she told John: "Back to the warehouse with him!"

"Release me," said John, "and I'll see your husband is taken care of."

"Hah!" barked Bess. "I'll kill you before I let you go. Master Catesby wanted you alive but I'm sure he'll settle for dead!"

"Catesby?" muttered John, as Bess steered them into a narrow alley between two warehouses.

"Bess," groaned Geoffrey. "I can't… walk…" He leant back against the warehouse wall, looking as if he might collapse at any moment.

"He needs a surgeon!" said John. "I give you my oath I'll fetch one, if you'll let me."

For a long moment Bess stared fondly at her husband then a look of utter contempt swept across her face. The speed with which she moved her blade took John by surprise. Raked across Geoffrey's throat, the bloodied knife was against his own neck once more, before John had time to react.

"But he was your husband…" breathed John.

"No, he was my brother," replied Bess, her tone revealing no trace of regret, "and now he doesn't need a surgeon."

"Your brother?" John could not hide his shock.

"As you said, he would have died anyway," said Bess. "As for you, I'd really like to have seen Catesby's face when I took you back; but you know, I think your head on its own will have to do."

He felt the knife blade press harder, but she rested a hand upon his chest and seemed to hesitate for a moment. "Pity, in a different life, I think you and I could have done well together…"

If he had any doubts whether Bess Fisher would carry out her threat, the past few minutes had eliminated them. Now she held him in a grip so tight he could not see how he could break free without her blade slicing into him.

Her eyes were locked upon his. "Sorry, my lord," she whispered, as a grim smile lighted upon her lips and the point of the blade pierced his skin.

Then her head was gone, cracked aside by a cudgel, and he found him himself looking into another face.

"Morning, lord," said Conal.

"Sweet Christ!" swore John, breathing out long and hard.

"No, only me," grinned the Irishman.

"I thought we'd never find you," groaned Will, taking his cousin's arm.

"I'm heartily glad you did!" John told him, looking down at the crumpled form of Bess Fisher.

"What shall we do with her?" asked Will.

"Is she still alive?" he asked.

"Aye," said Will, bending down. "She'll not wake for a little while though."

"Good!" said John. "Leave her there for the rats to chew on."

"She must die, lord," declared Conal, "for what she's done! For Monk – and for Nicholas… and his daughter."

John received the bleak news with a shake of the head. "Aye, but do you think our dear friend, Monk – of all people - would want me to cut her throat here in the street?"

"Maybe not, but she'd have done it to you, quick enough, wouldn't she?"

"Aye, that she would," agreed John, "but I'm not Bess Fisher… so for now just bind her hands."

"You don't understand, coz!" said Will. "She's killed half the household at the Black Ship!"

"Aye, but I'll not kill her like this. Just truss her up and leave her here; we'll fetch the local sergeant."

"They'll only hang her anyway," muttered Conal.

"Aye," said John, "most likely, they will."

"God be praised!" cried Hal, limping along with Alain.

"You alright?" asked John.

With a glance down at Geoffrey Fisher's bloodied throat, Hal replied: "I'm better off than him…"

"Good, then let's get moving – in case any more of Master Catesby's agents find us!"

13

8th October 1483, in the morning on the Margaret at Sluys docks

With growing apprehension, Isabel regarded the dockside from the deck of the Margaret.

"We'll soon be away," John told her. "Matthew has finished his business and we're just loading up the last of the provisions."

But after only one night in Finch's cramped cabin, Isabel wondered how she would survive many more. "I shall miss the ground beneath my feet," she murmured.

"It's just for a few days," he told her, "only a few days."

Meg laid a gentle hand upon her arm. "Come, coz, let's take a last walk on dry land, shall we?"

"But, is it safe?" asked Isabel.

"Aye, you'll never be out of our sight," John assured her.

She might have felt less anxious but for Bess Fisher's mysterious disappearance. Though John had left the wench tied up in the alley, by the time one of the town sergeants arrived to arrest her, she had vanished. At least that was what the fellow claimed, though John had expressed his own dark thoughts about that, for he reckoned that the Fisher woman could be very persuasive. The result, however, for the Elders, was continued unease.

Meg took Isabel's arm and they set off down the wooden walkway to the dockside to begin a slow amble along the wharf.

"When will all this end, Meg?" sighed Isabel.

"Hah, when will it end, coz?" Meg gave a savage laugh. "It'll end when you die!"

"Aye, that's what I'm afraid of!" declared Isabel.

"But God has kept us safe so far," Meg pointed out, "and you just have to believe in your man…"

"My man? Aye, I do, but now… another ship and another journey into God knows where…"

"Do you still love him, or not?" enquired Meg.

"I do," said Isabel. "I tried once before not to love him, and that didn't go so well…"

"Aye, you might have stayed in England as the dishonoured Lady Alice Radcliffe!"

Isabel could never forget those days in July. When all others - even her own parents - wanted to pack her off to a nunnery, she determined to take her own life. But for Meg, she would have; but Meg had offered a different path.

"Instead," continued Meg, "you followed your heart and sought another life."

So here the pair of them were; both on the run with their outlawed lovers. But their situations were not the same: love was driving Isabel along a path condemned by the church. By the Virgin, was there a mortal sin she hadn't yet contemplated?

Meg took her hand. "You can't decide who to love, coz. Love comes rushing at you, doesn't it?"

With a knowing smile, Isabel nodded. "Are we talking about my John, or your Thomas?"

Meg's eyes sparkled back at her. "Both, I think…"

"Aye, it comes at you like a bolting horse," said Isabel, recalling her first sight of John across the hall in the house on Grasche Street and their first halting, breathless conversation.

"And once you have it, you cling onto it because it's just so… exciting!" squealed Meg.

"Aye, you feel you daren't let it go," sighed Isabel.

"The blood roars through you and you're flushed before you even know why!"

"You long to be with him, yet you don't know what to say when you are…"

"And when he takes your hand, you tremble and feel weak at the knees," gasped Meg, "And, deep inside you, there's a change… in your belly… in your loins."

"And you know, that in that reckless moment you'll do anything," Isabel gave her cousin's hand a squeeze. "Anything not to lose him, anything to keep him safe… except, we can't keep them safe, can we?"

"No, coz, we can't," agreed Meg. "When I was taken by Slade as a child, I expected to be killed. I learned to live for each day and prayed that tomorrow would come. And it always did."

"But what if it doesn't?"

"Only God can decide that…"

"How can you live like that though?"

"How? Very easily," Meg assured her with a disarming grin. "I just remember a worse time – of which there have been quite a few! Only a few months ago, coz, you were set to throw your own life away – so I why worry if it ends now, or next week? You love a man who lives by his sword, so his life – and yours - will always be in the balance. Embrace that, or fear alone will kill you!"

Isabel could confess, to herself at least, that there were times when her younger cousin's powerful blend of wisdom and passion scared her witless. Surely it was impossible that Meg was still barely twelve years old. While they made their way back along the docks, Isabel was silent, reflecting upon her cousin's disturbing advice.

"Perhaps," she said finally, "I'm just not as brave as you, Meg, because I still can't help but fear the likes of Mistress Fisher."

"Then, by the Virgin, coz, you worry too much!" retorted Meg. "A life where you look for a Bess Fisher in every dark corner is no life at all!"

"But, she came into the place where we lived!"

"You have to embrace your fear," insisted Meg.

They had almost reached the end of the wharf and yet Isabel could see none of John's men close by.

"That's easy for you to say," murmured Isabel, "because you're not afraid."

"Aye," said Meg, "but I was once…"

When they turned about to walk back to the ship, Isabel tried to banish her fears by drinking in the sights and sounds of the port. Cranes strained to move large bales; and men, some stripped to the waist, dripped with sweat and grunted with the effort of loading, or unloading their goods. Bawdy women hurled out lewd invitations to every man – and even a few women - who passed by. Sellers of food and drink shouted their wares to those who disembarked from the ships, or simply loitered on the dockside. Here was all life: seamen, merchants, lawyers and landowners jumbled together with every sort of criminal in Christendom.

"We'll soon be on our way, in any case," said Meg, coming to an abrupt halt. "And Brittany has to be better than this shithole of a port."

"Such fine words you've learned from your Thomas," chided Isabel. "But coz – can you tell? I'm embracing my fear!"

Meg rewarded her with a grin and Isabel smiled back, but when a brawl erupted only a few yards away from them, she almost crushed Meg's fingers.

"Walk on, coz," said Meg, brightly. "They're not out to harm us, just each other."

"Aye, indeed," said Isabel, easing her grip on her cousin's bruised hand, "but remember how swiftly it happened before, when you were snatched by the Fishers!"

"Well, I'd like to think I'd notice Bess Fisher this time," said Meg, "but you don't need to worry - look ahead to the ship."

Isabel squinted at the Margaret, now only thirty yards away. "What am I looking at?"

"Alain, at the stern, with his bow already strung, watching every step we take."

"Oh," said Isabel, thinking herself such a fool.

"So you see, coz, we're still watched over by those who love us…"

When they reached the Margaret, John stepped off the ship to greet them, wrapping Isabel in a tight and very public show of affection.

"Lord!" The warning came from Conal behind them.

Twisting in John's embrace, Isabel stared across to the warehouses and her throat felt suddenly too dry to speak. There stood Bess Fisher, finger stabbing at the Margaret like a dagger – and she was not alone.

"Crossbows!" shouted Hal.

"Alain! Hal!" roared John, keeping his arms folded around Isabel. "Damn me! Finish the woman!"

Isabel saw Alain let fly an arrow and glimpsed Hal hurrying to string his bow, when John dragged her down to the cobbles. A sudden breeze seemed to snatch at her cap and she cried out in pain.

"Get aboard! All of you" shouted John, sweeping her up into his arms and rushing onto the ship. "Master Finch!" he bellowed. "I'd like to leave – now, if you please!"

While Finch bawled out orders to the crew, John took Isabel below to the cabin, followed closely by an anxious Meg.

"Are you alright, my love?" he asked, pulling off her bloodied cap to examine her head.

Though the wound stung and brought tears to her eyes, Isabel fought to stay calm; the quarrel could only have grazed her, or she would be stone dead already. She glanced at Meg who was mouthing: 'embrace it, coz'.

Putting a tentative hand to her scalp, she was relieved to discover only a little blood on her fingers. "Tis nothing," she said. "A bloody cap can be washed..."

"I swear to keep you safer from now on!" cried John.

Feeling the ship move a little under her, Isabel smiled back at him. "I'd be safe in a wooden box, John Elder, but I'll thank you not to put me in one yet. Meg will rub some salve on my head and the sea air will heal it in no time."

"Very well then, brave lass," he said. "I take it you're ready then to go in search of our Aunt Eleanor."

"Of course..."

"Aye, I hope you are too," Meg told her brother, "because seeking Aunt Eleanor is not a task for the faint of heart..."

Part Two: Weak Vessels

14

11th October 1483, at Brest in Brittany

Upon arrival in the port of Brest, John emerged from his cabin with renewed purpose and left the ship at once to begin making enquiries about the whereabouts of Henry Tudor. He assumed he would have to tread carefully, but it soon became very clear that he was by no means the first English renegade to seek out the heir of Lancaster. In the taverns around the port it seemed that almost anyone could tell him that Henry was now to be found further south at Vannes. Eager to move on, the arrangements he had so carefully set up to meet Eleanor in Brest now proved a hindrance.

"How long do you think we'll have to wait for your father's ship to arrive?" he asked Matthew.

"I saw him in London," replied the master of the Margaret, "but he wasn't due to leave for the southern ports for another few days since the Catherine needed some repairs – she's not a young ship, you know."

"Aye, but we can't sit just here waiting for weeks!"

"The Catherine won't reach Spain for days yet, so why don't I take you down to Vannes and then come back here to wait for the Catherine?"

"No, you can take us down to Vannes but I want your ship where I can see it – not miles away. Who knows how I'll be received by this Henry Tudor?"

"But," objected Will, "someone will have to stay here to tell my mother where we've gone. Having summoned her here, we can't just sail off and ignore her. I'd better stay."

"Let me stay, lord," suggested Hal. "You can spare me more than Will."

"God's teeth! I can't spare either of you!" complained John. "But… I'm not sure I can endure the pained look on Eva's face if we leave you behind, Will. But Hal, with more wit than I gave him credit for, must have realised that a certain lass called Mary will be arriving with my aunt. Your generous offer wouldn't have anything to do with that, Hal, would it?"

"No, lord," grinned Hal, "I hadn't given it a thought."

Leaving anyone behind on their own was a risk; but Will was right: they could hardly abandon Lady Eleanor without leaving word and, if there was any man his aunt would trust, it was certainly Hal.

"Very well," he agreed. "We'll return here once we've settled our business at Vannes, so make sure my aunt doesn't go wandering anywhere else, Hal."

Hal gave a shrug. "As if any man could do that, lord, but I'll try!"

"I'll leave you what coin I can spare – enough for a poor lodging at the docks at least."

"Thank you, lord, but I'll be alright," said Hal. "You just make sure this Henry Tudor's worth all the fuss, before you give up all our lives to his cause."

◇◇◇◇◇◇

Though the journey south from Brest was short, it was three days before they were actually admitted to Henry Tudor's base at the Chateau L'Hermine in Vannes. When he arrived, John found that he was not the only one seeking an audience with the young claimant to the English throne.

"So, is this… sort of Henry's royal court?" asked Meg, as they waited in a small anteroom to be admitted into the youth's august presence.

"It seems so," murmured John, preoccupied by the forthcoming audience with Henry Tudor.

"Not exactly a palace is it?" observed Meg.

But John's brooding thoughts had already taken him elsewhere to matters buried deep in his past. Since before he was born, the Elder family had fought for the House of York – aye, and plenty had died for it too! Their fealty to York went back to his grandfather; and his own father, Ned, had made his reputation in the service of the late king, Edward IV. To seek out the heir of Lancaster was to set all those past loyalties at nought. Even arranging to meet Henry at all seemed somehow like a betrayal. But, if he was honest with himself, the real difficulty lay not just in abandoning his old loyalties, but in the brutal truth that Henry Tudor had little real chance of challenging King Richard. It was a forlorn hope, but it was the only hope he had…

"It's not a palace, Meg," he agreed, "but then he's not a king yet either."

"Do you think he ever will be?" Meg pressed him. "Do you want him to be king?"

"I really don't know, Meg. Do you?"

"Well, I don't know him yet, do I?"

"When does a subject ever truly know their king though?" mused John.

"I know young King Edward - well, I knew him…"

"Aye, but this young man… he'll be different… He was not born to be king; why, his whole upbringing was a shambles of trouble!"

"Worse than mine?"

"Aye, sister, perhaps even worse than yours."

"Then I like him already," said Meg.

"I just wish we didn't have to meet him dressed in these soiled rags!" wailed Isabel.

Among the doubts John had envisaged from the two young women, the state of their clothing was not one he had even considered. But if Isabel feared that they would not shine sufficiently to impress the would-be king, he doubted she needed to worry. Most of those who attended upon Henry were likely to be rebels who had escaped from England with as little as he. Few of those exiles would have paused to consider their clothing requirements before taking flight. No-one he had yet seen at the chateau – neither man nor woman - was dressed in any sort of splendour or ostentation; indeed some were positively shabby.

Meg's observation was, as usual, correct: at first glance, Henry Tudor's exiled court was very small, poorly attended and sparsely furnished. It was hardly very reassuring and the long wait was beginning to annoy John. Who was this jumped-up earl who kept other lords and ladies standing about in a draughty room – not much of a king, surely?

His impatience threatened to boil over but just as he was about to burst into his host's presence, the door opened and he stood open-mouthed in shock.

"Aunt Emma?" he stuttered, bewildered at her presence in Brittany – and at the court of Henry Tudor - of all places.

Lady Radcliffe gave John only a cool nod of greeting before turning her eyes towards her daughter.

"Alice!" she cried.

"Isabel!" growled her daughter.

John could see that his aunt expected Alice to run to her and, perhaps Alice might have done, but Isabel did not.

It was Meg who, seizing Isabel's hand, hauled her across the room to her mother. When Isabel permitted her mother a chill embrace, Lady Radcliffe's eyes were brimming with tears. After the tense reunion, his aunt seemed to compose herself and eased her daughter and niece aside to face John once more.

"Is Sir Robert here?" he asked, but her icy stare gave him the answer even before she replied.

"Robert is dead," she said, her voice curt and formal.

"How do you come to be here, aunt?" he asked.

Ignoring his question, Emma said: "First, you must see his grace."

Noting her use of the term, 'his grace', he realised that at least one member of the Elder family had already accepted Henry, Earl of Richmond, as her king.

15

14th October 1483, at the court of Henry, Earl of Richmond in Brittany

Walking through into Henry's inner chamber, John found his host seated with half a dozen men clustered around him. The young man, who might have been some five or six years older than John, certainly looked the part, but the trappings of his pretended kingship were less convincing. He sat in a plain chair on a slightly raised dais and beside his makeshift throne, hung a limp and small – embarrassingly small – pennant. Though one or two of those who attended upon the Earl of Richmond, regarded John with interest, the rest radiated outright hostility.

Still reeling from the considerable shock of finding his aunt there ahead of him, John did not kneel, or bow. Instead he simply gave the sort of casual nod one lord might give in passing greeting to another of equal rank. The slight did not pass unnoticed and provoked several thunderous looks from Henry's companions. The earl himself, however, appeared to take no offence and merely glanced down at the letter which John had presented upon arrival at the château.

"So, Lord Elder," said Henry at last, "you have come to join our cause."

"Have I?" asked John.

"I assume you came here to swear allegiance – as countless others have," said Henry.

"Hardly countless, my lord," replied John, indicating, with a sweep of his arm, the far from impressive numbers in the room.

"Your grace would be a more appropriate form of address," warned an older man, who hovered closest to Henry.

"My uncle, Jasper," said Henry, with a hint of apology, "is the staunchest defender of my right to the throne."

"To the throne?" said John. "I see only two exiled lords – perhaps not even that, for you are no more Earl of Richmond than I am Lord Elder – and your Uncle Jasper hasn't been Earl of Pembroke for many a year."

"If I am just another lord," said Henry, displaying a hint of annoyance for the first time, "I wonder why you have troubled to come here?"

"The blood royal flows through him!" declared Jasper Tudor.

"Aye," said John, "but if he takes a false step, that blood – royal or not – will soon be flowing out of him."

"He is your lawful king!" insisted Jasper.

"Really? And what does the man my father vanquished at Mortimer's Cross know about lawful kings?"

Jasper took a pace forward, hand reaching for the sword at his belt.

"No, uncle!" Henry's low voice brought Jasper to an abrupt halt.

"I'd have thought this year has already seen rather too many 'lawful' kings," observed John.

"Men flock to my banner!" declared Henry.

"Men trickle to your banner!" argued John. "A few hundred renegades do not make an army of invasion!"

"The tyrant, Richard of Gloucester, must be-"

"Spare me the malicious gossip, please... Tyrant? He's scarcely had time to become a tyrant yet, has he? He's only been king for a few months!"

"He deposed his nephew, King Edward! What nobleman with any honour would depose his anointed king?"

"Well, to be accurate, my lord, King Edward V was never actually anointed," said John, "whereas King Richard has been – so I could put the same question to you."

"If you are Richard's man," snarled Jasper, "you'll be sorry you came here, John Elder!"

"Hah!" laughed John. "Richard's man? God's truth! I doubt anyone is less Richard's man than I! Gloucester is many things, but a tyrant? Well, perhaps he might become one, but not yet, I think."

"What do you know about it?" grumbled Jasper.

"I know better than you what Gloucester's done – by Christ, I watched him do most of it!"

"Then pledge your oath to me," said Henry simply.

"Why? I don't yet see a king before me; I don't see a man who has the fire in him to prise the crown from Richard's bloody hands - and keep it! And if I don't, then many others won't either. So, my lord, convince me; please, convince me."

"A king does not need to convince his subjects!" Jasper protested.

"This one does – because he has no subjects! He has no throne and he's not likely to get one any time soon!"

Henry stood up, stepped off the dais and began to pace up and down before John.

"Why should I try so hard to convince one trifling, outlawed youth of my fitness to be king?" demanded Henry.

For a moment, John hesitated, as if he stood on a cliff edge.

"Tell me why!" repeated Henry. "What is so special about you, John Elder? For I cannot see why my mother was so keen to have you come here at all!"

"Perhaps," began John, "because I can give you something that I suspect no other man can."

"And what pray is that?"

"Show me your fire and I'll tell you," said John. "Persuade me that you have the courage and wit to be a worthy king."

Though Jasper stepped forward again at that, Henry waved him back and John saw a spark of genuine fervour in the young earl's face.

"Fire?" said Henry. "If I lacked the courage and determination of a king, I'd already be dead. My royal blood has brought me nothing but fear and misery. God's truth! My lineage has been a millstone around my neck! As long as I've drawn breath, I've been in someone's custody and handed on faster than a leper's dog! Sometimes tolerated, sometimes hunted… and were it not for my good uncle…"

"You're not the only man to have a bloody childhood," said John, recalling his own.

With a solemn nod, Henry acknowledged the truth of the statement.

"Perhaps not, but I never sought the throne. By God, I would have happily returned to England as Earl of Richmond – indeed my mother was ever working for my return to court in the reign of the late king Edward. I would have accepted the young king, Edward V, too; but you see, John Elder, how God tests us all – even kings. How could I, any more than anyone else, foresee the path that Gloucester would take? Now the usurper has declared young Edward - and every child heir of York save his own - a bastard, so… am I to sit on my exiled arse and do nothing? No, it falls to me to challenge him."

"And how exactly are you going to do that?" enquired John, who was nevertheless impressed at last by the young man's passion.

"You refuse to join me, yet you ask for my plans?"

"Plans? Tell me no plans, my lord," said John. "Tell me instead what you can offer our broken kingdom."

Henry's answer was immediate: "I shall offer unity-"

"Hah! Unity? Who told you that? Blood of Christ, no-one even knows who you are! How can you possibly bring unity?"

"Because I shall wed the late king's daughter, Elizabeth, offering hope to both those who served him loyally and those who were ever faithful to the House of Lancaster."

"It would be a good trick," agreed John, "if you could do it... but I swore an oath to the heir of York, Edward V, lately lodged in the Tower with his brother. What if young Edward were to oust his uncle of Gloucester and reclaim the throne? What then?"

After a brief pause, Henry said: "If Edward V is rescued and restored, I shall accept him as my king – but only if he allows me to return to England and be granted the estates due to me as Earl of Richmond."

John was almost convinced by the youth, though wary of his die-hard Lancastrian advisers, such as his uncle Jasper, who now regarded John with an even more pugnacious stare.

"Are you telling us then that Edward V still lives?" cried Jasper, his voice no more than a hoarse whisper.

John said nothing and the silence between them stretched as taut as a length of tanned leather, before Henry sliced through it.

"No, uncle, he's not," he said. "He's telling us the opposite. Because, if Edward V still lived, this youth, John Elder, would not be here at all..."

Jasper stepped forward to seize John by the arm. "By God! Is that certain? Is the boy dead?"

Thinking again of that bleak night at the Tower was too much for John to bear and he angrily shrugged off Jasper's hand. Henry's uncle, interpreting John's silence as reluctance, pressed him further. "In the name of God, tell us, man!"

Disliking the glimmer of hope he saw in Jasper's eyes, John considered a denial, but this was no time for idle deception.

"I saw him dead," he murmured, choking a little as he said the words. "Not that I've any proof of it. I've no corpse to show you, or anyone else - even his mother, God help me."

"Yet you are here," said Henry, "and the word of a lord of unquestioned loyalty to York is sufficient for me. And, I believe – as does my mother, Lady Stanley - that it will be sufficient for many other men loyal to the late king. So, Lord Elder, if you no longer have your king, why not swear allegiance to me?"

"If you give me your oath now that you will marry a daughter of York," replied John, "then I will swear allegiance to you."

"That is a commitment to be made later before others," replied Henry.

"Give me your oath now," insisted John, "and by God, I shall hold you to it."

"His grace-" began Jasper, but John cut across him.

"His grace will not get my support unless he does! Either what you've told me is truly spoken, my lord, or it is not. Which is it?"

Jasper was in his face once more. "You dare accuse his grace!"

"Peace, uncle," said Henry. "There is no doubt about my intention, Lord Elder, but you are right: we do not know each other, so let us begin our journey together with oaths, not promises. To you now, I swear, before God, that I will take Elizabeth of York to wife as soon as I become king. Does that satisfy your doubts?"

"Aye, it does," said John.

"Then tomorrow," said Henry, "you will swear your oath of allegiance before others, including your aunt who brought letters to me from my mother."

"Ah," said John, "I was wondering, your… grace, what matters brought her here."

"And well you might, for one of those letters affects both you and your aunt. Very soon, we shall all be bound for England, my lord, but you will leave before the rest of us. I have a task for you… but more of that tomorrow, after I have received your formal oath of allegiance."

John gave a bow as he left, knowing that he had taken the plunge now; after only a few persuasive words, his allegiance had been transferred from York to Lancaster – or perhaps something more than either York or Lancaster… Aye, or perhaps he had committed his whole family and household to utter ruin…

16

15th October 1483, at Vannes in Brittany

The following day, as agreed, John gave his formal oath to Henry Tudor, after which his sister and cousins were presented to the king. But he was unprepared for the whirlwind of activity which followed hard upon his pledge of allegiance. When the brief ceremony was over, John had a private audience with his aspiring king with only Jasper Tudor in attendance.

"I need your firm commitment to my cause, my lord," Henry told him. "I intend to make my landing at Poole in Dorset. It is well-placed between two strong centres of revolt in Kent and Salisbury, but there is a problem among our friends in Dorset. If I cannot land there then I shall have to continue westward – perhaps as far as Dartmouth, or Plymouth, which means that the prize of London is that much further away. So, I would rather raise my standard at Poole, but to do so, I need to know that the rebel forces there are prepared and will support me.

"What is this problem with the Dorset folk?" asked John.

"If I knew that, I wouldn't need to send you there, would I? But your aunt will tell you what little we know."

"But how did she come to be involved?"

"All you need to know is that she is my mother's trusted envoy."

Henry's terse response told John that if he wanted to know any more about that matter, he would have to extract it from his aunt.

"How long do I have?" he asked. "Is your fleet is ready?"

"Very nearly," said Henry, "so you will need to make haste."

"I'll do my best, your… grace."

"Then if God supports our cause, I shall see you very soon in England, my lord!"

Soon after their meeting, Henry was seen leaving the chateau in a hurry, accompanied by his uncle Jasper and several others, who, John supposed, comprised a sort of council for the young man. God knew he would need one!

Events were moving a good deal faster than John had ever expected. To return to England so soon had seemed impossible, but now his fortunes - and those of the entire family - rested in the untrained hands of a would-be king, whom no-one knew - let alone trusted…

◠◠◠◠◠◠

When he left the king's privy chamber, his aunt was awaiting him.

"Well?" she asked. "What do you think of his grace?"

"I'll let you know in a few months' time," he replied. "I'm told we have a matter to discuss. I hope you know more than Henry just told me!"

"Since I've been waiting around here for weeks for you to arrive," grumbled Lady Radcliffe, "I'm only too pleased that we can start to make plans."

"Weeks?" said John. "But how did you know I'd come here?"

"I didn't! How would I know that? I'm only your aunt, but someone else was fairly certain you'd come."

He nodded. "That would be Lady Margaret sodding Stanley, I suppose. Why do I sense hers is the controlling hand here?"

Lady Radcliffe pulled a face. "Because it is!"

"She had no right to involve you!" he said crossly.

"That's a strange thing to say – given how you ensnared my entire family in your treason! In any case, I went to her – I had nowhere else to turn. Though it was not my idea to come here, she persuaded me. In truth, John, I didn't want to see you at all. I just wanted to see Alice. I blamed you for all that happened in July."

"God knows, I tried not to involve Alice in the plot…"

"Then you should have tried harder!" complained his aunt, but then her stern expression seemed to soften…. "But, since then, I've had a long talk with Master Hooper."

"In my experience, Hooper doesn't do long talks," he said.

"No, it was… painful for us both - awful." Her face seemed to pale at the thought of it. "The worst of all conversations: he did not want to tell me anything and I didn't want to hear it."

"It's a wonder the pair of you talked at all!"

"In the end, from what he said, I pieced together what happened to Alice… what you did – and didn't do… and how Robert came to be wounded."

"And did it help you?" asked John.

"I understand now that the fault was not yours alone… but did it help me? No, only Alice returning home could possibly help me."

"It was Alice's decision to go with me, aunt. Only she can change that."

"Do you want her to leave you?"

"Of course I don't!"

"Very well," she said, with a sigh. "But we must speak about Dorset. How much do you know?"

"I know nothing – but how do you fit into all this?"

"Lady Stanley had her own reasons for despatching me here."

"Which were?"

"Henry's rebellion has already begun," she told him. "When I left Dover, the men of Kent had already risen. By now, other revolts will have started all over the south and west: Newbury, Salisbury and Exeter. Men are raising armies to join with the Duke of Buckingham who will-"

"Buckingham?" cried John, incredulous. "You're not serious, aunt!"

"Aye, Buckingham… why not?"

"Buckingham is declaring for Henry Tudor?" laughed John. "I don't believe it!"

"I had it from Lady Stanley herself!"

"God's blood! Now I am worried, for I wouldn't trust Buckingham to hold his pisspot the right way up!"

"Well, he has pledged his support for Henry and will – as I was about to tell you - shortly cross the Severn with all his many retainers."

"Very well, let's say you're right and all these men are rising up against King Richard – they'll still be spread very thin."

"They will, but a little less so, I hope, with your help," said Emma.

"All I know is that I'm to go to Dorset to prepare for Henry's arrival. It seems that there should have been a rising in Dorset too. Was it foiled by King Richard's agents?"

"We don't know – only that its leader was found murdered. His grace wants you to take over command of the Dorset rebels."

"What? Surely a local man would be better?"

"There was a local man – now dead, as I said - but we have no idea whether he was killed by the king's agents or… by one of his own. Lady Margaret thinks they need someone from outside to rally the men to the cause. They believe the Elder name – your father's name - will still carry weight with some of the late king's supporters. Men remember your father well, John – well enough perhaps to stiffen their resolve."

John listened then in some bewilderment as his aunt explained how she was to act as a go-between with the rebels, to ensure they knew they could trust John Elder. To his amazement, she rattled on about how he would lead them and make Dorset a beacon for the rebellion. Gone was the reserved, respectable Lady Emma Radcliffe; instead an imposter had assumed her visage and was talking about stoking the fires of revolt - which he found rather unnerving.

"All they need is a leader," she concluded, "and, despite any misgivings I might have, the king believes you are what's needed."

"For once I share your doubts, aunt," he replied. "Why in God's name would Dorset folk follow me, a northerner? I'll sound just like one of King Richard's henchmen – and you'll be tarred too by your northern tones. And what do you – or Lady Stanley – know about rebellion? What do you know of war or fighting at all, for that matter?"

"It's not up to you; it's already decided!" she declared. "The rebels will be expecting me – and I know who to contact. So, you can't do it without me!"

"Aye, but it will be me who has to keep you safe!" he said.

"Not for long, because as soon as I have arranged a meeting between you and the rebels, my part is done."

"Aye, as ever, it all sounds so easy," he said, with a sigh.

"His grace will send you several more men at arms – courtesy of the Duke of Brittany – so you'd best decide where to put them. Since you will have much to prepare, would you like me to arrange lodgings here for Alice and your sister, Margaret while we're gone?"

"No need, aunt. They'll be sailing with us."

"But-"

"It's my decision, aunt. I'm not leaving anyone behind again. All the Elder affinity is sailing with me. I expect to meet up with Aunt Eleanor and Kate at Brest."

"Eleanor is going with us?" breathed Emma.

"Aye, she should be in Brest when we get there."

"God help us then," said Lady Radcliffe. "The arrival of my reckless sister is the very last thing we need!"

"She won't be anywhere near the revolt, aunt. We shall sail to England together and then the Catherine will take all the ladies west to Bristol whence they can travel overland to Ludlow. They have friends there, and since none of them has broken the law, they'll be safer there."

"Will you send Alice there too?" asked his aunt.

"Most likely..."

"But she could come with me..." Lady Radcliffe's hesitant suggestion lingered between them for a moment or two. "Will you not release your hold upon her?"

"I told you: she's not here at my bidding."

"I don't know that lass any more..." said Lady Radcliffe.

"Then talk to her, aunt. Make your peace with her. But at least you'll know she'll be safe with Eleanor."

"Dear God, when was anyone ever safe in the company of my sister?"

"Aunt Eleanor has inherited Felix's house in Ludlow; they'll stay there until the outcome of our enterprise is known."

"By Christ, how fortune favours her yet again!" groaned Lady Radcliffe.

"I'd hardly call being made blind in one eye good fortune, aunt?"

"No," agreed Lady Radcliffe, frowning. "I suppose not."

"Speak to your daughter," he told her.

17

15th October 1483, at Vannes in Brittany

Emma Radcliffe found her daughter walking in the chateau garden arm in arm with Meg.

"We must talk, Alice," said Lady Radcliffe.

"I'll leave you," said Meg at once.

"No, Meg, stay – by the Virgin," cried Isabel. "Please stay!"

Meg gave a half-smile. "Not this time, coz," she said and, pulling free of Isabel's grasp, slipped away to another part of the garden.

"Come then," said Lady Radcliffe, "Alice, explain to me what in God's name you are doing here… with your cousin John."

"Alice Radcliffe died in London-"

"By all the saints! Will you stop saying that?" cried Lady Radcliffe. "You didn't die! I know you might have – but you didn't!"

"Only because of Meg – and no thanks to you!"

"I didn't know you were going to try to kill yourself!"

"Aye, you did - and you left me to it!"

"I left it in God's hands!"

"Well, He did me good service because He sent me Meg!"

"Aye, and you took the advice of a child with no experience of life - against that of your own mother!"

"You're wrong about Meg," said Isabel. "Her short life has taught her a great deal. I've learned much from Meg!"

"Meg says this; Meg says that!" said Lady Radcliffe. "Meg's twelve years old! What does she know about anything? She was living on the streets - and in a whorehouse – when she was but nine years old!"

"Well, I've learned a few things from her!"

"Such as what, I'd like to know?"

"Well… how to avoid getting with child, for one thing!"

Just for a moment, even Emma's resolve wavered.

"Aye, some tutor Lady Margaret Elder is! Encouraging you to live in lust with your own first cousin!"

"I didn't intend to fall in love with John – who knows why God allows such things to happen? But, I think, in just one tiny moment, we were bound to each other… And John, risked all for me… saw me through the worst of times…"

"Hooper told me what Catesby put you through. It was monstrous – unforgivable!"

"Peace, lady, please," implored Isabel. "All those terrible things happened to Alice Radcliffe – not Isabel of Coverham."

Emma turned away and wept.

"Listen to me," pleaded Isabel. "We agreed this in London! You told all Christendom that your daughter Alice was dead. Disgraced and dishonoured Alice… is… dead! But, Isabel is alive… and she's here: living and breathing; here with you."

"But-"

"If you want to be reconciled, then be reconciled with Isabel and accept that she loves your nephew. But… know also that she would be honoured if you were to treat her as if she were a daughter to you."

Emma seized upon Isabel's hands gratefully, drawing her into a fond embrace from which Isabel almost immediately broke away.

"Alice has to be dead, mother, you understand? Because Alice could not possibly, in all conscience, marry John Elder; but Isabel can."

"What am I to say to that?"

"You could wish Isabel well – and, since she is orphaned, she would welcome any advice you might have…"

Emma shook her head in despair. "But what of Catesby? What if he learns who you have become? He has already ransacked our house, attacked me! Your poor, dead father will be attainted in the next parliament! Catesby still pursues us all…"

"Aye, lady, but John knows. He knows what's been done in Catesby's name and, when the time for retribution comes, your nephew will deliver it - and he will give no quarter. You may be certain of that!"

18

17th October 1483, on the Catherine in the Breton port of Brest

As the Catherine glided into the port, Lady Eleanor Elder scanned the wharves closely. After a while, unable to pick out anyone she recognised, she turned her attention instead to Augustine Grave. Not only was Grave her most constant companion and closest friend, but he was also her occasional lover. Ravaged by his ordeal during the summer, in London, Grave was not a well man; yet, as always, it was others who attracted his concern. Thus, he draped a comforting arm around the shoulder of Eleanor's grey-faced daughter, Kate.

Folk were, Eleanor decided, either at ease upon a ship, or not – and Kate was most definitely not. Her daughter's aversion to the motion of the waves had become apparent the moment they left the Thames estuary in July on their journey out to Spain. How long ago it seemed now that Master Finch had deposited Eleanor's small party on the dockside at Coruna. And she, like a fool, had expected the rest of the Elder family exiles to join her within a week or two at most. After two long months, she had still been waiting, but with ever-dwindling hope.

All that time, she, her family and a few assorted servants were lodged with the resident factor of her great friend, Felix, a prosperous Ludlow wine merchant. However, all too soon it became clear that the local man was far from enthusiastic about the considerable – and wholly unlooked for – burden upon his small household. Since Eleanor had no source of income, she resorted to hiring out her servants to others. Even so, their meagre earnings were not enough and she knew that if her nephew, John, did not come soon then she would be left with only one alternative: she would have to marry someone. What Master Grave would have made of that development was not difficult for her to imagine.

Another, even more pressing concern for Eleanor was the impact that her daughter – a burgeoning, sultry beauty of fourteen – had made upon the local men. Kate did not just turn the heads of the eager Spanish youths; she twisted them off at the neck. And, knowing her wilful daughter, it was only a matter of time before some foolish infatuation would unleash a shit-barrel of trouble for them all. Thus, when Finch arrived out of nowhere with the news that they were to leave Spain to meet the rest of the family in Brest, she could have kissed him. But, now that she was here, in Brest, she could not help a flutter of doubt, lest her nephew should let her down once again.

As the ship moored up, her eyes returned to the dockside and she gave a sudden squeal of delight. For there stood Hal – sweet Hal Ford, who had been a loyal servant both to her and her brother Ned before her. A moment later, as she looked in vain for her son and her nephew, she realised that Hal was alone.

For the young woman who stood beside her, her servant, Mary, there was no such disappointment for Hal was all she had eyes for. When he came aboard to pay his respects, though he spoke to Eleanor, he glanced at Mary whenever he could. She could not blame the two of them since the abrupt flight from London had separated them only a short while after they had formed an attachment. From Hal, Eleanor learned that her kinfolk were in Vannes and thus, again, she was obliged to wait – something Eleanor had never tolerated well.

⌂⌂⌂⌂⌂⌂

In the event, the wait was short and the following day the Catherine's sister ship, the Margaret, berthed alongside the wharf. The sight of John striding along the wharf with her son, Will, brought a rare tear to her eye. Her nephew, who she had known since the moment of his birth, held a special place in Eleanor's heart. Seeing him there, tall, strong and looking well, reminded her of his father, Ned. Yet when he leapt aboard the Catherine and came to embrace her, she noticed a change in him. She could see it in those haunted grey eyes: whatever had happened in those final hours at the Tower must have taken a heavy toll upon him.

Hugging Will to her, she looked at the two youths in admiration, for these two cousins, fast friends since childhood, filled her with pride. Following after the pair, came the rest of her kin, including – to her astonishment - her sister, Emma. There must be an interesting story there, she reckoned, but she doubted her diffident sister would reveal to her how she had contrived to find her way to Brittany.

In Spain, Eleanor feared her family were lost to her forever - aye, that was the deepest cut: not knowing if they still lived. After the despair of the escape from London, this reunion in Brest seemed all the sweeter. Whatever private demons might still haunt every member of the Elder family, it was a day for celebration for them all - and too, for those who served them.

She was pleased that John insisted that for one evening at least, they should all gather aboard the Catherine to rejoice in their survival and drink to those who had been lost. The evening was much enhanced when James Finch - Matthew's father and the master of the Catherine – was persuaded to tap one of the tuns of sweet wine being carried aboard his ship. Long into the night as flaming torches slowly burned down, they enjoyed each other's company, passing on their news, both good and bad. For some - such as Hal Ford and Mary - they had only a few hours to forge a closer bond than they managed before they were so cruelly parted in July.

Eleanor observed with a little disquiet the close intimacy between her nephew and niece, Alice. Yet, too often, folk had been swift to judge Eleanor herself – and never to her advantage. So, she tried not to do the same to others. Nor did it escape her attention that Will, whose reputation with the lasses had, sadly, become notorious, was being served most attentively by a sweet-looking wench called Eva. Perhaps he would he find some solace there…

To Eleanor it seemed that the evening passed all too quickly, though she was careful to avoid, for the most part, her older sister - beyond expressing regret upon hearing that she had been widowed. In all, they exchanged barely a dozen words but, it was for the best, she thought. Whenever the pair met, it often began promisingly, but it never ended well.

As for what was to happen next, John had made it quite clear that the two ships would travel together only as far as the Dorset coast. The Catherine would then continue to Bristol where it would not only unload its cargo but also the young ladies: Alice, Meg and Kate who, along with Lady Eleanor, would make their way overland to Ludlow. Meg's handsome young guttersnipe, Thomas Skirett, would go with them too, partly because they might need a man in Ludlow, but chiefly because Eleanor suspected that no-one had the energy to argue about it with Meg. She also hoped, for Mary's sake, that she could persuade John to part with Hal.

As for what John intended to do in Poole, let alone what Emma's mysterious part in it was, Eleanor was left to guess. He told her about the revolt but only to explain why he needed to see the three youngest ladies safe. He made no further mention of the lass, formerly known as Alice, so Eleanor remained ignorant about his intentions there.

"The less you know about what I'm doing, aunt," he told her, "the safer you'll be if events go against us. You will be secure in Ludlow giving the king no reason to act against any of you."

Eleanor made no argument because she knew very well that Meg would confide everything to her later on during their journey to Bristol.

The next morning, despite both crew and passengers still suffering from the ill effects of too much wine, the two ships sailed out of Brest harbour on an early tide. The excitement aboard both ships was almost tangible and the welcome change in all their fortunes filled everyone with renewed confidence and vigour.

Eleanor too, felt the gloom of recent months lifting – until, a few hours into their voyage, the two vessels sailed into a thick bank of fog. Almost at once they lost contact with each other and all attempts to hail their sister ship failed. In a few hours, Eleanor's early optimism dissipated in the cool, damp air.

While the Catherine floated slowly through the sea mist, Eleanor, along with all the others, listened in silence for any sound which might reveal the position of the other ship. It occurred to her though, that as long as both ships remained silently listening, it was unlikely that anyone would hear very much.

She gave a sudden gasp. "Voices," she cried. "I swear I heard voices, Master Finch!"

"Quiet, lady!" snapped the ship's master.

"But I heard them!" insisted Eleanor, until Finch's fierce glare forced her to be still.

He moved to stand beside her. "You heard… someone…" he said softly.

"But, who else could it be?" she hissed at him.

"Could be any ship," he replied. "Lady, it's been hours since we last saw the Margaret."

"That long, truly?"

"Indeed, so it could be anyone – it could even be pirates…"

"Pirates!" Eleanor had never expected pirates. She thought it possible the ship might sink, or be blown off course, but pirates? No. The Catherine was old and not very large; her sails were almost threadbare in places and every one of her creaking deck timbers was scarred or split. Surely the old lady would sink out of pure fright if pirates tried to board her!

"So, how can we know who it is?" she asked.

"We can't," said Finch, "not yet, anyways. Whoever it is, they'll be drifting, like us; the wind's dropped off…"

"But if it is pirates…"

"If it is pirates, our best hope is that we slide by them… quietly, my lady."

"You have a rich shipload of wine aboard," she observed.

"I do - and they'll take that - but by God, they'll take your daughter too, lady – maybe even you."

"Aye, I dare say the scum would use Kate badly, wouldn't they," she murmured. "What do you mean '*even me*'?"

"They'd likely not use her at all, my lady - a young, untarnished beauty like her, they'd probably just sell her on. They'd get a good price in Malaga - or one of the other heathen ports down south…"

"Oh," was all Eleanor could reply, as she waited in the murky stillness, disturbed only by the gentle lap of the water and an occasional groan from the elderly ship.

When, from time to time, a wisp of conversation floated towards them, she held her breath and fought to drive from her head the image of Kate being haggled over at some foreign slave market.

"Who are these pirates?" she whispered. "Are they French?"

"French, Breton, Flemish – even English," replied Finch. "Pick any one. One day they're honest traders, the next they're the worst of thieves. All men can be pirates on their worst days, my lady..."

"But that can't be right."

"Right or not, lady, it's what happens."

With terrible suddenness a vessel loomed out of the mist and raked along the side of the Catherine.

"Stand to!" bellowed Finch, snatching Eleanor away from the ship's side.

As the two ships converged, their upper timbers splintered and screeched, as if in agony.

Eleanor hardly caught a glimpse of it before the two ships parted company as abruptly as they had clashed.

"You gotta a blade, lady?" enquired Finch.

"Aye..."

"Then go below to your daughter and keep that blade in your hand!" he urged.

Eleanor hurried to the cabin and peered inside to find Grave and Kate huddled together with Mary.

"Don't tell me that was the Margaret we just hit!" cried Grave.

Eleanor gave a curt shake of the head. "Stay in the cabin, no matter what you hear."

"Lady?" said another voice.

She spun around to find the two young friends of Thomas Skirett from the London gutter. 'Spindle', and his lass, 'Jug', had thrown in their lot with her – a decision she reckoned they were most likely regretting around now. 'Jug', as her vulgar name suggested, had plied her trade on the streets of the city until only a few months ago. Hardly surprising that now, far from the life they knew, the pair looked frightened out of their wits.

"Pirates!" announced Eleanor and, without further explanation, she bundled the wide-eyed girl into the crowded cabin and slammed the door shut.

"Stay here at the door and have your knife ready," she ordered Spindle, before returning to the main deck, to reflect that she really must find out their real names. Amusing though it was at first, she could hardly keep referring to them as if they were someone's private parts!

When she reappeared at his side, Finch eyed her crossly. "Christ save us!" he protested. "I told you to stay below."

"Aye, Master Finch, you did," agreed Eleanor, as she faced him down with a gleam in her good eye. "But there's no sense in keeping a sharp blade out of the fight is there? And, besides: one-eyed, renegade ladies don't have to do as they're told."

Finch responded only with a weary shake of the head, but Eleanor, thriving on excitement, was keen to prove that her efforts to recover her health in the warmth of Spain had borne some fruit.

"I don't see any pirates," she told Finch. "In faith, in this I can't see much of anything!"

"They're still close…" he murmured.

"Will they fly a flag, or pennant?" she asked.

"Might do… might not. …"

"But they could be English!"

"Hah!" laughed Finch. "Don't mean they're your friends, lady…"

Finch's voice trailed away as he watched mesmerised, along with several others of his crew, as Eleanor tore a great gash in her kirtle. She recalled that, in her younger days, she had found it allowed her more freedom to move in a fight. Enjoying the rapt attention of the crew, she gave a wicked grin, as she slowly lifted up one ragged edge of the kirtle to retrieve her well-honed knife from a black velvet sheath nestling against her tanned inner thigh.

"Christ's balls!" groaned Finch.

Then, knife in hand, Eleanor sauntered over to take her place at the ship's side where three men at arms and several other crewmen already stood. A moment later she was oddly pleased when young 'Spindle' joined her, armed with a cudgel.

While she waited, she brushed a nervous hand over the grubby brown patch presented to her by Finch when they left Coruna. Its previous owner, according to the ship's master, had died wearing it but, dead man's legacy or not, she was grateful for the scrap of worn leather to mask her sightless left eye. According to Grave, it made her look more menacing than ever; which, of course, she took as a great compliment.

She was forced to admit – if only to herself - that she was still struggling to view the world through only one eye. When she complained – as she admitted she was wont to do at the least provocation – Grave would gently remind her that one good eye was rather better than none. Few men could silence her as effectively as Grave - strange how affection could bring her to her knees.

Without warning, the ship they had encountered earlier, ghosted into view again and grated once more along the Catherine's side. She saw now that it was larger - three-masts, like the Margaret, rather than the Catherine's two, standing black against the mist - and it rode a little higher out of the water, she thought. Lining its side, crewmen brandished weapons and bellowed insults. Next moment, a dozen or so of the pirates, waving cudgels and knives, leapt through the air towards the Catherine's deck. Though Eleanor watched, motionless, she felt a surge of blood coursing through her body as if a fire, long-extinguished, was being rekindled.

One second the two vessels were grinding against each other and the next they lurched apart to open up a grey chasm between them. For many of those who jumped, the gap proved fatally wide and only three men reached the Catherine's deck. One of them, a tall man, with a mass of unkempt hair and a thin beard, landed squarely in front of Eleanor, his sword raised.

Feet planted upon the deck, she gripped her knife more tightly, poised to defend herself, until the ships crashed together again in another bruising kiss. Though her opponent stared at her, he did not attack. She hoped he was distracted by her appearance, but more likely it was the chilling screams of his comrades being crushed between the two colliding hulls.

Eleanor too was slow to react and, when she did lunge at him, the Catherine gave a sudden list and tipped her backwards onto the deck. Though she rolled into a crouch ready to spring at her adversary, he had other concerns for a breach had opened up once more between the two ships. With several uncertain steps, he retreated towards the Catherine's splintered rail. Though his own vessel already lay a full two yards away, he vaulted from the rail and Eleanor, scrambling to her feet, just caught a glimpse of him clinging to the side of his ship.

For some reason she did not quite understand, she was pleased that he had made it. The brute would probably have killed her and abducted her daughter but, in that moment, she could only admire his bravery and agility, as he scrambled up to his ship's deck. Without thinking, she saluted him with a wave of her blade and he, in turn, made an extravagant, and she suspected quite lewd, gesture in reply, before he and his vessel disappeared once more into the fog.

An uneasy silence returned as the crew waited for another assault. At any moment Eleanor expected the pirate ship to loom over them out of the murk, but it did not. In fact they did not see it again and Eleanor was appalled to discover that she felt more than a trace of regret when her bearded seaman did not reappear.

"You've met the ship's master then," muttered Finch. "René de Merckes."

"You know him?"

"Can't miss him, can you?"

"I scarce noticed him," murmured Eleanor.

"We've had our differences, you might say, René and me…"

"Perhaps pirates aren't so bad after all," mused Eleanor.

"Hah! Not so bad? You might think a bit different, lady, if they hanged you from the yards, spilled out your guts and threw your carcass into the sea!"

"If they did all that, Master Finch," laughed Eleanor, leaning back at ease against the oak foremast, "I doubt I'd be thinking much at all…"

Ignoring her, he turned sharply aside to snarl at a crewman by the ship's side. "Keep a close eye on that lead!" he bawled.

"What's he doing?" she enquired.

"Do you never stop asking questions, lady?"

"I like to know what's happening," she said, with a frown. "I like to be… prepared."

"Well, if you must know, he's making sure we don't rip our hull to shreds on Breton rocks," said Finch. "That help get you prepared, does it?"

"Aye, thank you, Master Finch; it does!" she replied sweetly. "So the pirates have gone now?"

He gave a sudden grin. "You sound disappointed, lady."

"No," she lied, "just asking…"

The dripping fog, however, took longer to ward off than the pirates and remained with them for the rest of the day. Sometime during the night it finally cleared and the following morning a gentle breeze blew up. Finch pointed out to her the coast of Normandy but, as far as Eleanor knew, it could have been anywhere. To her, one distant finger of grey-brown land looked much the same as any other; yet it was at least a smear of hope amid the great expanse of water.

"God favoured us yesterday, my lady; just be thankful for that."

"Oh, I thank the Virgin every day for delivering us, Master Finch," said Eleanor, stretching her arms up to the sky and arching her back to loosen her stiff and aching joints.

Finch bellowed out a string of orders to his longsuffering crew then turned to Eleanor.

"My lady, I fear your… somewhat… ragged appearance is unsettling my crew, so do you think you could get that servant girl of yours to… you know, sew you up again, if you please?"

"Of course, Master Finch, I shall do whatever you ask, but what if the pirates should return?"

"Oh, I think you frightened them off the first time, lady…"

So, for the rest of the morning she sat undisturbed upon the small scrap of stern deck with only Mary in attendance. While her servant struggled to repair the butchered kirtle, Eleanor watched the faint smudge of grey land disappear until soon she could see no land at all.

When the offending garment was mended, Finch joined her on the stern deck and she remarked: "I can't see the land anymore - and I rather miss it."

"Long as I know where it is, my lady, that's all that matters," he told her.

During the late morning the others crawled up onto the deck in ones and twos. Grave ushered Kate to the ship's side where, as was her habit, she hurled the sparse contents of her stomach into the sea. Watching the pair, Eleanor smiled at Grave's patience, showing with every word and gesture how much he cared for the lass. Just as well, since Eleanor, despising weakness in herself, struggled to tolerate it in others – even her own daughter.

When Finch moved off, no doubt to tongue-lash his crew again, she saw Grave escorting Kate in her direction. Delivering what she hoped was a sympathetic smile, Eleanor waited for the pair to join her. A grimace from Grave warned her that a smile alone might not be enough.

"I hate this ship!" railed Kate. "Why in the Virgin's name did you bring us aboard again, mother?"

"We've only been back at sea for a day or two, my dear," she said. "And was it not worth it to see your brother and cousins again?"

"Will spent the whole time drooling over that Flemish whore he's picked up and my cousins are strangers to me now."

"Not Meg, surely!"

"Meg most of all, with her coarse lover trotting behind her everywhere she went – and she's younger than I am, mother!"

"Aye, Kate, but Meg is… Meg…"

"Oh aye, of course, Lady Margaret is special… God's breath! I'd rather have stayed in Spain. I was content enough there - and I was even learning some words!"

Aye, but what words, Eleanor wondered?

"How much longer will the journey take?" asked her daughter.

"Master Finch says that with fair weather like this we might reach Poole in a few days and Bristol in a week."

"Another week!" cried Kate.

"Well, you'll just have to put up with it!" scolded Eleanor.

"The time will pass, Kate," soothed Grave.

Aye, thought Eleanor, but it would pass at snail's pace both for mother and daughter; for it seemed they were forever destined to be at odds. Whatever few skills of motherhood God had bestowed upon her, they were clearly inadequate for the task.

That evening, for once, they were all together and, after the perils of the previous day, Eleanor quietly gave thanks that the disparate members of her party had survived to witness the falling sun bathe the dazzling sea and sky with the warmest of amber glows. Captivated by its simple beauty, she reckoned that, despite all their past trials and looming uncertainties, they were indeed blessed to behold such a sight.

She did not, however, feel quite so blessed in the middle of the night when the wind strengthened and a sudden squall blew up. Kept awake by the ceaseless groaning of the ship's timbers, she heard the watch change every four hours or so and soon became attuned to every small scuffling and scratching sound. Best not to tell her daughter about the rats, she decided.

By dawn, the keen wind had not decreased at all and the crew had to work hard to keep the vessel sailing true.

"Are we safe, Master Finch?" she asked the master.

"At this time of year, my lady, you never know what to expect," he told her. "You can have flat calm, as you've seen, or you can have a boiling sea! But don't you worry, the Catherine's seen all this before — and at least we're making good distance!"

Within hours the wind strengthened further, driving their vessel even harder before it. Despite Finch's protestations of confidence, the fierce wind began to toss the ship hither and thither and the crew were obliged to lower some sails lest they should lose them. While they laboured to keep both the ship and its goods intact, the passengers faced a stark and unenviable choice: seek refuge in the grim, dark cabin below at the stern, or remain on deck at the mercy of the relentless wind and rain.

Towards evening, after an entire day of violent winds, Eleanor began to have genuine fears for their survival; for it did not take an experienced mariner to see that the crew were already exhausted.

That night, as Grave, Kate, and the two London waifs huddled below, Eleanor resolved to remain above deck.

"You can stay below if you wish," she told Mary.

"Pah! Too damned cramped down there, my lady," declared Mary. "You can hardly breathe!"

So Mary stayed there with her mistress and, as always, Eleanor loved her for it.

"If you two are going to stay up here then more fool you," Finch roared, tossing them some rope, "but you'd best tie each other down!"

Grim-faced, the two women bound themselves to the ship and each other, determined to spit in the eye of the raging tempest. The tempest, however, apparently unconcerned by their defiance, hurled even more ferocious winds against them as if bent on forcing them over the side.

"It's the wrath of God, my lady!" screamed Mary. "It's caught up with us at last!"

"We've been in worse places, Mary!" replied Eleanor, bellowing to raise her voice above the gale. And so they had – in fact she had made a habit of being in the worst of places, but there was something quite different about this savage storm that sent its towering waves crashing down upon the ship. If it truly was the wrath of God, then Eleanor feared she could expect little compassion at His hand.

"Perhaps we should pray, my lady?" cried Mary.

"You can do whatever the hell you like!" screamed Eleanor, clutching her servant to her as the rigging shrieked and timbers all around them cried out for mercy.

It was just about then that a great shaft of wood swept past them and disappeared into the sea: the Catherine had lost her main mast.

19

22nd October 1483, at dawn on board the Margaret

It had been a long night aboard the Margaret, as the vessel was buffeted by storm winds and high seas.

"Where, in God's name, are we?" demanded John, his voice croaking out of his salt-scarred throat.

"A long way from where we ought to be, I fear," said Matthew, with a weary sigh.

"Is anyone hurt?" asked Isabel.

"No, my lady," replied Matthew, with a reassuring smile, "nothing more than a few cuts and bruises."

"By God, what storms!" said Meg, "and your poor ship…" She waved an arm at the deck strewn with wreckage.

"Well, your brother's ship actually," Matthew pointed out. "And yes, I'll admit it looks like a shambles now, but most of the debris can be cleared easily enough. With a few repairs and a fair wind, we'll soon be on our way again."

"It looks bad enough to me," grumbled John, surveying the broken spars, torn rigging and smashed items of cargo.

"Believe me; it could have been much worse," said Matthew. "The masts are still in one piece – and only one of the water barrels was smashed."

"By Christ!" cursed John. "This voyage has been a disaster from the first day – ever since we lost the Catherine! And I still don't understand how that happened either!"

"In sea fog, my lord, you've only to steer a few yards away from another ship," explained Matthew, "and, before you know it, she's gone."

"But… God's blood, we've only just been reunited with them all!" he groaned. "And we can ill afford any delay…"

"Oh, do cheer up, brother," cried Meg, taking him by the arm. "We're still alive, aren't we? Now leave poor Matthew to his work!"

Feeling Isabel's more gentle grip upon his other arm, he succumbed and they bore him away from Master Finch.

Even so, his patience was sorely tested when the repairs took far longer than Matthew expected and all day long the Margaret wallowed on a flat calm sea. By dawn the next day, the ship was repaired, but they found not a breath of wind to take them to England. By the end of that day, even Matthew seemed downcast.

"I fear we could be stuck here for days," he lamented.

And they were: for it was the best part of another three days before a light breeze sparked a little hope. The following day the Margaret stalked the elusive wind in the hope of gaining a little more speed but in vain and Matthew estimated that they had covered only a few dozen miles in the whole day.

"The Catherine must be well ahead of us now," said John. "When they reach Poole, they won't know what to do! I wish now that I'd told Aunt Eleanor what we're about in Dorset. "

"It's just possible the Catherine is moving as slowly as we are," reasoned Matthew, "so they may not reach the Dorset coast much ahead of us. And even if they do, my father will simply take the ship into the port and they can wait for us there."

"Aye, perhaps, but time is wasting, Matthew," said John, "and, each day it wastes, our hopes of success in Dorset dwindle further."

20

22nd October 1483, aboard the Catherine at sea

Lady Eleanor lay tethered to the stern rail; her clothes, though saturated many times, were already drying stiff with salt. Her cap was long gone, leaving her mass of red hair matted and salt-laden. The boiling sea Finch had dared to name was now but a gentle swell. The storm was over, but if, in the end, God had stayed His mighty hand then His wrath had still taken a terrible toll of the Catherine and her crew.

Leaning forward to survey the main deck below her, Eleanor could only thank the Virgin that she was still there at all. Of the main mast, only a torn stump protruded from the ravaged deck. The mast itself, rigging and main sail had disappeared without trace and, though the foremast seemed intact, only a torn rag of sail clung doggedly to the yard. Of the numerous tuns of wine that were stored both above and below deck, only a solitary barrel remained intact; the rest were either lost overboard, or so badly damaged that the wine would be spoiled. Sundry other goods once neatly stacked on deck were just gone – all lost.

The damage to the vessel and its cargo was the least of it though, for bodies littered the deck and though a few still lived, Eleanor knew at a glance that several did not. Already the surviving crew members were scavenging for pieces of cloth large enough to use as shrouds. When Mary untied the ropes which had saved them both, Eleanor stumbled below on trembling legs to the cabin, where she found the others alive but bruised and wracked by sickness. Even the stoic Grave looked a pale and beaten man.

For the rest of the morning, no-one found much to say, though Eleanor noted that one or two of the crew gave them dark looks. When she questioned Finch about it, he mumbled that many sailors thought it was unlucky to have a woman aboard.

"Hah!" she replied. "And I suppose when there's no woman to blame, they blame evil spirits!"

"And why wouldn't they?" he growled at her. "Strange what you'll believe when all seems lost..."

Eleanor looked him in the eye. "Is all lost then?"

His bleak countenance told her the thrust of it, but she forced him to elaborate.

"Fifteen men killed, or lost overboard, in one night," he told her. "Fifteen good lads - and two more injured so bad they're like to follow them under the waves."

"But some were so young..."

"And they won't be getting any older," said Finch.

"Will any of us?" she asked.

Finch shrugged. "We lost the mast, main sail and most of the ship's load – and any food we had is spoiled."

She had already seen all of that for herself but when he spelled it out, it sounded somehow even more catastrophic.

"But at least we still have some water and a little beer," he said.

"Can we still make it to Poole?"

"Don't know... but those winds were battering us in the right direction at least. We can't be far off the English coast..."

"And we still have one mast and a small sail."

"Hah! Just about," he conceded, "and we can still steer, thank the Lord for that! But how long it'll take us to make landfall is any man's guess."

"So, do we still try for Poole?"

"Not sure where to head, my lady. If I'm right, the storm drove us west and a touch north. The winds and currents might yet take us to the English coast, right enough. If St Nick's watching, we might make Poole – we could put in there for repairs – if St Nick's watching…"

"And if he's not watching?" murmured Eleanor.

"We could be washed along the channel, driven onto rocks somewhere… almost anywhere…"

"What can we do then, Finch?" she asked. "What do I tell my daughter?"

"You tell her to pray, lady," whispered Finch. "You tell 'em all to pray, for our fate – whatever it will be - is far out of my hands now."

For the rest of that day the Catherine, shrouded in gloom, limped across the sea aided at times by a brisk, warm breeze from the south-west. That afternoon Eleanor gathered her flock once more upon the stern deck. Better, she decided, if things went badly to spend whatever time remained with those she loved.

Most worrying was the deteriorating health of her daughter who had eaten next to nothing since they sailed from Brest and kept little enough of that in her belly. Weak and listless, her once quite buxom daughter grew thinner each day. She seemed already devoid of hope for her eyes took on a curious, dull look as if she was in another place. Perhaps she was, thought Eleanor - how swiftly the body surrendered, when the spirit failed.

By sharp contrast, Eleanor was astonished to find that the London pair remained unwaveringly cheerful. When she remarked upon it, Spindle simply replied: "When yer used to goin' 'ungry, lady, you soon learn to keep breevin' till yer next feed comes along!"

"Aye, Master Spindle," she said, "but perhaps some are just born to survive…"

"Or, they're chosen by God," complained Mary, "who always seems to have His favourites…"

"Mary, I swear you've spent too many years in my service," murmured Eleanor. "When did you become so… bereft of faith?"

"The day I left Hal Ford in Brest," replied her servant and then clapped a hand to her mouth. "I shouldn't have said that…"

"Why not?" said Eleanor. "Everyone knows you're besotted with Hal!"

"They don't!" said Mary.

"They do!" said Spindle, Jug and Grave all at once.

"Oh," said Mary, turning her reddening face away. "Well, he's not here, so what does it matter? What does anything matter? I'm never going to see him again, am I?"

Wracked by guilt and regrets, Eleanor began to succumb to a persistent throbbing in her head. When, at the end of the day, the last traces of sun began to fade, Eleanor took succour from the gentle, comforting squeeze of Grave's hand. But her relief was short-lived for even her obstinate self-belief was melting away as fast as molten iron in a blistering hot furnace.

"Stay strong, my dear," whispered Grave, reading her mood as accurately as ever, "for do we not always draw our strength from you?"

When most of the others went below, Eleanor sought out Finch who was wearing a surprisingly cheerful expression.

"Do I see the light of hope in your eyes, Finch?" she pleaded. "Please tell me I do…"

"Pray and be hopeful, my lady," he replied. "That's always my way."

Eleanor's raised eyebrows probably revealed her doubts about Finch's professed optimism, of which she had observed precious little evidence before.

"If I'm right," he said, "we should make Poole by late tomorrow."

"But we've no food left..." cried Eleanor, "and Kate's so weak."

"With water we can last for days," Finch assured her. "I'm not saying it'll be easy, but 'tis right to hope, is it not?"

Eleanor frowned. "I shall pass on your hope to the others, Finch, though I should confess that hope has never worked especially well for me."

"Then have faith in the Lord, my lady, for He does determine all."

"Aye, Finch, He does; but, in my experience, He more often comes to the aid of the strong... than the hopeful!"

With a rueful shake of the head, Finch ignored her bleak assertion and went to oversee what remained of his crew as they continued to bring some semblance of order out of the chaos. She admired their heart, their sheer tenacity – for it was a tireless determination to survive which matched her own.

At dawn Eleanor dozed, half-awake, imagining a death at sea. How many times had she faced death, she wondered? But not this way, for drowned at sea was not a fate she had ever thought very likely. Was it better to starve to death or drown, she wondered idly, as she drifted back into an uneasy sleep?

"Land ho! Land!"

When the hoarse cry woke her, Eleanor unearthed a last stubborn flicker of resistance and staggered her way down the steps to join Finch at the ship's port side. Her chafed lips parted in a defiant smile, for even she could see the land which, though still distant, was unmistakable – the same sort of grey smear Finch had pointed out earlier in their journey.

"Where are we?" she demanded.

"Need to be closer to be sure," said Finch.

They must have watched the land for more than an hour before Eleanor made the stark observation: "It's not getting any closer, Master Finch."

But of course, he already knew that. "It's the damned currents!" he declared. "The more we steer landwards, the more the sea pushes us east – and with that great rip in our foresail, we can do sod all about it!"

Later that morning one of the crew gave a shout. "That's Dorsetshire!"

"You sure?" cried Finch.

"Sailed these waters as a lad, master," confirmed the seaman.

"Where then?" Finch seized the man's arm. "Portland Bill?"

"Aye, Portland, Master Finch!" cried the fellow, seized with emotion.

"Think we can get to Poole after all?" asked Finch.

"Currents can be bad around here," said the crewman, as if beginning to doubt himself.

"True," agreed Finch.

"Afore Poole, there's a few coves, but… there's steep cliffs all along mind – and offshore rocks…"

"And if the tide's wrong," said Finch, "we could catch our keel on the reefs out here…"

"In the name of Christ!" barked Eleanor, who had been following their exchange from the stern deck, "Do you have any good news?"

The two seafarers fell silent for a moment.

After a deep sigh, Finch nodded. "If we can get past Handfast Point, into Studland Bay – that's a safe anchorage. But there's a strong pull past the headland."

"If we can get that far," said the crewman, "we might even put into Poole harbour, but-"

"By the Virgin!" croaked Eleanor, "Must every word you say come with a damned 'but' after it!"

"-all hangs on the tide," finished the crewman.

"The tide now, is it?" railed Eleanor. "Is everything against us?"

"Ebb or flow, my lady," Finch told her, his own voice as brittle as hers. "It's the toss of a coin now…"

Yet, the land was closer and too close to surrender to despair just yet, decided Eleanor, as she returned to the others. Though her head still ached and her stiff limbs complained every time she moved, she would not yield yet – nor would she permit her ailing daughter to do so. Each time Kate drifted away into sleep, Eleanor woke her with a cruel jab in the ribs.

"Stay awake, Kate, and fight, damn you! Fight to stay alive… for just a little longer, please…"

Grave, perhaps unsure whether to scold or praise, remained silent.

"I don't care if she lives to hate me," muttered Eleanor, "as long she lives…"

Even the Londoners had nothing to say, every last spark of their God-given resolve now extinguished.

As the afternoon wore on, Eleanor sat watching grey clouds gather overhead, bringing the possibility of rain; but by midday, no rain had come and the clouds began to disperse once again. Finch beckoned her down to the main deck so, leaving Kate in the care of Grave and a young seaman not much older than her daughter, she stood up, only to sway before catching herself on the splintered ship's rail. Although long ago used to the rhythm of the ship's movement, lack of food had sapped her strength more than she was prepared to admit. The dull, but unrelenting, pounding in her head did not help. Thus, with a little more care than usual, she descended once more the few steps to the main deck and joined the master at the ship's prow.

"I didn't want to say it too loud, my lady," Finch murmured, "but at the rate we're moving, we'll most likely round Handfast Point in the night – or, if we don't round it, we'll smash into it… Whether the tide's in flood or not, there'll likely be fierce races."

"Races?"

"Strong, local currents, pushing or pulling at us – but this old ship can't escape them. After the battering the poor girl's taken, it's a wonder she's still afloat at all."

"So, there will be… races – what of them?"

"At best, the races might push us into Studland Bay but… they might just dash us against the rocks. Whether they'll bring us good or ill, only the Lord can tell."

"Then I fear the Lord will need His wits about him, Finch."

"Aye, my lady, and so shall we. It's a heavy sea, not too rough, but heavy all the same. If we get past the point and into the bay, all well and good; but, if we don't, we'll run aground - or worse, we'll break up. If we do hit, my lady, there'll be no time to think – or talk."

"So, what must we do?"

"If we run aground, stay aboard. When dawn comes we may find ourselves in a safe place."

"And if the Catherine breaks up?"

"I'll call out: 'abandon the ship'…"

"And then what?"

"You get your folk off the damn ship anyway you can!"

"Didn't we have a small boat?"

"Did have, but in case you hadn't noticed, the storm ripped that away too…"

"So, we just go… into the sea… in the darkness…"

"Best jump and get well clear. If she turns over, you're not getting off at all."

"But we'll not be able to see anything…"

"No, nothing. I'll do what I can, my lady, but shipwrecks don't follow no plan - best just pray for a safe passage…"

"I've said enough prayers, Finch," she said, disconsolate, because this was a fate that raw courage alone could not overcome.

"And I, my lady," agreed Finch, "but a few more can't hurt…"

She clasped his hand. "Thank you, Master Finch, for telling me all."

"As you said, lady, it'll help you if you're prepared…"

When she returned to the others, she found that most had drifted again into a stupor – all save Spindle who gave her a nod and Mary – of course, Mary, who would most likely be chained to her mistress' side till the day that one – or more likely, both - of them perished. Poor Mary should be spending her days on dry land in the arms of Master Hal Ford, not squandering them in the company of her ungrateful bitch of a mistress.

Grave was asleep with Kate cradled in his arms and this time Eleanor did not wake them. Better they slept now, she thought. In fact, if the moonless night went badly then perhaps it was better that none of them ever woke up.

The sleep of oblivion, however, was not – and could never be – an escape for Eleanor Elder. For hour upon hanging hour, she remained at the ship's rail with Mary, seeing nothing but listening to the waves' persistent slap against the Catherine's hull. Every so often the sound was punctuated by the voice of the seaman who dipped the lead weight into the water and called out the depth. Of course, if an isolated, rocky outcrop tore out the ship's bottom then such a precaution would not be worth a peddler's curse. Still, as the ship plodded on through the tireless waves, the rhythm of his calls was somehow reassuring– until he stopped.

The Catherine shuddered from a sudden impact and somewhere – somewhere right beneath Eleanor's feet - there was a dull, but audible, crack. For a moment the tired ship seemed to hesitate, trembling, upon the lip of a wave before plunging down into the next trough. When she rose up once more, Eleanor hugged Mary to her and wept with relief as the Catherine clambered over the next swell. But with every heave of the sea, the ship's movement grew more sluggish until she gave a deep groan and from the stern came a sudden squeal of alarm that pierced Eleanor's heart. Kate.

Snatching Mary's hand, she turned to run to the stern deck but beneath their feet the planks twisted and lifted, tossing the two women down onto their backs. A chaos of snarling voices, rushing water and splintering timbers filled the darkness around them. No bellowed order of "Abandon the ship!" came from Finch, but Eleanor, sitting up to her waist in the seething water, did not need to be told that the Catherine was sinking fast.

The bedraggled pair hauled each other along the sloping deck, scrambling up yard by yard. The stern could surely not be more than a few feet away, but when Eleanor's fingers grasped the end of a splintered plank, she cried out in despair. The raised deck had gone! Indeed the whole stern of the ship had disappeared, just sheered away in the black void. Suddenly Eleanor felt cold - colder than she ever expected. Her legs were so numb she could crawl no more and the bitter knowledge that her daughter was lost crushed her spirit. It had all happened in an instant — just as Finch warned that it might.

The ship's master was suddenly at Eleanor's side, hand outstretched.

"My Kate!" she screamed at him.

"My best young man was at her side!" roared Finch. "Let's get you off the ship!"

Gripping Mary's hand, Eleanor reached for his arm, only to lose sight of him as he and the entire main deck dropped by several feet. The ailing vessel dipped her bow under the waves, taking their squirming bodies with it and plunging them into the sea. Dragged down by their heavy, saturated clothes, they screamed like terrified children until the sea closed over their heads and filled their gaping mouths with black water.

Part Three: Handfast Point

21

22nd October 1483, at the house of the Mayor of Poole

The mayor of the burgeoning port of Poole, Roger Cayne, waved his friend and comrade, Richard Morton, into his privy chamber.

"Richard! I wasn't expecting you this morning," he said. "Is something wrong?"

"Wrong? By God, yes, Roger!" stuttered Morton. "Indeed, something is very wrong!"

"Well, sit, my dear fellow, sit," urged Roger. "Will you take a drink of spiced wine?"

Richard shook his head and then slumped down onto a chair, head in hands.

"Come then, my friend, compose yourself and tell me what has got you so agitated."

Taking a deep breath, Morton began. "Last night I received a visit from my kinsman, Robert, who was on his way to-" Morton broke off to lower his voice before continuing. "-on his way to Exeter to join the rebels there. In London, Robert visited Lady Margaret Stanley – she is-"

"Yes, yes, Richard," interrupted Roger, "I know who the lady is, but please continue."

Morton glanced around the chamber while Roger resisted the temptation to shake the man by the throat. If there was a more anxious fellow in Poole, Roger had yet to meet him.

"She passed on to my kinsman some news… alarming news, Roger…"

"Yes?" prompted Roger.

"About our leader, Sir John Savage!" cried Morton.

"But since Sir John rode off to Kent, a month ago, we've heard nothing from him – or from the men of Kent for that matter," said Roger, "despite my many urgent enquiries!"

"Until now," groaned Morton, "and it turns out that he never even arrived in Kent!"

"Well he certainly didn't return here!" declared Roger.

"No, but - if we're to believe Lady Stanley," said Morton, "the reason he never arrived is that he was murdered on the road!" whispered Morton. "All these weeks we wondered where he was and it turns out he's been lying in a damned ditch since very soon after he rode out of here! He must have been killed weeks ago!"

"And Lady Stanley told Robert all this?"

"Yes, I told you."

"But, Richard, can we believe it, do you think?" asked Roger.

"Well Robert believes it – and he's a lawyer who's not easily fooled," said Morton.

"I meant no slur against your kinsman," said Roger, "but if this is true, it deals a deadly blow to our hopes of rebellion here in Dorset."

Since Roger had, in fact, been expecting the news to break for some time, he struggled to feign surprise. When Morton mentioned Sir John, Roger feared their leader might still somehow be alive; so now at least he could rest easy on that point. The three men he had despatched after

Sir John had clearly done their work well – as they had claimed.

"We are finished here then," lamented Roger. "Our revolt has crumbled before it's even begun."

"No!" cried Morton, "I've delivered only half my news! There's more!"

"More?" said Roger, wondering what else there could possibly be to say.

"Yes, we're to expect a messenger from Lady Stanley."

"A messenger?" snapped Roger, wrong-footed for the first time. "What for?"

"I don't know, Roger. Robert just told me to expect a messenger. I am to go to St James' Church in the town at midday every day until the envoy arrives. He'll show me a silver ring as a token that he truly comes from Lady Margaret."

"It all sounds a little too mysterious to me, Richard," said Roger, "and even if it is true, can we trust Lady Stanley? Her husband is King Richard's Steward."

"We have to trust someone, Roger!" said Morton. "Surely the men of Dorset cannot let others take the lead in this? I've heard the Kent rebels are already making a noise, while we sit on our hands here in Poole – leaderless and badly adrift!"

"But what does Lady Stanley know of our affairs?" said Roger. "It is we who take all the risks while she sits weaving her web safely far away from the perils of rebellion. And how are we to rise up? When? Where? Henry of Richmond was supposed to be in England by now – yet where is this rebel earl? And - as you said yourself – we have no leader!"

"So what do you think I should do, Roger?" Morton was trembling as he spoke.

"You'd better tell the others what you know, but perhaps not about the messenger. Best we keep that to ourselves – after all, Sir John's murder cannot just be chance. It's possible that one of our own has betrayed us to the crown?"

"Much as I hate to believe it, Roger, I fear you may be right."

"But, let it not be said that I left you to bear this heavy burden alone, Richard. If any messenger should arrive, come to me at once, and I'll do everything in my power to settle matters."

Morton wrung Roger's hand gratefully before bidding him farewell. After he left, Roger wandered out, deep in thought, to the small courtyard at the rear of his house. His attempt to forestall the local rebels had been effective so far because without a leader there would be no revolt. However, if the interfering Lady Stanley did send someone, he would need to take prompt action. He smiled. Thanks to his trusting friend, Richard Morton, Roger was now well placed to intercept any messenger. No doubt Morton would trot along and tell him when the unknown person arrived. With all the town's resources at his disposal, Roger felt confident that he could take care of the rest.

22

24ᵗʰ October 1483 close to dawn, in Studland Bay, Dorset

Eleanor lay on a stony shore with Mary draped around her waist and cool water lapping against her legs. Spitting out the contents of her mouth – grit or sand, with a trace of some green weed - she hauled herself up onto her elbows. Fighting back nausea, she eased her weary body from Mary's loose grasp and sat upright. She stared out at the sea, which she could hear and feel, but could not yet see very well. For an anxious moment she feared she had lost her sight once more, until she worked out that it was not yet dawn.

Mary had not stirred and, in a sudden panic, Eleanor bent down to examine her, running her hands over her servant's body, seeking wounds or broken bones.

"That's my bruised arse," groaned Mary.

Eleanor pulled her hands away. "I just thought…"

"I know," murmured her companion, "but I'm alright. You hurt, lady?"

"Hurt?" croaked Eleanor. "No, not hurt. All that matters is finding Kate and Grave… and the others. That's all that matters."

She attempted to shout out Kate's name, but her dry throat denied her.

"We should rest our bruised legs till it's light, my lady," said Mary. "We can't see anything yet!"

"Aye," wheezed Eleanor, "I know, but while we rest, others could be dying…"

She stood up and took several faltering steps along the beach only to stumble over a rock and fall headlong. Crawling on all fours to reach her, Mary gripped her hand tight.

"We'll find them, my lady, but we can do nothing yet."

Eleanor remained with her, waiting for the dawn; one moment snarling at the sea, the next sobbing onto Mary's shoulder. At the first glimmer of dawn, they began to scour the shoreline. Since they had washed up in a very small cove, it did not take long. They discovered another member of the ship's company, but the crewman's head rested at an impossibly sharp angle to his neck. As the sky lightened further, the pair found themselves alone on the empty beach.

Fixing her gaze upon what she supposed must be Handfast Point, Eleanor expected to see the remains of the Catherine perched there upon the grey rocks. But there was nothing - not a spar of timber, nor shred of sail - to mark the ship's passing. Perhaps the vessel went down on the other, westerly, side of Handfast Point, but she could not see a way around where the waves broke upon the headland.

Was this high tide, or low tide? She knew only what little Finch had told her about the tides but, judging from the debris lying higher up the beach, it was somewhere in between high and low tide. They could wait to find out, but if the tide was still coming in then they could be trapped in the tiny cove. Behind them, a grubby white rock face stretched skyward and a glance at the eroding cliff edge showed where great shards of rock had broken away to plummet down onto the cove below.

Above the cliff, she glimpsed the top of a wall. Was it the top of a tower? It might be simply a house, or perhaps a church; but whatever it was, it must be sited dangerously close to the cliff edge. In any case, it looked impossible to reach from where they were down on the beach. They needed help but to get it, they would have to find some local folk.

Trudging from the point to the other end of the stony cove, they found they could clamber over some slippery rock pools into a much wider bay beyond. There, to their delight, they saw two figures sitting on the sand and one immediately raced to greet them.

"Right pleased to see you, my lady!" cried Spindle, and she heard the relief in his voice.

Eleanor nodded a grim acknowledgement to mask her disappointment. Though she was pleased to discover other survivors, she had thought at first glance that it was Kate and Grave. Even so, two more souls were safe, she told herself but, when they reached the London pair, she saw to her dismay that the lass, Jug, was far from safe.

"She's broke 'er leg!" lamented Spindle. "I splinted it with some bits of wood I found..."

To her credit, the pale-faced lass made little complaint, with only the occasional sharp intake of breath, or low-voiced curse. All the same, despite her fortitude, she would be walking nowhere; she would have to be carried.

"Have you seen any others?" asked Mary.

"A fella walked past," said Spindle.

"What do you mean 'walked past'?" asked Eleanor.

"Never mind 'im!" cried Spindle. "Jug needs 'elp!"

"Aye," said Eleanor, with a sigh, "so do we all..."

"We need water too, my lady," said Mary.

"I know that well enough!" grumbled Eleanor. "You stay with Jug," she ordered. "Spindle, come with me and we'll see if we can find a way to the next cove."

Almost at once they found another of the crew – one of the younger ones. Though death had left no mark upon him, yet he was dead all the same – drowned, Eleanor supposed. Further along the shore they encountered another poor fellow, alive but bleeding from a head wound. Dazed and confused, he said nothing but shied away, giving them fearful looks.

"That's the one I saw," murmured Spindle.

Seeing no-one else close by, they told him to wait and help would come. Whether he understood, Eleanor could not tell, but she hurried on towards the far end of the cove, praying they could find a safe path around. But even from thirty yards' distance she could see that it was hopeless, for the waves were already dashing against the foot of the sheer cliff.

Turning her back to the stony shore, Eleanor stared long and hard, once more, at the cliffs.

"It's just there!" she cried. "There's a wall up there – so there must be people who could help. Sweet Virgin! It's right there, but how can we get up to it?"

Spindle eyed the cliff warily. "You finkin' of climin' up that, lady?"

"Unless you can fly, Master Spindle!" snapped Eleanor, unable to disguise the bitterness in her voice.

"It's… it's gotta be too steep, ain't it?" he said.

She began to cast about for a path up from the beach to the top, but could not discern a route against the smooth rock.

"Aye, it surely is," she replied. "Thank you, Master Spindle! Come on, we'll have to try the water."

"Yeh, p'rhaps we can wade round, lady," suggested Spindle.

She nodded without enthusiasm. "Go and see how deep it is," she told him.

Whatever Spindle lacked, it was not courage. He scrambled across the rocky shore and went straight into the water. At once he sank from sight.

"Oh, Holy Mother help us!" cried Eleanor, rushing onto the rocks after him. She feared the worst until a frantic arm shot out of the sea near enough for her to seize him and pull him back to the shore.

"You can't swim?" she said.

"No, course I can't!"

"Well why in the name of Christ did you jump in then?"

"You told me to! And I gotta get some 'elp for Jug…"

She slid her legs over the rough outcrop and dangled them into the sea.

"What're you doin', lady?"

"I can swim," she replied. "Come on, I'll help you."

But Eleanor had not swum for many years and only then in the small pools fed by Yorkshire becks. When she plunged into the cold water, it so took her breath away that she could scarcely remember how to swim at all. Even so, it was not as deep as she feared – at least not yet.

"Come," she ordered, taking him by the hand. "Try to find the rocks on the sea bed with your feet!"

"I don't fink there are any," said a terrified Spindle, as he entered the water again.

"There are!" she insisted. "A tall lad like you should have no trouble. Anyway, I can't carry you!"

"I could be swept away," he grumbled, before swallowing some water.

Still clutching his arm, she guided him around the headland into the next bay and the pair scrambled with dripping clothes onto the stony beach.

"That wasn't so bad," she said, though with little conviction, for her shivering body was wracked with exhaustion.

Scanning the length of the bay, she saw no-one. Surely there should be fishermen about, or were they already at sea? She stared offshore and began to imagine she could see specks upon the water. If they were boats, they were too far away to help. The tide was certainly coming in for at the far end of the beach, they found deep water after only a few steps. Eleanor tried to swim around but the incoming waves kept driving her back and eventually she gave up and waded ashore, cold and dispirited.

The pair squatted on a patch of gritty sand and stared up at the cliff once again. In this bay it seemed to Eleanor that the sloping cliff was a little less vertical and not so high. It was topped by a line of trees and in several places a cleft of green against the murky white rock promised hope of a way up.

"So," she said finally, "the cliff it is."

"I still don't like the look of it," said Spindle.

Facing him squarely, Eleanor said: "Can you see any other way off this wretched beach?"

"Lady, I don't see a way out at all!" moaned Spindle. "And I 'ate goin' up high!"

Eleanor's response was savage. "Well, I suppose it depends how much you care for that lass of yours, doesn't it? She needs your help, Master Spindle – and I need your help if I'm to live long enough to find my daughter!"

Prodding the youth in the chest, she added: "So just how much do you care for her, Spindle? How much?"

Leaving the question rattling around his head, she left him and set off up the rocky slope on her own. The poor lad was right, of course, for she could see no path either, but that would not deter her from trying to claw her way up. Yet each time she tried, her fingers slipped on the milky white rock and, though she managed to climb a few feet, she would then slide back down almost as far. The rock face felt uneven: smooth here and there, but sometimes crumbling at her touch. Soon her torn and sodden kirtle was soiled by earth and chalky dust but she cared little, knowing that every faltering step might take her closer to help.

With relentless intent, she dragged herself up until she reached a narrow ledge. There she came to a halt, gasping for breath. She was not yet even half way up, yet she felt drained of all strength. Fully recovered, she might have succeeded but, weakened as she was, she had to concede that the ascent was beyond her.

Hearing a muffled curse below, she realised that Spindle, despite his fears, was also attempting the climb. Two fools then, she thought: she, for being reckless enough to climb, and he, for being witless enough to follow. Yet, when he clambered up onto the ledge beside her, he looked a great deal stronger than she felt.

"I fink… we can do this… arter all, lady," he said, his words punctuated by deep, rasping breaths.

"Do you?" she groaned in disbelief.

"Yeh, we done the worst bit! Look, there's tree roots we can grab 'old of."

The youth's unexpected optimism bolstered her own fragile self-belief.

"Lead on then," she said softly.

But when he stood up and carried on, her limbs refused to respond. Seeing her distress, Spindle reached down to offer his hand. After all the time she had spent in Spain trying to regain her strength and vigour, it was galling to feel so weak. Oh, to be young again, she thought, as his strong arm hauled her to her feet.

"Come on, lady; you can do it!" he urged. "Fink about Lady Kate."

Despite all, Eleanor's face broke into a grin, for who could have foreseen that she would ever be clambering up a Dorset cliff face accompanied by a London guttersnipe.

"Lady Katharine, to you, Master Spindle," she muttered, but she kept a tight grip on his reassuring hand.

As Spindle suggested, the rest of the climb was neither as steep, nor over such a crumbling surface. Tenacious plants had colonised the rock face and their strong roots aided the pair's progress to the top of the cliff. There they sank down upon their knees for a moment's respite before starting to make their way along the wooded clifftop. When they came across a well-used track, they almost cried out with relief.

"Nearly there, lady!" Spindle encouraged her.

As they shambled along, Eleanor tried to crane her neck to see down to the cove below.

"By the Virgin," she said, "if we'd stayed there, no-one could have seen us from up here."

Soon they emerged from the trees and, ahead of them Eleanor saw an old flint wall in need of repair and beyond it a tower – perhaps a small keep.

"Thank God," she whispered.

Spindle supported her weight as they staggered through a gap in the crumbling wall towards the gateway. When Eleanor leant against the rough stone beside the gate, her legs felt like they were made of wool.

While Spindle banged upon the gate with his fist, she gazed up for any sign of life but the building looked old, deserted and uncared for.

"Oh, no," she groaned. "Don't tell me that, after all that, no-one lives here!"

Spindle was still hammering on the gate when she slid down the wall to the ground. The last thing she felt was the stone grazing her head as she passed out.

23

24th October 1483, close to dawn on the Dorset coast

Eyes tight shut against the world, Kate Elder just wanted to give in and accept the inevitable; instead she coughed up another mouthful of salty bile. Each time the sea tugged at her kirtle, she expected to pass under the waves forever. But the young seaman's tenacious arm held her up – just high enough for her to draw in yet another spluttering breath before she was sucked back down again by the unrelenting sea.

"Nearly there, m'lady!" he cried.

Nearly where, she tried to ask, but swallowed half an ocean instead. As she choked up the water, her saviour raised her a little higher and she clung fast to him - this young seaman whose name she could not recall.

When the ship disappeared from under her, she reached a hand out to Grave but he was gone in an instant – gone with the ship – gone with her mother… The shock of the cold water plucked her from a drowsy torpor only to suck her into an icy, black whirlpool of terror. But then this youth, with scarcely a beard upon his chin, dragged her to the surface. From that moment on, he held her in a firm embrace; but now she could feel that he was tiring – Holy Mary, how could he not be? It would be a lot easier for them both if he just stopped trying, she thought. Why didn't he just let her go? Her meandering mind was jolted awake when her rescuer thrust her once more to the surface.

"Stay with me!" he bawled at her.

Where did he think she was going, she wondered? But she nodded and stared up, wide-eyed, into the night sky. Thereafter, only his constant cajoling kept her from drifting into oblivion. All she wanted to do was sleep, but his cruel nagging would not let her. And so it went on, and on… until his efforts to keep her afloat became gradually more erratic and his own head dipped beneath the surface more often.

Then he was shouting at her again – would he never leave her be?

"Lady!" he cried, smiling at her. "Lady!"

"What?" she gasped, choking in some water yet again.

"I can touch bottom, m'lady!" he said. "And it'll soon be dawn!"

Banishing her despair for a moment, she eyed the sky; was he imagining that it was lightening a little? Only when her foot struck a rock and she felt firm ground beneath her feet, did she begin to countenance what he was saying. Then she grinned back at him, for at last Kate truly believed she might be delivered from her ordeal by sea.

Hugging the crewman to her and feeling his rough chin against her cheek, she rejoiced that she was still alive. But dead ahead of them, in the half-light, she glimpsed a vertical cliff face only moments before the surging waves tossed their tired bodies against it. Though she cried out, her companion held her fast and, hauling her along to a fissure at the base of the rock, he gently laid her down. As she gulped in the salt air, her fingers scrabbled at the narrow yard of gravel beach.

Lying there exhausted, with the water tumbling over her legs, her elation turned to despair when she started to think about the others.

"Kate!"

Her head jerked up to see Augustine Grave smiling down at her. At once his hands seized her to pick her up and fold his arms around her.

"Kate!" he cried, weeping with joy. "Thank the Lord! I'd almost given up hope!"

"Grave," she could only croak at him, all but spent as she trembled in his embrace.

"Here," he said, "there's a cave. Come on."

He led her into a space under the cliff and sat her down on a large lump of rock. It was as well he did for her cold, stiff legs had not an ounce of strength left in them.

"You're safe now, Kate," he assured her. "Safe – and there's a trickle of water in the cave - fresh water seeping through the rock!"

She smiled up at him, gave a sudden shiver and passed out.

◊◊◊◊◊◊

Voices roused her from a deep and troubled sleep.

It was the crewman who had rescued her shouting: "Master Grave! Master Grave!"

Raising herself up to see what the excitement was about, she saw Grave laughing and, fleetingly, it struck her that she had not seen him laugh for months.

The crewman who had borne her through the shipwreck – she must ask his name - pointed just off the shore where, in the morning light, she could make out a boat coming in.

By the time Grave came to help her up, she was already up on her knees, though starting to shiver with cold.

"We're saved, Kate!" cried Grave. "I prayed for it, but I never expected it to come so swiftly!"

Willing hands helped Kate and Grave onto the small craft but, since it already carried two men, there was no room for her young seaman.

167

"We'll come back for you!" cried one of the boat's crew and the youth waved an acknowledgement to them.

"What's your name?" shouted Kate. "I don't know your name!"

"'Arry!" he yelled back.

After their brief exchange, the crewmen, with practised skill, manoeuvred the vessel out to sea and then took it around some rocks, above which she caught sight of a stone fortress.

"Where are we?" asked Grave.

"Handfast Point," replied one of the sailors.

"We have friends to search for," Grave told him.

"We'll take you to our master first and get you dry. He's a seafaring man is Master Clynt. He'll know what to do."

Kate was past caring where they went now, as long as it was towards some land, for already the swell was making her feel queasy. Drifting away in her utter weariness, she took in nothing more until the boat ground up onto the shore and she was lifted out of it. Welcoming voices greeted their arrival as they stumbled up the beach. She smiled sleepily at Grave who wrapped a reassuring arm around her.

Several figures ran towards them – by the Virgin, they were eager to help, she thought. Only after Grave shouted a warning did she notice that those racing across the beach were armed with cudgels. Before he could shout another warning, Grave was clubbed down by the strangers.

"No!" she screamed.

Dropping down onto the stones beside Grave, Kate gave another scream and began to crawl away along the shore, but her assailants caught her easily and pulled her to her feet. When she buckled at the knees, several men passed her from one to another, spinning her around and pulling at her tangled hair. Though she tried to resist, she had no fight left in her, even when they pawed at her breasts with their rough hands.

"By God, that's enough! Leave her be!" The new voice must have carried much weight for at once the men released her and she fell, weeping, onto the gritty sand.

"Thank you, sir," she whimpered. "Thank you…"

"Stay there," he barked at her.

"But look to my friend," she pleaded, moving to Grave's side. "He's hurt!"

"Oh, I am looking at him," said the stranger, staring down at Grave.

"Master Grave is very dear to me," she said. "Please help him…"

"Master Grave?" echoed the stranger, with a shake of the head. "Well, well, how the world doth turn. Never thought I'd set eyes on him again…"

"You know him, sir?" asked Kate.

"Oh, I know Master Grave very well – and I've an idea who you might be too. I tell you, girl: this is quite some day for me. The Lord has truly surpassed all my expectations!"

"I don't…"

"Your dear mother still alive, is she?"

"You know my mother too?" Kate was beyond puzzled. Could this man have met her mother in London?

"Oh, yeh, Lady Eleanor Elder and me – we're old friends, we are. Perhaps she mentioned my name: Elias Slade."

Kate blinked up at him where he stood with the morning sun at his back – a dark, looming presence ringed in amber. She said nothing, for her mother had done a good deal more than mention him. Kate knew all about Elias Slade and what she knew made her tremble with fear.

"Where exactly is your mother now?" Slade asked.

"I don't know…" sobbed Kate, a cold hand clutching at her heart.

The wretched sea had spared her, only to deliver her into the hands of her mother's worst enemy.

24

24th October 1483 in the late afternoon, at Handfast Castle in Dorset

Eleanor awoke lying on a bed in a gloomy chamber. It was not a very soft bed, but she was accustomed to that – and lately she had slept on far worse. As she came properly awake, she became aware that under the woollen blanket all her clothes had been removed, even her shift. By whose hand - and how long had she lain thus? And what had become of Mary and the others?

Utterly careless of her nakedness, she leapt from the bed, only to fall at once over the slumbering body of Mary.

Her servant yelped in fright, or perhaps pain, and then scrambled to her feet.

"My lady!" she cried. "Sweet Virgin! What are you doing?"

"Looking for my clothes, you fool!" shouted Eleanor.

Mary, staring across at the open door, said nothing more.

Eleanor turned to find a man in the doorway, his eyes fixed upon her – yet not so fixed, for she felt them journey slowly down her body.

"Take care you don't wear your eyes out!" she snarled at him. "Aye, I'm a woman and I'm undressed. Cope with it!"

"Not entirely undressed, my lady," he replied, lifting his gaze to her face. "You still have a rather impressive patch over one eye."

"My lady!" cried Mary, sweeping belatedly into action to secure the bed blanket around her mistress.

171

"Thank you, Mary," growled Eleanor, "but I think the gentleman has already seen all there is to see."

"This is our host, my lady," said Mary, "Sir Simon Cayne."

He smiled at her embarrassment. "Welcome to my home, Lady Eleanor."

She gave him a curt, awkward nod. "I was travelling with others," she said, still discomfited by her circumstances.

"Taken care of," Sir Simon reassured her.

"We were shipwrecked." She hesitated, her throat still sore from an excess of salt. "There are others to find…"

"So I'm told," said Sir Simon. "Among them, your daughter - I've had a man out searching, but the light's going again now. Tomorrow, he'll search again."

"One man?" protested Eleanor.

"One man is all I have, my lady; but on the morrow, we shall do better."

Slumping down onto the bed, Eleanor surrendered to her frailty.

"Take some more water," advised Sir Simon, "but take it slowly. You were exhausted when you came here… In the morning, we can talk again."

"The morning? Which morning?" murmured Eleanor, bewildered. "But it'll be too late…"

When he closed the door behind him, she would have harangued Mary but she did not have the strength nor, if she was honest, did she have the will.

"You should sleep, my lady," soothed Mary, coaxing her back onto the bed and rearranging the blanket over her. "I know I need to!"

"Aye, but…" conceded Eleanor, "we'll never find them if we lie here…"

"First, we must rest, lady," said Mary.

"I know," wept Eleanor, "I know we have to rest... but it'll be too late..."

"Aye, lady, I was resting till you trod on me! But at least we've dry land beneath us now, eh?"

"Not my Kate though," muttered Eleanor. "God knows where she is, or if she even lives!"

"We'll all search tomorrow, lady."

"Aye, very well." Sleep almost took her until a stray thought occurred to her. "How did Sir Simon know my name? Did you tell him?"

Mary gave a sigh. "I thought you might notice that. Well, I fear that, in his haste to get help for us, young Spindle might have told Sir Simon a great deal more than you would have liked – but please don't blame him, my lady."

"Good Christ! How could I blame him, Mary? The youth got me up here; without him, I'd have died on that damned beach, or fallen off the cliff."

"Mmm, strange, my lady," said Mary, with a sly grin, "that's more or less what he said about you..."

"Give me some water and be quiet," ordered Eleanor.

⌂⌂⌂⌂⌂⌂

Though Eleanor was desperate to start the search for her loved ones, the following morning did not start well.

"I cannot wear that!" she declared.

"Well, you have to wear something, my lady!" said Mary, throwing the kirtle onto the bed and folding her arms.

"But not that!"

"He's giving you his dead wife's clothes," whispered Mary.

"Is that supposed to make that insipid rag any more appealing?" raged Eleanor, wandering about the room wearing only a tight linen shift – which, she realised belatedly, must also have belonged to Sir Simon's dead wife.

"Hush my lady, he'll hear you!" hissed Mary.

"Are you telling me to be quiet as well, you impudent little bitch - a pathetic wretch I dragged off a hillside in Wharfedale? You are like a millstone I can't throw off!"

"I know you're not angry with me," said Mary, in that particularly irritating, whining tone she employed when attempting to placate her mistress.

"Do I not sound angry enough then?" roared Eleanor.

Casting about for an object to throw, her hand lighted upon a pewter candlestick. She raised it above her head to hurl at her servant, but before she could do so, it was snatched from her grasp. Whirling round, she found Sir Simon standing beside her, having retrieved his candlestick.

"Blood of Christ, don't you ever knock?" she cried.

Face flushed, her eyes blazed at his before he could look away and an uncomfortable silence followed during which Eleanor inspected the hem of his late wife's shift.

"Well, my lady," said Sir Simon at last, "I'll let you finish... dressing." And after carefully restoring the candlestick to its place, he went out.

"By the Virgin," moaned Eleanor, sitting down on the bed, head in hands.

Mary held up the kirtle. "Shall we try again, my lady," she said, unable to keep the sweet tone from her voice.

"Not only is it the most drab cloth imaginable," observed Eleanor, "but it's just too small!"

"Aye, I suppose his poor wife was less... blessed in the chest area than you ... but let's try it, shall we?"

"I just want to find them, Mary," murmured Eleanor. "That's all. And I could do without all this... all this..."

"I know, my lady – as do we all. So, the sooner you dress..."

With grim acceptance, Eleanor allowed Mary to lace up the kirtle, though her servant was obliged to apply a good deal more force than usual. Eleanor grunted in discomfort, but she was by now resigned to it and prepared to tolerate almost anything to get started on her search.

When they were done, Mary stared at her with a weary sigh.

"What is it now?" grumbled Eleanor.

"I was just thinking… here we are, washed off a ship and dragged over rocks, at the mercy of sea and storm, yet, while I look like a sorry old rag, you always manage to look like the most handsome woman in all Christendom…"

Eleanor's expression softened and she pressed Mary's hand. "If I have any trace of good looks, it is entirely down to you, Mary, not me. And for your pains, you endure so much grief at my hands…"

It was the closest Eleanor would ever get to an apology and Mary's answering smile told her that all was forgiven between them.

⌂⌂⌂⌂⌂⌂

As soon as she descended the spiral stair, Eleanor understood what a small household Sir Simon kept. More than that, the whole place smelt of neglect and decay. They broke their fast in a moderately-sized, but sparsely furnished, hall which she suspected was rarely used for dining – or anything else for that matter. The rickety table in the centre of the space was so small it could barely accommodate three or four diners and Eleanor feared that her creaking chair might collapse at any moment. She was relieved when the simple meal was over and her host led her down a flight of stone steps to a small, cobbled yard outside. The stables might once have housed eight or ten mounts, but now alas there were only two - both of which were saddled and waiting by the gateway.

"Your servant told me you ride well," said Sir Simon, "so…"

"Aye, my servant appears to have told you a great deal about me," said Eleanor, noting that no ladies' saddle had

175

been provided. "But this will suit me well enough. Now, if you please, I've delayed so long already…"

"Rest assured, my lady, that no time has been wasted. My man and yours have been out since dawn and later this morning they'll take a boat out and work their way along the coast to Sandwich Bay."

She nodded, tight-lipped, reluctant to contemplate once more the slim chances of finding Grave or Kate. "Sandwich Bay?"

"If your ship sailed from the west and broke up off the point then some survivors might have reached the shore – there are a few caves in the cliffs, so you never know… If anyone's there, they'll find them."

"But where shall we look then?" she asked.

"We'll ride down through the woods to Studland Bay – a little further along from where you were washed up," he said. "That's the most likely place to find any more survivors or…"

"…bodies?" she said.

"Indeed, my lady, but let's hope for better than that, shall we?" urged Sir Simon. "There are many coves along the shoreline. I've sent word out into the village; your friends may already have been found by fishermen."

"If we had another mount, my servant, Mary, could have helped," said Eleanor crossly. "She should be helping!"

"I believe, my lady that she is tending to the injured," said Sir Simon.

She winced at the note of censure in his voice. God curse her! Of course someone had to look to Jug and the injured seaman – and she had not even enquired about them! What ailed her? Was it grief that made her so selfish, or was she always so? She resolved to remain silent lest she say any more to confirm her callous stupidity.

Sir Simon misinterpreted her silence. "Lady Eleanor, I apologise if I seem too familiar, but your man omitted to tell me your full name."

"Did he?" said Eleanor, making a mental note to congratulate Spindle later.

"So? May I ask…?"

"Sir Simon, you have been very kind, but my circumstances are not all they might seem," she replied. "My name alone might bring some trouble upon you. You did not ask me to stumble upon your house, so perhaps it is better you do not know my name."

"Am I to conclude then that you are… pursued?"

The poor man looked so crestfallen that she almost relented; but no, it was in his interest as much as hers that no-one knew that the outlaw John Elder's aunt had landed in Dorset. Knowing only a little of what her nephew was planning, she knew she must be cautious – for all their sakes.

"I am not pursued," she told him, "nor wanted by the law – whether sheriffs or anyone else. Let us just dispense with formal titles: you call me Eleanor and I'll call you Simon. Does that suit you?"

"If… that's what you want," he said, "that suits me very well for I'm not a very formal man."

Nonetheless, she knew that if she remained at Handfast Castle for any length of time, a fuller, more convincing, explanation would have to be given. With a complete stranger, only so much could be taken on trust!

Simon led the way through the woodland, sparse close to the castle but thicker further down the track where autumn was already beginning to colour the leaf canopy. Though here and there hazel coppices allowed some light in among the birch and hawthorn, Eleanor could see nothing of the sea shore as they rode down. When the pair emerged from the tree-covered slope, Simon turned right down a rough track which took them to a broad bay.

A surprising number of folk were about: some fishermen had drawn boats high up the beach where a few women sat mending damaged nets. Eleanor's heart missed a beat when she saw several men hauling a wooden spar from the waves, though whether it was part of the Catherine, she could not tell.

Apparently guessing her fears, Simon explained: "If a ship sinks out to sea, it'll most likely go to the bottom out there, but if it breaks up near the point, the debris will be scattered around this bay, and even as far as Poole harbour."

She gave a curt nod, not trusting herself to speak, as her damp eyes scanned the shoreline.

"To be honest, Eleanor," he said, lowering his voice, "if anyone was washed ashore here, these folk would already know about it."

"Aye, but would they have told you?" she asked, eyeing several of the drawn and sullen faces.

"Yes, they would. They wouldn't tell you, but many of these people are my tenants. They're poor and they scratch out a living however they can, but if I ask, they'll tell me – and I have asked…"

She nodded, for was it not always the way? She was an alien to them; they cared nothing for her or her kin but, whether through fear or respect, they would do their lord's bidding.

"We'll ride further along," he said, "along to the salt pans where other folk live and work."

By midday, they had ridden past the shallow salterns and all along the shoreline of the bay, but no-one they met reported any sign of survivors. By the time they explored the spit which traced a finger of gravel out into the harbour Eleanor was mired in gloomy despair.

"Come," he said. "We'll return on the western side of the spit."

"But, surely they would be less likely to reach that far?" she said.

"True," he admitted, "but you need to see the extent of the harbour to understand…"

They rode several more miles until he pulled up and dismounted. "We'll rest the mounts here," he said, "while you see what you're up against. This is Red Orde Quay and from here you can see clear across the harbour."

She stared out over the muddy foreshore where several islands lay close by, but beyond them stretched what seemed a vast expanse of water across which several ships of considerable size were sailing.

"That is Poole harbour," Simon told her.

"All of that?"

"Indeed, but you can't even see the whole of it."

They walked along the shore for a few hundred yards before returning to the quay.

"No-one from the Catherine could have made it this far," she murmured.

"Perhaps not," he said, as he helped her to remount. "But perhaps our servants have fared better."

Eleanor found no comfort in his words, only a growing numbness in her belly, as they rode across an area of heathland into Studland village, past a small stone church and back up through the forest along the track to the castle.

"If… someone has not reached the shore by now," she ventured, "how long… could they…."

"How long could they live?"

She nodded, watching his face, for she already sensed that Simon was not a man who dealt in falsehoods.

"Not long, I fear; hours perhaps," he said, with a sigh. "In faith, Eleanor, not much longer than it took you to find

Handfast Castle. But, with God's help, they'll have already made it ashore – all we have to do is find them."

She welcomed his candour, but it only served to inflame her grief. Especially since, when they returned to his house, the glum faces of the servants revealed the disappointment of their day.

"Found one of the crew," said Spindle, "dead though, 'ed stove in – nobody else…"

"It's still possible that your folk were picked up by a passing vessel," said Simon.

"At dead of night?" scoffed Eleanor, utterly dispirited.

"Or perhaps at first light," said Simon. "It's possible, my lady, a ship bound for Poole, or Wareham, might have discovered them. I've instructed the Wareham bailiffs and my brother, Roger, the mayor of Poole, to send word to me here if any of the ship's company is found. I'm afraid that all we can do now is wait."

"Wait?" cried Eleanor, feeling that she had spent most of the summer waiting for someone! "Should we not go to these places and see for ourselves?"

"To what end?" he cautioned. "You could be chasing across Purbeck in every direction except the right one. I assure you that if anyone is found – alive or dead – I'll be told at once. In the meantime you should rest. Why, you're quite grey from exhaustion. Today's ride, I fear, was too much of a trial."

"Hah!" said Eleanor. "If I don't find those I love, then I assure you that my trials will have only just begun!"

25

25ᵗʰ October 1483, at Holes Bay in Poole Harbour

Kate awoke in a panic, fumbling at the blanket that covered her. To her surprise, after her rough handling, she found herself in a bed – a narrow pallet bed, but comfortable enough. She half-expected to be a prisoner yet she was not even bound; perhaps it was all a mistake... Could she have dreamed it all? Getting up too quickly, she swayed and leaned against the wall, until her head began to clear. Two cautious paces took her to a tiny window but since it was close-shuttered, it offered no view of the world outside. At least it allowed in the light of day, but for how long had she slept?

Hearing footsteps outside the door, she clambered back to the bed. A barefoot youth entered with a bowl of steaming liquid and a chunk of black bread. The latter he tossed in her general direction, before placing the bowl on the bare floorboards beside the bed.

"Am I a prisoner?" she asked.

When he made no reply, she persisted: "Tell me where am I then."

With a nervous look around as if someone might suddenly appear through a wall, he spoke softly: "Just stay in 'ere and keep quiet; that's all you need to do."

"And if I don't?" she muttered.

"Please yourself, girl, but I'm supposed to tell you that if you make any trouble, your friend - Master Grave, is it? - will feel their wrath."

Shuddering at the thought, she nevertheless retrieved the hard piece of bread as soon as he left. Taking up the bowl, she dipped pieces of bread in the lukewarm, cloying liquid. Ravenous after emptying her stomach day after day aboard ship, she gulped down the lumps of sodden bread. But, when she crammed the last few morsels of bread into her mouth and poured in the remaining soup, she felt bloated. But at least, she reflected, she had food – and she was on firm ground, free from the endless, sodding heave of the ship – not to mention the endless, sodding heaving of her stomach!

After eating she sat on the bed, uncertain what to do next. She was unharmed, so perhaps her captors intended to keep her that way, yet she knew enough about Elias Slade to worry about what he had planned for her. But then how could he have any plan – after all, he could not possibly have known that she would wash up at Poole. Her arrival must have been as much of a surprise to him as it was to her.

Yet, for all that, his hatred of her mother meant that he would not hesitate to do her harm. So there was no point in pretending all was well, because it most certainly was not. Only one thought sustained her: if both she and Grave had survived then it was possible that her mother still lived too. Grave's presence was a great source of comfort to her, though his safety might now depend upon her own good behaviour. Until she could learn more, there was little she could do except wait. However, since impatience was one of the few qualities Kate had inherited from her mother, the rest of the day seemed to last a year.

It was not until the early evening that she was visited again and on this occasion taken downstairs to a cellar. The chamber's darkness was only alleviated by several stubs of candle, but in the harsh, flickering light she saw Grave once again. The sight of him was almost too much for her to bear, for he was tied to a wooden post, where he had clearly been subjected to the most terrible beating. At once she rushed across to him, sobbing as she took his broken and bloodstained hands in hers. Though his eyes were half-closed and his face cut and bleeding, he managed a faint smile of recognition.

"Why have you done this to him?" she raged at Slade.

"We just had a bit of a talk," said Slade, "and we fell out - his doing, not mine."

"And I suppose now it's my turn to be tortured!" she yelled at him.

"No, girl, no-one here's going to hurt you!" replied Slade.

"What?" Her confusion seemed to amuse him. "Why not?"

"You're too valuable to me and my friend here." He gestured to another man who, until then, had remained in the shadows.

"Master Diggory Clynt, merchant of this town," announced the stocky stranger.

"Now listen, girl," Slade told her. "You'll do as you're told or this wretched old tosspot here, Master Grave, will be punished – you understand me?"

Kate gave a surly nod. "I've been told."

"But do you understand, girl? You make a noise, he gets cut; you try to leave, he dies…"

"Aye, aye, I know what you're saying!"

"Good, because as long as you behave, you get to sleep in a warm bed and he gets to stay alive."

"What do you want with us?" asked Kate.

"Master Grave here has much to answer for – as does your mother – a foul pox upon the bitch! The pair of them ruined me – and you know it! I saw it in your eyes yesterday; but you, on the other hand, could be useful - and I reckon your mother would do a lot to get you back."

"She's most likely already dead!" Kate spat at him.

"She might be… but that she-wolf has a habit of turning death's blade aside. We'll see soon enough whether she lives or not."

"And if she don't," chipped in Clynt, "we'll sell you to one of the heathen traders – and trust me, you'll fetch a fine price! Bit of a new life for you…"

His words sent a shiver through her and she stood up to stroke Grave's face.

"Don't despair," he muttered. "And don't give a thought to my fate… I'm already dead…"

Unable to find any words to say to him, she simply kissed his bloodied cheek. With a scowl, Clynt seized her arm and pulled her away for the youth to lead her back up to her chamber. This time, once inside, she heard a bolt drawn across the door. It seemed that Slade, having revealed her fate, was not taking any chances. Though Grave had told her not to worry about the consequences for him if she tried to leave, she could not imagine how she could even try to escape. With no idea where she was and no-one to help her, she could only hope that her mother had survived.

26

26th October 1483, in Poole Town

The ferry crossing had been rougher than usual – or so Simon told her. To Eleanor, it seemed interminable. At Poole Quay, when the port bailiff met them, he spoke not of survivors, but of bodies… only bodies. Several of them had been washed up in the harbour so, of course, she had agreed at once to inspect them. Even though it was most likely they were local folk who had met with some misadventure, she thought there was always a chance... But now the task was almost upon her, she began to doubt her own resolve. What if, among the soulless corpses, she found Kate, or Grave?

Swallowing a dark brew of hope and fear, Eleanor donned a passive mask as she followed the bailiff from the quay with Simon. Eyes fixed upon the street ahead, she concentrated only on treading a straight line. When she stumbled on the cobbles, Simon took her arm and she leant gratefully upon it.

"How many are there?" she murmured.

"Four bodies have been recovered," replied the bailiff.

"Bodies…" The fellow might have been discussing a catch of fish, she thought. She wondered, but dared not ask, whether among the bodies there was a lass; a dark-haired, beautiful lass. And more than once she muttered to herself: "Please God, let it not be Kate."

They stopped before a stone-built town house. "This is the house of my brother, Roger, my lady," Simon told her.

"The mayor of Poole," added the bailiff.

"It's a fine house," she murmured.

"As a favour to me, he's kindly arranged for the… bodies to be laid out here in private," explained Simon.

She scarcely noticed the hurried introductions to Simon's younger brother, Roger, aware only of a tall, prosperous-looking man who looked very little like Simon.

"Thank you, Master Cayne," she managed to mumble.

"There are three men and one girl," Roger told her. "But, my dear, I fear this is truly no task for a lady."

"I've seen corpses before," she replied. "Just lead me to them and then leave me alone."

"My lady!" Simon and his brother protested as one – so perhaps they did have something in common after all.

But, with a face carved from stone, she faced the pair of them down. "I have to be certain, don't I – for good or ill? So, just let me do this; and I shall find it easier alone, believe me."

After a further show of reluctance, Simon led her through a passage and out into a courtyard. Crossing the yard, they passed into a paved and roofed area. A row of four shrouded bodies filled the space – one a little smaller than the other three. Waiting to lift each shroud for her was a lone servant.

"Please leave me," she told him. "I can do it."

Just for a moment he looked as if he might protest, but her fierce one-eyed glare persuaded him to obey without argument, though she noted that the Cayne brothers remained at the other side of the yard.

Taking a deep breath, Eleanor faced the four shrouds. Though her eye was drawn inevitably to the smaller corpse at the far end of the row, she did not go there first. Stepping forward, she swiftly uncovered the first man and winced at the state of him. She had steeled herself to see a man's face battered by wave and cut by rock, but she had not expected the loss of an eye and an ear – torn away, she supposed, by some sea creature. Letting the shroud fall, she found herself trembling and reached out a hand to the bench to steady herself.

Hearing one of the brothers take a step towards her, she growled: "No, stay there… if you please."

Since the first dead man was unknown to her, she replaced the shroud over him and moved along the row to uncover the next. She could not help a sudden gasp, for his was a face she knew at once, though it too had taken a terrible pounding. He was a burly young lad from the Catherine. Finch told her at the end that his best man was with Kate and she wondered whether this was he. Her eyes flicked across towards the final, female, corpse. Could her daughter have been with this youth when he died? With an effort, she dragged her gaze away from the dead seaman and murmured a simple prayer; he deserved more, but that could wait a little longer. A tear or two dropped onto his face before she lowered the cloth over it once more.

"Oh, Kate," she sighed and, missing out the third body, stepped straight over to the smaller, slighter one. Because, having seen the crewman, she just had to know at once. Hand shaking, she reached out and lifted one corner of the linen. She almost closed her eyes but then, with one savage movement, she swept aside the whole cloth.

The fine, pale features were undamaged, unblemished, as if the girl might simply have fallen asleep - though the water had plumped up her face a little.

Eleanor leant forward and sobbed over the corpse.

"My lady," pleaded Simon.

"No!" snapped Eleanor for, God forgive her, she was weeping tears of relief, not sorrow; for this poor, lifeless lass was not her daughter - someone's daughter, aye, but not hers! With reverence, she laid the linen cloth down, taking care to cover the body fully once more.

Moving back from the girl to the final corpse, she uncovered the body of an older man. She said not a word as her knees buckled, only stopping herself from falling by sinking back against the wall. Though Simon rushed to her side, she recovered and pushed him aside. This was not a moment she wished to share with anyone else.

"Leave me!" she cried. "I must get some air!"

Before anyone could stop her she pushed past them all, ran out of the yard into a covered passage which led her through the wall at the back of the house. Outside, she expected to be in a privy yard but found herself instead in a narrow lane that reeked of fish and urine. Few folk were there and she gulped in the stale, foetid air until she could slow her breathing a little. Then she staggered away until she found her way back to the busy quay, where she spent a few moments pacing slowly along by the water, staring out at the harbour.

Grave was dead! Her rock was gone! The man who had suffered every one of her tiresome outbursts and tossed them gently back at her was gone… Grave, her soul mate, was gone. Though the wharf was crowded, rarely had she ever felt more alone.

But she knew that Simon would not leave her alone for long and when a voice called out: "Lady Eleanor!" she turned around to look for him. Then in the milling throng of people she caught a glimpse of a face – not Simon, a different face - and one glimpse was all it took. The scar across the cheek and the bitter eyes glaring back at her - still, even after all these months, thirsty for revenge. Elias Slade, of all people, was here - was so close that he could almost reach out and touch her. So Poole was where the villain had run to…

While she stood transfixed, he stepped closer, close enough to thrust a dagger through her aching heart if he had a mind to. But he had no need for a blade, when he had words that cut even deeper.

"Poor old Grave," he said with a sly grin. "I think his heart wore out."

"No!" whispered Eleanor.

"You haven't lost a young girl, have you?" he added. "Because I've found one."

"No!" Her tortured scream stopped everyone on the quay in mid-stride.

Only then did she turn and flee. Stumbling away from him, fighting the urge to retch, for never had she felt such fear. He had killed Grave! And he still had Kate - her sweet Kate!

Simon caught her in his arms. "Eleanor, thank God I've found you! You look terrible. It was your daughter, wasn't it?"

"No, it wasn't… Kate," she strangled out the words, biting back the bile and defying the dread that threatened to overwhelm her. She swept her frantic eyes left and right across the crowd of puzzled faces staring back at her, but Elias Slade was not amongst them.

"It wasn't her?" said Simon.

"He's here," she whispered.

"Who's here?" Simon looked about them, confused.

Just for an instant, the thought crossed her mind: had she imagined Slade? No, she had seen him; he was there and all now was changed.

"You were so upset," said Simon, "I feared it could only be your daughter."

"It was the third man," mumbled Eleanor. "His name was Augustine Grave and he was very dear to me… There are few men I could ever say that I loved, but he was one of them…"

"I'm so sorry, Eleanor," he said.

"But down here, in the crowd on the dockside, there was someone else," she told him.

"Someone from your ship?" asked Simon.

"No, someone from my past..."

"You're not yourself..."

"No, I'm not," she murmured, "and I may never be again..."

"You can talk to me, Eleanor – for I know grief too. Talk to me."

Talk to him? How in all God's Christendom could she begin to explain? How could she possibly make her new and trusting friend understand the threat that Elias Slade presented? Here was a man who had shattered the Elder family, butchered and maimed so many - a brutal murderer, whose kinfolk had in turn been killed by the Elders in a bitter, vengeful struggle, until only Elias survived to escape their revenge. But now he was back... and he would want to exact full retribution...

"My apologies, Eleanor!" cried Simon, full of remorse. "I see that you are stricken by grief – fool that I am!"

How could she tell him about Elias Slade – or any other part of her turbulent past – without laying bare her very soul? He could never understand what made her as she was and, if this gentle knight who sheltered her without question, saw her stripped down to her savage core, he would surely look upon her only with loathing.

He was still holding her in a close embrace, still talking, poor man - still trying to soothe her. "I fear it has all been too much for you," he said. "I shall take you back to Handfast at once!"

"Aye, but what about Grave's... body?" she whispered.

"Worry no more about that," said Simon. "I shall arrange for him to be brought to Studland and buried at the church there."

But, as he led her across the quay, Eleanor could not even focus upon Grave; instead with every step she took, her eyes roved hither and thither, scanning the streets and glancing behind to see if Elias Slade was following. If he was, she did not see him. But then, when he fled bleeding from Ludlow, she never expected, even in her bleakest nightmares, to see him again. And now, without even laying a hand upon her, he was slowly killing her.

27

26th October 1483 in the afternoon, at Roger Cayne's Poole house

In Roger Cayne's hand was an unexpected, and rather messily scrawled, note from the Poole trader, Diggory Clynt. Clynt invariably called himself a merchant, but even trader was a generous description for a man who was suspected of piracy and thieving on an extravagant scale.

Since Roger's election by his fellow burgesses as town mayor, his world ought only to collide with Clynt's when laws were broken. Clynt had once been his client and, as Clynt's lawyer, he ignored some of the man's more dubious activities, but as mayor his own actions came under rather closer scrutiny. Thus any written communication from Clynt was most unwelcome. On the other hand, Clynt was known to be a wealthy man, and Roger, as an elected official, was duty bound to assist any man whose wealth benefited the town.

Having no wish to invite trouble, Roger had maintained a safe distance – until now. He was a little relieved when he saw that Clynt's missive was a simple introduction to the bearer: one of Clynt's partners, called Elias Slade. Slade bore an ugly scar that disfigured what might otherwise have been a handsome face and he carried himself like a knight rather than the low-born villain he clearly was.

"I'm a busy man, Master Slade," said Roger, "but, as a courtesy to my former client, Master Clynt, I can give you a few moments. If you seek legal advice, I can suggest several competent men in the town."

A sly smile crept across his visitor's face. "Oh, I'm not here to take advice, Master Mayor," replied Slade. "I'm here to give you some."

Being used to the rough and rambling speech of seafaring men like Clynt, Roger was more than a little surprised by Slade's swift response and confident demeanour.

"You arranged for a lady to see some dead bodies this morning," continued Slade.

"That's privy business, Master Slade, not yours," said Roger, bristling with annoyance at the fellow's intrusion into a private matter. "Now, are you going to tell me why you're here, or shall I just have you thrown out?"

"It so happens, Master Cayne that the lady you met this morning is very much my business. Know who she is, do you?"

For the first time Roger hesitated before speaking, his finely-tuned instincts registering a flicker of warning. "We were only briefly introduced," he replied. "There was little time…"

"Staying up on the point, she is - with your brother, I've heard."

"Also none of your business," said Roger, feeling his anger rise. Who was this pumped-up dog to poke his nose into Cayne family affairs?

"Cosy," remarked Slade, with a knowing leer.

Since Roger had tried earlier in the day without success to prise the identity of the woman from his brother, he was now a little curious about what the stranger might have to say about her. It was most certainly in his interest that his elder brother remained in his present state: widowed and childless. The last thing he needed was some fertile harlot ensnaring him with the charms of her voluptuous body – which the lady in question certainly appeared to possess.

Perhaps this Slade fellow might be able to supply a few useful details after all.

"I take it you know the lady?" asked Roger.

"Oh, yeh, Master Cayne, I know her – and her family - very well. Very well indeed."

"Well, who is she then?"

"That'll depend on how much you're willing to pay to find out."

Of course, thought Roger that was to be expected, since useful information always came at a price, especially from a man in league with Diggory Clynt. But he did not intend to shower rewards upon this Slade ruffian. "If you came here to extort from me," he said, "then you may as well leave now."

Slade did not move. "The lady has just lost her lover, poor old Master Grave. I dare say she'll be seeking comfort elsewhere now. And well, she is staying with your brother, isn't she?"

"You need to leave before I have you tossed out into the street," warned Roger, beginning to suspect that the man knew nothing worth paying for.

But Slade just grinned. "Someone told me that you take a keen interest in all that your brother does. A wealthy widower like him… looks ready for another wife, doesn't he? She's a fine looking woman too…"

"Spit it out, man: who is she?"

"She's a devil in woman's form, Master Cayne," growled Slade, "but, tell you what, now we've agreed that you want what I know, let's decide how much it's worth to you, shall we?"

"What do you want?"

"You're the mayor of this town, aren't you?" said Slade.

"As well you know."

"Let's just say I'd like you to use your influence."

"Have you committed some offence?"

"I may have," replied Slade, "but there will be more… offences on the way surrounding this lady…"

"I can't pervert the course of law to suit a common criminal!"

Slade stood up. "Then our business is already done, Master Cayne," he said. "I'm sure the lady will be no threat to you at all-"

"Sit down," ordered Roger. Slade disgusted him – a man with all the subtlety of a bolting horse – yet, sharp-witted enough, for all that. "What, exactly, do you want?"

"This woman… her ship was wrecked…"

"I've heard that."

"An old ship that broke up on Handfast Point…"

"So?"

"Diggory and me, we salvaged what we could, but there wasn't much of her left. Best let that vessel lie, eh? If anyone asks, you've never heard of it."

"Pah! What does one more wreck matter?" scoffed Roger.

"Diggory and me, we've no interest in the ship; only some of those it carried. So, as I said, if anyone asks, you've not heard about a ship going down at the point."

"Agreed. What else?"

"I'll tell you about this woman and you give me a free hand to deal with her – as I see fit."

"I'll certainly not be a party to any crime!" protested Roger.

"As… I… see… fit," repeated Slade, "and I'll want a paper to protect me and mine from the law."

"I don't want any harm to come to my brother," declared Roger.

Slade had a glint in his eye when he replied: "Well, Master Mayor, we both know that's not true, don't we?"

28

27th October 1483, in the early hours of the morning at Handfast Castle

In a daze, Eleanor wandered out of her chamber on the second floor of the keep, then down the spiral stair to the floor below where a wooden walkway linked the main building to a watchtower at the very tip of Handfast Point. Only when she ventured out onto the bridge and felt the wooden boards beneath the bare soles of her feet, did she come fully awake. Standing there, knowing the sea was just there beneath her, she let the cool night air chill her, numbing the bitter memories of the day. She ought to sleep, but sleep was more elusive than ever…

She wandered further along the bridge towards the small tower where once, she supposed, men might have been posted to stare out over the dark waves that rolled and crashed against the base of the chalk cliffs. Only the widowed Sir Simon and his servant, Master Palmer, dwelt there now, rattling around in this little mausoleum of a castle. Even the cook came up from the village each day. The arrival of Eleanor and the others had more than doubled the population of the place overnight.

Creeping along the walkway she climbed a swaying wooden stair to the tower battlements where the wind was much stronger - that same wind from the south west, which had driven the Catherine onto Handfast Point and changed all their lives forever.

Startled by a sudden movement behind her, she almost cried out but relaxed when she saw her host. Behind him was an open door which she realised must give him immediate access to the rampart from his chamber.

"I'm sorry if I disturbed you, Simon."

With a shake of the head, he replied: "I don't sleep much anymore."

"My coming has forced you to stay out in this remote chamber?" she asked.

"In truth, I often stay out here," he confessed. "The chamber where you are, I used to share with my wife. As it's where she breathed her last, it is not a place where I am at ease… But you must be too cold out here. Come into the warmth, please."

He offered his hand to guide her down the short flight of steps but she hesitated, unwilling to be drawn into his chamber. It revealed a trust on his part that was misplaced since he knew nothing about her and, if he had, he might well not be quite so welcoming. All the same, it was a raw wind that stung her skin with cold, so she took his outstretched hand, warm against her chilled fingers.

Only when she saw the shutters did she realise that his chamber must once have been a guardroom of some kind with arrow loops facing outwards. The only furniture in the room was a narrow bed with a single blanket thrown back.

"Please, my lady," he said. "Take the bed – I mean only for warmth…"

"I could not."

"But you're shivering!" he protested. "You've had a terrible day and you need more rest than I do. I'll not sleep any more tonight."

"I doubt I will either," said Eleanor.

"But your loss is still raw, and, whatever you may think, rest will help you."

So, she acquiesced, for he meant well and she could hardly stand there arguing about it all night. And she had to admit it did feel better, for a little of his warmth remained under the blanket he pulled over her.

"I will leave you to rest," he said.

"No, stay," she replied. "Sit on the bed and talk to me."

"After today, I wouldn't know what to say to you."

She patted the foot of the bed. "Talk about something else; tell me about your wife."

So he did. His wife, Sarah, was a merchant's daughter from Wareham and, as Simon painted a loving picture of her, Eleanor began to feel even guiltier that she had been so disparaging about the woman's clothes. Sarah had died in childbirth along with the child she hoped to bring into the world. It had been ten years, but he spoke of it as if it had only just happened. After a while, perhaps sensing that he had rambled on for too long, he stopped abruptly.

"I'm boring you," he said, patting her hand gently, "and most certainly keeping you awake."

"You never married again," she said.

"I was always thinking of taking another wife," he said, "but, a good wife is hard to find in a small place. I think the right woman would just have to fall into my life…"

He snatched his hand away. "I'm sorry! That sounded as if… and I didn't mean… I certainly wouldn't, after the day you've endured. Not that you don't attract me – because you do. What am I saying? Forgive me, please!"

A long silence stretched out between them.

"Dear God, you re mortified, aren't you?" he whispered. "I'm so sorry!"

She reached out for his hand. "Dear Simon, I assure you I'm not in the least troubled by anything you've said. You should have a wife – someone to bring this dusty old castle to life. A woman you can love once again, but Simon… I'm not that woman."

⌂⌂⌂⌂⌂⌂

Later that day, in the evening, Eleanor decided that she must tell him everything. It just seemed dishonest not to do so, since he had confided so much in her. She aimed to speak to him after their frugal supper of bread, cheese and ale, but the more she thought about it, the more she just wanted to get it over with. So, as they sat down alone in the hall to eat, she began her story and, once she started, their plates of food remained untouched on the table. She could not eat and the longer she talked, the less he seemed interested in his food. As night fell, a crushing darkness closed in upon the single, waning candle flame between them.

She had hoped to choose what to tell and what to conceal - a forlorn hope. In the end, her words just spilled forth in a torrent of broken dreams and ill-judged decisions which had brought her to where she was now: in a pit of despair. Though she had no intention of confessing her worst, her bloodiest, acts, somehow she did. He needed him to feel her sense of loss and desperation, but Simon Cayne was not a priest who could hear her confession and absolve her from her sins. He was an honest, ordinary sort of man whose face grew ever paler in the harsh candlelight.

Most unnerving of all was that, while she talked, he made not a single comment or interruption. She hoped he might reach out a hand, but no, there was no gentle touch of reassurance. When, at last, she stopped, only a face of stone stared back at her. She expected some reaction to her outpouring - an outburst, aye, or even an expression of disgust, but what she got was silence. Then he simply got up, walked out of the hall and retreated across the walkway to his chamber. It was the shock, she supposed, but thank the Virgin she had only shared with him the past two years or so. God's teeth! Her entire life story would surely be more than any man could stomach!

Poor Simon, who had imagined her as a frightened, vulnerable lady in need of his protection – perhaps even his love - now knew the truth of it. Now he understood that, in a blink of that emerald splinter which served as her one good eye, she was capable of the most appalling violence. Lifelong heartbreak and betrayal had woven steel shards through her spirit - that was what Eleanor Elder was. Perhaps, if Simon Cayne had known all that, he would never have opened his door to her in the first place. It would have been far better for him, she thought, if he had just cast her back down onto the stony Purbeck shore to die.

Listening to his steady, measured footsteps trudging across the wooden bridge to his chamber, she wept. She told herself that she was weeping for Grave, whose tightly-wrapped body had arrived at Studland in the late afternoon. She told herself that she was weeping for Kate, but, in part at least, she knew that she was weeping for herself. She had confessed all and begged for Simon's help. What more could she do now, except bury Grave and move on in the hope of saving her daughter.

Part Four: Seeds of Revolt

29

28th October 1483 in the late afternoon, at Catesby's House in London

Bess Fisher studied the lawyer closely, noting with quiet amusement how Catesby kept her waiting as he needlessly shuffled documents across his desk.

"Mistress Fisher," said Catesby eventually. "Or is it Widow Fisher – I get so easily muddled when I consider your family… history. You have a most interesting past, don't you? Remind me, what was your dead husband's name?"

When Bess declined to answer he continued. "He met a rather abrupt end, didn't he?" mused Catesby, "a bit like your brother – though your husband was not a man who usually got caught up in brawls…"

"Tis thought he did disturb a thief," said Bess, "who, in trying to make his escape, lost his head and stabbed my poor husband in the eye."

"Lost his head," murmured Catesby, "still there was no coming back from that wound, was there? But you didn't keep his name…"

"I don't pretend to have liked my late husband much, Master Catesby, so I took my father's name once more: Fisher."

The lawyer stared at her, face void of respect.

"Your brother came well recommended," he remarked. "Sir James Tyrell is a useful ally to have - but you, on the other hand, were recommended by no-one. And you seem to find the devil in all things…"

"True enough, Master Catesby, I'm drawn to sin as a new-born lamb craves its mother's teat," said Bess, a bitter edge to her voice. "But… I must be good at something, or you wouldn't have dragged me out of that Newgate shithole where you threw me two weeks ago."

"Perhaps you should have stayed in Flanders," grumbled Catesby. "I put you in Newgate because you did not report to me at once upon your arrival – as agreed and expected..."

"I scarcely had a moment before your ruffians leapt upon me!"

"But you were not going to, were you, Bess? So tell me now, what happened in Sluys?"

Catesby's tone carried a deal of menace. Several agents he had sent to assist the Fishers in their efforts to capture John Elder had all perished in Flanders and now he wanted her to account for the deaths and her own failure. Without other witnesses, she could tell him whatever she liked, especially since her brother, being dead, could hardly gainsay her.

It was a struggle, but Bess managed to squeeze out a tear or two by pinching her leg as hard as she could. "My poor brother," she wept, "is dead by the hand of the outlaw, John Elder. We had him, Master Catesby! We had him!"

"But you lost him!" snorted Catesby. "And all I have is three dead men, a lying little whore and an empty purse!"

"My brother was a brave man!" she declared. "A little more faith in us and you'd already have that damned outlaw you want so badly!"

"Your brother was a weak fool!" replied Catesby. "But I'm not – and, by the way, I know full well how you pulled upon his strings! So, now that he's gone, what are you made of, Bess Fisher?"

So, it was honesty Catesby wanted, was it? "It was never Geoffrey who made the decisions, Master Catesby – when steel was needed it was my steel, not his."

"Steel, really? Because all I see is a murdering harlot with mounting debts. So, why shouldn't I throw you back into Newgate?"

"Because I found John Elder, didn't I, while you were still blundering about looking for your own arse? So, I've proved what I can do - any service you want. If you can say it, I can do it: theft, seduction, murder – just as long as you take care of all my debts."

The lack of hesitation before Catesby spoke again brought her much relief, for it confirmed that the bastard lawyer had intended to employ her all along.

With a scowl, he stood up. How men loved to assert themselves, she thought.

"I'm giving you one last chance of redemption," he announced. "I want you to find a woman for me."

Bess could not help a smug grin. "For you?"

"Climb out of the gutter, woman!" retorted Catesby. "If I needed a whore, I could do a lot better than you!"

"Your pardon, sir," said Bess sweetly. "But, I am ever at your service…."

"Yes, you are," replied Catesby. "So try not to forget it."

Seeing the lawyer's impassive face and dark, narrowing eyes, Bess amended her initial assessment. She must tread more softly; Catesby was no fool and the likes of Bess Fisher would be utterly expendable in pursuit of the king's wishes.

"What is she then, this woman you want to find?" asked Bess.

"Lady Eleanor Elder is John Elder's aunt."

Bess pulled a face. "Oh, good… and what's she done?"

"Nothing yet, that I can prove at least…"

"So why does she matter?"

"Because she's very close to her nephew and left London in haste in the summer at much the same time as he did – surely no accident. I'd wager all I have that she was snarled up in his treason before and still is now – like the rest of her cursed family!"

"As you will, Master Catesby; so, where do I start?"

"It's been reported to me that she is in Poole."

"Is that in England?" asked Bess.

Catesby gave a weary sigh. "It's in Dorsetshire, Bess, which I take it you've never visited."

"I'm sure I can find it, but how will I know her?"

"My man in Poole will tell you where she is and you'll watch her."

"Why can't your man watch her then?"

"He has more important things to do. You just watch her – nothing else. Don't write your own little story this time, Bess."

"Very well, but what might she be doing in Dorset?"

"In his last dispatch, my agent in Brittany, who is watching the traitor, Henry Tudor, sent word of a new arrival there – John Elder. Having arrived suddenly, he stayed for a few days and then left in the same manner. The rumour was that he was heading for Dorset – how strange a chance it is then that his favourite aunt has turned up there of all places. If he makes contact with any of his kin, it will be her."

"I'll watch her very close, Master Catesby," Bess assured him.

"If there is any sign that she is involved in sedition – secret meetings, or letters sent to anyone, you must find a way to intercept them."

"Very well and what do I do with Lady Eleanor if she is guilty of treason?"

"You do nothing. Her fate lies in the hands of another."

"Oh, who?"

"Not your business, Bess. You just do as you're told."

"I'll want my debts settled for this," said Bess.

"If you carry out your task – as instructed," said Catesby, "then I believe we can agree that your debts will be paid in full."

Bess smiled in quiet understanding, but her smile turned sour when Catesby added: "I'm sending two men with you."

"I work better on my own-"

"Only since you managed to get your brother killed!" he retorted. "But I'll have no argument; you will go with two of my men or you'll go back to Newgate!"

"Dear me, Master Catesby," cried Bess, "a girl might think you don't trust her!"

"A girl would be correct." There was no humour in Catesby's voice. "Should you see John Elder, you must tell my men at once! But you are to concentrate on Lady Eleanor; they can watch her nephew."

"When do I leave then?"

"Now, because, if John Elder intends to stir up trouble, he'll arrive in Dorset very soon. My men, the brothers Snagg, are waiting outside with a mount for you."

"The brothers Snagg?" Bess gave a low snigger. "Did you make that name up?"

"You will tell them everything and they'll keep me informed," Catesby reminded her, as he moved to the door.

Standing up, Bess took silent pleasure from the fact that she was a little taller than he was.

"You'll have to ride hard," he said, "because you'll need to reach Basingstoke by this evening and Ringwood tomorrow."

"Sounds wonderful!" said Bess. "I love riding hard!"

"After that though, Poole is only a few more miles."

"I can't wait to meet the brothers Snagg," said Bess.

"Take great care, Mistress Fisher," warned Catesby, "because if you cross me in this, you'll hang. My fellows have orders to drag you back here by the hair if you don't behave - after which you'll be thrown into a cell with all the other whores until a rope can be made ready. Is that a sharp enough spur for you?"

"Oh yes, Master Catesby," said Bess. "Quite sharp enough, I assure you."

30

29th October 1483, at Handfast Castle

Eleanor sat alone in her chamber; broken, bitter… Grave and the crewman from the Catherine had been buried, but Simon had barely said a word to her throughout. Although he had done all that he had promised he seemed ever more distant. Her honest submission appeared to have gained her nothing; she had sacrificed his good opinion of her for nothing!

Now he knew her secrets – all those that mattered at least – she was utterly in his hands. Perhaps he was already reporting her crimes to his brother who, as mayor, could easily order her detention. By the Virgin, they might come for her at any moment! And she had lost another day – another day that Slade held Kate and she had done nothing to find her!

Well, she had waited long enough. "Mary!" she cried.

It took only a moment for her servant to enter the chamber. "My lady, whatever is it?"

"How is the girl - I refuse to call her 'Jug'?"

"Sarah," said Mary.

"Sarah, really? Well, how is she?"

"She's broke her leg, my lady; so she still can't move much."

"That's a pity, for we need to leave – I think perhaps in some haste."

"Well, Sarah can't go far, my lady."

"Either she comes with us, or she stays here."

"But why must we go anywhere?"

"Because I believe Sir Simon will betray us."

"No, he won't!" scoffed Mary. "Why, he's done nothing but help us from the start!"

"Aye, that's true," she agreed.

"Then why would he suddenly turn against us?" demanded Mary.

"Well, perhaps because I might have told him just about every foolish thing I've done in the past two years…"

"Oh, fuck!" exclaimed Mary. "Why in the name of Christ would you do that?"

"I needed his help, so I gambled… that honesty-"

"Not much of a gamble, lady, with all you've done!" observed Mary.

"Aye, perhaps, but I always had cause!" declared Eleanor. "You know I always acted in defence of others!"

"Aye, I do know that, my lady, but he must think you're the most Godless woman in Christendom!"

"Hardly the most Godless!" protested Eleanor.

"Close enough for him, I should think!"

"Aye, so now do you agree that he'll betray me?"

Mary pulled a face. "I'd better tell the others to be ready to leave, but I know Sarah can't leave and Peter-"

"Peter? Who's Peter?" said Eleanor.

"Spindle! Spindle's name is Peter!" said Mary. "Damn me, my lady, it was you wanted to use their right names – you could at least try to remember them!"

"I've had… other matters to think on," said Eleanor, not at that moment caring a toss for their names. "Aye, well, what about… Peter?"

"Well, he won't leave without Sarah."

Eleanor shook her head. "No, of course not - nor would I ask him to. Just me and thee then, Mary, unless you intend to desert me too…"

Slapping the chamber wall with the flat of her hand, Mary rounded upon her mistress.

"I just don't know how you can even think that – let alone say it to my face!" she cried. "By Christ, if I'd wanted to leave you, I could've done it any time! The Virgin knows I always had reason enough! I could have left you when you were blind, couldn't I?"

"Very well, I understand; you're loyal," said Eleanor, "and I thank you, but don't dribble on about it. If you're coming, find us some food to take."

"So we're going to steal from him now, are we?"

"Oh, get out and tell… Peter to saddle two horses!"

"You do know, don't you, that we don't actually have any horses and stealing them is a lot worse than stealing a loaf?" Mary pointed out.

"Have I not been clear enough?" asked Eleanor, her voice close to breaking. "There is nothing I won't do to find my Kate!"

Mary threw up her hands and hurried out leaving the door wide open.

As Eleanor was shutting it, she heard the castle gates being opened and the sound of a horse in the cobbled yard. By Christ, it might already be too late! Well, they might take her, but she wouldn't make it easy. If she could get down the stair in time, she could wait down in the cellar until Simon ushered his visitor into the Hall. Once they were in there she could dart back up the stair and then down the outside steps, seize the recently arrived horse – which would still be saddled in the yard – and make her escape. With luck the gates might even still be open. She would have to leave the others – even Mary - but, in any case, the girl did not deserve to share the fate of her mistress. None of them had done any wrong and they were good servants. Simon would see them safe, because that was the man he was.

When she began to descend the stairs, she heard no voices so, with luck, she reckoned she could sneak down into the cellar unnoticed. Treading light and fast, she reached the foot of the stair undiscovered, relieved that there was no sign yet of Simon, nor the new arrival. It would take only another moment to slip down into the cellar to wait. But at the very moment she reached the landing adjacent to the hall, Simon appeared at the top of the outside steps, accompanied by his brother, Roger.

"Good day to you, Eleanor," said Simon, "though you rather take us by surprise."

The mayor's arrival confirmed her worst fears and she faced the two men, open-mouthed.

"Roger, you remember Lady Eleanor," said Simon.

"Hardly likely to forget her, brother," grinned Roger.

Eleanor dropped to her knees. "Please, Simon, forgive me… give me at least a little more time to find my Kate…"

"What is he supposed to forgive?" asked Roger at once.

To her surprise, Simon crossed the landing, took her hands and pulled her up at once.

"Nothing," he said swiftly. "The poor lady has been grieving for Master Grave, as is to be expected. There is nothing to forgive and I am only too pleased to help you in your search for your daughter. That's why I've asked my brother to lend his support."

"My lady," Roger assured her, "I am eager to put myself at your service."

"Come, Eleanor, join us in the hall. Roger knows most men in the port and I was just asking him about the fellow you saw, Elias Slade."

"Of course, as mayor, I encounter men like Slade all the time," said Roger. "Poole is such a fast-growing town, my lady, that such men are drawn to its wealth like maggots to a ripe orchard."

"You believe you can find him?" gasped Eleanor.

"I've never been more certain of anything," replied Roger, "but… I should counsel a little caution. Such a man, I fear, will not submit quietly. We must proceed with care for, if I were to find and arrest the villain, perhaps one of his confederates might still harm your daughter."

"But what else can we do?" asked Simon.

"Make a trade!" said Eleanor at once. She had no idea where the idea came from – but the moment she said it, she knew it would work. "Me for Kate – Slade will agree to that."

"No!" protested Simon. "We cannot do that! I'll certainly not allow you to put your own life at risk."

"It's my life!" insisted Eleanor, "and it's what Slade wants, so he'll agree!"

"I can't permit it, Eleanor!" said Simon, grasping her hand.

"Permit it?" she cried. "Then you can't have been listening very well the other night!"

Simon, looking as if he'd been whipped, dropped her hand and fell silent.

"If I may, brother," interrupted Roger, "I think the lady may be right."

"What? No!" protested Simon.

"Hear what I propose before you dismiss it, Simon," said Roger. "We need to tease this villain out, but of course Lady Eleanor won't be put at risk. We'll simply agree a place to meet and I'll have men at the ready to seize Master Slade."

"But it's still a great risk," said Simon, "not just for Eleanor, but for her daughter too!"

"Aye, it's a risk, Simon," murmured Eleanor, taking his hand once more, "but it is the only way we can find her. Slade will never give her up easily, of that I'm certain."

"Why don't we see if I can track down the villain," proposed Roger. "If we find him, then you can decide how to proceed."

"Very well, brother," agreed Simon. "But make no arrangements without speaking to us first."

"Of course, but I shall move with all speed, for my mission has ever been to drive men like Slade from our fine town."

31

29th October 1483, late afternoon, approaching Poole Harbour

"Is this it, at last?" asked John.

Matthew Finch nodded.

"By God's grace, I thought we'd never get here!" said John. "What a journey!"

"Indeed, my lord," agreed Matthew. "A journey of feast or famine - fog-bound, then windless for days and finally, bedevilled by storms. Such is the world of the sea-farer!"

"But have you ever been becalmed for so long?"

"Five days?" replied Matthew, "Oh, I've known worse."

"Worse? Surely not?"

"Yes, down in Biscay – but this time it was the storms which cost us more..."

"Aye, and the repairs!" agreed John.

"But, at the last, God gave us a fair wind and here we are – so we should be thankful we're delivered safely."

"Aye, and I do thank God for that but, Matthew, I pray we're not delivered too late! God's teeth! His grace could have arrived here before us - and we've first to find the Catherine! The sooner the ladies can sail on to Bristol, the safer they'll be!"

Though there had been a light sea mist that morning, it was clearing by the time they approached the harbour entrance. Matthew Finch was able to judge his course clearly enough which was as well, for he had already warned his crew to watch out for the shallow waters beside the main channel into the harbour.

"Just how shallow is it?" asked John.

"How far do you see with your eyes shut, my lord?" countered Matthew.

"Not far - so you don't know?"

"The channel can vary over time – especially with higher tides or storms. I've only been here once before and that was last year on the Elizabeth – a smaller vessel – and her master almost ran her aground then!"

"Do you think they've had storms here too – like we've had?"

"It's likely," agreed Matthew, as the ship glided though the harbour entrance on the afternoon tide. "Best make the most of this fine weather, eh?"

"Aye, we've much to do," agreed John, "but the most urgent task is to set our agent safely ashore. Point me out the place where you thought we might land Lady Radcliffe."

"You wanted somewhere quiet, or where a privy arrival would pass unnoticed?"

"Aye."

"Well, most of my recollections of Poole are a little clouded by the ale I consumed during my last visit, but I seem to remember it as a rough port. I should think quite a lot passes unnoticed, but the place you want is probably Baiter."

"Why Baiter? What's at Baiter?"

"Sod all that matters, believe me. It's where they buried their plague victims – and I dare say they've buried quite a few more who never had the plague!"

"Sounds like just the place for a boatload of mercenaries to land!"

"It's close enough to the town, but outside the wall - though, as I recall, the wall is more ditch than wall…

"You don't sound very fond of this place, Matthew."

"Fond of it? No, I'm not. It used to be a haven for south coast pirates – and, for all I know, it still is. It certainly attracts more than its fair share of cutthroats! And another thing: once we drop anchor, folk in the port will start wanting to know what we're doing here: what we're carrying. So, if you agree, while you're seeing your aunt ashore at Baiter, I'll take Will and find the port bailiff, who'll no doubt be rubbing his hands in the hope that we've a rich cargo aboard. I'll tell him that we've no goods to discharge, only minor repairs to carry out. Then we'll see if the Catherine is in the port – or has been sighted by any other ships."

"Hah! The only rich goods we have are the ladies," said John. He meant it as a jest but Matthew was not laughing.

"You should know, my lord, that there's a market for young white-skinned girls in ports like this. They snatch them to sell in the slave markets of southern Spain."

"By Christ, Matthew, don't tell them that," laughed John, "or they'll be wandering the quay just to get more attention!"

"I'm serious, my lord!" Matthew's rebuke was sharp. "Girls are more often than not picked up on the quay – or in one of the taverns – and, before they know it, they're at sea – with no hope of returning home!"

"My apologies, Matthew, for I see that this is no small matter…"

"That's Baiter," said Matthew, jabbing his finger at a low-lying stretch of the coastline to the east of the main docks. "And this is as close as I dare go. Look, you can already see the mud banks now the tide's turning."

"But there are a few wooden wharves along there," observed John.

"Yes, but you can only use them at high tide – and not with a ship of this size."

"Very well then," said John, "let's launch the boat and take a look."

Lady Radcliffe, who had appeared beside Matthew, stared across at Baiter. "Charming place," she murmured.

"Not very inviting, aunt," said John, "but I'll take a look first with Master Hooper and then, if it will suit your needs, we'll send the boat back for you."

◇◇◇◇◇◇

When the small boat scraped onto the shore, John leapt out only to sink up to his knees in thick mud, to the amusement of several scruffy youths who had sat watching his vessel land.

"Oh good," he muttered, as Hooper and Conal joined him to trudge across the stinking mire to firmer ground.

Baiter did its best to live up to Matthew Finch's description: it was a foul and evil-smelling shithole which had clearly become home to the poor, the criminal and the downright murderous. Buildings of any substance were few and far between and every one reeked like a privy. Whatever villainy one desired, John reckoned it could be obtained with ease at Baiter, but perhaps in that respect, it was not so different from areas outside the walls of many towns. Nevertheless, landing in broad daylight with two other men at arms, he expected his arrival to be greeted with suspicion – or at least draw some reaction – but no. Clearly, those who inhabited Baiter were very familiar with new arrivals and had learned not to ask questions of strangers – especially heavily-armed strangers.

Taking care to avoid the offensive array of dung heaps, shallow graves and rubbish pits, they headed west towards the town where they discovered the wall easily enough. Matthew's assessment again proved accurate for the town 'wall' consisted of a ditch with a timber palisade on top which in most places a small child could have breached simply by leaning upon it. The ditch might once have been

216

quite deep but so much detritus now filled it, that it was possible simply to walk across to the palisade. In fact in some places, there was no longer a fence of any description and, in others, small, squalid hovels had been constructed right across the ditch.

It took little effort to identify the gate into the town from Baiter, though John wondered what purpose it served – it certainly couldn't keep anyone out. Although a serjeant propped himself against it, he appeared to take no interest at all in the folk who sauntered to and fro past him.

Poole looked like a town which was growing so fast it was outgrowing its old boundaries. At some point the men with all the wealth would have to turn their attention to stricter controls on trade and movement - not to mention the construction of a complete stone wall. But in the present boom, he knew that the drive for profits would mean that local ordinances would be flouted at every turn.

His aunt should have no difficulty in entering the town from Baiter, as long as she was accompanied by Hooper and armed with whatever information Finch was able to give her about her destination.

Having seen enough, John retraced his steps to the Baiter shore and sent back the boat for Lady Radcliffe. By the time it returned with his aunt and Hooper's comrade, Master Grim aboard, it was late in the afternoon. The tide, he noted, had receded further and he prepared to carry his aunt across the swathe of mud. But before he could do so, Hooper stepped forward to pick her up himself. So be it, thought John, reckoning that his aunt would rather be beholden to Hooper than her errant nephew.

"You'll need to make haste, aunt," he told her.

"Aye," she said. "Pity you didn't!"

"Curfew's not too far off and, though you can enter the town through the broken fence, it's probably best that you don't."

"I know that," she said curtly.

"And remember: don't give your own name-"

"Do I look like a simpleton?" she hissed at him. "I'll use Hooper's name – and he'll know where I am at all times and his comrade, Master Grim, will come here with any news for you. Sweet Christ! I know what I'm doing, John!"

"Aye, of course you do, aunt," he replied.

Even so he disliked abandoning her, believing, despite her protestations, that she would be utterly out of her depth. Though he had every trust in Hooper, he worried that even the loyal man at arms had little experience of the world of deceit and subterfuge into which he and his mistress were about to venture.

Before he returned to the ship, he remained upon the shore watching the three figures pick their way through the smouldering fires until he lost sight of them.

"What have you gotten yourself into, aunt?" he murmured softly.

◇◇◇◇◇◇

Matthew paused for only a moment after Lady Radcliffe left in the boat for Baiter and then set off for the port with Will. Though he studied the ships along the quay carefully, he could not discover one that resembled the Catherine. By the time they had sauntered around the docks, Matthew was certain that the Catherine was not in Poole – yet he knew with equal certainty that his father would have taken the ship to the port and waited there for the Margaret to arrive. Since it must surely have arrived before them, where had the Catherine gone?

A visit to the port bailiff proved unhelpful since the bailiff only confirmed that no ship called the Catherine had docked there in the past week.

"Could it be somewhere else in the harbour?"

"Could be up in Holes Bay," suggested the bailiff. "Got boatyards there, but it's mostly too shallow. Might have sailed up the river to Wareham, I suppose?"

But Matthew could not see why his father would have continued up the river Frome to Wareham when they had agreed to meet at Poole. But another, darker, question needed to be asked.

"What about… wrecked ships?" he pressed the port official. "Have you any reports of a recent shipwreck?"

"Shipwrecks?" said the bailiff, as if the term was new to him. "Don't think we've had many of those in the last few months."

"Who would know if a ship had been wrecked close by Poole?" asked Will.

"Well, I would, of course – and the other bailiff would – oh, and the mayor too – and, if any bodies turned up, a surgeon might be called upon too. But you say you were caught in a storm, so the ship you seek might have been driven anywhere by the same storm. It's a small chance it turned up here."

"Except that it was bound for Poole and its master was an experienced man," insisted Matthew.

"Well, if you don't like what I've told you, you can take it up with the mayor - Roger Cayne. He lives in the big stone town house near the Wool House. He's the man to ask – you go and ask him."

"My thanks," said Matthew stiffly, for the bailiff's manner was far from helpful. "Perhaps we'll seek out Master Cayne on the morrow."

"You do that, friend," grumbled the bailiff, "but he'll tell you the same as me: no ship called the Catherine has docked here."

Exchanging a weary glance with Will, Matthew returned to the ship. "It's too late in the day now," he said, "we must get back to Baiter to pick up your cousin, but I fear we'll have to come back."

"Why didn't Lady Radcliffe just leave the ship here?" asked Will. "It would have been much easier."

"Yes, but I rather think the whole point, Will, is that she's not seen to come in by ship – and certainly not on the quay where every arrival might so easily be observed and reported, eh?"

32

29th October 1483 in the evening, at a tavern in Ringwood, Hampshire

At least the tavern offered some warmth, thought Bess – and it was dry! From Basingstoke they had found the road washed out by the recent rains and had ridden their backsides sore taking a longer route. Thus Bess was not only soaked through, but her arse was rubbed raw and she was utterly miserable. The final stroke came when they discovered that the inns in Ringwood were full and they were reduced to taking a small chamber at a lowly tavern.

Far from happy, Bess was even less enthusiastic when the Snagg brothers determined, with a knowing snigger between them, that the cramped upstairs chamber would be sufficient to accommodate all three of them. She was under no illusion what the brothers expected to happen in that room when they all bedded down on the narrow pallet bed. During the long ride, they had made frequent references to several – admittedly rather admirable - features of her body. Though she supposed that Catesby had described her to them as a whore, she did nothing to discourage their interest, for it was exactly what she hoped for.

She almost felt a little sorry for them, for they were really rather endearing, especially the younger brother, Seth – in a puppy-like way. But the previous night she had wormed out of them who they would be meeting in Poole; so now, with that vital knowledge acquired, it was time to drown the unwanted puppies.

Considering the coming night would demand all her strength and wit, she regretted that she was not at her sharpest. The sparse meal they ate of pottage, accompanied by bread which had been baked to the edge of destruction, did little to restore her. Much ale was consumed by the brothers and Bess too gave every impression of being seriously drunk. Thus she made no protest when Seth gave her torso a thorough examination with his hands, but when Tom, the elder brother, embarked on a similar voyage of discovery, she pushed him away - gently at first, but then with more vehemence. Abruptly she broke away from the pair, announcing that she would retire upstairs.

As expected, both men soon followed – though neither was content. Seth resented the intervention of his brother which had brought an unwelcome end to his fondling and Tom was furious that his own advances – unlike Seth's - had been firmly rejected.

Thank the Lord it was so easy, thought Bess, as she watched the two men enter the chamber. A jealous man was such a weak man…

"Seth, my dear," she said, turning her back to him, "would you unlace my kirtle for me?"

Only too pleased to lay his hands upon her once more, Seth responded with alacrity, his eager fingers loosening her bodice in a few short moments. Slowly, teasingly, she turned in his arms, allowing him to ease her out of the kirtle. Behind Seth, Tom stood, grim-faced. How much restraint, she wondered idly, did the older man possess? Dressed now only in her linen shift, she decided it was time to test him out. She took Seth's hands from around her waist and guided them onto her breasts, allowing him to stroke her there, whilst she stared over his shoulder at Tom and pursed her lips in the shape of a kiss.

As Seth leant closer, pressed hard against her belly, she hesitated. The youth was actually quite handsome… but sadly, any liaison between them would not end happily. Pulling abruptly away from him, she was pleased to observe the shock on his face when she stepped past him to his brother.

"Older brothers first, perhaps," she whispered in Tom's ear.

Needing no more encouragement, Tom embraced her willingly, pawing at the thin linen she still wore. A sideways glance at Seth troubled Bess, for it appeared that he was not going to intervene against his brother. That was a nuisance... for it meant she would have to work a lot harder.

Kissing Tom full on the lips, she pulled him down onto the pallet which creaked under their combined weight. Once Tom was on top of her, she allowed him to lift her shift up past her thighs. He fumbled with his breeches and finally managed to drag them down along with his braies. He was so well-endowed that again, just for a moment, she was tempted; but no, that would not do either – get a hold of yourself, Bess Fisher, you wanton bitch!

"No, no! You're hurting me!" she cried out in alarm. "Get off me! Seth, help me! Please! Help me!"

But Seth did not move and for the first time she harboured serious doubts. Had she misjudged these two so badly?

"Seth!" she wailed again, weeping. Tears usually worked exceptionally well, but no, the weak little turd was still rooted to the spot and Tom was already thrusting at her. Shit! A brother's love clearly outweighed the youth's passion for her! Oh sweet Christ, if she had lost her touch, this evening was going to turn out very badly for her indeed!

She groaned - and not just from Tom's earnest thrashing – but because she would have to bear some genuine pain to turn this disaster around....

"Tom!" she screamed. "Stop!"

"Peace!" warned Tom. "What's got into you, woman? You were willing enough just now! You'll wake up the household."

As she squealed and writhed under him, she reached down for his belt.

"Peace, you foolish whore!" growled Tom, slapping her on the face.

Thank God! She almost said it out loud as at last she laid her hand on the hilt of Tom's knife and, in one swift movement, thrust the blade up under his ribs. Warm blood spilled onto her as he screamed in pain and anger.

Pushing him aside, she displayed her bloodied belly before abandoning Tom's blade on the pallet.

"He's stabbed me, Seth," she whimpered. "Will you just stand there and watch me die?"

For an instant she thought he might just do that, so she added in a desperate whisper: "Now we can never be together, dear Seth…"

When Tom rose, wild and murderous, from the floor, Seth snatched up the knife from the pallet. "You selfish bastard!" he raged. "I was always content with your leavings – but now you'd deny me even that!"

Tom turned an astonished face towards his brother. "No, Seth, what are you thinking?" he moaned.

"Bastard!" shouted Seth and plunged the knife into his brother's neck. As his bewildered brother clutched at his arm, Seth stabbed him again and again in the chest and ribs until Tom collapsed onto the floor boards, already wet with his blood.

"Help me," sobbed Bess. "Help me, Seth. I'm dying…"

He flew to her, abandoning the knife to wrap his arm around her, to support her swooning body.

"Let me look to your wound, Bess!" he cried. "I know it's a bad one."

"I fear it's mortal, Seth," she murmured, though she kept a hand clamped firmly over the 'wound'.

"Pray for my soul when I'm gone, will you?" she added. A nice touch, she thought.

"No, no, Bess; let me look at it. There's always hope!"

"No, Seth, not always," she said, with a sad smile. "Sometimes, there really isn't…"

By then of course her other hand had retrieved the knife, which she drove so hard through his right eye that she felt it strike the back of his skull. She wanted to give him a swift end; he deserved that much from her.

While she was cleaning herself up, she was already working through her account of the brothers' vicious struggle. Looking down upon the corpses, she murmured: "Drag me back by the hair, would you, Master Catesby? I don't think so…"

33

30th October 1483 at noon, at the Church of St James in Poole

In vain, Emma Radcliffe slammed shut the church door to keep out the rain, but it steadfastly refused to stay closed. Now the storm was worsening, the dark clouds hovering above the town pressed still lower. Inside the church, the smell of rotting timber pervaded the whole building. A rivulet of water ran across the narrow nave and several drops of water landed on her cap. With its leaking roof, the damp and fragile wooden structure was in desperate need of repair.

Just for a moment the wind picked up, aiming a stray punch at the feeble walls which caused them to shudder. But Emma had only a brief moment of doubt, for she knew that St James would be watching over his humble place of worship. Its priest though was nowhere to be seen – more than likely seeking a warmer, drier place to pray. Emma could not blame him, though it occurred to her that if the flimsy edifice were actually to fall down, then perhaps the growing wealth of the town would provide for a new, stone-built church.

Because the sky was so dark, it did not seem much like midday but she thought that by now it had to be. Her man, Morton, was late. Finding a dry bench, she indulged in a grim smile, for it seemed hardly any time at all since she had met Lady Margaret in a London church very different from this place. Now, here she was: no longer simply a grieving widow but... what? The agent of an exiled lord - or just a traitor to her lawful king? Perhaps both caps fitted... but

226

could she do it? Could she carry it off, as Lady Margaret believed she could? Or would her nephew's all too obvious doubts be justified?

The main door gave a warning creak before it was flung open. Shaking the rain water off onto the flagstones, a black-cloaked figure hurried in. As she turned to face him, Emma was suddenly terrified.

"God give you good day, goodwife," said the newcomer, who looked surprised to see her.

At once all rational thought sped from her head and she mumbled the vaguest of greetings - tongue-tied before she even began! Was this the man she was due to meet or not? By the Virgin, he could be anyone!

"Are you quite well?" enquired the stranger.

"Aye," she managed to spit out.

"You're from the north then?" he asked.

So, already that much was clear to him. John had warned her, but, of course, her foolish pride ensured that she paid little heed to anything he said.

"I think that rain might be easing off," he said, pushing at the door to look out.

"I doubt it," replied Emma.

That's right you fool, she berated herself, give him a few curt words, why don't you? Because that'll help to build trust! She was puzzled by his awkward manner until she realised why; he was willing her to leave! Not for a moment did he imagine that she might be the agent of Henry Tudor he was expecting to meet. He paced back and forth across the nave, looking even more nervous than she felt.

Unable to suppress a little laugh, she found that, somehow, it calmed her fears. With a sigh, she walked over to him and held out her hand so that he could see the silver ring upon her finger. He peered at it, gave a start and then stared at her with a look of utter disbelief.

"It's you?" he muttered.

"I am certainly me; now, who are you?"

"Richard Morton, but… you're not who I was expecting."

"Who were you expecting?" she asked.

"Well, a sort of… man."

She nodded; taking no offence, for it was only to be expected. If her own nephew was surprised she had been chosen, it was unlikely this stranger would be any less so.

"You were expecting a messenger," she told him, "and it's said that women are less noticed, and thus more effective in evading capture."

"But… how are you, a woman, to lead us?"

"You should try that question with my sister," murmured Emma. "But you're right: another will come to lead you. I am here to ensure that both you - and he – can meet safely. You should see me as a conduit."

"A conduit?"

She wondered if she was speaking the same language as Morton – but perhaps her northern accent was troubling him. "As a conduit carries water, I carry messages," she explained.

"Ah," he said, eyes nervously exploring the dark interior of the church. "Then you bring word from the Earl of Richmond?"

"I do," replied Emma. "After we heard of the death of your leader-"

"So, it's really true then?"

"Aye, of course - else why would we be meeting here at all?" snapped Emma.

"For a messenger from a friend, you have a sharp tongue," grumbled Morton.

"Aye, your pardon, Master Morton, but I've had a long journey to get here," she said. "Did you know the man well?"

"Well enough," said Morton. "But I still can't see how anyone knew who he was - or where he was going? Most of us didn't even know the road he intended to take."

"Well then, I come to the first part of my message: you have a traitor amongst you."

"Well, I confess, some of us have already suspected it," agreed Morton. "But if no-one can be trusted, then what are we to do?"

"Your name was given to me as a man I could trust. But you must not reveal anything you know to anyone else – or at least to only a very small group of your leaders, men you can trust with your life – and the lives of many others!"

Morton gave a sombre nod. "So, who is to lead us then?" he asked. "Is it the Marquis of Dorset? He has lands hereabouts."

"No."

"Oh, well, who is it then?" he asked, visibly crestfallen.

She was not supposed to tell him, but she decided the fellow was so shaken he needed a little encouragement.

"It will be Lord John Elder," she said, "the outlawed son of the great York lord, Ned Elder."

His face brightened at once. "Ah, I've heard of the Elders!" he said. "I think that news will give our men some heart."

"But," she insisted, "you are to say nothing of Lord John until he arrives. Do you understand?"

"Oh, of course – I need no more urging upon that point, I assure you!"

"Aye, well, all our lives hang upon not talking to the wrong people," Emma impressed upon him.

"How goes the revolt elsewhere? We live on gossip alone here."

"I know little more than you," she said, but again, seeing the disappointment in his eyes, she offered him something more. "Listen, you will play an important part in the revolt, for the Earl of Richmond himself will shortly be arriving here."

"The Earl of Richmond here – in Poole?" cried Morton.

"Hush, man! In God's name, keep your voice down!"

He nodded, still shaking from the import of her last revelation. "At last the men of Dorset will take pride of place alongside the earl," he breathed. "So, what do you want me to do next?"

"You are to gather your local men to meet Lord Elder."

"What, all of them?"

"No, your leaders – those who will muster others – will suffice. But remember; only trusted men can know what I've just told you. Make the arrangements and then meet me here to pass on the time and place.

"It may take a day or two to get them all together," said Morton. "Some are not men of Poole – they live a few miles distant.

"Well, move as fast as you can, or the landing will take place without you!" she urged.

"Indeed, goodwife," he agreed, but made no move to leave.

She stared at him. "Go on then. You go first."

"Very well," he said.

The poor man was still shaking when he shuffled out into the driving rain – which had not yet let up. After watching him cross the street and head towards the quay, she waited in the church for a long time, hoping that the rain might eventually stop. Since it did not, she gave up waiting in the end and made her way to the inn where she had rented a small room. It was a risk, of course, staying in the heart of the town but it was better than being cooped up on the ship any longer. Bad enough that she should have to endure living on a ship, but the cramped cabin was altogether too much.

Thoroughly elated, she was smiling as she hurried to the inn, anxious to see Hooper and tell him how well it had gone – after a shaky start. Perhaps, after all, she was better suited to subterfuge and secrecy than her nephew supposed.

34

30th October 1483 late afternoon, at Roger Cayne's House in Poole

"You should have come in by the rear door," chided Roger Cayne.

Elias Slade gave a dismissive wave of his hand. "Never mind that," he said. "What have you got for me?"

"My dear Master Slade, I have a gift for you: Lady Eleanor wishes to deliver herself to you."

"Meaning?" Slade's suspicious manner prompted a smile from Roger.

"Exactly what I said: the lady wants to give up herself to take the place of her daughter - who I believe you are holding prisoner? It might have been useful if I'd known that."

"The girl's a… guest of Diggory," said Slade. "Don't want me to tell you every 'guest' he has, do you?"

"Certainly not!"

"Anyway, we're not trading the girl for her mother. We want both – there's profit in it for Diggory."

"Spare me the details, Slade. I don't want to know. I'll just tell you the time and place - the rest, I'll leave to you."

Slade looked doubtful. "Eleanor Elder's no fool; why would she agree to a trade without men at her back?"

"She believes that she has no choice; but also, I may perhaps have led her to think that she will have men at her back…"

"Who'll that be then? Your soft-headed brother?" laughed Slade.

"Very likely, but I might have led them to think there would be others…"

"But there won't be?" said Slade.

"No."

"So, she has no-one to go with her save a few servants?"

Roger shrugged. "I couldn't possibly tell you such things, Master Slade. Why, it would be a gross breach of trust."

"You're a cunning bastard, Master Mayor, I'll grant you that," said Slade. "Hah! 'Gross breach of trust?' I like that - I'll have to store that one away."

"But mind me, Master Slade, there must be no pitched battles - or I should have to act against you."

"Doubt you'd want to try that," warned Slade. "Besides I have your scrap of paper…"

"Very well then, but make sure it's all done swiftly and quietly."

There was a sudden knock on the chamber door and Roger gave a start.

"This time you must leave by the rear door," he ordered, "and keep out of sight!"

"I'm not some leper!" growled Slade. "I'm a man of business!"

"Well get out and be about that business!" ordered Roger, crossing the room to draw back a curtain behind which lay another door. "Leave through there. I'll send you word when all's arranged."

For a moment longer Slade stood his ground. "This town's growing fast, Master Cayne," he said, "and it's folk like me who are building it up – best you remember who your friends are."

Despite Roger's glare, Slade took his time to leave and there was a further knock on the other door by the time he had finally departed.

Roger found his clerk waiting upon the threshold with another visitor – a familiar, though unexpected, one.

"Richard!" Roger waved his comrade into the room. "Have you heard yet from any mysterious messengers?"

"Well, yes, Master Mayor, that's exactly where I've just been – with Lady Margaret's envoy."

"Envoy, is it? What envoy?" enquired Roger, wondering how he did not know of such an important arrival in his town. God knew he paid his spies enough!

"I was to wait at the church every day, you see-"

"Yes, yes, Richard, you told me that before, but this time I presume someone actually turned up?"

"Indeed – and a shock, I can tell you?"

"Why?" demanded Roger, alert at once. "Has some prominent nobleman come to lead us?"

"No, it was a woman," whispered Morton.

"A woman?"

"Yes, indeed, Master Cayne – a woman!" breathed Morton.

"And do you think this female envoy is listening to us now, Richard?"

"Er no, how could she be?"

"Then for God's sake, stop whispering and tell me what she said."

For the first time, Morton seemed hesitant. "I don't know; she told me not to tell anyone, you see… but then I thought, well, I have to tell the mayor. What if it's a trap and I'm arrested – or, God help me, killed? So I thought I should at least tell you."

"Indeed - as we agreed, Richard, if you recall. We need to look out for each other, you and me. So, tell me: who was it that you met?"

"Well, I don't know – she didn't say… she had a northern accent though."

"Did she have red hair and green eyes?"

Morton looked puzzled. "No, dark hair – I didn't notice her eyes."

Even a fool like Richard Morton would have noticed Eleanor Elder's eyes, so it clearly wasn't her. Who else then? A stranger - someone who had just arrived in the town.

"Well, what did she say?"

"Lord John Elder is to lead the Dorset rebels."

"What?" cried Roger.

"Ned's Elder's lad – the outlaw."

"Hmm, I scarcely know of the father, let alone the son," said Roger diffidently, hoping that Morton had not registered his initial excitement.

"He wants a meeting – I'm to gather all the leading men in the enterprise together-"

"Is that wise – all together in one place? It could be a trap."

"How else can all our comrades meet him?" asked Morton. "The question is: where to meet?"

"Somewhere quiet and out of the way," said Roger. "I'll give it some thought, Richard. Come to me tomorrow and we'll agree a place."

"I'm so grateful for your help, Roger," said Morton, standing up to clasp Mayor Cayne's hand. "I'll admit, I was feeling the weight of it a bit – especially with Henry of Richmond landing here."

Roger gripped Morton's hand more tightly. "What did you say?" he cried. "The Earl of Richmond is landing here in Poole?"

"Yes, just saying his name makes it seem suddenly very real, doesn't it? What some wouldn't give to know that, eh?"

"Indeed," agreed Roger, thinking how fast he could get word to Catesby in London.

"Have you told anyone else?" he asked.

"Of course not! Careless words are our enemy, Roger. But now I've met the envoy, I'm a little reassured. For the new king to come here himself – what an honour! At last, we'll be in the vanguard of the revolt!"

Indeed, thought Roger, and those in the vanguard were usually the first to feel cold steel splitting open their bellies. "Best keep our feet on the ground, eh, Richard? Let's wait and see, shall we? Come to me tomorrow!"

As Morton reached the door, he issued a further warning. "Not a word though, Roger, to anyone else," he breathed. "As we said, 'tis likely we've a traitor; so we must keep such matters close."

"You may rely upon me, my friend," Roger assured him. "I shall not betray your trust to anyone."

Morton hurried out and Roger permitted himself a chuckle. Poor old Morton, never had any man thought himself so discreet and yet proved such a regular source of valuable information. Today Morton had positively showered news upon him and the mayor knew exactly which little nugget to act upon first.

He scribbled a hasty note and was about to summon his clerk when the fellow knocked at the door once again.

"What is it?" asked Roger, exasperated.

"There's a woman at the door."

"What woman?"

"Wouldn't give a name just said you'd be expecting someone from London."

"What, a woman?" By God, how many more mysterious women were going to arrive in Poole? There were already far too many! "Are you sure?"

The clerk drew himself up to his full height and replied stiffly: "I may be old, Master Cayne, but I think I still know a woman when I see one – and there's no mistaking this one."

"Yes, yes, alright, show her in and then take this note to 'you know who' at the docks."

"Not him again…" mumbled the clerk.

"You are still in my employ, are you?" growled Roger.

"Yes…"

"Well, hurry back," snarled Roger, "or you won't be!"

He glanced out of the window. It would soon be dark – soon be curfew indeed - so it was rather late for a woman to call upon him. But then if she was from Catesby, he supposed it might be urgent. Surely it couldn't be the same woman, could it? What an unlikely afternoon it was turning out to be!

The moment he saw his next visitor, he was quite stunned by her beauty. It was clear that she had recently arrived, for she had not delayed to change out of the clothes in which she had ridden. So he was right: it must be urgent.

"Please, my dear, sit at your ease. I am the town mayor, Roger Cayne."

"Widow Bess Fisher," she replied and her lack of a northern accent told him at once that she was not the same messenger that Richard Morton had met.

"You are most welcome, Widow Fisher."

"I have to tell you, Master Mayor that I am relieved to be here at all. Master Catesby sent three of us and only I have survived, by God's grace, to reach this town."

"So you are from Catesby?" he said. "But what happened to the others?"

"Set upon by rebels on the road, Master Cayne," lamented Bess, "and my two poor protectors defended me to their very last breath, hiding me away safe before they were brutally overcome. Such fine men they were…"

"Hmm," grunted Roger, weighing up the woman's tale.

Though he could admit to himself an immediate attraction to the woman, he was not one to be easily fooled.

If she was truly from William Catesby she would have to prove it before he would even consider trusting her. Women, after all, were known for their deceitful ways.

"Did Master Catesby tell you what you are to do here?" he asked.

"Indeed, I'm to watch Lady Eleanor Elder for any sign that she may be in contact with her nephew John, the renegade lord."

He almost laughed aloud, for that part of her task seemed already redundant. He questioned her closely about the Elders – in particular John, of whom he knew almost nothing and now needed to know everything. Bess seemed to know quite a lot – presumably Catesby had rehearsed her so that at least some important information might lodge in her woman's head. Though she told him she had pursued John Elder to Flanders, he did not, of course, believe a word of it. The idea of a woman doing what she claimed was quite ludicrous but he could allow her a little indulgence.

What was he to do now about the exchange of Eleanor Elder which was supposed to happen on the morrow? It was not exactly in this woman's interests for she needed Lady Eleanor to be free to act, free to be observed talking treason with her nephew. On the other hand, if Richard Morton was to be believed then John Elder might just save them a deal of trouble by handing himself to them. Roger had to consider how he could best use the tools he now had at his disposal?

Despite his reservations, this woman, Bess, looked as if she might be up for a little closer work with him in the days to come. She certainly possessed everything he looked for in a woman – well, that sort of woman - because no proper lady would be grubbing about as an agent of Catesby unless she had a very disreputable past.

He laughed out loud suddenly and Bess gave him a quizzical glance, allowing her lips to part slightly, which stirred his loins and banished one or two more doubts.

"Lost in my own thoughts, my dear Widow Fisher – Bess, if I may call you Bess."

She nodded acceptance while he reflected how exhilarating it was to be in possession of the whole story. One man knows part of it, another knows part of it, but real power lay in knowing all of it…

Bess smiled at him. "Perhaps Master Cayne, you can suggest somewhere, close by, where I might spend the night. I confess I could fall into any bed this very instant!"

"Really?" Roger was on his guard at once. "Well, my dear, I'm certain we can make that happen, but perhaps not tonight. I must introduce you to the man who first alerted me to Lady Elder's presence here in Poole."

"Must you?" sighed Bess.

"Oh, yes," replied Roger, "and I'm sure he can find a suitable bed for you."

35

31ˢᵗ October 1483, at the sea shore in Studland Bay

On a clear morning, you could see right across the bay, but this was not such a morning. Heavy rain had lashed Studland and the whole harbour area for the past few days. Thus, even now, long past dawn, the rain continued to fall and the sky remained gloomy.

In a futile attempt to calm her nerves, Eleanor drew in several deep breaths as she waited among the low trees above the shoreline. Simon Cayne, sword and knife at his belt, stood beside her, yet his presence did nothing to allay her fears. He was a good man; but, by the Virgin, how many other good men had she seen die trying to help Eleanor Elder?

God's truth, she had tried to persuade him not to come! Yet, despite her pleas that he should remain at the castle, here he was. As if reading her thoughts, he rested a hand upon her shoulder and pointed out into the bay. She nodded, seeing the two small boats on their way towards the beach. In one of those approaching vessels would be her daughter and she screwed up her eyes in an effort to pick out the girl. Though it was only a guess, she reckoned that Kate would be the slighter of several cloaked figures in the second craft. One way or another, she decided, this would be the day that Kate Elder would be freed.

"Where are your brother's men?" she whispered.

"They'll be here," Simon told her.

"You're certain?"

"My brother has never let me down, Eleanor – never. They'll be taking shelter wherever they can along the shore; so don't you worry about that, my dear."

She gave a sigh, for there it was again: that moment when a man told her not to worry; the moment when, experience taught her, it was time to start worrying in earnest.

When the first boat crunched to a halt on the stony foreshore, the sight of Elias Slade leaping out to wade ashore sent a shiver running through her. Sensing her apprehension, Simon gave her hand a gentle squeeze. She responded with a weak smile, for she was far from reassured.

By the time Elias came to a halt ten yards from the water, there were four armed men with him but the second boat, with Kate aboard, remained a dozen or so yards offshore.

"Stay there!" Slade shouted at the other boat but, against the swirling sea, it required all oarsmen's skill to hold the boat in the deeper water.

Taking a few paces forward, Eleanor and Simon emerged from the cover of the trees but, although Elias must have seen them, he stayed where he was.

"You wanna do this trade then, lady?" he called out.

Eleanor scanned the windswept treeline to left and right, but of Roger Cayne's men there was no sign. "Where are they?" she hissed at her companion.

"They'll be here," murmured Simon, but the look on his face told her that he too was starting to have doubts. "Roger's never let me down, Eleanor…"

"Aye, but he might let me down…" she said.

"Well?" bellowed Slade. "Am I taking your girl away again then?"

"No!" cried Eleanor. "I'm coming!"

"We can't do this alone!" whispered Simon. "You were never supposed to actually carry out the trade! He could kill us both – and your Kate!"

She gave a shrug and kissed him on the cheek. "I was always prepared to do it, Simon," she said. "And, now we're so close, I'm not leaving her. You just keep her safe for me – swear to me you'll do that!"

"Of course, but-"

Eleanor was already on her way out into the stinging rain. It was enough for her to know that Simon would keep his word and Kate would be safe. Buffeted by the wind and rain, she continued walking towards Slade until, when she was about twenty yards away, she came to a halt.

"Bring her in, Elias!" she shouted, her words snatched at by the blustering gale.

Just for a moment, he seemed to hesitate but then waved to his comrades in the second boat who swiftly manoeuvred their vessel into the shallows. When Eleanor saw Kate wrestling with those who held her, her eyes glistened with pride. That was her lass!

At a gesture from Slade, Kate's captors released her and Eleanor watched in anguish as she clambered over the gunwale and fell into about a foot of water. Struggling to her feet, the girl stumbled forward, swathed in her sodden cloak. With a groan, Eleanor saw that every step was a great effort for her.

"What have you done to her, Elias?" Eleanor cried, taking several more paces forward.

"Your daughter's well enough, lady," snapped Slade. "Now, you just keep walking to me and all will be settled as agreed."

Kate looked anything but well; her hunched figure wandered up the beach as if dazed, while the wayward breeze propelled her further from her mother.

"You'll soon be free, Kate!" cried Eleanor, willing her lass to keep going. "Simon, help her, please!"

"Hah! Got another poor sod shackled to you, have you?" laughed Slade. "But don't be too hasty, Master Simon - and you just keep walking to me, lady."

Eleanor glanced behind her to ensure that Simon was making his way towards Kate. She breathed more easily now for very soon Kate would be safe – and that was all she desired. In her right hand, she carried her knife, reversed to keep it hidden from sight for as long as possible. She had no doubt where that blade would be going the moment Kate and Simon were clear of the beach.

Risking another glance at her daughter, she frowned. The way Kate was bent over, she must be hurt, or terrified. If only Eleanor could see her properly… one last time.

"Kate!" she cried. "Don't worry; Sir Simon will look after you!"

Just for a moment, the girl straightened and stood tall.

"Your turn now, Lady Eleanor," warned Slade. "To the boat, if you please."

Eleanor nodded, but with her eyes fixed upon Kate, her heart was in turmoil and her steps faltered.

"Lady," growled Slade. "Let's not make this too hard, shall we?"

But Eleanor, unable to draw her eyes away from her daughter, began to walk towards her.

"What are you doing?" Slade roared into the wind. "I've kept my part in good faith!"

"Indeed you have, Elias," she shouted back. "You've looked after her so well that she's grown taller!"

"What?" yelled Slade.

"Run, Simon!" shrieked Eleanor, turning to retreat back up the beach. "We've been deceived!"

"But what about Kate?" he cried, barely a yard from the girl.

"That's not Kate!" screamed Eleanor.

Even as she said the words, the hunched figure swept aside her cloak and in a blur of movement, flashed a blade at Simon. Too late, he tried to back away, but her knife ripped into him. For a few more steps, he managed to stay on his feet, but then fell to his knees.

"Leave him, Elias!" demanded Eleanor, knowing she could not reach Simon in time. "You have me! You don't need him!"

"Ah well, lady," chuckled Elias, "that's true enough, but I reckon that hellcat over there's made some other… arrangement about poor Sir Simon…"

With a cry of rage, Eleanor stumbled towards the woman who now stood over Simon as he struggled to crawl away.

"No!" she cried, hurling herself at Simon's assailant, as she knelt to deliver a mortal thrust. Tumbling down onto the pebbles, the two women spat and lashed out at each other. Though Eleanor kicked her opponent hard in the midriff, she seemed hardly to notice. Rolling to her feet, she struck with such swift precision that Eleanor struggled to turn aside a raking slash at her breast. With sudden alarm, Eleanor realised that her adversary was both younger and quicker than she was.

The pair circled each other, watchful and wary until, as if by some mutual instinct, they flew at each other, seizing hands, twisting and squeezing to prise free a knife. For a while they wrestled thus, close as lovers and drenched by the rain. In strength, at least, the two seemed well-matched.

"Bess Fisher," grunted her opponent, as her cheek touched Eleanor's. "Perhaps… your nephew… spoke… of me?"

"When I've done with you, no-one will ever speak of you again!" snarled Eleanor. "I'll feed what's left of you to the crows!"

"Charming!" breathed Bess.

When Eleanor spat in her face, Bess butted Eleanor's forehead with her own. In a moment of dark panic, Eleanor's vision clouded and she feared the blow had robbed her of all remaining sight. But then it cleared and she found that Bess, staggering weak-kneed, was feeling the effects of her own blow. Eleanor forced a grim smile: the bitch had clearly not encountered a head quite as hard as that of Eleanor Elder.

Both women took a pace back and faced each other in a simmering stand-off whilst, around them, Slade and the others formed a ragged circle. As they continued to stare at each other, Eleanor was all too aware of Simon bleeding out only a few feet away from her. His wound was grievous yet she could do nothing for him.

"You can't weep and fight at the same time, girl," advised Bess, darting her blade forward to cut at Eleanor's thigh.

"Looks like we've got us some entertainment, lads!" laughed Slade.

"They want a show," said Bess, so quietly that only Eleanor could catch her words. "Oh, do let's give them one!" She was still speaking when she launched a series of lunges at Eleanor's stomach and ribs.

These, Eleanor suspected, would merely be feints while Bess probed for weaknesses and, she lamented, by Christ, it would not take her long to find them! Eleanor had not picked up a knife in anger for months – unless you counted the pirate, but she hadn't done him any damage!

Jerking her mind back from its wandering, she realised that, in that careless moment, Bess Fisher could easily have killed her, but she hadn't. Her opponent was taller, leaner and quicker – so why had she not pressed home her advantage?

"You didn't take your chance," said Eleanor.

"You weren't ready," said Bess, as they moved around each other once more. "Where's the pleasure in that? But there'll be another, for you've not much skill with that blade, have you?"

"I'm a little out of practice," replied Eleanor, "but I warn you: I'm never beaten…"

"Oh, I can believe that, but then every victor loses in the end, don't they?"

Facing along the beach, Eleanor could see what lay beyond Bess and slowly she became aware that a small crowd was gathering in the lee of the trees. At first she thought they might be Mayor Cayne's men but, as they edged closer to the circle of men, it was clear they were local folk. When some recognised their lord, Sir Simon, lying on the beach, there were murmurs of disquiet.

Slade must have noticed them too for he shouted: "Bess, come back to the boat!"

"Piss off!" cried Bess. "This fight is going all the way to the end!"

"Get Lady Eleanor, lads!" bellowed Slade.

Realising this was her one chance, Eleanor kicked out with her boot as hard as she could. Bess, distracted by Slade's intervention, took the blow on her shin and, with a howled curse, dropped like a stone. Two from the ring of men pounced upon Eleanor at once, but she stabbed at one and lurched past the other, almost tripping as she staggered towards the crowd, now only a dozen yards away and seething with hostile intent.

Dimly, she was aware of the shouts of Slade's comrades and the murmur of the onlookers but, soaring above them all, came a foul torrent of abuse from Mistress Fisher. When Eleanor turned around, she saw Elias Slade and his men retreating to their boats, hauling with them a screaming Bess, who left no-one in earshot in any doubt what she would do to Eleanor Elder when she next got the opportunity.

Swept up by the crowd, Eleanor was carried forward to where their lord of the manor lay. Some pursued the fleeing villains, hurling stones at them as they launched their boats out into the bay. But the rest surrounded Simon, easing Eleanor aside to examine his wound. Several seemed to know what they were doing and all Eleanor could do was look on, powerless to help. After a time, two women announced that the knight could be moved and he was hoisted up by a host of willing hands. As they bore him to a wagon, Eleanor was left to trail disconsolately behind them. Where the primitive vehicle came from she had no idea, but soon they hoisted her into the wagon beside their fallen lord and proceeded to push it into the village.

The rest of the day passed in a bewildering blur for Eleanor. Perhaps she was still stunned, for her temple certainly ached from the blow. She allowed herself to be led hither and thither, wherever Simon was taken, as if they thought her to be his lady. He was laid in the village tavern upon a table strewn with straw and all too soon spattered with his blood. While they waited for a surgeon to arrive, Eleanor pressed his cold hand in hers, stroked his pale brow and whispered words of comfort as his own lady might - if he had one. When the physician examined him, she remained, as did one of the women, whom she discovered was the local midwife.

Eleanor, no stranger to wounds, already knew that Simon would die – if not now then later - perhaps hours later… perhaps days, but he would die because such belly wounds killed most folk. Her judgement was reflected in the faces of the men and women who had tried so hard to save him; they knew it too.

Later in the afternoon, Simon was taken once more to the cart, this time with a pair of oxen yoked to it, and borne to his home at Handfast Point, to die...

Only when she was back at the castle and a sleeping draught had been administered to Simon, did Eleanor dare to reflect upon what had happened. Only when wrapped in the consoling arms of Mary, did she give vent to her utter despair.

"It was never a trade," she moaned. "It was always to be a kill – and not just me... Simon's death must have been part of it from the start..."

"But weren't his brother's men to be there?" asked Mary.

"Aye," murmured Eleanor, her mood bleak. Roger Cayne's promised men had never appeared – but now of course, she saw that they were never supposed to.

36

31ˢᵗ October 1483, at St James Church in Poole Town

Though it was scarcely a hundred yards from the inn to the church, Emma still managed to get thoroughly soaked. Once again the clouds had descended upon the town overnight and now, at midday, the rain still obscured most of the harbour from sight. Scurrying into the church, she shook the rain drops from her cloak, though it would make little difference to how damp she felt.

She expected Richard Morton to arrive late; but where was her nephew? What, she wondered, was the point of her labouring to arrange a meeting if neither party possessed the wit, or will, to attend?

When the church door banged open, Emma gave a start, but it was only Morton. Slamming the door shut again he stood shivering in the entrance, dripping steadily onto the stone floor. In another church it might have mattered, but not here since there were already numerous pools of water from the leaking roof.

"Well, at least one party has braved the weather," she remarked.

"My apologies for being late," said Morton. "The rain…"

"I fear that your new leader must also be delayed," grumbled Emma, struggling to control her annoyance.

"Perhaps the rain-"

"The rain is the same for us all!" scoffed Emma, dismissing Morton's attempt to excuse her nephew. Just once, she thought, the others members of her family might do what was expected of them.

"Should we wait, do you think?" asked Morton.

"Aye, because without Lord Elder, I fear we can take this no further."

"Then wait no longer," said a voice from the furthest dark recess of the church.

Emma gasped and Morton spun around in panic, as John Elder emerged from beside the rood screen to join them.

"What are doing?" hissed Emma, her face white with anger. "Why didn't you tell me you were here?"

"Your pardon, aunt, I wanted to see who was coming," he replied.

Since his clothes looked dry, Emma saw that he must have been there for hours! He was damned cautious; she had to give him that.

"So," she said, "Master Richard Morton, this is Lord John Elder."

"Master Morton." John acknowledged the nervous rebel with a cursory nod. "I've been sent here by the Earl of Richmond to help you prepare for his landing."

"And right glad we are to have you here, my lord," replied Morton, causing Emma to wince at the man's obsequious manner.

In her eyes, her nephew had done little yet to earn the respect of the Dorset rebels – or anyone else for that matter. He was not his father – and never would be. Added to which, it was she who had so far taken all the risks in meeting the rebels. Though the skills of a woman might not be highly valued, she was determined not to relinquish her role of negotiator so easily.

"Master Morton, do you have a suggestion for a meeting place?" she asked.

"Yes, in fact one of my most trusted comrades has suggested the castle on Handfast Point."

"Aye," said John, "we saw it as we approached Poole. Who owns it?"

"Are we using real names?" said Morton, lowering his voice.

Emma hesitated.

"Well I am and so are you!" declared John. "We are surely past all dissembling now! I need to know exactly who I'm putting my trust in – as do all of your men."

"Aye, you're right, of course," added Emma. "The time for ciphers and subterfuge has long passed."

"Very well," said Morton. "The castle is owned by the Cayne family and because it's out of the town, it will be easier to gather our men without being noticed."

"Aye, it sounds very suitable," agreed John.

John sounded enthusiastic, thought Emma. Perhaps he really could pull this off…

"So," she said, assuming control again, "let's agree the other details, such as when we shall meet."

"To get all our fellows to Handfast will take a day or two, for some will have a journey to do," explained Morton.

"Aye," agreed Emma, "and the cursed rain will make travelling more difficult – or at least a lot slower."

"When then?" asked John.

"The soonest would be… the day after tomorrow?" suggested Morton.

"That would be Sunday then," Emma pointed out. "Is that good or bad?"

"It's good!" said John. "My father fought half his battles on Sundays! And besides, we can't afford to wait any longer."

"The town has a week-long fair from All Souls Day – which, from custom, will fall on Monday," said Morton. "But many folk may choose to be on the move after mass on Sunday – will that help disguise our intent, do you think?"

"Let's pray it does!" said John. "We need all the assistance we can get!"

"Very well," Emma agreed, if a little reluctantly. "Now we shall need someone to meet us when we land on Studland."

"That had best be me," said Morton. "I'll be waiting for you on the beach near the village. There's a clear track that we can take up to the castle from the bay."

"Well, that seems to conclude the arrangements," said Emma.

"One matter," said John abruptly. "If the Cayne family own land, they must have some sway in the town."

"Well, Roger Cayne is one of our staunchest supporters," said Morton, "and he's the town mayor!"

"And yet he does not lead your rebels…" mused John. "Do you not think that's strange, Master Morton? If he is so prominent, would he not be a natural leader?"

Annoyed that John was questioning the commitment of men he did not yet know, Emma glared at him and steered Morton away. "I'm sure your friend has his reasons, Master Morton," she said, "and we will no doubt meet him in two days with all the others."

"Yes, yes, of course," stuttered Morton, as if the full import of what they were discussing was only just making an impression upon him.

She had hoped that the man would be uplifted and given renewed confidence by the meeting but instead, when he took his leave, Morton looked even more scared than before. Watching him plunge out into the welter of rain, she risked a glance at her nephew. She was not surprised to see by his expression that he was mightily unimpressed by the man who claimed to represent the rebels of Dorset.

"You are concerned about Morton?" she asked.

"Aye," he breathed, "That was the face of a man who discovers on his wedding night that he's married the most beautiful woman in Christendom but has no idea what to do with her."

"Not quite how I would have put it," murmured Emma.

"By Christ, aunt, if they're all like him, we might as well surrender now!" he grumbled.

"I'm sure others will show more heart," said Emma.

"Let's pray they do – I still can't see why Mayor Cayne isn't taking the lead..."

"While it's true that some others in his position have done exactly that," said Emma, "we can hardly condemn the man for not doing so. And remember, they already had a local knight in command."

"Aye, before one of them murdered him!"

"We don't know who murdered him, John!"

"Aye, but one of them did. They have a traitor in their midst, aunt. Forgive me if I put my trust in those I know, for the time being."

"I do hope this rain will ease by then," groaned Emma.

"Rain will be the very least of your worries!"

"Nephew, you know nothing at all about my worries," said Emma.

"No, probably not, aunt," he conceded. "Come, Hooper and Grim are waiting close by with my men. We'll take you **to** the Margaret."

"Oh aye, back to the Margaret ... I simply can't wait," she said, following him out into the rain.

37

1st November 1483 in the late morning, at Handfast Castle

Simon Cayne was still alive, but that was the best that could be said. At the church of St Nicholas in Studland village, the good folk of the manor had offered up their prayers on his behalf. Eleanor too, though unwilling to leave his side for long, had slipped into the castle's tiny chapel to add her prayer for his recovery – though she suspected that Simon was far beyond even the Lord's help.

Lying in bed, his face pale as a wax effigy, he looked dead already. The black wound in his belly continued to fester, despite copious quantities of wine, herbs, poultices and every kind of evil-smelling salve the physician could devise – or perhaps because of them. For once Eleanor, knowing nothing of such matters, wished her sister had been there. Emma's head was crammed full of medicinal remedies, acquired in her youth – in a different, better, time…

Leaving the near lifeless figure, Eleanor dragged her guilt from his chamber onto the narrow battlement she had visited a few nights earlier. This time though, it was daylight; it was also stormy, but it was not the first time she had sought to lose herself in the heart of a storm. After a short time the rain eased, leaving only the undiminished gale blowing hard against Handfast Point.

Simon told her that the castle was gradually crumbling away beneath them, so perhaps the storm would be enough to finish the task. At that moment, a part of her wanted the whole tower to sheer away and plunge her down onto the rocks below. Yet, surrender was not her way… Like the wind-worn, white cliffs, bullied and battered by the raging wind, she would not be cowed. She would hold firm until she could fight back.

There in the buffeting wind, enveloped in a great woollen cloak that Mary had unearthed from Simon's chamber, Eleanor put her mind to what must happen next. Simon's brother, Roger Cayne, had been summoned, but was yet to arrive – if the treacherous villain dared to come at all. When his brother died, Roger would inherit all, including Handfast Castle and she was under no illusions. When that moment came, her life would be worth nothing. So what she needed now was a miracle.

Staring out across the bay through the ragged curtain of rain, she searched for sails. The Margaret had left Brest at the very same instant as the Catherine, so they should have arrived long ago! What she would give now to have her two brave, young warriors beside her: her son, Will, and nephew, John. Several vessels had come and gone through the entrance to Poole harbour in the past few days, but her untrained eye could not tell one distant speck of ship from another. She slapped her hand against the wet stone in frustration, for even the town of Poole was now utterly obscured from view, buried somewhere under the oppressive cloud.

Was it possible the Margaret was lost in the same storm that wrecked the Catherine? Aye, that was her greatest fear: to have lost most of her remaining kinfolk in one savage twist of fortune – and not even to know it. Then she would truly be alone with her fears – aye, alone and with no hope of rescuing her daughter.

Only when the unflagging wind began to snatch her breath away, did she surrender to the elements and return inside. Throwing off the sodden cloak, she went to see

Simon and found his servant, Master Palmer, waiting for her.

"He asks for you, my lady," said Palmer.

Dutifully she went to sit at Simon's bedside and Palmer left the pair alone. When she clasped his cold hand in hers, she could discern no obvious change in his condition. Defeated, she let fall his hand and got up to leave, only to see his eyes flicker open as he reached out for her.

"Simon?" she whispered. "Are you feeling a little better?"

With a wan smile, he shook his head.

"Then rest!" she told him. "Save your strength."

With another feeble shake of the head, he croaked at her: "Some… matters must be settled, dear Eleanor."

"Hush," she said. "There's no need for haste."

"I pray you, believe me, there is…"

"Don't speak," she insisted. "Just rest and get well."

"We both know," he groaned, "I'll never 'get well'… and there are things you must be told."

"Not until you are stronger, I beg you!"

"And I beg you to listen," he murmured. "When you poured out your secrets to me, I should have trusted you. I should have told you my secrets then."

She opened her mouth to protest, but he squeezed her hand so she did not.

"For I too have secrets." he told her. "Several months ago, my brother and I found common cause with a local knight. We planned… a rising in Dorset… against the new king."

"What?"

"But, our leader was killed… treachery, but…"

"Hush!" pleaded Eleanor, gripping his hand ever more tightly. "You're killing yourself, Simon! There is no need to tell me all this now!"

"But there is!" Simon's voice became a rasping wheeze, now so faint that she had to bend close to hear him. "Men are coming…" he breathed. "After the beach… it can only have been my brother who betrayed us… and he's still betraying us! Men are coming, I tell you… You must warn them!"

"Don't worry about that," said Eleanor, stroking his face, hot from the fever.

"And… you must leave…"

Eleanor wanted to reassure him that she would not leave, because soon her nephew would come. If there was a traitor then John would root him out, but even as the words formed in her mind, she saw that Simon's head lay still, his mouth no longer moved and in no time the last glimmer of life left his eyes.

Spent of all feeling, Eleanor rested her head upon his breast. Simon Cayne was a good man, betrayed by his own brother, who very soon would come to Handfast to claim his brother's body and his inheritance. With a sigh, she remained there as the light faded, until Palmer returned to light a candle. She watched the faithful servant absorb with dignity the fact of his master's death.

"I don't know what to do, Master Palmer," she murmured.

"What is there left to do, my lady?" replied Palmer. "Master Roger will decide now…"

And, of course, he was right; because whatever Simon wanted her to do, she could not stop Roger Cayne. Even if she fled, where could she run to? The mayor of Poole had the resources to hunt her down if he wished - aye, and to condemn her too.

38

1ˢᵗ November 1483, at Roger Cayne's Privy Chamber in Poole

When Roger studied each of their faces only Bess, he noted, was willing to meet his stare while the two scoundrels, Clynt and Slade, wore expressions which veered between the bored and the downright truculent.

"I hope you're all pleased with your work," he said, "because, between the three of you, you've left an unholy muddle for me to sort out!"

"Leave me out of this," declared Clynt. "I weren't even there!"

"Really?" said Roger. "Well, let's not forget, Clynt, that it was your refusal to release the girl which made this so difficult!"

"I found that girl, so you've no business depriving me of my profit!" snarled Clynt. "And you were glad enough of the chance to rid yourself of your brother. Is it my fault if this careless bitch weren't up to it?"

"Hah!" spat Bess. "I did what I was paid to do – which is more than the rest of you!"

"But did you, my dear?" grumbled Roger. "Because I'm told my brother's not dead!"

With a trace of a smile, Bess replied: "But he will be, Master Cayne. He will be very soon, for my blade ripped open his belly. It was only Eleanor Elder that stopped me finishing him off – and she was Slade's business, not mine!" She stabbed an accusing finger at Elias. "Whatever went awry was down to him, not me. If he hadn't dragged me away, I'd have killed Eleanor Elder too!"

Slade gave her an icy smile. "When I need advice from a murdering whore, Bess Fisher, I'll let you know. Till then, you just keep right out of my way."

"Enough! God's teeth, enough!" barked Roger. "What's done can't be undone but, from now on, your petty squabbles must end or you'll answer to me! And by me, I mean the full weight of the law!"

"Your threats don't trouble me, Master Mayor," said Clynt, laughing in his face. "What are you going to do? Lock me up? Hang me? Who'll you get to do your grubby work then, eh?"

Roger's tone hardened further. "I don't need to hang you, Clynt. I'll just impound your ships and your goods - perhaps even take over your boatyards? Try making some profit then! I've given you all fair warning. So, hark now and mind my words – or you'll regret it."

With a sigh, Slade turned away from the others. "Very well, Master Cayne," he said.

"Clynt?" asked Roger.

Clynt gave a shrug which Roger took as acceptance of his authority.

He did not ask Bess. "Your work here is done, Mistress Fisher," he told her.

"Done? I don't think so. I want Eleanor Elder!" she demanded. "And John Elder too!"

"You'll get payment for what little you've done," said Roger, "but when my clerk has given you the sum agreed, I suggest you leave Poole at once."

"What?" cried Bess. "You're cutting me out?"

"Cutting you out? By God, woman, you were never in!" said Roger.

"But I'm worth two of these bastards!" she said.

"What nerve!" said Slade. "You even struggled to carry out the one task you were given. So, be glad you're being paid for it and be on your way!"

"Go on, you common little drab," added Clynt, "be off with you… back to the gutter!"

Her cheeks flushed with anger – sweet Jesus, how ripe she looked, thought Roger – but he could not trust her and, for a man in his position, it was just too great a risk.

"Now would be an excellent time for you to go…" he said. "Christ knows why Catesby sent you in the first place."

Though she simmered in protest for several moments, she had no choice but to submit. Sweeping from the room, she crammed all her resentment into a resounding crash of the door as she left. The three men smiled with relief, pleased to see her go.

"I hope you are both clear now that there is more at play here," said Roger, "than your small profit, Clynt - or petty revenge, Slade. There is sedition… there is revolt…and it must be dealt with, above all else."

"What do the likes of us care who wears the damned crown?" said Slade.

"Because the crown," replied Roger, using his last reserves of patience, "is a fat teat that will flow with profit - for those who know how to milk it. A grateful king will reward his most loyal subjects – and how will he know who to reward and who to punish? Who will he ask?"

"Why, the local mayor," murmured Slade, with a knowing grin.

"Indeed and Master Catesby has already promised me a great deal including a new town wall of stone-"

"By Christ, Cayne, what do I care about a few stones in a wall?" snapped Clynt. "There's no profit for me in stone walls!"

"What about customs and tolls then?" asked Roger. "What if you were granted the right to import certain goods with little, or no duty to pay? And there is the small matter of five hundred marks which the king has now offered for the capture of any knight leading the rebels – and John Elder is more than just a knight, is he not?"

"Ah," agreed Clynt, "now that does get my interest...."

"Alright, alright. True enough: it's a worthy sum," agreed Slade. "We get your point, Master Mayor, so let's not sit talking about it all day. What do you want us to do?"

At last, thought Roger, compliance; but he'd had to work damned hard for it. Without a little more muscle, he could not take on the rebels. Though he had sent for assistance from Catesby, he feared it would be days before any more of the king's men could be despatched. As far as he knew, most were with the king in the West Country, or else putting down the Kent revolt.

"Very well, to business," he said. "Some Dorset men are planning to rebel and will be gathering even now at Handfast Castle. I am told that not only will Lord John Elder arrive to lead the rebels but it is even possible that Henry of Richmond will-"

"Who's he?" asked Slade.

"He is the traitorous turd around whom all these rebellious flies gather. It's not yet certain he'll land here, but if he does, we must capture him, for that is a prize the king would pay very handsomely for. But I go ahead too far; first, we must go to Handfast Point and take the castle whilst there are only a handful of rebels there. Once my brother is dead, the castle becomes mine so there'll be little resistance. When John Elder turns up, we take him and kill any men he has with him."

"You make that sound very easy," remarked Slade. "Met John Elder, have you?"

"No, not yet, but-"

"He ain't going to fall down on his knees, Master Mayor; and if he comes well-harnessed and men at arms with him, then you'd best start praying."

"But we'll have the castle and he won't have enough men to take it, so we can trap him in the open ground outside."

"If you say so," agreed Slade. "Handle it as you please, and I'll do my part, but don't take that youth lightly – I did that once to my great cost!"

"Yes, yes, I hear you," said Roger, eager to put an end to the discussion. "To more practical matters: Master Clynt, you'll provide me with boats to cross to Studland to confront the rebels - and let me have some of your lads too."

Clynt looked wary. "And what do I get for all that?"

"You get the chance to move Kate Elder onto one of your ships docked at the quay - without interference from her mother, or me. The town will be crowded with the All Souls' Fair that starts on Monday. More than that though, you'll get your share of whatever reward the crown decides to shower upon us."

"Fair enough," agreed Clynt.

"Slade," ordered Roger, "you will cross to Studland with me and lead your own men alongside Clynt's."

"And what about the Elders?" asked Slade.

"The outlaw, John Elder, must be taken - alive if possible, not least because Catesby will want to have a long talk with him. As for his aunt, she's yours – but her fate needs to be a… privy affair."

"Oh, it'll very privy," Slade assured him. "Just her and me; privy is just how I've imagined it for the past year."

Part Five: All Souls

39

2nd November, in the early afternoon, in Studland Bay

By the time the Margaret glided into Studland Bay, Will was relieved to see that the storm winds, which had lashed the ship while it was anchored in Poole Harbour, had at last abated. Nevertheless, he noticed that Matthew Finch still kept a close eye on the western sky. Seafarers, he suspected, were ever watchful for a change in the weather; and, after his recent experiences, he didn't blame them.

At the ship's rail, Will's cousin, John stood ready to embark his shore party into the waiting longboat.

"Sure you don't want to take me with you?" asked Will – not for the first time.

"Better you go with Matthew in search of the Catherine - and your errant mother and sister," replied John.

"Aye, you're right," said Will, "and I shan't rest, coz, till I've found them. But you could take the rest of the Bretons."

John gave a firm shake of the head. "This is our first meeting with these rebels; I don't want to terrify the poor bastards at first sight! Even eight of us seems like too many! In any case, you may need a little muscle when you make some more enquiries at the port - and you've to keep my Meg and Isabel safe."

"That's what young Thomas is for, isn't it?" laughed Will.

Thomas, however, gave barely a murmur of agreement in response.

"You alright, Thomas?" asked John.

"Yeh," replied Thomas.

Having observed Thomas during their voyage, Will was not surprised by the youth's diffident tone. But now John had his eye fixed firmly upon the lad.

"If you've got something to say, Thomas Skirett," growled John, "then by Christ just say it; but you'll address me as 'lord' when you do!"

"I only thought, lord, that I could do more…" said Thomas, squirming under his lord's intense scrutiny. "I can fight, you know… lord."

"Aye, true enough, you can scrap like a street beggar," replied John. "But you can barely hold a sword, let alone use it in a mêlée. And just because you've lain with my sister, doesn't mean you can do as you please in this household!"

Watching Meg's face turn slowly from pink to red, Will feared an explosion was imminent. Since he judged that such an outburst would help no-one, he nudged Isabel beside him. "Take her below, coz!" he whispered and Isabel dutifully pulled away a reluctant Meg.

"Lord," said Thomas, "I didn't mean to…"

"You'll do as you're told by me, lad," said John. "No-one else rules here but me – and especially not Lady Margaret Elder!"

"I know, lord," conceded Thomas, with head bowed. "I know."

"Let's get you all safely ashore, shall we?" suggested Matthew, with a timely intervention.

"Aye to that, Master Finch!" was John's terse reply.

"How long will you be, coz?" asked Will.

"Not sure," said John, "but one day should be enough. You've time to go back to Poole, but bring the ship back to the bay tomorrow afternoon. I hope to God we have a clearer idea what can be attempted by then! It doesn't help that we've no idea when Henry might arrive – if he's coming at all!"

As John descended to the boat, Matthew called down to him: "We'll be back tomorrow, my lord. Let's hope we've some good news to give you about the Catherine!"

Will watched from the ship's side as the small boat was rowed across the short stretch of water and disgorged its passengers onto the shore. Matthew was already preoccupied with plotting their route back to the harbour entrance, for there were more vessels passing into the harbour now.

Once the small boat was recovered, the ship turned to sail back out of the bay. Swinging around in a wide arc to pick up a breath of wind from the south west, the Margaret headed along the bay towards the harbour entrance. Staring back at the group on the shore, Will had to admit he would much prefer to be there alongside his cousin, even on that lonely beach, than spend any more days aboard the ship.

Along the coast, he saw several fisher folk, draping nets to hang from the low trees. Beyond those lay a flat shoreline of salt pans ending where a short sand spit jutted out into the bay. When Will glanced into the inlet contained by the sand bar, his eye was drawn to a black, half-submerged object close to the shore.

"What's that?" he called out to Matthew, but he could tell from the young master's lukewarm reaction that anything he sighted was likely to be of little consequence.

"Not much to see there, Will," said Matthew. "An old hulk, perhaps?"

"Hulk?"

"A wreck – or part of some ship lost months, perhaps even years, ago. Storms often move such things about."

"Couldn't be the Catherine then," said Will, relieved.

"No," said Matthew, but then he gave a sigh and bellowed out a string of commands.

"What?" asked Will.

"It's probably nothing worth looking at," grumbled Matthew.

"Fair enough," replied Will, "so why have you turned back then?"

Matthew pulled a face. "Well, now that you've mentioned it, I'll have to look, won't I? That's just me, I'm afraid."

By the time the ship had turned, whatever Will had seen was already some distance away.

"What did you see?" asked Meg, joining them at the rail with Isabel.

"Not sure," said Will.

"It's very small," said Matthew. "Most likely part of a fishing boat, but no harm in taking a look…"

"Could it be the Catherine?" asked Isabel.

"Doesn't sound like it," said Will.

"We'll be well into the shallows over there," warned Matthew and, as the Margaret completed her turn, he shouted to a crewman: "Let's have the lead there! I've no wish to run aground."

"You've convinced me already," said Will. "Let's carry on to Poole."

"We've turned now," said Matthew, laying a conciliatory hand on Will's arm. "We might as well get a bit closer, eh?"

Giving a wide berth to the sand spit, they sailed a little way into the inlet.

"There!" said Will, pointing out the object.

"Ah, I see it better now," murmured Matthew.

"What is it?" asked Will.

"Don't know," replied Matthew.

As they edged closer, the crewman with the lead weight gave a sudden shout and Matthew took the Margaret back out into deeper water again.

"Sorry," said Will. "It just looks like a mess of timber now, doesn't it?"

"Let's take the boat in, shall we?" said Matthew.

"Really?" laughed Will.

"We're here now and the tide's high enough for us to stay here awhile. I doubt we'll get another chance."

"Alright then, let's do it!" cried Will.

As several crewmen rowed them towards the shore, Will noticed that Matthew was staring thoughtfully at the lump of debris floating in the shallows.

"Still looks like a mess of old timber," said Will, but, as they drew alongside, even he could tell that it was part of a wreck, though what part he had no idea. "What do you think?

"It's… how did you describe it? It's a mess of timber – part of a ship's deck."

"Could it be from the Catherine?" asked Will.

"Doubtful," said Matthew. "As I said, storms can lift up parts of a wreck and move it anywhere…"

"They must get a lot of wrecks around a harbour like this," said Will, "but at least if it's old, it can't be the Catherine, can it?"

He felt oddly disappointed, even though it was the best outcome; the last thing he wanted was to discover that the Catherine was indeed wrecked!

"Sorry to drag you over here," he told Matthew, but the master was already looking further along the inlet.

Will followed his gaze and found the object of Matthew's attention. "Something else?"

"Another part of this wreck, most likely," said Matthew.

They rowed closer and jumped into the shallows to examine it.

"Not deck this time?" said Will.

"No, a ship's prow, Will…"

"Is it?" said Will, staring at the wooden hulk. "Doesn't look like it."

"That's because it's upside down," murmured Matthew.

"Looks old, like the other one," said Will. But his mouth felt suddenly very dry, as he watched Matthew, waist deep in the water, continuing to inspect their discovery.

"Matthew?"

"It's not as old as the other bit, Will," murmured Matthew, with a sigh.

"You don't think it could be…"

Bending down, Matthew ran his fingers over the wooden planks "I don't think, Will; I know. It's the Catherine…"

"But how can you be sure?" protested Will.

"She was the first caravel I ever saw…

"I'd know every inch of that ship… anywhere - and in any condition," cried Matthew, his voice breaking. "Christ knows, Will, I spent half my life upon it! It's the Catherine, I tell you!"

His anger burst through his usually calm demeanour. "This prow must have been driven ashore during yesterday's storm… but the ship was wrecked days ago – perhaps longer."

"Could they have got off the ship, do you think?" mumbled Will. "My mother, my sister… your father?"

"Christ and the devil!" cried Matthew, slapping his bare hand against the sodden timbers in a rare gesture of rage.

"At the quay, we asked that bastard bailiff about wrecks, yet he said there were none!"

"But could they?" repeated Will.

"Look at it, Will!" stormed Matthew. "Just look at it. This is just a fragment! Even you must see that the Catherine's been smashed to pieces!"

"Better not tell the ladies that!" cried Will.

"Why not?" groaned Matthew. "They'll see it in our faces anyway..."

⌂⌂⌂⌂⌂⌂

He was right; the news of the destruction of their sister ship spread gloom among the whole ship's company. The mood aboard the Margaret turned grim, as the Elders were obliged to face up to the loss of their kinfolk. Many of the crew also had friends, or kin, among the Catherine's complement. Thomas went about the small vessel cursing to the heavens at the knowledge that he might never again see the few friends who remained from his former life on the streets of London.

"We'd all bin better off stoppin' in London town!" he cried. "It was safer there!"

"Perhaps the rest of the ship is still in one piece and has been driven ashore somewhere else," suggested Meg.

Will considered sparing her the worst but Meg Elder, he knew, would always want the truth, however terrible.

"My lady," explained Matthew, "with her bow split open, it's very likely that the rest of the ship was also badly... broken up... I fear, almost at once... She would have gone down very fast."

"But we don't know what happened yet, for certain, do we?" said Meg, "Nor how long ago? Perhaps they were only struck by yesterday's storm!"

"No," said Matthew, "a week, at least, I'd say..."

"Aye," said Will, "but they'd have launched their boat, wouldn't they?"

"I don't say that some didn't survive," said Matthew, "only that we should prepare ourselves to learn that some did not…"

"We must search for survivors," cried Isabel. "That's what we should do!"

"Anyone who survived would have been ashore days ago," Matthew told her.

"Aye, but where are they then?" cried Isabel. "Why were they not at the port?"

"Quite right, coz!" said Will. "Whether or not there were survivors, someone in that damned town knows about this wreck!"

"But, you asked," said Isabel, revealing her innocence, "and did they not say they knew nothing of a wreck?" She looked at the others in utter disbelief. "Why would they tell us nothing when they knew we were looking for our family?"

"Plenty of folk in these parts might profit from a ship running aground," said Matthew. "God knows, the Catherine had goods aboard worth stealing…"

"Then we must go back to the quay and ask again," said Meg.

"Don't you worry, coz," Will assured her, "that's exactly what we're going to do! And I'll not stop until I've found out what happened to those aboard!"

Adding her own iron-shod words, Meg, said: "Aye, and if we must break a few heads to loosen tongues, then so be it!"

Her look of stern determination left Will in no doubt about the lengths to which his young cousin would go to know the fate of those she loved so well.

"I shall be with you every step of the way, Will," declared Matthew, "to learn what's become of my father."

Meg began pacing the deck – a worrying sign, thought Will.

"When we go back into the harbour," she told them, "we won't anchor in the channel; we shall sit the Margaret alongside Poole Quay until we get some answers!"

40

2nd November 1483, in the castle at Handfast Point

Eleanor heard someone ascending the steps with a measured, confident tread; but, of course, it was as she expected.

"I tell you, Mary; I've had enough," she said. "I've just… had enough."

"That doesn't sound like you, my lady."

Though her servant's words were intended, as always, to soothe her mistress, Eleanor could see that Mary too only had ears for the thud of boots on the spiral stair.

Eleanor stared at her chamber door.

"It's too much, Mary," she murmured. "Losing Grave… and Simon too! And he's only lying dead because Eleanor Elder stumbled into his life!"

"He's dead because his own damned brother had him killed, my lady, that's why!" declared Mary. "You know that – why do you scourge yourself so? That man would have found some other 'excuse' - look at what's happening now – and that's not because of you!"

Roger Cayne had just arrived, with a score of armed men. From the window in her chamber Eleanor had caught just a glimpse of poor Simon's body being bundled into a cart in the yard. No doubt it would be hastily conveyed to St Nicholas in the village, to be even more hastily buried.

The footsteps stopped outside the chamber and, when the door swung open, Eleanor took Mary's hand in hers. Mayor Cayne stood upon the threshold, regarding Eleanor with obvious distaste.

"Lady Eleanor Elder…"

"Aye," agreed Eleanor. He deserved all her hatred, but just at that moment she could not seem to conjure up her customary venom.

"Lady? From what I've seen and heard, more of a whore than a lady," observed Roger.

"Say your piece," said Eleanor, "and spare me the judgement of a man who has his own brother killed! God's blood, you are well named, Master Cayne…"

His instructions were terse and precise. "You will remain here – in this room - until I return. Then we'll see what's to become of you."

"Why not simply release me? You have no use for me…"

"No, I don't," agreed Roger, "but someone else does…"

"Slade…" breathed Eleanor.

"An old friend of yours…"

"Do you know where my daughter is?" she asked.

"Yes, I do," he told her.

"Then I beg you to tell me!"

"She's about to sail for Spain," Roger told her. "She's going to start a new life there, as a whore…"

"Please," begged Eleanor, falling upon her knees, "if you have any sway, could you not spare her that? Could you not have her freed?"

But Roger Cayne merely smiled. "I've more important matters to consider than the fate of your miserable daughter, woman. Now, stay in here, or I'll have you whipped!"

When he had gone, Mary opened the door a crack and closed it at once.

"A guard?" asked Eleanor.

Mary gave a silent nod.

"Dear Christ, what a danger we two must be…" said Eleanor, though she had never felt less dangerous in all her life.

She gave a shiver before lying down on the bed where Mary folded her in her arms.

"Usually, I can see some hope," she whispered, "but this time, I fear there is none; we are quite alone."

Though she heard movement in the courtyard, she remained on the bed. It would be Mayor Cayne and most of his men leaving, along with the cart carrying his butchered brother.

"I know you better than anyone else alive, my lady," said Mary. "And I know that when you seem beaten, that's when your enemies should fear you most…"

It must have been an hour or so after the mayor left that Eleanor heard the gates open again. A little later on it occurred once more and then several more times during the morning. Intrigued that others were arriving, she began to wonder who they could be. If the mayor's guards were letting these men into the castle, then surely they must be his allies?

What was it that Simon had insisted on telling her on his death bed? 'Men are coming… Men are coming and you must warn them…' But warn them about what? His brother, Roger? There had certainly been no sounds of fighting, or even voices raised in argument.

With a sigh, Eleanor sat up on the bed. As long as she was confined to her chamber, she would discover nothing about the new arrivals and she owed it to Simon to do something.

"Mary," she said.

"Aye?" replied her servant warily.

"Let's see if they'll allow you out."

"What? No, lady!" said Mary. "What for?"

"I need to know what's going on downstairs."

"Why take the risk?" cried Mary. "Remembering, my lady, that it'd be me taking the risk!"

"Whoever has come here this morning, it can only be about the revolt," sighed Eleanor. "Simon was trying to tell me how his brother had betrayed them, but I didn't understand – I still don't. Sweet Virgin! Where's my nephew when I need him? He's the one who's supposed to be unravelling this mess – not me!"

"So you think these new fellows may be rebels, my lady?"

"Perhaps, but we need to find out."

"Well, I don't know how, my lady."

"I have an idea," said Eleanor.

Mary grimaced. "I had an awful feeling you would have…"

"I want you to ask the fellow outside if he wants some ale."

"I couldn't care if he never drinks ale again, my lady!" replied Mary.

"Aye, nor I, but… someone pouring ale – not just for him outside our door, but also for those in the yard, or at the gates, or even in the hall… might hear a little more of what's going on, don't you think?"

"Aye, my lady" agreed Mary, "I'll see if he'll let me."

Eleanor took her hand to pull her back. "I know I ask everything of you, Mary," she warned. "But you just have to listen… and take care… and hurry back… safe."

With a sharp nod, Mary opened the door and went out.

⌂⌂⌂⌂⌂⌂

It turned out that the man at arms outside Lady Eleanor's chamber was partial to a drop of ale and gave Mary his blessing, albeit grudgingly, to go down to the cellars. Mary reckoned it must have been many years since Handfast Castle last boasted an alewife. The small quantity of ale consumed in Sir Simon's time was brewed at nearby

Corfe Castle and brought up by wagon to be stored in the cellar at Handfast. When Mary went down there to examine the barrels, she found them mostly empty or in poor repair. Only one barrel looked freshly tapped, so she filled up a large jug to the brim and set off to serve first the guard outside Lady Eleanor's chamber.

Despite her considerable effort in bearing the heavy jug up the steps, the recipient seemed far from grateful and acknowledged her with only a surly grunt.

"Shall I serve the rest of Master Cayne's men?" she asked.

"Yeh, go on," he growled. "Then get your fat arse back up here!"

Greeting his discourteous manner with a bleak nod of acceptance, she retraced her steps down to the alehouse in the cellar and filled two more jugs. Taking one jug up the stair to the hall, she saw that the door was open. When she risked a look inside, a burly figure suddenly filled the doorway.

"What are you looking for?" he barked at her.

"Well, you," stammered Mary, flushing with guilt.

"What are you doing wandering about?" he demanded.

"Bringing you this!" she said, holding out the jug to him, "though I don't know why I bothered!"

"Hmm," he grunted. "Well, that's more like it! But, go on – you'd best clear off now."

Though she only had time for a glance inside the hall, it was enough to count seven or eight men - all seated on the floor, disarmed and bound tight by the hands. It was long enough also to register the pleading expression on at least one face.

"Hey!" The guard summoned her back before she could take more than a couple of steps.

"What?" she said, her nerves making her tremble with fear.

"Get some more," he ordered.

"You want some more already?" she gasped.

"No, for them, you fool!" he pointed vaguely towards the yard.

At that instant she could have kissed the oaf, for he had given her licence to do exactly what she wanted from the start. But first, Lady Eleanor needed to know what she had seen so far.

When she ascended the steps to the chamber once more, the guard greeted her with a grin; clearly the ale had mellowed him a little.

"I've still got some others to serve," she told him.

"What you doing back up here then?"

"Just telling my lady where I'll be for a while…" she replied, with a nervous smile.

He gave only a grunt as she passed him, but as she opened the door, she felt his hand on her arse. Flashing him what she hoped might appear a willing look, she went in and shut the door.

"Tosspot!" she hissed at the door, before recovering her composure. "Sorry, my lady."

"A fair verdict, I'd say," said Lady Eleanor. "So, what did you find? Have you seen what's happening? By the Virgin, I feel even more blind than usual up here!"

"I'm quite safe, thank you, my lady," replied Mary. "I'm sure you meant to ask that first…"

But her lady's solemn face warned her to get on with her report.

"There's not much to tell anyway," said Mary. "Master Cayne's left at least four men here, I think."

"But did we not hear others come?"

"Aye, another eight men - but they're all stopped up in the hall."

"Stopped up?"

"Aye, they're in the hall with their hands tied; and the door's guarded, so they can't be friends of Master Cayne, can they?"

"And there's no sign of Master Cayne yet?"

"Nope. I suppose he's still burying Sir Simon?"

"Aye, I suppose that too… but who are these new men and why are they here?"

"I've got to go back and serve the other guards in the yard," said Mary. "I might learn more from them."

Lady Eleanor, patting her arm, looked her in the eye. "You're all I have, Mary; be sure you come back to me."

41

2nd November, on Studland towards Handfast Point

Though John expected that Morton would meet them the moment they landed in Studland Bay, he did not appear – indeed no-one appeared. Despite his Aunt Emma's immediate concerns, he decided that it made little difference. Morton had told them how to reach the castle from the beach and the track to Handfast Point was clear enough from there. Given the history of treachery amongst the rebels, Morton's absence was worrying but it changed nothing. John still had to meet the rebels.

"Richard Morton said he would be here," complained Lady Radcliffe. "So where is he?"

"Did you trust him?"

"Aye, though he seemed a timid fellow," she replied. "I'm sure he's no traitor, John."

"But yet, timid men make untrustworthy friends, aunt, and – in case you've forgotten – this is a deadly matter we're involved in here!"

"I know that well enough!" she retorted, stiff and defensive.

"High treason, aunt, is what we are about!" he told her. "High treason, for which, men - aye and women too - can be hanged!"

"I may be a woman, but I'm not a fool!" she cried.

"Aye," he said with a sigh. "Come; let's find out what's at Handfast Point, shall we?"

As a precaution, because the path was obscured by woodland as it rose towards the clifftop, John sent Hooper and his man, Grim, to scout ahead. Glancing around at the men who remained, he took some reassurance: Hal, Conal and Alain would, he knew, follow him into purgatory, and the two Breton mercenaries looked up for some bloody work if it was required. Even so, he was beginning to wish now that he had brought Will and the rest of the Bretons with him!

"You take the lead, Hal," he ordered, "and watch for Hooper coming back."

"Lord," acknowledged Hal, trotting on ahead, as they set off from the foot of the slope.

Hal had not gone far when he came to an abrupt halt.

"Lord!" he cried, pointing to a half-concealed body in the bracken alongside the trees.

"Aye, now why am I not surprised?" muttered John, bending down to inspect the corpse.

"Is it Morton?" gasped his aunt.

"It is," confirmed John.

"Struck down from behind," said Hal, "then throat sliced through."

"Aye, thank you, Hal," said John, frowning at the archer.

But his aunt was clearly not so easily shocked, for she knelt down beside the body. "Poor man..." she whispered.

"Aye, poor us too," growled John. "Alain, string your bow. Conal, stay close to Lady Radcliffe now! Until we find Master Hooper, she's all you worry about."

Noting Lady Radcliffe's dismissive glance at the Irishman, he told her: "You don't leave his side for an instant, aunt – for any reason – you understand?"

Turning away from Morton's corpse, she gave a curt nod.

"First, let's get off this track," he said. "Hal, find me a path through this damned forest."

"Why are we leaving the path?" demanded Lady Radcliffe.

"It didn't serve Master Morton very well, did it?" replied John. "And I'm sure it won't be any safer for us."

"But who would want him dead?" she asked.

"Only the rebels knew we were coming, aunt..."

"The traitor, you think?"

"Let's not forget what happened to their first leader – it's clear at least one of these rebels is not a rebel at all!"

Hal flitted out of the trees. "Stony stretch ahead, lord – we can leave the track there."

"Aye, that should suit us well enough."

For another dozen yards or so, they followed Hal until he veered off the track to the right, away from the coast. Taking his aunt by the arm, John guided her through the bracken and thin trees away from the beaten path. Conal was only a step away from her and the rest followed, careful to walk only across the exposed outcrop of chalk. If any man tracked them with genuine skill he would find their trail in moments, but it was all they could do. Walking in single file behind John, they covered perhaps fifty yards before he called a halt.

"Are we lost?" asked Lady Radcliffe, her nervous eyes darting in all directions.

"No, aunt, not yet," replied John.

"But you don't know this forest at all," she said.

"We know forests, my lady," said Hal, "and our lord knows better than anyone how to fight in them."

"Fight?" She recoiled at the suggestion.

"Thank you, Hal," said John. "Aunt, I'm sure you'll not be in danger but, if you are, be glad you have that hairy Irishman beside you."

His Aunt Emma looked anything but reassured. "But why have we stopped?" she persisted. "Shouldn't we get further from the path?"

"No, we wait here," he said.

"Wait?" hissed his aunt. "By all the saints, what are we waiting for?"

With a shake of the head, John replied: "I need to hear when someone's using the track - Hooper and Grim perhaps, not to mention any others who might be about… So, make yourself comfortable, aunt – and keep quiet. We may be here a while."

Despite their circumstances, he could not resist a grin when Conal settled himself down barely a foot from his charge inducing a shudder from his aunt.

The long absence of Hooper and Grim worried him, for he could ill afford to lose two of their best men at arms. And yet, he still had no knowledge of the terrain they had to cross to the castle, nor who might stand in their way.

"Hal," he murmured, "scout through the forest and up to the castle. You're looking for men – enough of them to be a problem for us, eh?"

"On my way, lord," said Hal, with a parting grin, as he disappeared into the trees.

"Why do you keep sending them all away?" hissed Lady Radcliffe. "Soon there'll be no-one left!"

"Oh, peace, aunt!" he groaned.

In vain he strained to hear the sound of Hal making his way into the forest, but of course there was no sound. Despite the terrain of tall bracken and dry, crackling twigs underfoot, Hal was the fastest, lightest mover of them all; he was also John's most skilled tracker – and, for good measure, the deadliest of archers. John almost felt sorry for anyone who might encounter Hal in a dark forest.

"What if someone else finds us… before they return?" asked Lady Radcliffe. "What do we do then?"

His aunt's growing anxiety raised fresh concerns for him. If their plans went awry, how would she cope? For, in his experience, plans nearly always went awry.

"You, aunt, will stay perfectly still," he told her. "You don't cry out, you don't scramble away into the trees; you stay with my friend here. Doing so might just keep you alive."

White-faced, she met his eyes for the first time that morning and gave another curt nod, settling herself onto the thick pad of fallen leaves which Conal had thoughtfully gathered for her.

In the tense silence which descended upon the small, waiting band, John considered what threat they might be facing. If he needed any further evidence that someone was trying to foil the Dorset revolt, then Richard Morton's murder provided it. Such a betrayal could only come from someone who was close to the leadership – someone who presumably knew now all that Morton had been told by his aunt.

"Aunt," he said in a low voice, "what did you tell Master Morton the first time you met him?"

If she looked pale before, his question made her bottom lip tremble.

"Everything, nephew. Everything..."

"Including Henry of Richmond's landing?"

"As I said: everything..."

So, the traitor had to be close to Morton and Morton had referred to Mayor Cayne, whose family owned Handfast Castle, as a trusted friend. Only to such a man would Morton have revealed what he knew. Yet, it was equally possible that Mayor Cayne – like Morton – was being duped by the rebel traitor. If so, then he too would be taken by surprise – as would any other rebel leaders who turned up for the planned gathering at Handfast. All the king's men had to do then, was wait for John's group to arrive.

It didn't take a wise man to work out that Poole was a very possible landing place for the rival king; his aunt had merely confirmed it to the traitor. If they captured John, they could ambush the unsuspecting pretender, Henry Tudor, the moment he landed.

Studying his aunt's tear-stained face, he cursed his new lord, Henry, and the youth's mother, Lady Stanley, for putting his aunt in such a vulnerable position. She was no king's agent! It was not as if her presence was even required now that the one man she knew was dead. Had the Margaret still been anchored in Studland Bay, it would have been a simple and probably less dangerous task, to escort her back to the ship. But the Margaret was long gone and he had no way of recalling her before the morrow. Lady Radcliffe's presence, as he had feared from the beginning, would be a hindrance. By deploying Conal to protect her, he was depriving himself of his most effective warrior.

His thoughts turned unbidden to his wife, Lizzie who had perished in just such a forest and in similar circumstances. The memory of the loss wounded him afresh, as a blade twisting in his belly. God's teeth! Why could the Elder women not stay where it was safe - like other women? Did they not understand how desperate he was to protect them?

From away to his left, on the track, came the sound of tramping feet. Alain, posted nearer the path, threw him a warning glance and he nodded.

"No-one stirs," he whispered.

△△△△△△

Having worked his way through the trees in a great loop, Hal reached what appeared to be the farthest extent of the forest to the north. There the small village of Studland lay, easily marked by the church tower of St Nicholas, but he could see no gathering of men at arms there who might present a threat. From where he stood, the beach lay out of sight; if anyone else had landed there after them, he would not know it.

Disappointed not to have encountered Hooper and Grim, he moved back into the woods again and began to work back through the forested area towards the clifftop castle at Handfast Point. In places, the forest canopy was quite low, with hazel and birch growing more thickly, which slowed his progress. At last though, when the trees began to thin out, he picked his way forward more easily and glimpsed a flint wall ahead. He reckoned he must be quite close to the point now for, to the west of the castle wall, there was an area of heathland which he guessed must extend along to the cliffs he had seen from the ship.

Now for the tedious part of his task: observing comings and goings and trying to judge what was going on. Searching for a suitable place from which to watch, he finally selected one of the taller beech trees. However, there seemed to be little to observe. True, Handfast Castle was only a small place but there was surely always work to be done. Then, with a curse, he thumped his fist upon his chest. It was Sunday! He'd forgotten it was Sunday; so there would be no work undertaken in field or forest!

Yet, he thought, even on a Sunday, people still move about… The church would have held a mass earlier on — folk from the castle must have attended that — unless there was a chapel up there… Having wrestled with all the possibilities for several minutes, Hal was about to return to his lord to report that all was quiet at the castle, when he heard movement behind him — and not so far away either.

"Keep your wits sharp, you mindless motley!" he muttered to himself. "Or you'll be joining Master Morton!"

Listening keenly now, he reckoned that several men were approaching his position — but from different directions. Shit! That was the trouble with trees: it wasn't always easy to pinpoint where folk were! Someone was coming from the east — the clifftop path he would have taken with Lord Elder perhaps - while others, more distant, were following the treeline from the west, nearer to the heathland.

His bow strung ready, he remained standing beside the beech, waiting to face whichever threat reached him first. Then he saw one of them, making his way furtively towards his position. Blowing out his cheeks, he carefully nocked an arrow to his bow. Still, he hesitated for he had no idea who the fellow was – he might kill one of the very rebels his lord was trying to reach. Too late, he heard a footfall behind him.

42

2nd November, aboard the Margaret at Poole Quay

"Where first?" asked Will, when the ship was safely berthed at the quay.

"You and I, Will," said Matthew, "are going to find that shit of a bailiff who lied to our faces last time!"

But neither could take a step towards the gangplank before Meg, Thomas and Isabel came up from the cabin.

"Here we are then," announced Meg.

"You're not going, coz," said Will flatly.

"Aye, well you just watch me – and where I go, your lord and mine has decreed that Thomas shall go too."

"I'm Kate's cousin too," protested Isabel. "I should be there as well!"

But for once, despite Meg's stubbornness, Will was not about to concede so easily.

"No!" he insisted. "Neither of you are coming. John would kill me if anything happened to either one of you."

"But-" began Meg, but Will cut across her like a thrown axe.

"No arguments!" he warned. "Just stay here and keep your eyes open."

"What does Matthew say?" chirped up Meg. "He's the ship's master; it's up to him."

"No, it isn't, Meg," retorted Will. "So, just for once: please, be told! Thomas, you make sure these two stay on board. Bind them with ropes if you have to, but keep them here!"

Though she pulled a face, Isabel, at least, appeared to accept his decision.

"And Thomas, be on your guard," advised Will. "We may well not be among friends here. We'll take two of the Bretons with us, but those who remain here will help keep you ladies safe."

Following Matthew off the ship, Will left Meg seething in silence at the ship's rail with Thomas.

Before they had covered more than ten yards, they found the port bailiff striding towards them. "You can't berth there!" he yelled. "You've no business there – I've another ship coming in any time now!"

"Well, she'll have to wait," said Will, seizing one of the bailiff's arms as Matthew took the other.

Between them they marched him, despite his vigorous and noisy protests, back to his customs house, or rather the ramshackle shed which purported to be a customs house. Though other seafarers and dock workers looked on, they made no attempt to assist the officer in his distress, for those who collected port tolls were rarely the most popular of local officials.

"The mayor shall hear of this!" the bailiff railed at them, as they bundled him inside.

"We really don't care," said Matthew, "because you, sir, are a liar. You lied to me when I asked you if there had been a recent wreck."

"I don't know anything about-"

But the official did not get any further before Matthew slapped him across the cheek.

"I don't!" he cried. "I can't tell you what I don't know!"

Matthew hit the man again, a jabbed punch to the jaw and he fell into a heap on the wooden floor.

"I don't know!" he bleated. "I truly don't, masters!"

Giving a disconsolate shrug, Matthew said: "I think he's telling the truth, Will."

"Do you?" asked Will, his face impassive. Lifting the perspiring bailiff to his feet, Will leant him against the timber wall then, drawing out his knife, he placed its sharp point at the bailiff's chest.

"My good friend here, thinks you're telling the truth," he said, "but I like to be sure; so let's be clear: what you're saying is that you can tell us nothing about the wreck of a ship called the Catherine? Nothing at all…"

"No, by Christ, nothing!" pleaded the bailiff.

Will gave a nod as if satisfied but then tore aside the man's woollen shirt and pressed the point of his blade onto the bare chest.

"I used to be a mercenary once," he told the official, "and my old captain, now what was his name? Anyway, his name doesn't matter much, but what he always said was: if a man doesn't tell you what he knows with a knife through his belly, then he never knew much to start with."

Studying the man's face, he moved his blade further down and pressed it harder until it pierced the skin.

"Wait!" cried the bailiff, sweat dribbling down his ruddy cheeks and dripping from his jaw.

"Remembered anything yet?" asked Will, pushing on the blade until it penetrated close to an inch into the bailiff's flesh. Blood was trickling from the wound and mingling with sweat to meander down his belly.

"No," screamed the bailiff. "Help here! Murder!"

"I think that's enough, Will," warned Matthew.

"Cry out another time, master bailiff," declared Will, "and my knife will gut you, here in your own little world… Time to stop lying now, don't you think?"

The bailiff looked to Matthew. "He'll kill me…" he moaned.

"I think he probably will," lamented Matthew, "if you don't tell us all…"

"No, not him – the mayor, I mean the mayor will kill me!"

"I'll kill you, long before you ever see the mayor again!" barked Will.

"I don't know what's behind it all," muttered the bailiff. "I just did what the mayor told me to do – that's all. That's my job."

Will removed his blade and sat the bailiff down "And what exactly did the mayor tell you to do?" he asked.

"I just helped carry the bodies to the mayor's house and put them in the cellar… that's all…"

In a sudden move, Will swept his blade to the bailiff's throat. "Whose bodies?" he snarled, his voice trembling as he put the question.

"I don't know, I tell you! I didn't hurt anyone! Beyond helping that morning, my part was very small: if anyone asked about the wreck, I was just to say there wasn't one…"

"You speak of 'bodies'," growled Matthew, "but fellow, these are folk – like you and me – who've been taken by the sea. Among them could have been my own father…"

A glance at his comrade told Will that even the usually placid ship's master was barely controlling his anger.

"Where shall we find your mayor then?" demanded Will.

"He has the large house beyond the Wool House, but there's only his man there now."

"Where's the mayor gone then?" asked Will.

"Don't know – all he told me was: 'He was on the king's business.'"

"Did he now? Well, we'll go and have a few words with his man," said Will. "Don't go away," he said and turned away. But then, turning back, he crashed his fist against the bailiff's temple. "Better to make sure, eh, Matthew?"

Reaching the mayor's fine house would not have taken long but for the crowds which seemed to be growing by the hour.

"Why's it so crowded?" asked Will.

"The All Souls fair starts tomorrow," said Matthew. "I suppose merchants and others are coming in. That's why the bailiff wanted the Margaret moved away. It's going to be a busy afternoon!"

They were obliged to push through the press of folk who had started to gather around the cook shops, or had spilled out of the taverns set back from the quay. Will slithered across wet cobbles already slick with sheep shit. The culprits, herded now into temporary pens, bleated their innocence while impatient stockmen roundly cursed them.

By the time they finally reached the mayor's house and Matthew knocked politely upon the door, Will's patience – always a commodity in short supply – had run out. He battered upon the door just as it was opened by a tall, thin man – tall, thin and at that moment quite incredulous.

"What did you do that for, you fools?" he complained. "I was coming!"

Prodding the man repeatedly in the chest with an accusing finger, Will forced him back along the short passage.

"Tell us about the ship that was wrecked a few days ago," Will told him.

"Very well," agreed the servant. "What do you want to know?"

"You're not afraid to tell us then?" said Matthew.

The man gave a shrug. "Well, do you want me to tell you, or not?"

"Of course we do, but no-one else has talked without some… persuasion. They're all scared of your master, the mayor."

"Master Roger Cayne is the town's mayor, that's true enough," said the clerk, "and I am his servant, but he is also one of the most unpleasant men I have ever known. Since I've every intention of leaving his employ very soon, I'll willingly tell you what I know."

From the moment he began, Will and Matthew were shaken, and not a little unnerved, by his words.

"A lady came to look at the corpses," began the servant. "Four had been washed up in the harbour."

"What lady?" demanded Will.

"She came with Master Cayne's brother, Sir Simon. I think they called her Lady Eleanor – didn't hear another name."

Will sank against the passage wall; absorbing the knowledge that his mother was still alive!

As Lady Eleanor's visit to identify her companions was described, Will groaned, suspecting that Augustine Grave had been amongst the dead, yet still hope burned for both young men since there was no news of any others.

"And do you know where Lady Eleanor is now?" asked Will, breathless.

"She returned to Handfast Castle, I believe, with Sir Simon Cayne-"

"Wait," said Will. "You're telling us that Lady Eleanor is at Handfast Castle?"

"As far as I know; the two folk that your lady recognised were later sent to be buried close by there at St Nicholas, I believe, although…"

"Although?" asked Will.

"News came last night of some trouble over there; it seems Sir Simon was hurt badly."

"And so the mayor, his brother, has gone to him?" said Matthew.

There was sadness in the fellow's eyes as he nodded. "He's gone over to Studland alright – but most likely not for his brother's sake."

"What makes you say that?" asked Will.

"Because I should think he's taken enough men at arms with him to invade France!"

Will and Matthew exchanged a look. Was Roger Cayne one of the rebels going to meet John at Handfast, or was he in fact the traitor going to stamp out the revolt before it even began?

"Thank you," said Will, "but you might not want to be here when the mayor returns…"

With a broad grin, the servant replied: "If he is taken down then I would rejoice to be among those who witness it."

Clapping the man on the back, Will led the others out in swift steps.

"Back to the ship?" asked Matthew.

"Aye," said Will. "We must get back to Studland this very afternoon!"

"Not this afternoon, I fear," said Matthew. "The tide's low now and the channel out of the harbour is crowded with ships and other craft of all sizes coming in. The moment we leave the quay, several vessels will be jostling for our berth. I dare say at least one wouldn't baulk at forcing us out of the main channel onto the mud."

"But John could be in trouble!" protested Will. "They all could be!"

"I know, Will, but no man can change the tide! Better we wait and go at high tide rather than risk grounding the Margaret."

"Right then – but early tomorrow," said Will, "and I mean as early as possible."

"On the early tide then," agreed Matthew. "And that at least will give us time to think and prepare."

"Aye – and to pray we're not too late!"

They boarded the Margaret, if not with enthusiasm then certainly with renewed purpose, only to discover that, in their absence, Meg, Isabel and Thomas had left the ship.

"By God!" raged Will. "I should have bound the foolish pair to the mast!"

43

2nd November 1483, at Poole Quay

All Bess had to do was watch. Stay close and watch. She would get her chance – a chance to pay back that slug, Diggory Clynt. Though it was Roger Cayne who cut her out, it was Clynt's parting compliment which rankled most. Call her a common whore, would he? Even now, a day later, the accusation made her shimmer with rage. Certain enough, she could be a whore if she needed to be – but never, ever, was she a 'common' one!

That insult would cost Master Clynt dear - very dear. He would wish he had not crossed Bess Fisher at all; because Bess knew things. Bess listened and absorbed all the little details... such as Clynt's intention of shipping out young Kate Elder this very day. How helpful the boastful Clynt had been in telling her, only the day before, where his fine ship was berthed beyond the water gate at the west end of the quay. Perhaps he thought she wasn't paying attention, but it took more than a thief's grubby fingers on her arse to distract Bess Fisher.

Though Mayor Cayne had sent her away, she did not expect him to let her leave Poole, since she knew far too much about his activities outside the law and he was most protective of his precious reputation. Fearing that he would have men watching for her at the Town Gate, she had paid a boy to tell the guards where Mistress Fisher was hiding. Watching the lad flee from the gate confirmed her fears; they knew her name at once which meant that they were waiting for her. If they caught her, the rope would be her fate.

Now, the only other way out of Poole was by ship and she could be certain that Clynt's hired men would be looking for her. Unless she pulled off something truly brazen, she was dead. Hence, an outrageous idea took root in her mischievous little head. The risk was appalling – with no clear prospect of success – but Bess would need allies to escape the hangman. What better ally against the likes of Cayne and Catesby than an avowed enemy of them both?

She already knew that John Elder had a ship, though she imagined that the outlaw would sooner hang her from the mast than let her aboard. But, having witnessed, at the very closest quarters, Lady Eleanor's savage determination to recover her daughter, Bess reckoned that Kate Elder would be a prize valuable enough to trade for safe passage on the Elders' ship. But of course, it was a gamble…

Since Clynt was keeping the girl at his boatyard in Holes Bay, he would have to bring her across to the quay by boat. So Bess set herself to watch the west side of Poole's docks, where a multitude of narrow, wooden jetties thrust out into the mud and shallow, murky water. But Bess knew which jetty Clynt habitually used, so all she had to do was wait.

What was Kate Elder to her? Nothing. She had only set eyes upon the girl once, when she was introduced to Elias Slade at Clynt's boatyard. She was a beauty - about that at least, Clynt was right. Yet… the thought of a young girl being sold to the heathens didn't sit well with Bess. No girl deserved to be sold by a man to anyone - heathen or Christian; for Bess knew, as many married women knew, what it meant to be traded to a man! No girl deserved that – not even the daughter of Eleanor Elder! Yet, she told herself that she was not doing it out of her dislike for the trade; no, it was simply a means of escape.

During the morning she hoped to loiter unobtrusively among the taverns and cook shops along the waterfront, but so far nothing was working out quite as she intended. Instead of a quiet quay on a Sunday morning, there were crowds everywhere, because Bess had forgotten all about the sodding All Souls Fair. It was bad enough that most of the townsfolk who attended morning mass at St James decided to take a walk along the quay. But now their numbers were swelled by all those coming in for the start of the fair on the morrow.

All sorts of small craft were ferrying folk in from around the harbour. Larger ships too were disgorging their goods by barrel and sack – and all had to be transported somewhere. The crowded docks might hamper her attempt to steal Kate away because Clynt could use the throng to mask the transfer of his prisoner. The small vessel that brought in the Elder girl would be just one of scores of such boats! Even if Bess spotted it, she would have very little time to snatch the girl, since it was only a dozen or so yards from the jetty to Clynt's ship.

She was still lamenting her circumstances when the craft carrying her quarry arrived. She almost missed it, her view of the jetty partly obscured by a crowd of laughing seamen clustered around a juggler. Bess hated jugglers at the best of times – she couldn't see the point of them. By the time she spotted Kate, the girl was already being pulled up onto the jetty. She looked half asleep – they must have dosed her with some potion or other…

Knowing she had to move fast, Bess barged her way through the sailors, steeling herself to ignore every drunken hand that explored her as she passed. Her eyes were fixed upon Kate Elder, but to her dismay, she saw that there were four of them with the girl. Virgin's breath! Four men to take one girl! Two, she might have taken out, but four… it made her task quite impossible…

She came to a faltering halt amid the crowd of seamen, her daring plan already in tatters. Several of the sailors, taking encouragement from her hesitation, began to paw at her. With a blade half-concealed in the sleeve of her kirtle, she could easily have unmanned the culprits if she cared to, but another thought struck her. What she needed now was some confusion and panic; and if there was one thing Bess was good at creating, it was confusion.

"Oh, masters!" she cried, pointing to Kate, who was being half-carried across the wharf. "Help me! Those brutes are stealing away my little sister – to sell to the heathens!"

Breaking away from her hopeful admirers, she ran at Kate, screaming: "Kate! Kate! It's me, Bess!"

Though the girl looked up at the sound of her name, her face showed no recognition at all – which was hardly surprising. When Bess reached the men holding her, she resisted the urge to strike at them - better to appear simply the innocent and helpless young woman. So, instead she seized Kate's arm, screaming: "Let her go, you villains! Let her go!"

Her cries reached some distance along the quay and many heads turned towards the cause of the commotion. One or two of her amorous seamen had followed close behind her. No doubt they shared Clynt's opinion and expected a free poke if they helped her. Even so, when they saw that the two men holding Kate were accompanied by two more muscled seamen, their enthusiasm began to wane - until one of Clynt's men made a mistake. He pushed one of the sailors backwards. Though Bess scarcely noticed him fall, she heard the crack of his skull on the cobbles and the resulting roar of anger, as his comrades hurled themselves into the fight.

This was her chance – and since she would not get another - she must risk all against the two men who still clung to Kate. Stabbing one of them in the belly, she twisted out her blade and launched herself at the other who dropped Kate's arm to reach for his knife. Bess slashed at his throat, cursing as her strike missed its mark and merely cut into his shoulder. Her first victim, clutching at his midriff managed one mighty swing with his cudgel before he slid down onto the cobbles. Ducking to avoid the club, Bess was relieved when it only ripped off her cap. Her second victim had his blade out and despite his wounded shoulder, he lunged at her. She swayed to avoid his thrust and stabbed at his groin. With a yelp, he backed away and disappeared under a crowd of sailors.

Delighted to see that the seamen were giving Clynt's dogs a well-deserved beating, Bess seized Kate's hand and dragged her away from the quay. The bewildered girl seemed incapable of haste and they covered only a dozen yards. By the time they reached the corner of the Wool House, they were forced to stop, but not because of Kate. Feeling light-headed, Bess found her legs unusually weak. Glancing down at her right hand, she was astonished to see blood dripping from it.

"Oh, shit!" he muttered.

In the speed of the moment, she had felt the cut, without realising that by cruel mischance, the villain's blade had sliced across her wrist. Staggering on several paces further, past the Wool House, she looked back for any sign of pursuit. With a gasp of relief, she saw that a larger brawl had broken out and Clynt's men had to be lost within it.

For a few moments, she leaned her back against the stone wall to rest, raising her arm to try to stem the flow of blood. Kate glanced across and met her eyes – thank the Virgin, the girl looked a little more alert now.

"I'm Bess Fisher," she told Kate.

"Bess Fisher?" The girl's voice trembled with fear. "But didn't you…"

"I'm going to get you out of here," said Bess.

"But why?" breathed Kate.

"Do you want to get away or not?" moaned Bess.

Kate gave a shrug, "Your hand's cut," she observed.

"Only a little blood," murmured Bess. "Come."

But when Bess set off again into a narrow alley, she crumpled to her knees almost at once. For a moment or two, numbed by the shock of the wound, she stared, fascinated by the blood that trickled down her fingers to splash onto the cobbles. Only when Kate shook her by the shoulder, did she force herself to her feet again. Taking Kate's hand, she squeezed it hard.

"You need to bind me up, girl!" she hissed." Do you understand me?"

Kate gave a slow nod but did nothing.

"Your kirtle!" urged Bess. "Tear a strip of cloth!"

But though Kate attempted to rip her kirtle, she seemed unable to find the strength to do so.

"Good… fine…" snarled Bess. "Do it your fucking self!"

With her left hand she reached under her own kirtle and seized a handful of linen shift. Tugging hard at it, she tore off a short length and handed it to Kate.

"Now bind me up, girl!" she ordered. "Bind me up! Now!"

The terrified girl did her best and the flow was at least reduced. It would have to do, thought Bess, for they could not stay there, so close to the quay. Even so, it would take a little while to get back some of her vigour.

"Just a few moments, Kate," she said, gulping in deep breaths.

Kate made no reply, but gripped her arm. Bess followed her gaze back down the alley and saw the fellow heading for them, knife in hand. With a sigh, she pushed off the wall and thrust Kate behind her. If she was fresh she would have gone at him, but she had no strength left for any sort of fight – enough for one killing blow perhaps, but there was no chance of achieving that.

In despair, she took a hesitant step forward, only to find Kate walking past her.

"What are you doing?" cried Bess.

"I never expected to get away..." said Kate, offering her arm to her captor.

With a grin, he shook his head, but gratefully accepted her surrender.

"Stand over there," he told her, "while I see this bitch to her grave."

But Kate remained by his side and flicked her eyes back to Bess. With a jolt, Bess realised that perhaps Kate Elder had more of her mother's spirit than she had so far seen. The instant she gave Kate a nod, the girl tugged at the man's arm to pull him off balance. Laughing at her feeble attempt, he simply tossed her aside. At the last moment, he must have sensed Bess closing upon him for his head snapped round just as Bess lurched forward. All she could do was plunge her knife at a startled eye and hope for the best. When he reeled away from her, clutching his face, for once, Bess was already on the ground.

This time she did not linger to inspect her handiwork but allowed Kate to help her up. Though neither of them possessed the energy to run, the pair stumbled off along the alley.

"Holy Mary!" cried Kate. "Where shall we go?"

Bess couldn't think ... she had it all planned, but the next part seemed elusive now... where were they going? She couldn't remember, because her blood had been spilled; and, deep down, she knew she was losing too much – far too much...

In the end, it was Kate who drew her rescuer away into a darker side alley and hauling her along until they reached a warren of filthy lanes. There the pair collapsed, exhausted, in a heap.

"You're still bleeding!" cried Kate.

"I know I'm bleeding!" moaned Bess. "So, why don't you do something about it, girl?"

While Kate worked to bind the linen tighter around her wrist, Bess lay helpless. She couldn't ever remember feeling so weak. Oh, shit, great plan, Bess! Step one, rescue the Elder girl; step two, bleed to death!

44

2nd November 1483, on Poole Quay

"Will's going to be so furious with us," cried Isabel.

"That 'e is!" grumbled Thomas.

"Oh, for the Virgin's sake," said Meg, as she led the three across the quay and on up the High Street. "We're just going to have a look, that's all. We have to look, don't we – or why did we come to the quay at all?"

"But it's so crowded, Meg," said Isabel. "How do we know where Aunt Eleanor would go if she were shipwrecked?"

"Well, I've been thinking on that: she would have to lodge somewhere, wouldn't she?"

"If she got here, she would," groaned her cousin.

"If she still lives at all!" declared Thomas.

Meg seized his arm, glaring at him. "Thomas! My Aunt Eleanor will be alive, somewhere – I promise you that - and don't you ever think different!"

"Come on then," conceded Thomas, meek in the face of her passionate rebuke. "Where d'you wanna go?"

Meg, as ever, was not a creature who harboured doubts: "I want to go to every inn and tavern where she might be staying."

But after an hour or more, even Meg had to concede that the All Souls Fair was making their task impossible. For with so many more folk staying in Poole, no innkeeper was interested in answering questions, however vehemently Meg put them. Soon the streets were so full with stalls and people that even she was ready to admit they would have to return to the ship empty-handed.

"What about an alms-house?" suggested Isabel. "Or – I know – the church!"

"Now that's the first sensible thought you've had," said Meg, seizing upon the idea.

"No!" cried Thomas. "We 'ave to get back, Meg! They'll be worried to deff."

"I saw the top of a church on the west side as we came up the High Street," said Meg, ignoring his concerns. "It's almost on our way back!"

"But, it's not!" protested Thomas.

"Look, you can see it from here, Thomas," said Isabel, pointing it out.

"You sure 'bout this, Meg?" groaned Thomas. "Alleys like this can be rough."

"God's breath, Thomas, you should feel at home in such alleys; you were born in one!"

"Yeh, I'm just sayin'…"

"Well don't, my dear," said Meg, taking his arm, and planting a tender kiss upon his cheek.

With a sigh, he kept hold of her and offered his other arm to Isabel. "We best 'urry then."

Though they had already walked further than Meg promised, she now led them off the busy High Street, confident that she would find a lane that would cut through to the church.

"Just keep that church in sight," she insisted, hauling them onward.

But soon the alley narrowed so much, they could no longer see the top of the church. Fearing that Thomas might have been right, Meg began to regret her impetuous decision. But, unwilling to confess her reservations to Thomas, she decided they had already gone too far into the tangle of lanes to turn back now. With a silent prayer to the Virgin, she carried on with Isabel's hand grasped tightly in hers while Thomas dropped back to walk a little behind them.

When the alley turned towards the quay and widened out a little, relief washed over her. She was so pleased to see the church appear ahead of them that at first she did not notice the two figures huddled in a dark corner of the alley.

"Meg?"

The cry stopped her dead and she spun around at once to peer into the gloomy recess.

"Who's there?" she cried, though she knew the voice as well as her own.

"It's me…" said a bedraggled figure, crouched in the mire.

"Kate?" Meg whispered.

"Aye," answered her cousin.

Meg ran to her but stopped a yard short. "You!" she spat the word at Bess and drew out her knife.

Isabel and Thomas hurried to her and stared in disbelief at the sight of a bloodstained Bess Fisher in the protective arms of Kate Elder.

"What is this, Kate?" growled Meg.

"She saved me," murmured Kate.

"Do you know who that is?" rasped Meg, "She's-"

"Bess Fisher. I know."

"But we told you!" cried Isabel. "At Brest, we told you what she did!"

"Aye, I know that too," replied Kate, "but still… she saved me. I was a prisoner, without hope, Meg, on my way to being a slave… and she rescued me - at great cost to herself!"

"But…" Even Meg could think of nothing appropriate to say to that.

"And she's lost so much blood," said Kate.

"Not as much as she's spilled!" snapped Meg.

Bess Fisher, who had lain unconscious, now stirred a little.

"I bound up her wrist," said Kate. "I know I could have left her to bleed, but it didn't seem right… and I'm so tired now."

Thomas helped Kate up but she was so weak, he was obliged to support her against his shoulder.

Kneeling beside Bess, Meg carefully prised out the knife from her fingers. Bess opened her eyes and took only a moment to recognise Meg.

"Oh, shit," she murmured. "Had to be you, didn't it? Do it then, girl; finish it – for I'm beyond fighting - at least it'll not be at the hand of a man…"

Meg shook her head. "It's not my decision. It's up to my brother, Lord Elder."

"Ah well," spat Bess, "do it now then… because we all know what he'll say, don't we?"

Meg examined the cloth bound around her wrist and bound it tighter still.

"My cousin's likely saved your life, Mistress Fisher."

"A fair trade then," murmured Bess softly, "for I did surely save hers…"

"I was to be sold like a slave to the heathens in Spain!" wailed Kate.

"Yeh, and you still will be," grated a man's voice, "only now you'll have two more girls for company."

"Oh shit!" moaned Bess. "Diggory Clynt… Get me up!"

"Stay there!" ordered Clynt. "My, how my day turns for the better!"

Meg, seeing that Clynt had four others with him, looked straight at Thomas. "Run!" she mouthed at him. "Get Will!"

But with a shudder of despair, she saw in his eyes that he would not leave her. "If you stay…" she started to say, but Thomas pushed her back to Isabel and Kate and drew his sword.

"Thomas Skirett!" she shrieked at him and watched, in a daze, as two men attacked him with cudgels. Her brave lover acquitted himself better than she could have hoped, wounding both men. But when Clynt joined the fight, there could be only one victor. With casual, practised ease, he slashed his sword across Thomas's chest then carved his blade down into the youth's left shoulder. Thomas, blood already darkening his shirt, darted a look of anguish at Meg and let his sword fall.

As Clynt prepared to deliver a killing blow, Meg launched herself at his exposed back, but her short blade seemed to have little effect against his heavy coat and he shrugged her off as if she was nothing.

"Thomas!" she yelled, as Clynt thrust his sword into Thomas's breast. "No," she whispered, falling to her knees.

Clynt grinned down at her. "Fond of the young sod, were you?" he asked.

One of Clynt's men saw Bess Fisher lying still on the ground and kicked her in the side and she rolled, lifeless, towards Clynt.

"Dead is she? Save Master Cayne hanging her then, won't it?" he cackled. "Right then ladies, get up and get over here – you," he told Meg, "can drop that knife too."

But Meg, though her heart was ripped apart, found the sliver of steel in her spirit. Bess had her eyes wide open – eyes that were pleading with her. So, she complied with Clynt's command and tossed the knife at his feet.

"Now, lads," he said, "That's how you do it, you see. You just have to ask, eh?"

Bess Fisher moved with the speed of a viper, snaking out a hand to snatch up Meg's blade. Clynt had barely turned to glance at her before she delivered a venomous thrust up into his groin. As he began to scream, Meg rushed forward and wrestled the sword from his trembling fingers.

"Help!" cried Clynt to his comrades, shaking with agony. "Don't just stand there!"

He batted Bess aside with a flailing arm and clutched at his bleeding wound. Meg, taking advantage of the confusion among his men, swung Clynt's sword at his head. Though she struck him hard enough to knock him clean off his feet, she had no skill with the heavy sword. Severely wounded he might be, but he was far from finished for her blow was struck with the flat of the blade. While Clynt's men rallied around his writhing body, Meg hauled Bess back into the corner where Kate and Isabel cowered. Standing over them, she held the sword out before her.

"Bear me to a surgeon, you fools!" Clynt was roaring, but despite his anger, he was weakening. If Meg could see it, then his men must have seen it too.

"I'll geld any other man who comes for us!" Meg ground out each word, her face an unwavering mask of anger.

"Get me up, damn you!" cried Clynt, dragging himself across the muddy alley. "And kill that little bitch!"

The two men already cut by Thomas exchanged worried glances, but the other pair were clearly made of sterner mettle. One stepped forward a long knife pointed at Meg, while the other moved to help Clynt.

"You should have finished him," groaned Bess, lying spent beside her. "He'll show no mercy now…"

Seeking a way out, all Meg could see around her were heads poking out of nearby houses. The locals, it appeared, welcomed any new source of entertainment and though a small crowd was gathering in the alley, no-one offered to help the girls. Clynt's sword felt heavier by the moment, but she dared not relinquish it.

Supported by his comrade, Clynt tried to stand but wept with the pain of it and soon lay back down again. "Fetch me a surgeon, damn you," he bellowed, "else I'll bleed to death! And, by God, why is that whore still standing untouched with my sword in her hand?"

One of the wounded men backed away from his master and ran off, crying: "I'll get the surgeon!"

Wise fellow, thought Meg; but the remaining three, encouraged by the baying crowd, took a step towards her. With a final stare down at Thomas's torn body, she took the hilt of her weapon in both hands and tightened her grip. Watching the three men close in warily upon her, she forced a smile. More than once her Aunt Eleanor had told her: 'You're your father's daughter, Meg Elder.' And, though her father was only a distant legend to her, Meg knew well enough what her aunt would do.

Lowering the sword a little, she waved them on while her eyes tracked their every move and gesture.

"I know street rats when I see them," she taunted. "I used to be one."

"Give it up, girl!" ordered one of those wounded by Thomas.

Instead she raised her weapon once more and delivered a chilling warning: "You won't be the first man I kill – or the last!"

"You tell them, Meg," murmured Bess Fisher, from behind her.

But Meg was under no illusions: she would be joining her lover all too soon, but she would make it as costly for her attackers as she possibly could.

The crowd that now filled the alley was roaring its approval as the three men rushed at her. Small, swift and lithe, Meg darted between two of them, shrieking as she raked her sword across the nearest belly. Dancing back through them, she scattered them again, but as she stood again by her cousins, she could scarcely lift the heavy weapon.

Bess must have seen her distress. "Meg!" she cried. "Take this!"

Dropping the sword, Meg snatched her short knife from Bess's outstretched hand. But in doing so, she allowed her opponents to move in closer. Slashing wildly with the blade, she leapt through their ranks one more time, but, though she evaded capture, one of their cudgels struck her forehead. Suddenly faint, she staggered and a trickle of blood ran down into her right eye.

"Oh," she said, with a sigh, sinking onto her haunches.

With the jostling men and women around her demanding blood, her opponents were eager now for the kill and she was too dazed even to sway aside as one swung his cudgel at her head.

The shaft of wood, however, met only a steel blade and snapped in two. By the time its bearer had recovered from his shock, Will had sliced his sword under the man's ribs. To Will's left, Matthew Finch parried a cudgel blow with a club of his own. When the two heavily-armed, Breton mercenaries weighed in, the skirmish came to an abrupt and bloody end. Clynt scrambled to escape by crawling along the foot of a wall, but Will, raging from the sight of Thomas lying dead a few yards away, hacked him down. Though Clynt raised an arm to defend himself, Will buried his sword up to the hilt in the man's chest.

The crowd's noise dropped to a low, grumbling murmur.

"You see this turd of a man?" yelled Will, "Be warned: if another hand is raised against us, we'll hack it off!"

In the face of such savagery, many of them fled at once. While Matthew helped Meg up and Will looked to the other girls, the Bretons kept an eye on the dwindling crowd.

Will's sister, Kate leapt up into his arms, tears of joy flooding her cheeks.

"You've saved us, Will," cried Isabel, hugging her cousin in a close embrace.

When he saw Bess Fisher, his reaction echoed that of Meg.

"You were the cause of all this, I'll wager!" he growled at her. "Well I can send you to hell too now, Bess Fisher!"

Meg shook her head to clear it, but it just made it hurt even more. Even so, she put out her hand to Will's chest.

"No coz," she muttered. "Mistress Fisher saved Kate; and she saved me – by the Virgin, that murderous bitch kept us all alive!"

45

2nd November 1483, in the early afternoon in
Studland Wood

Signalling Alain to follow, John headed through the trees towards the track. The closer he got, the more he wondered at the amount of noise the oncoming men were making. But who were they? Part of the rebel group he was to lead - or the ones responsible for Morton's murder? He simply had no way of knowing.

Barely a dozen yards from the path, he came to such an abrupt halt that Alain almost bundled straight into him. On the far side of the track piss was steaming up from the bracken where a tall figure stood - a man he never expected to see again – not anywhere… but, most certainly, not here. And the sight of that man alone was enough to twist and knot every fibre of his body as blind fury threatened to engulf him.

White-faced, John gripped a nearby branch, wanting only to crush the life from it; but, despite the forlorn urge to hurl himself at the villain, he held himself in check. Even so, all thoughts of Henry Tudor's revolt were swept aside for here, a mere few yards away, was Elias Slade - the man who had not only killed his brother, but also abducted Meg and single-handedly destroyed half his household.

Alain too stared at Slade in disbelief and flicked his eyes to his lord, asking the question. But John, feet planted like pillars in the undergrowth, gave a slow, stern, shake of the head. What miracles had God worked to bring this man here, to wild Studland in Dorset, so far from their last encounter in Ludlow? Last time the devil had, at the very end, escaped retribution, but he would not escape John a second time. Only the knowledge that his Aunt Emma was nearby, forced John to stay his hand. He could not afford to start a bloody, rolling skirmish in the woods against men whose strength he did not yet know.

Nevertheless, Slade's presence made up his mind about the men on the track: any man who followed Slade was an enemy of John Elder. Next moment, Slade moved off up the track after his comrades and the moment was gone. Breathing in deep lungfuls of the damp forest air, John remained unmoving among the browned fronds of bracken.

"Lord?" whispered Alain.

"Aye," said John, with a slow sigh. "Go after him and find out how many he has with him."

With painstaking care, John retraced his steps to the others, where he found his aunt, gripped by fear and starting at every wavering shadow in the undergrowth. Before he could offer a word of reassurance, however, he heard several others approaching.

"Might be Hal," he said, with more confidence than he felt.

But it wasn't Hal; it was Hooper and Grim who brushed aside the undergrowth to join them.

"By Christ, Master Hooper, you took us unawares!" said John.

"Well, who else would it be?" grumbled Hooper.

"Never mind; what have you found out?"

"The castle gates are shut tight but there are men up on the heath," he reported. "Though who all the buggers are, I couldn't tell you."

"What are they doing?" asked John.

"Just hanging about – like they're waiting for something..."

"Or someone," said John. "We saw others moving up on the coast track-" He broke off as Alain slid to a halt alongside him.

"I counted a dozen, lord," said the archer.

"Aye," said John, with a glance at Conal, "and among those dozen was Elias Slade."

"By Christ, lord," muttered Conal. "We can't let him slide away this time!"

"That man is here?" breathed Lady Radcliffe.

"Aye, he is, aunt," said John. "So, it seems we've one group of men by the castle and another on its way there. But are they allies, or enemies, I wonder? Somewhere up there we should find our rebels – but I'd expect them to be inside the castle...."

"So, what do you want to do?" asked Hooper.

"I'll leave Lady Radcliffe in your care once more while we try to join up with the rebels. Follow us up, through the trees, but stay well-hidden; I don't think this will be easy."

Half-expecting an argument from his aunt, John was relieved when she gave a nod of agreement. Instead it was Hooper who drew him aside to express his doubts.

"This isn't what we expected," he warned. "We are far too few to match these numbers"

"Aye, we are, but we should find some friends in the castle."

"You think Slade's for King Richard?" asked Hooper.

"Slade is for no-one but Slade," said John. "And, believe me, whoever he's fighting for, I shall kill him. But, if this goes badly, the Margaret will be back tomorrow to take you and your lady away to safety."

"Perhaps I should lend you Master Grim?" suggested Hooper.

"You may have need of him yourself," grinned John, clapping Hooper upon the shoulder in a gesture of farewell.

Determined to overhaul Slade, John set off up the coast path in swift pursuit. So fast were they moving that they were almost caught out. Since the woodland path followed an almost straight route, the last of Slade's men was suddenly clearly visible ahead. Had he seen them and managed to shout a warning, any slim chance of surprise would have been lost.

John called a brief halt and gathered the others around him.

"Alain, you're our shield," he said, "so drop back ten yards - and keep sharp! Remember, all of you, we don't need to kill every man, just force a path through to the castle gate. And whatever you do, don't stop!"

"What about Slade?" demanded Conal.

"If I get the chance, I'll kill him," said John.

Clasping arms with each man in turn, John drew out his sword. Feeling the weight of it in his hand always seemed to give him confidence. Though it was not his father's great battle sword - for that was still safe aboard the Margaret – it was fine steel nonetheless. Beside him stood Conal, scian in hand, and eager for the coming fight.

"On then," murmured John.

Since the slope was steady rather than steep, they soon picked up their pace again and in no time they were closing once more upon the last man. This time their quarry, very likely alerted by the tramp of their boots, suddenly turned. But, even as his mouth opened to cry out, a shaft loosed by Alain caught him full in the throat and hurled him backwards into the bracken.

John's sword swept aside another man before he could utter a sound and, though others cried out, John's men at arms were soon through them, surging on in their relentless ascent. Several more men at arms, no doubt alerted by the shouting, stopped to face them across the track ahead. One spun around as an arrow tore into his shoulder, while John and Conal crashed between the other two, with their two Breton comrades cutting and slashing after them.

Five men down, thought John, and not a scratch yet! Ahead though, waited a knot of men and, to his delight, he recognised Slade amongst them. These men looked better harnessed but, of course, Slade would only surround himself with the best.

With the two groups only a few yards apart, Alain loosed another arrow and, though it flew harmlessly astray, it was enough to unnerve Slade's men who scattered into the trees. John didn't blame them: in a forest, a good archer might easily pick them off one by one.

"Close up, Alain!" he shouted, waiting for the archer to join them as each of his men peered into the trees beside the track.

Cursing the elusive Slade, John cried: "On, lads! Remember: these men don't matter; our goal must be to join the rebels!"

"But what about Slade?" complained Conal. "He matters, lord!"

"Aye, he does! But he'll want a reckoning with me, as much as I do with him. So, he won't be going far…"

Forcing his aching limbs to carry him faster up the track, he was pleased to find that Conal, after a few truculent snorts of disapproval, was following. They covered the remaining distance in only a few minutes, emerging from the forest with alarming suddenness. Ahead lay the perimeter wall of the castle at Handfast Point. Having seen it from aboard the Margaret, John was less impressed from a distance of fifty yards. The low, crumbling wall that faced them was broken down in several places and had seen no repair for many a year. Passing through one of several well-used gaps, they made straight for the castle gate.

There his simple plan swiftly began to unravel. Hurrying towards them from the heathland to the west of the castle, were a dozen or more men. They had to be those Hooper had seen; and, armed as they were with clubs and knives, they looked like locally-recruited men.

"Have a care," he warned the others. "We can't be sure yet whether they're friend or foe."

"We could be sure if they're dead!" grumbled Conal.

"Gently, my friend," John told him. "We don't want to kill our allies now, do we?"

"If you say so," said the Irishman.

"Keep heading for the gate!" shouted John, but even as he said it, the pack of crudely-armed men spread out to block their path and John's small band were forced to stop.

"Fight or run, lord?" enquired Conal.

"Neither!" replied John. "Alain, keep your bow at the ready and watch for Slade coming up behind us. Conal, watch my back, if you please!"

"Pah! When have I not?" grumbled his comrade.

When they neared the waiting line of men, one stepped forward.

"Halt!" he shouted. "State who you are and what your business is here!"

"By whose order?" demanded John, still advancing, albeit more slowly.

"Roger Cayne, Mayor of Poole!"

For the first time that morning, John felt a little relief and was heartily glad that Morton had warned him that Mayor Cayne was on their side. He walked forward to greet the mayor, hand outstretched. "I confess I'm pleased to see you here, Master Cayne, for there are men in hot pursuit of us."

Roger Cayne, however, did not reach out to take his hand; instead, he drew his sword.

With faltering step, John said: "Hold fast, Master Mayor, I'm Lord John Elder. Did Master Morton not tell you that I've come to lead the revolt?"

"Indeed he did, Lord Elder, and that fool, Morton, has already paid for his treason."

In a few words, Cayne's reluctance to take a lead in the revolt was explained.

"So, it was you who betrayed your comrades..." said John.

"Betrayed? Hardly, for as an agent of the king's law in these parts, suppressing revolt is one of my heavy responsibilities," replied Mayor Cayne. "Now, if you and your men would care to surrender..."

"You're a long walk from Poole, Master Mayor," said John, holding his ground. "You've no commission to act here."

The mayor smiled. "I have the authority vested in me by Master William Catesby in London, but more than that, I have the men and you don't..."

From the edge of the trees a harsh voice roared. "Hold that bastard, John Elder!"

John did not turn but fixed Roger Cayne with a stare. "Are you a friend of that man?" he asked. Though his voice was quiet, he knew that the significance of his question would not be lost on his own comrades.

"Master Slade is... assisting me."

John nodded, for all now was clear: since Mayor Cayne was blocking his way into the castle then the rebels had be within. If he could get close enough, they would surely open the gates to him. Yet, caught between Mayor Cayne's local men and Slade at his rear, his own few men were probably outnumbered by three to one. Hesitation now would kill them all.

"At them!" he roared, and with Conal beside him, crashed into Mayor Cayne's men to carve a gaping hole two yards wide for the Breton pair and Alain to follow through. Even so, one of the Bretons caught a cudgel blow to his head and only the efforts of his fellow Breton and Alain saved him from further injury.

"Keep going!" shouted John, clattering his sword into several more of the mayor's poorly armed men to clear a path to the gates.

Reaching the gateway alive was the first part of the task, but they were a man down and surrounded. Unless the rebels opened the gates, the combined forces of Mayor Cayne and Elias Slade would bludgeon them to death.

In vain John stared at the nearby gatehouse, but though he and the others bellowed for the gates to be opened, there was no response from within. A hasty look up at the castle walls revealed no-one on the ramparts. A terrible thought occurred to him as they battled for their lives: what if this place was exactly what it looked like: a deserted ruin?

With fresh alarm, John saw that yet more men were coming on from the heathland behind Cayne – only three men, but it would likely be enough to finish them.

"Lay down your arms now, or take your fate!" bellowed the mayor.

"We're just too few," he murmured to Conal, as the circle of armed men began to close in upon them.

"Pah! Half of them only have clubs and knives…" observed Conal. "They fear our steel, lord - it's too soon to cry quarter yet!"

Staring beyond Master Cayne, John gave a rare smile. "Did I say I was crying quarter, old friend? We know about Slade, but let's test the mayor's mettle!"

Surging forward, John launched an assault directly at the mayor himself. Blow followed savage blow, scattering lesser men before him until he faced Roger Cayne. Though the latter stood his ground, his comrades, John noted, were hanging back to see how their master acquitted himself.

"Let's settle this between us, Master Mayor!" cried John.

But Cayne, backed away, shouting: "Strike him down! He's only one man!"

But none answered the mayor's call to arms.

"Either defend yourself or get thee gone!" roared John.

"Stand firm!" Cayne called out, but already his men were falling back towards the trees.

"Lord! Slade…" warned Conal.

"Don't you worry about Slade," said John, pointing across to the three men hurrying towards them from the heath.

A moment later, an arrow flew past him and thudded into flesh, producing a cry of anguish. When another swiftly followed with the same result, John smiled to hear Slade's voice raised in anger.

Conal raised a dark eyebrow. "You saw Hal coming then?"

"Aye, and he's brought a couple of friends!"

The arrival of another archer sent the mayor's part-time soldiers fleeing into the forest in disarray. Slade's efforts to rally his contingent fell on deaf ears, as each man sought to escape Hal's deadly shafts. Several joined the mayor's men in the shelter of the trees.

"Conal," ordered John, "keep hollering at that gate, because it's our only way out of here! I'll warrant that Hal and Alain have only a few arrows left between them!"

At that moment, two men at arms emerged from the trees, cutting their way through the mayor's retreating men. With them, they brought Lady Radcliffe.

"You've seen them off then," remarked Hooper, sauntering past the old wall to join them at the castle gate.

"Aye, but even so, this isn't a safe place," grumbled John. "I told you to wait!"

"With all those men running about, she'll be safer up here in the castle," argued Hooper.

"Aye, she would be – if we could get into the damned castle!" said John.

"I can hear you, you know," groaned Lady Radcliffe.

With a grunt of frustration, John turned away and noticed, for the first time, those who had arrived with Hal.

"God's teeth, James Finch!" he grinned at the ship's master. "How do you come to be here? And where have you hidden the Catherine – not to mention my Aunt Eleanor?"

The welcome smile upon Finch's face darkened at his question.

"By God's grace, John… my lord, the Catherine went down…on the rocks by the point."

"What?"

"I was plucked from the sea, like my shipmate, by fishermen. God save us - we've only just made our way up here – and we've yet to see another soul who survived the wreck!"

Reeling from the blow, John lowered his voice. "Blood of Christ, Finch! Are you telling me they're all lost? Aunt Eleanor, my coz, Kate and Grave…"

Finch shook his head "Young Harry here, reckons that Master Grave and Lady Kate made it ashore - a local boat picked them up, but it never came back to get Harry."

"And my aunt?" asked John.

"We don't know. We were taken to Swanage – along the coast to the west. We were making our way to Wareham, but at Corfe Castle they told us that Sir Simon Cayne - up here at the point - had sent round for any news of shipwrecked folk. So… we thought there might be others up here… and then we sort of found Hal…"

Still trying to absorb the crushing news, John clasped Finch's hand. "Well, I'm not sorry to see you, Finch. Let's pray that others made it safely ashore."

"Lord!" cried Conal.

"What?" barked John, unable to keep the fresh despair from his voice.

"The castle gates are still barred shut."

John stalked across to the gate where Conal and Hal had been banging hard and bellowing but without any response. Hal looked as if he might explode at any moment, so John pulled him away from the gate and ordered Conal to cease his hammering.

"Has Finch told you about the Catherine?" he said to Hal, but the archer's bleak expression told him all.

Gripping his loyal servant by the shoulder, John said: "My aunt and your Mary, they've been in worse scrapes before, haven't they?"

"Have they, lord?"

"Aye, they have! And you know better than any man how tough those two women are!"

"Perhaps they were once, lord," murmured Hal, "but now, I don't know; your aunt's not the woman she once was…"

"Good Christ, Hal! Have a little faith in them, eh?"

46

2nd November 1483, at Handfast Castle

When she returned from the cellar with more ale, Mary nodded to the hall guard as she descended the steps to the yard outside. It was cooler than she expected and she had to brave the cold breeze which skimmed across the cobbles, but the yard was exactly where Mary wanted to be. Handing over one pot to the gatekeeper, she set off for the far end of the wall where the final man leaned. The light woollen shawl around her shoulders offered little warmth and she was already chilled by the time she reached him.

"By God," he said, with a grin, "this is a right welcome jug! Thank you, goodwife."

"By the Virgin, it's cold for you out here!" she said, though her shivering was not caused by the cold alone.

"Damn true, woman!" agreed the guard. After a particularly long swallow, he added: "Wouldn't say no to another of these!"

Following his request with a rumbling belch, he draped an arm around Mary's shoulder. "And a bit of company would warm me up, eh?"

"If I can get away," she said, reluctant to give him too much encouragement. Casting her eyes around the yard, she realised that she was out of sight of the other guards and felt particularly vulnerable. If he chose to take advantage of her, there would be no help coming. Whatever she imagined might happen, a sudden burst of noise from beyond the wall drove any such thoughts from her head – and most likely his too.

"Who's out there?" she hissed.

"You just go and get some more ale," he warned, pressing the swiftly emptied jug into her hands. "And leave such other things to me and my fellows. Go on; get me another pot of ale!"

If she lingered a moment longer, he would cuff her about the head for her pains. So she turned away, her sultry smile turning to a grimace of disgust as she set off in haste back across the yard. But outside the wall, the sounds grew louder – sounds of struggle - and, despite her fears, she slowed a little to listen.

Half way across the yard and unable to make out what the snarling voices were saying, she had learned nothing. When the gatekeeper spotted her, he beckoned her over. With a groan, she prayed that ale was all this man wanted.

"Like another?" she called hopefully.

He was giving her an enthusiastic nod, when another fearful hammering pulled his attention back to the gate.

"Who is it?" she whispered.

But he ignored her question and, with the cries of those outside echoing in her ears, she was left to ponder who they could be.

"You're not going to open those gates are you?" she asked, finding trepidation all too easy to feign.

"Just get the ale, woman!" he snapped, aiming a boot at her behind.

Scrambling away, she banished her idle thoughts until the thundering upon the gate ceased and a single voice cried out for the gate to be opened. Her whole body started shaking and she staggered to a halt, unable to stop herself from turning back towards the voice.

"Move off!" shouted the gatekeeper, "Unless you want my boot at you again!"

Like a startled deer, she stumbled away on unsteady legs, back up the steps to the hall, but not down to the cellar for more ale. Instead she fled up to the second floor, past the startled guard and into the chamber where an impatient Lady Elder awaited her.

"You've been away so long! Where have you been?" demanded her mistress.

"I've been serving ale to men who don't deserve it!" cried Mary. "But they're here!"

"Roger Cayne's back?"

"No. Lord John's here!" said Mary. "He's outside the walls!"

"How can you know that?" asked Eleanor. "Did you see him?"

"No, lady," wept Mary, "but I heard Hal's voice clear as I hear yours! And, lady, where Hal is, Lord John is – isn't he?"

"You're sure it was Hal?" Eleanor pressed her.

"Do you think I don't know that voice, my lady? I know every tone of it…"

"Aye, of course you do," soothed Eleanor.

"But they're trying to get in," cried Mary, "and, by the Virgin, I think they may be hard-pressed!"

Lady Eleanor gave a sigh. "Aye, now I see some sense in it all. Sir Simon was one of the rebels – and John was coming to Poole to lead the Dorset rebels, so this is a place my nephew might well come to, sooner or later."

"So Mayor Cayne is trying to stop the rebellion?" asked Mary.

"Aye, Mary. By the Virgin, almost the last words Simon said were that he feared his brother would betray them again - and he surely has!"

"No wonder the men in the hall look so afeared, for they must know that only a rope - or worse - awaits them."

"But if my nephew is just outside, Mary…"

"But he can't get in, my lady!"

"Aye, and Roger Cayne's guards will keep that gate tight shut until he tells them to open it."

"But Hal… their cries sounded terrible, my lady…" groaned Mary.

"Then we must do our best to help them!"

"But how?" whispered Mary.

"We'll have to take out some of the guards," replied her mistress simply.

"But there are four men at arms!"

"Aye, but one at a time, Mary, we outnumber them…"

"Sweet Virgin, my lady, we've no weapons!"

"Well, we do have one," said Eleanor, reaching under her kirtle to retrieve her blade.

"By Christ!" said Mary. "Do men never search you?"

"Hardly ever," smiled Eleanor. "So, call in the one outside. Say I'm ill."

"What, now?" asked Mary.

"No, tomorrow, girl! Aye, now – are we not in haste?" replied Eleanor, lying down upon the wooden boards.

"Here we go then," said Mary and, taking a deep breath, she flung open the door. "Oh, master, I beg you help my mistress! She's fallen and I swear she's near to death!"

Pushing Mary roughly aside, the guard stepped into the room where he found Lady Eleanor lying upon the floor, moaning.

"What ails her?" he asked.

"How should I know?" cried Mary.

"So she dies, or she doesn't die – it's all one to me," he said, turning to go out.

"Well, it's not to me!" snarled Eleanor, kicking out at the back of his knees.

With a cry of anger, as his legs folded under him, he went down on his back, landing awkwardly next to Lady Eleanor. Though he was a big man, his fall winded him and Eleanor whipped around her knife, using all her strength, to punch it into his throat. As his body writhed beside her, she forced the blade down with both hands through the muscle and fat. Legs and arms thrashing wildly, he tried to slap her hands away. But as she worked the knife to and fro, blood began to spurt from his throat and run down over his chest. Despite the splashes on her face and breast, Eleanor did not relax her grip on the knife until all movement ceased. Then, with bloody hands, she wrenched her knife from his gullet.

Mary quailed to see the grim, blood-streaked mask of her mistress looking up at her.

"Where are the other servants?" asked Lady Eleanor, wiping her face with the back of her hand.

"They're locked in a storeroom, lady, I think; but we can't get to that without going past the hall," explained Mary, struggling to look at her mistress who had unwittingly smeared more bright blood across one cheek.

Lady Eleanor's bloodstained hands seized her by the shoulders. "You've seen blood before, Mary. Now go! Go and fill your jugs of ale!" she ordered. "I'll meet you at the hall door."

After only a moment's hesitation, Mary sped down the steps to the first floor, her head filled with dread images of ripped out throats and hands stained crimson. Tripping, she almost fell down the narrow spiral stair. Resting a hand against the cold stone, she tried to calm herself by taking a single, slow breath, before going on down to the cellar. Since the barrel was almost empty, pouring the ale took longer. Sweet Virgin! Her mistress would be chiding her once again for her tardiness.

47

2nd November 1483, in the afternoon outside Handfast Castle

"They're coming again!" announced Conal.

"God's truth! A little respite would have helped!" cried John, seeing the newly arrayed line of men approaching out of the woodland. Alongside Slade, ominously, strode Mayor Cayne – so their forces were now combined.

Glancing at his two archers, John saw that Alain had strung his bow and nocked an arrow, but his bag now hung limp and empty.

"Hal?" enquired John.

"Almost out of arrows, lord!" snapped Hal.

"Well, use what you've got to slow them down!"

Hal obliged and loosed his final shafts at the nearest men.

"By Christ, lord," muttered Conal, "but we really are too few to hold them…"

If the gates remained shut John faced a simple choice: fight or surrender. The presence of his aunt would normally have dictated the latter path. But not only was his aunt branded a traitor, like the rest of them, but also a spy. If taken, she could well hang along with everyone else. Yet, to fight on was the bloodier option; men would die and keep dying until they no longer had the will to resist.

Turning to Hooper, John said: "Protect Lady Radcliffe at all cost!"

"I don't need you to tell me my duty, Lord Elder," grumbled Hooper, taking up a position with Master Grim by the castle gate, against which Lady Radcliffe now cowered.

The remaining men at arms, joined by Finch and young Harry, formed up in a shallow half-circle of resistance. All around them, their enemies began to creep forward.

If he could kill Slade, John thought, then he could break the spirit of their opponents. But, if he went after Slade, his weary comrades would have to hold everyone else at bay; and he was not sure that was even possible. He would be risking all their lives on a single throw of the dice… except all their lives would be forfeit in any case. Better to fall at this gate than die the cruel death of a traitor.

"Surrender, Lord Elder!" cried Mayor Cayne. "You're trapped!"

"Lord?" enquired Conal.

"Hal," said John, looking the archer in the eye. "Hold this line for me, if you please. Conal and I are going hunting…"

With a nod of resignation, Hal said: "We'll do our best, lord. Pray God you send Master Slade to the fires of hell for me!"

"It's time, Conal!" said John, drawing out his sword once again.

Clasping his lord's arm, the Irishman replied: "Lord, 'tis well past time!"

As one, they made a great lunge forward, crying: "An Elder! An Elder!" THe suddenness of their attack threw the front rank of their enemies into utter confusion. Battering aside any man who would not yield ground, they cut a bloody swathe towards Elias Slade. But Slade, clearly unwilling to be drawn into a fight with the pair of them, pressed more men forward to block their advance. John's only consolation was that every man that came for him was drawn away from his comrades at the gate.

Heavy, muscle-draining, blows were exchanged as the two warriors raised the intensity of their onslaught. In a blur of steel, the Irishman's razor-sharp scian prodded, sliced and tore at man after man, bleeding them till they dropped. Cracking a chin with the hilt of his sword, John then chopped the brutal blade down on an unprotected neck before stabbing it through a gambeson to burrow into reluctant flesh. With Conal still at his back, John hacked his way towards Slade but as he closed upon him, he felt a stab of pain. From nowhere, the thrust of a knife blade grazed his ribs. He halted for moment to catch his breath, while Conal despatched the would-be assassin. Though his wound was by no means mortal, it would hamper his movement a little.

His quarry now stood only two yards away; but, having seen him receive a wound, Slade was no longer backing away. Slade no doubt smelt victory and next moment John found himself clashing blades, face to face with Slade.

"Nasty little wound, you've taken," cried Slade, aiming a ranging slash at John's shoulder.

"Not enough to stop me killing you!" railed John, parrying the blow and forcing his adversary back.

"Give us some yards here!" bellowed Slade and several of his men stood back from them, all save Conal and another heavily-built warrior who, like the Irishman, seemed born only to fight.

Though they lacked plate armour to protect them from mortal blows, the two pairs of men hacked at each other without cease. If they failed to parry every slash, cover every feint and block every move, they would be hurt – and hurt badly. If they were too slow, or delayed for a fraction of a second, they would be down - and once they were down, each man was certain his opponent would never let him back up.

Conal, wrestling hand to hand, gave a sudden exultant roar as he seized his opponent's sword arm and then buried the fine steel scian into the man's chest. Both men fell as the Irishman struggled to wrench his weapon free.

Distracted, John half-blocked a wild slash from Slade which, instead of taking his head off, barely clipped his shoulder. But sensing an advantage, Slade pressed him harder, desperate to finish him while the Irishman was still down.

Slade was a skilled swordsman, reliant on speed and finesse, which John knew he could never match. Only by using his strength, could John hope to win. Launching a bitter assault at his adversary's neck and shoulders, he tried to drive him back. But Slade, despite the wounds he received in their last encounter the year before, had lost none of his speed or agility. Sweat ran down John's cheeks as he strained every sinew to match his opponent's pace and guile. Raging at himself to knock the villain on his arse and finish him, John simply could not find a way to do so. So many times he had envisaged how he would kill Elias Slade, that it was horrifying to discover that he was just not good enough to do so.

Cut off from Hal and the others, John could only judge how they fared by their cries of triumph or rage. Facing away from the skirmish by the gate, he did not see disaster coming. Only when Conal, still down on his knees, roared a warning, did he know that something was badly wrong. If Slade was forcing him further from the gate, then that was where he ought to be. But, without laying himself open to Slade's flashing blade, he could not turn and retreat.

Though it seemed like hours, it could only have been seconds until Conal was back on his feet again and running at Slade. Faced with both men at arms, Slade was compelled to give ground and John risked a glance back to the gate. Fearing that he might have lost one of his men at arms, he saw that he had lost two. The wounded Breton – brave to the end – had been struck down again; close by him, Hooper was dragging a scarcely moving Master Grim back to the gate.

At once John and Conal retreated and Finch, a formidable man with a sword, rushed forward to aid them until the three men reached the gate, breathing hard. Striking out at Mayor Cayne, Finch succeeded in battering him to the ground, only to find himself outflanked by several others. In the confusion, he took a crack on the head from the hilt of a sword. Dragging him back, John leant him against the wall beside Lady Radcliffe.

"Aunt!" he yelled. "Bind up his head!"

Eyes wide open in shock; his aunt began examining Finch's bloodied scalp.

But what use was any of it now, thought John? Since he had failed to kill Slade, their position was now truly hopeless.

The rebellion in Dorset was over before it had begun; if Henry Tudor ever arrived there, he would find his rebel leaders at Baiter hanging from a line of freshly erected gibbets.

48

2nd November 1483, at Handfast Castle

With dwindling patience, Eleanor waited in the shadows on the spiral stair. She had already dawdled there for several minutes – what in God's name was Mary doing? Fear trampled upon fear in its haste to fill her heart with anxiety. By the time Mary joined her, Eleanor was seething with pent up fury and alarm.

Mary took one look at her mistress. "What's wrong, lady?" she whispered.

"What's wrong?" hissed Eleanor. "I've been hanging here on the stair, scarce daring to breathe! What took you so long?"

"It's a slow business!" retorted Mary. "You wanna do it?"

"Mind your place!" snarled Eleanor, snatching one of the jugs. "I'll take this into the hall and try to free the men there."

"On your own, lady? But he's a big fellow and well, what's he going to think, seeing you covered in blood?"

"I'll worry about what he thinks; you take the other jug to the gatekeeper. You need to keep him busy in case there's any noise from the hall."

"What about the other guard further along the wall?" whispered Mary. "I can't keep them both busy with one jug! I'll have to fetch another for him!"

"There's no time! You'll have to offer him something he wants more than ale!"

"No!" declared Mary.

"Peace lass! Keep your voice down!"

"But I can't do it!" protested Mary.

Eleanor's bloodied face was suddenly two inches from hers, eyes blazing at her. "Your Hal is dying outside that gate; do you want to help keep him alive or not?"

"He'd never ask that of me!"

"Well, I would – and I am!" growled Eleanor. "And every sodding moment we waste here, the more likely all our menfolk will end up dead! By Christ, lass, you only have to keep the guard's attention, not marry him!"

"But what if I can't?" cried Mary.

"You're a clever lass; find a way!"

"Aye, alright then; I'll try…"

"Good," grumbled Eleanor, "because I'll be doing every other damn thing!"

From where the pair stood, face to face, they heard the wild Elder battle cry ring out and met each other's eyes.

"May God protect you," breathed Lady Eleanor, touching Mary's cheek with her hand. "Now, go!"

As soon as Mary hurried away to descend to the yard, Eleanor tore open the top of her kirtle, stepped off the stair and walked along the short passage into the hall where the guard was pacing between the tables. Mary had not exaggerated, for the fellow was tall and well-built. Looking up at his thick set features and bulging neck muscles, she gave a heavy sigh of disappointment, for this was not a man she could kill by stabbing him in the neck.

Holding out the jug with an obviously shaking hand, she said: "For you."

But he ignored the jug and instead stared at her bloodied features and clothing. "What the fuck happened to you?"

"Your friend upstairs… happened…to me," cried Eleanor, setting down the heavy jug on the nearest table to let her shoulders slump forward.

"He cut you?" muttered the guard.

Falling against him, Eleanor left him no choice but to catch her. He obliged, holding her up in his strong arms for several moments before gently setting her down upon a bench.

She must finish him swiftly, or all was lost; but to do so, she would need to be close, so very close.

"Where are you hurt?" he asked.

"My left breast," replied Eleanor, pulling aside enough of her bloody kirtle to spark his interest, "but it's nothing..."

"Best I take a look," he said, needing no invitation to explore the general area of her wound.

Fixing him with what she hoped was a helpless look, Eleanor allowed him to bend forward and forage more widely around her chest. Then she reached up to his cheek, a tender touch. Gripping his chin lightly with her hand, she murmured: "I think, at heart, you're probably a good man... so, I'm sorry..."

He grinned at her. "No need to be-"

Sweeping up her other hand she plunged her blade at his right eye and almost missed. The small blade slid off his nose first, before driving down into the eye. She wasn't sure what to expect – a scream of anguish and pain, or a brief struggle – but there was nothing, for he died before he could even blink. As she let his lifeless body slide away from her onto the floor, a wave of regret struck her, but she thrust it aside. There was no time now for guilt, or shame – those would haunt her later, if there was a later...

Retrieving her knife, she hurried to the prisoners and began to saw through their bonds. Having freed two, she surrendered the blade to them and they freed the rest.

"We must open the gates!" she told them. "At least two of Mayor Cayne's men remain."

"Who are you?" demanded one of the prisoners.

"I'm the one that just freed you!" cried Eleanor.

"But who is at the gates?" cried one.

"We've been betrayed once today already!" declared another. "How do we know it isn't the traitor himself?"

"Because it's my nephew out there!" said Eleanor.

"How do we know you're not a traitor?"

"Sweet Virgin!" cried Eleanor. "Why would I release you if I'm not on your side?"

But her wild appearance panicked them and they forced her to sit down, while they satisfied themselves about her. Retrieving their weapons from the heap on the floor, they regarded her warily while she fumed in disbelief.

"Listen to me!" she cried. "We have perhaps only moments, before your cause – and mine is lost!"

⌂⌂⌂⌂⌂

Mary left her only pot of ale with the sentry at the gatehouse, who looked a good deal more worried than the last time she had seen him. Walking further around the yard, she looked for the remaining guard. He had moved to lean against the wood store, but looked up as she approached. His initial smile faded as he noted that she had brought him no more ale.

"The ale's all gone," she told him.

He nodded. "So, why did you come back then?"

Sweet Virgin, why indeed, she asked herself? "Didn't you ask me to?" she said.

Taking her hand, he pulled her closer; close enough to smell the sweat on him and something else – a taint she knew all too well. She already had the stench of blood in her nostrils; you didn't serve Lady Eleanor Elder for long without recognising it! This fellow reeked of blood, steel and leather – because that's what a man at arms smelt of. Someone had told her that once, a long time ago, she recalled, as his rough hands began to explore her. There was no subtle gentleness in his mauling, just a base elemental groping.

For him, she was only the means by which he might scratch a persistent itch – and, God help her, she was letting him, because that was what her lady asked of her – no, required of her. But her mistress was right: if it took that to save Hal, what did it matter? It would not be the first time she had been taken against her will, though that had been long, long ago – long before Hal - before even Lady Eleanor…

"You don't seem too keen," he said, pulling at the top of her kirtle.

"Why the hurry?" she murmured, staying his hand. "You got somewhere else to be?"

His response was to take her by the chin. "We ain't going to be sweethearts, girl!" he scoffed. "You came back here – and we both know why – so don't get all shy about it now. That won't do, will it? So, let's get to it, 'cos, yeh, I have got other things to do."

Releasing his hand, she allowed it to prise free a breast from her kirtle. Pressing her back against the hard flint wall, he pulled her clothing up to her waist. She knew what she must do, and it was no more than many a serving girl had to do every day - if not in the Elder household.

How did her mistress seem to do it without effort - or regret? But then Lady Eleanor always had a blade… and Mary did not, though she couldn't recall ever using one in anger. Even so, when she felt his bare flesh touch hers, long-suppressed memories reared up from her childhood and a surge of panic seized her. Her whole body tensed and she held her breath until a slap across her face broke the spell.

"What do you think you're doing?" he growled.

"No," she murmured.

"No?" he echoed, pausing for a moment. "Listen, you're nothing, girl; you don't matter."

With an effort she shook her head to clear it of the bitter reminders of her youth. She had to concentrate! All she had to do was distract him until her mistress and the others came to her aid.

"Hey! I already made my mind up, didn't I?" she spat at him. "But I didn't say I wanted my arse cut up on the flint, did I? What's wrong with the wood store?"

"I'm supposed to be in the yard, that's what's wrong with it!" he argued. "There's a lot going on in case you hadn't heard!"

"Aye, but that's outside the wall," said Mary, "and we're inside, aren't we?"

Gripping his hand in hers, she pulled him towards the wood store with his breeches and braies still wrapped around his ankles.

"Come on, it's only a few yards!" she said, coaxing him to follow.

"Alright then, girl," he said, "let's get inside, but we'll have to be quick."

"Not too quick, I hope, lover," she added, opening the low door to draw him inside. "Do want to unlace me some more?"

"Christ no, I'm well past that," he cried. "Just hoist up your kirtle and I'll do the rest!"

Rolling her over onto her back, he pushed her down onto a stack of logs.

"Oh, shit!" she said. "Now I've got splinters in me!"

"Don't mind that, girl," he laughed, "you'll soon have something bigger than a splinter in you!"

That was the moment when she felt his strength and it dawned upon her that, whatever she had planned, or wanted, to do, he was going to have her anyway.

49

2nd November 1483, at Handfast Point

"My name is Thomas Audley," said the first man she had released. "Now, please sit down, mistress. You seem to know all about our business, but we know nothing of you."

"Master Audley," said Eleanor, "I am Lady Eleanor and my nephew, John – Lord John – has come to Handfast to lead the Dorset rebels!"

"So you tell us, mistress, but all we know is that we came here today to meet our new leader; not one of us knows who that is to be – only Richard Morton has even met the man. So how is it that you know and we do not? Did you come here with him?"

"Not exactly," said Eleanor, "but I did in a way…"

"Nothing you say makes sense. For all we know, we could be letting the king's men in here."

With a glare sharp enough to skin a hare, Eleanor said: "The king's men are already in here! There's one lying in front of you on the hall floor!"

"Tell us about your nephew…"

"Ask him yourself; he's outside the damned gate!"

They regarded her in stony silence until, with an angry sigh, she conceded.

"Lord John Elder, outlawed by King Richard, soldier… son of Ned Elder-"

"Ned Elder?" said one of the others. "Why didn't you say that before? I fought with Ned Elder at Tewkesbury - Ned's lad would be alright."

"Aye, if he still lives," thundered Eleanor, "because while you chew words here with me, he and his men are outside dying! Now, do I have to drag the damned gate open myself?"

Visibly chastened by her latest tirade, they gathered up their weapons, and set off out of the hall. But on the threshold, further doubts seemed to assail them.

"Perhaps we should search the keep first in case there are other guards," suggested Audley.

"Enough!" raged Eleanor and snatching her knife back from the fellow that held it she marched out of the keep, down the steps and into the yard.

The gatekeeper saw her coming steadily towards him and, seeing the small blade in her hand, gave a chuckle.

"What are you going to do with that?" he asked.

But as she drew nearer, he saw the blood on her clothing, face and hands and drew back a little.

"Do you like my attire, fellow?" asked Eleanor. "See this blood I wear? It's the blood of two of your comrades – and I've every intention of adding yours to it!"

Perhaps her demeanour and appearance made up his mind… or it may have been the crowd of rebels who eventually trailed down out of the keep after her. Either way, he fled from the gate.

Alone, Eleanor could not lift the heavy bar across the gate, but soon the others arrived and at last the gates were opened. The first person, Eleanor saw as the gate was flung open was her sister, Emma, crouched beside James Finch, who was bleeding from the head.

"Oh, good Christ, sister!" cried Eleanor. "Let's get him inside!"

At the sound of her voice, John's head snapped around to see her.

Watching him, with Conal and Hooper, shielding their comrades from the blows raining upon them, Eleanor felt a fierce pride in her nephew. With difficulty, Roger Cayne's men were forced back until the wounded men could be helped inside. Still shaking his head in disbelief, John slammed the gates shut, aided by a strong shoulder from Conal. Once Hooper had fitted the bar across the gates, the exhausted men dropped down to rest, while others had their wounds tended to.

"Mary!" shouted Eleanor. "Go and find the other servants!"

But Mary made no reply for she was not close by as she always was. Then Eleanor remembered where Mary was.

⌂⌂⌂⌂⌂

Attempting to hide her utter panic, Mary tried to slow down her amorous assailant with words.

"You're all I've been thinking about since I left you," she moaned, "but, let's take our time."

But, gasping in shock as his fingers crept into her, she realised he was far beyond words. In desperation, she tried to reach down his leg, feeling for his belt where she thought she might find a knife. But she only succeeded in stroking his bare thigh, which led to an even more disturbing development. Now, with him hard against her, she was at the mercy of his lust, knowing she would just have to let him pump his unwelcome seed into her.

Outside, the clamour of voices grew louder and… somewhere out there, she prayed, Master Hal Ford still lived.

Grinning broadly, the man on top of her was busier than ever: one hand massaging her breasts, while the other made forays where no man should venture – save perhaps Hal… Sweet Hal, who had lain with her aboard the Margaret, the night before they left Brittany. Had it been possible, she would have stayed with him then; but at least the vivid memory of him gave her a brief moment of peace. Whatever happened now, the words they said that night would live with her forever.

"I'll wager that feels good, eh, girl?"

But it didn't; it didn't feel good and it didn't feel right. "Oh, sod it," she groaned and, leaning her left leg to the side, she opened herself up to him. "Hitch up a bit and let me help you…" she cried.

"Now you're for it, girl!" he whooped.

"Oh. I am," she murmured, "I am truly for it!" Stretching both hands behind her head, she arched her back. "Wait, I'll move my other leg…"

"I'm ready!" he wheezed.

"Oh, believe me, you've never been more ready for this," she panted, "and it's all about the…"

She brought her right knee hard up into his groin. "…timing!"

As he yelled in agony, she scrambled out from under him, crawling out of the wood store on her knees. Relief overwhelmed her and she staggered to her feet on the cobbles, only to discover the gatekeeper standing in front of her.

"What've you done to Hawker?" he bawled at her.

"Hawker?" She had never even asked the guard's name and now she felt her lips tremble as she tried to say the word; for Master Hawker was still moaning his misery in the wood store. Suddenly aware of her near nakedness, she tried to placate him. "Just a little quarrel, friend," she replied. "He's alright…"

"He don't sound like he is!" returned the gatekeeper.

She heard the footsteps first, thudding towards her across the cobbles. He heard them too and looked back nervously towards the gate.

Lady Eleanor appeared first, but Hal overtook her - the two people she loved most in all of Christendom – and behind them followed Conal and Master Hooper.

"Mary!" shouted Hal. "Mary!"

"Shit…" breathed the gatekeeper, tossing down his weapon. "I didn't touch her!" he cried. "I didn't!"

"He didn't!" agreed Mary, but she was quite pleased when Hal punched him on the chin all the same. It seemed only fair, she thought.

"Are you alright?" cried Hal, taking her by the shoulders.

Not caring that her hair was wild and loose, nor that her legs were bare, nor even that her breasts were poking out of her kirtle, Mary puffed out her cheeks and looked up at him.

"I've known better times, my love," she murmured, "but I'm fine now…."

And after that she didn't care what happened to any of them, because Hal swept her up in his arms – in front of everyone – and embraced her like a lover… or, perhaps, a husband.

Part Six: Under Siege

50

3rd November 1483, in the Solar at Roger Cayne's House in Poole

When Roger Cayne met with a scowling Elias Slade in his solar, their grim faces told a wretched story. With all the advantages he held, Roger could hardly believe how badly the day before had gone; but Slade was swift to apportion blame.

"I warned you!" he grumbled. "I told you that John Elder wouldn't be so easy to despatch!"

"Well, you certainly didn't manage to do so, did you?" countered Roger. "But, you were right enough… though you might have warned me how he would react to your arrival!"

"Old story, Master Cayne, but it's enough to say there'll be no happy settlement between the two of us…"

"Are you still committed to our cause then?" asked Roger.

"Why wouldn't I be?" said Slade.

"I thought after Diggory Clynt's death…"

"I've still got a score to settle; that's not going away… and, there are still profits to be made…"

"Indeed," confirmed the mayor. "So, what's your strength now?"

"It'd be a lot better if that fool Clynt hadn't got himself killed," complained Slade. "And all over some stitch of a girl!"

"But, he did," said Cayne wearily. "And you will benefit from his share of our... business. So, my question stands: how many men can you raise?"

"With mine and what's left of Clynt's, I reckon about forty – but only a handful of those are real fighting men, I mean proper, harnessed men. The others are handy in a tavern brawl, but – as you've seen - John Elder's men at arms will cut them down without raising a sweat."

"All the same, Elias, numbers matter. I can muster perhaps as many as fifty – but, like you, I fear they may not stand against seasoned soldiers."

"I thought you sent to Catesby?"

"I did - days ago!"

"And?"

"And nothing..." said Roger.

"John Elder's ship will be back over at Studland by now," observed Slade.

"So?"

"So, he could get clean away - and I'm not losing that bastard again!"

"If, as my late friend, Morton, suggested, his purpose was to prepare for Henry Tudor's landing then I doubt he'll leave yet."

"True enough," agreed Slade.

"Our problem is: how to defeat him," declared Roger.

"I've been thinking about that," said Slade. "We may not have men who can fight him in open battle, but we have more than enough to keep him stopped up in that castle – starve him out if we must. We can keep him there a long time."

"And what if, while we are starving him out, Henry Tudor arrives with an invasion fleet and sweeps us aside with his army?"

"If we keep John Elder in that castle then Tudor will have no idea where he and the other rebels are. And, if he sends men ashore blind, we'll meet them on the beach because – as you said - we have the numbers. I don't hear many cries of support in Poole town for this Henry Tudor."

"But those on John Elder's ship in Studland Bay could easily tell Tudor where he is."

"They could," conceded Slade, "but we could put a stop to that too…"

At that moment and, without any introduction or warning, the door was thrown open and a giant of a man stepped into the room.

"God give you good day, sirs!" he boomed.

Staring wide-eyed at the beast who had invaded his privacy, Roger searched in vain for a glimpse of his truculent servant whose continued absence suggested that he might finally have deserted his master.

"Who the devil are you?" demanded Cayne, attempting to revive his authority in the room.

"Sir Walter Nevil!" the knight announced brightly, "henchman of the king and kinsman of the queen!"

"Really?" said Roger, unable to disguise his surprise.

"Do you doubt my word, you rogue?" roared the knight.

"Er, of course not," said Roger. "It's just that I wasn't expecting Catesby to send anyone quite so quickly."

"Catesby? Sir Walter Nevil is not despatched by mere lawyers – no, not all. He serves royalty and is here by order of King Richard, not at the behest of his little dog! I may come from Master Catesby but I am not sent by him! Now, which of you is the mayor?"

"I, Sir Walter, am Roger Cayne, Mayor of Poole. And this is my close ally and associate, Master Elias Slade. Between us, we command the men of the town."

"Glad to hear it!" enthused the knight.

"Now, you will need some lodgings," said Roger, "though with the All Souls fair it won't be-"

"Pah! Already taken care of," interrupted Sir Walter.

"But… how?"

"The landlord at the Black Dog was kind enough to take us in – indeed he was most welcoming after a brief discourse with the flat of my sword!" Sir Walter's guffaw rattled around the small chamber.

"How many men did you bring, Sir Walter?" asked Roger, trying to make his enquiry appear casual.

"Eleven, Master Cayne. I always ride with eleven of the very best men at arms – always; no more and no less. A dozen of us to root out the king's enemies wherever they may be hiding, eh?"

Roger was tempted to ask the knight what happened when one of his prized eleven was killed, but he quickly thought better of it.

"Where are these rebel scum then?" enquired Sir Walter.

"Across the water."

Sir Walter looked horrified. "They've already gone back to France!?"

"No, no, Sir Walter, a little closer than that," said Roger. "They're at Handfast Point beyond Studland."

"Handfast Point? Studland? Some pissing small places, I'll warrant. Am I right?"

"Indeed 'pissing small places' on the other side of the harbour," confirmed Roger.

"Very well, Master Mayor, find me some vessels to carry my men and horses across."

"It shall be done, Sir Walter. By tomorrow, we'll have all our men – and yours - outside Handfast Castle."

"This castle – how strong is it?" asked the knight.

"Hardly worth the name castle," replied Roger. "Its ancient gates will splinter at the merest touch of a battering ram. Why, a man such as you-"

"A knight…" corrected Sir Walter.

"Indeed, a knight such as you should have little trouble in taking such a crumbling outpost."

"Good, send me word later," said the knight. "I shall be at my lodgings." Then, as an afterthought, he tossed a sealed letter to Roger. "That letter will confirm my credentials – not that you need it, since you already have my word."

Only when the formidable knight had stomped out, did Roger breathe normally once more. Breaking the seal, he opened the letter which it turned out - despite the knight's bluster – was indeed from William Catesby.

Roger skipped through a few brief opening remarks, pausing only to laugh when Catesby authorised him to hang Bess Fisher. Since the bitch had helped to butcher Diggory Clynt – amongst others - it hardly mattered to him that she had also killed the two men Catesby had sent to keep her under control. Perhaps he should have retained her services after all. Until now, his allies had been dwindling by the day. Sir Walter's arrival, however, gave him renewed confidence.

Catesby told him that recent reports from Brittany suggested that Lord John Elder was on his way to Poole – by God, when would Catesby tell him something he didn't already know? It seemed that only the fear that Henry of Richmond might also land at Poole had forced the dispatch of Walter Nevil, of whom Catesby wrote:

'Walter will make three claims – that he is a knight, a henchman of the king and a kinsman of the queen. No-one has yet sought to challenge him on any of these three unlikely assertions but, as you will, no doubt, have noticed, he is tall, built like an oak and very effective. My advice is not to believe a word he tells you; instead, employ him like you would a hunting dog. Set him on the scent, wait for the carnage and don't get in his way.'

"Well?" enquired Slade.

"It seems our prayers have been answered," replied Roger. "Sir Walter and his men can do the bloody work while we offer our earnest support – from a safe distance..."

"But, mind, we can't have good Sir Walter claiming the price on John Elder's head, can we?" said Slade. "Nor any other rewards... and we must think about that ship..."

51

3rd November 1483, just after dawn at Handfast Castle

Sitting in Sir Simon's chamber, which his Aunt Eleanor seemed to have adopted as her own, John stared at the windows. Perched above the grey chalk cliffs, the room offered views out to sea through its three arrow loops. One faced due west towards the rising outcrop of land beyond which lay Swanage, where Master Finch had been taken after the shipwreck. Another opening faced south where, as John himself knew, there was only sea as far as a man could sail. Thus, he was concentrating his attention on the third, east facing, loop but eventually he turned away in disgust.

"No sails?" said Lady Radcliffe.

"A few sails," he conceded, "but none large enough to be the Margaret."

"Perhaps Matthew anchored inside the harbour last night," said Lady Radcliffe.

"Hmm, I suppose but, with so many uncertainties, it would help to know that we had a ship close at hand."

"We will have, John," she said. "Be patient."

"Patient, aunt? Henry of Richmond could arrive here at any moment and we still have no secure place for him to land – nor do we actually have the size of rebel army that our would-be king is expecting!"

"You won't have any sort of an army," observed Eleanor, "once those men who were imprisoned here decide to be on their way."

"You think they'll leave this morning?" he asked her.

"I don't know why they bothered coming at all," grumbled Lady Radcliffe, "if they're going to run away at the first little trouble."

"Yesterday, they were facing a terrible death, sister," said Eleanor.

"So was I – so are we all, still!" protested Lady Radcliffe.

Staring at each of his aunts in turn, John gave a disbelieving shake of the head. Why in God's name could the ill-matched pair never travel a common road? Whenever their paths crossed, their rancorous rivalry, fuelled he supposed by lifelong jealousies and resentment seemed to override all else. Having abandoned any hope of reconciling the two, he was now obliged to use the only tool he had left - his supremacy in the family - to crush them both. Did it bring harmony? No, not at all; but it made him feel a great deal better.

So, they would snipe and they would posture but, after a time, they would listen and obey.

"All they lacked was a leader," said Lady Radcliffe, "and now they have one."

"It's not that simple, Aunt Emma," said John. "These men have been betrayed from the very start – how would you feel?"

"Aye, but you are here now, so all that can be put to rest."

"But can it? Men who now know they were mistaken in trusting a lifelong acquaintance are hardly likely to put their trust in a stranger, are they? And a northerner too, by God!"

"But they must!" insisted Emma.

"Why? Why must they? Because you tell them so?"

"Because... King Henry needs them!"

"King Henry? There is no King Henry, aunt - not yet – and never likely to be if he lands here in Dorset! If he lands at Poole, he'll not get off the quay! The mayor will oppose him and we are far too few to help him."

"But he will have an entire fleet with him, John!" insisted Lady Radcliffe. "More than enough men at arms to sweep aside Master Cayne's rabble!"

"I fear I'm the cause of this disaster," said Eleanor. "If it were not for my ill-timed arrival, Sir Simon would still be alive, Grave would still be alive… and Kate would not be a prisoner."

"Aunt, Sir Simon was already committed to the rebellion – his life lay in his brother's hands long before you arrived. We came here to help him and the others, but perhaps the fate of this revolt was always beyond anyone's help."

"Perhaps," she conceded, before walking out onto the battlement.

"Take care out there," he warned. "The stonework is-"

"Weak? Aye, it is, but I know every inch of it, nephew."

"Of course you do," smiled John, praying that her melancholy mood would not persuade her to hurl herself onto the rocks below.

One aunt driven by mindless optimism; and the other wracked by guilt and grief. What was he supposed to do with the pair of them? Frustrated that neither seemed to grasp how precarious was their situation, he made his excuses and left them to their thoughts.

Crossing the wavering bridge to the keep he reflected upon their chances of holding the castle against their enemies. When he was outside he thought the main castle walls looked formidable enough but from the inside their catastrophic flaws were all too obvious. Few recent repairs had been made to structures which appeared to have been built hundreds of years earlier. Handfast Castle was in its death throes and no-one would be more aware of that than Roger Cayne.

Hurrying down the stair through the keep to the yard outside, John met Conal and Hal on their way up.

"You've scouted the whole area?" he asked.

"Yes, lord," said Conal.

"And?"

"Our friends have gone but, as you expected, lord, they've set two men as watchers."

"You left them alone, I trust?"

"As you ordered."

"Any sign of the Margaret in the bay?"

"Not yet, lord."

"Let's hope Will and the others arrive soon for you can be certain that it won't be very long before the mayor returns and Master Elias Slade will be with him."

"I live for that moment, lord," declared the Irishman. "He'll not escape this time!"

John nodded, though he thought there were only so many times one could make such a claim. Conal's blind faith was beginning to sound worryingly similar to that of his Aunt Emma.

"Very well," he said, "continue the repairs to the main wall and Conal, keep every man alert. Hal, a word with you, if you please."

Once Conal hurried off, John led Hal out into the courtyard. "How is Mary?" he enquired.

"She's feeling better, lord," replied Hal. "Much more like herself, but…"

"But?"

Hal said nothing.

"God's breath, speak up, Hal. It won't be the first time you've set me straight!"

"Lady Eleanor should never have put her at such risk, lord…"

"We were all at risk yesterday, Hal. If what Mary did gained us even a few moments then it was worth it. Two guards at the gate might have made a fight of it. You were out there, who else might have been killed if the fight had lasted even a little longer?"

"Several, I know that, but she…"

"You're not thinking about Mary, are you?" said John. "But someone else you once loved – cut down by the hand of Elias Slade…"

"Perhaps, lord, yes, but only because I fear the same outcome."

"You've lost no more than I, Hal – or many others here. Christ's blood! My Aunt Eleanor has lost more than anyone."

"But such deeds are not the work of women, lord!"

"Would you or I have employed a woman thus?" asked John. "No, we would not because we seek to keep our womenfolk safe. But, Hal, brave women seem to think much like brave men. Do they seek to hide themselves away? No. Women like Lady Eleanor, aye and Mary too – ask only how they can help their menfolk.

"But they risk themselves too much!" cried Hal.

"Aye, they do. Are they afraid? Aye, they are. Might they be killed? Aye, they might, but still they will fight for their men and their household – and we should thank them for that service, Hal. We should thank them for it…"

For the rest of the morning John supervised the work to strengthen the castle walls whilst at the same time having private conversations with each of the rebels who had been released by Lady Eleanor.

Piecing together what they told him, he realised that they were a varied crop of men from several different areas of the county. What quickly became clear to him was that these men could not possibly raise a rebel army in Dorset between them. A few gentlemen and tenant farmers just did not have the resources or the numbers of men for such an undertaking. Some of those present might be prepared to fight and a few were clearly trained to do so, but most were not.

To each man in turn he put the question: if Henry Tudor landed in Studland Bay tomorrow, would you take up arms to support him? Whatever answer they gave, he ignored it. He had only to look into their eyes to know what they would do and what he saw there did not fill him with confidence.

Morale was not helped by the arrival of a messenger in the early afternoon. Both horse and rider were lathered from exhaustion, for they had covered the distance from Salisbury in half a day. With him, the messenger brought catastrophic news for the rebellion. Yet, John felt no sense of shock that the rebellion's figurehead, Henry Stafford, Duke of Buckingham - had been captured and taken for execution before the king at Salisbury. Though John had a poor opinion of the duke, who until recently had been an ardent supporter of King Richard, there was no doubt that the Buckingham name leant considerable weight to the revolt and his death dealt the rebel cause what felt like a mortal blow.

If the duke's death wasn't worrying enough, the news that King Richard himself was only fifty miles north of them gave him cause to consider whether their position in Dorset was still tenable. According to the messenger, the king was bound for the south west, to Exeter, where the rebels were amassing an army but, John wondered, might he not come by Poole? The port was well situated for an invading fleet so, at the very least, there was every chance that he would send reinforcements to his loyal mayor.

What was he to do now, in the face of this new setback, thought John? But before he had time to digest the news, there was a cheer from one of the ramparts: the

Margaret had been sighted in the bay below. It was a boost he badly needed: with his ship nearby, all possibilities still remained – especially the chance to see the ladies safely out of the castle. He gave a wry smile – for it might not be so easy to persuade them to leave their beds for the pleasure of more uncomfortable nights aboard the Margaret …

Within the hour Will arrived at the castle bringing with him the remaining Bretons and a barrel load of other news – some of which went a long way towards lifting the gloom. The survival and liberation of his sister, Kate, was a major cause for celebration. But God was surely toying with them, for bad news fell upon good with the speed of a swooping hawk when Will reported the death of Thomas Skirett. John could scarcely believe it and felt the loss keenly, especially since the last words he exchanged with the youth had been harsh – undeservedly so. Yet the burden of leadership buried such concerns; everyone now wanted to ask the same question and it was his cousin, Will, who summoned up the nerve to put it to John.

"Well coz, now that we are all together once more, what are we going to do?"

Since John had been thinking of little else all day, he knew the answer well enough, for none of the recent events changed what he must do, merely how he must do it. It was not an answer that would please anyone for it offered only more uncertainty and risk.

"We wait," he said. "The fighting men will remain here and hold the castle until Henry of Richmond arrives or, until we can no longer hold it. In the meantime, the ladies and the servants will go down to the Margaret and stay there."

Will gave a chuckle. "I doubt my mother, or Aunt Emma, will be happy about that decision!"

"Aye, I know," agreed John. "But, God help me, Will, I'll take no argument on this.

Of course, both aunts refused to go to the ship, until John roared at them that he would have them taken there: bound, gagged and tied to a mule if they did not go willingly. A little to his surprise, the two older women accepted his decision without further words and the following morning, on 4th November, the small column of women and wounded was escorted down the forest track to Studland Bay to be ferried out to the Margaret.

James Finch, grinning despite his battered head, led them all on foot, leaving the few horses at the castle. Sarah, whose broken leg was now less painful, was able to walk down with the aid of a wooden crutch that Peter made for her. Though John knew that Mayor Cayne's watchers were still there, he was content to ignore them. Perhaps when he heard that there were no women left at Handfast, he would understand how serious John was about holding onto it.

From Studland's stony beach, the Margaret's small boat took several hours to ferry them all aboard and only when all were safely transferred, did John breathe a little easier. While the women retreated to the ship, several of the rebels left for their homes. They offered their reasons for leaving sheepishly, but John was in no mood to press them into service and was genuinely surprised that more did not leave.

Seven men remained to join John's men at arms in defending Handfast Castle until their new prince should come. Three of the most enthusiastic, Masters Will Twynho, John Cheverell and Thomas Audley, professed their commitment to the cause and prayed for the safe arrival of Henry Tudor. They almost had John persuaded of the likely success of their venture, but he, the eternal pessimist, remained unconvinced. He shared neither their belief, nor their confidence; because he knew Elias Slade would return to Handfast.

But, as it turned out, no-one foresaw what would happen...

52

5th November 1483, at Handfast Castle

John knew that if Mayor Cayne and Elias Slade arrived before Henry Tudor, he would have to defend the castle – a task which had nothing at all to recommend it. Handfast was simply too large for such a small group to defend; added to that, its walls were weak and damaged, its gates were worn and it possessed no cannon.

At dusk the evening before, John had walked the castle wall with Conal and George Palmer, the late Sir Simon's servant, who had stubbornly refused to abandon his master's home. At first John noted the weak spots but by the time they finished, he had lost count. Instead he focussed on the strongest element the castle possessed, its three storey keep which could only be breached through a single doorway at the top of fifteen stone steps. Though the keep was very old, the masons who built it had done their work well. The stone, which he learned from Will Twynho was from the nearby Purbeck quarries, had lasted well.

Unfortunately, anything made out of wood had not survived so well. Day and night the men laboured to strengthen the main gates and the great door into the keep. Made of stout oak, they would once have been as hard as iron but now, after years of neglect, they were dried out and split with age. In places the timber was softened by rot and almost impossible to repair without more time than they had. All they could do, beyond some basic shoring up, was make a barricade of sorts to reinforce the gates. Though it would not stop the attackers gaining entrance to the castle, it would at least slow them down when they did.

Water from the well, which was in the yard, was carried up to the hall and some was stored in the tower beyond the walkway. If the castle was breached they could retreat to the keep and when that was captured, they might make a final stand on the tower perched on top of the fast-decaying lump of chalk. Just to reach it they would have to scurry across the narrow, half-rotten footbridge. In the unlikely event that they survived all that, there was no escape from the tower itself - except by jumping to their deaths onto the rocky shore below which was not an inviting prospect...

"Do you think we'll have enough water?" asked Will.

With a wry smile, John replied: "I don't expect us to last out long enough to run out of water, coz!"

Will gave a shake of the head. "You need to have more faith, John – that's always been your trouble..."

"No, coz, this family has always been my trouble..."

It would be their third dawn at Handfast with no sign of the return of Roger Cayne. A few began to believe that the mayor was a beaten man, lacking both the will and the fighting men to recapture the castle. Some were now convinced of it, confident that God had seen the justice of their cause and given them His blessing. Most were no longer concerned about the difficulties of defending the castle and instead awaited the imminent landing of their new king. This dawn, however, did not see the arrival of Henry Tudor.

John saw them coming from the top of the keep: men, horses, heavily-laden mules, even a wagon edging inexorably up the forest track from Studland. By God, there were a lot of them; and, as always, war was about numbers. When the assault came, he would be ready for it – at least as ready as he could be. No matter how brave you were, or how strong you were, numbers always made a difference –

and John knew that he did not have the numbers. Fifteen men might be enough to hold out for a time perhaps, but fifteen men could not win. If Henry Tudor did not come very soon, it was certain that Handfast Castle would fall.

It took their enemies several hours to bring their whole force up to Handfast Point and establish the siege. Suppressing a humourless smile, John watched the men at arms using the ancient ruins of the outer wall to shield them from any attack from the castle. If only they knew that the defenders had little to hurl at them but rocks!

It was not long before the predictable barrage of abuse began – all part of the customary tactics intended to unsettle a besieged enemy. Though John ignored the insults and threats, his new rebel friends, less schooled in warfare than his own men, seemed much dispirited by what they heard. They had dared to hope and, in John's experience, when hope was swept aside, little else remained.

"Battles are won with muscle and blood," he told Will Twynho, "but sieges are won and lost in your head. Don't let them beat you, Will, before you even start to fight."

Always, John was searching for Slade, but to his surprise, it was not Elias Slade, nor even Mayor Cayne, who bellowed out a terse string of conditions for their surrender. It was a massively-built, heavily-armoured knight who introduced himself as Sir Walter Nevil. With him were several other men, similarly arrayed, which changed the situation – and not for the better. As he feared, the king had sent reinforcements in the shape of a man who was not only supremely confident, but also seemed accustomed to leading men in battle. This would be a very different fight from the skirmish outside the gates.

Hal, perched high up on the keep, was already yelling a warning when the first crossbow quarrels snapped against the stone of the castle ramparts. But his alert came too late for one of the Bretons atop the rampart beside the gate.

Thrown back off the wall, he fell heavily across the barricade and though they retrieved his body, he was already dead. Thus, after only a few minutes, their numbers fell to fourteen. After that, John knew, it was only a matter of time…

Glancing up at Alain and Hal with their bows at the ready, Twynho cried: "Why in God's name don't they shoot back?"

"Because they know better," said John. "It took them hours to retrieve the few arrows they have; they know when to use them – and it's not yet."

"But shouldn't we try to stop them getting in!" cried John Cheverell.

"We shall, John, but we can't afford to lose any more men on the rampart; we'll wait for the fight that matters."

"But-"

His protest was cut short by a thundering crash at the gate. By Christ, this man Walter Nevil wasn't wasting any time!

"They've brought up a damned tree trunk!" called Hal from above them.

Aye, thought John, we noticed. "You know what to do!" he called up in reply, before wincing as the next blow cracked one of the centre timbers of the right hand gate.

"Make ready!" shouted John, unsure whether his voice was carrying above the raucous din being made by their opponents on the other side of the wall. Reassured by the arrival of Conal and his cousin, Will on either side of him, John drew his sword and inhaled deeply – always a good idea to breathe while he still could.

Next moment, the pair of gates was shattered into dust and splinters as the hefty shaft of oak burst through them. Its momentum took it two yards through the gateway, dragging several heaving bodies with it. At once two arrows arced down from the keep to pin two straining attackers to the trunk. Since it was impossible to drag their battering ram back out, the besiegers were obliged, if they wanted to gain entrance, to clamber over both the great log and the hapless men skewered to it.

Struggling past their stricken comrades, Sir Walter's harnessed men forced a path towards the barricade. Their initial attempts to push it aside failed, as John knew they would. Next they would attempt to scale the barrier for it was a mere four or five feet high at the most. But while they tried to rip out some of the timbers, barrels and masonry with their hands, John and his men battered them with axe and sword, until they were forced to fall back through the gateway.

While his comrades assailed the retreating men with scornful jeers, John scanned the castle yard and saw George Palmer by the chapel wall waving his arms about wildly. Unable to hear what the servant was shouting, John hurried across to him.

"They're hacking away at the wall!" he cried in alarm.

"Aye," muttered John, "that makes sense – our friend, Sir Walter, seems to know what he's doing…"

"But what if they break through?" whispered Palmer. "What shall we do?"

"Just pray they've no black powder, Master Palmer! Stay here and keep a watch – and tell me at once if it appears they'll open up a breach!"

Trotting back towards the main gate, John felt more at ease; somehow, it helped knowing what was coming – helped to dispel the fear… By the time he was back at the barricade, so were the enemy and this time with the great brute, Sir Walter, at their head. A mighty wedge of armoured might smashed into the left side of the barrier and the sheer force of the impact forced it apart a few inches.

One knight managed to squeeze into the first gap but then, trapped there, he found it impossible to beat aside the many blows directed at him. Despite the frantic attempts of his fellow knights, the brave fellow was cut and pounded a dozen times by a combination of Will and Conal. After a short time, the mortally wounded man simply bled to death, to become just another part of the obstacle which blocked the castle entrance. Unwilling to continue their assault where his broken corpse remained, his enraged comrades turned their fury against other sections of the barrier, hacking timbers aside with axes. In their midst, Sir Walter fought like a man boiling over with rage, his great pollaxe chopping away at the barricade until he was able to prise it apart. Wherever Sir Walter went, John moved to face him.

While the knight and his men worked on John's right flank, two men armed with crossbows arrived inside the gate and took aim to the left.

"Crossbows!" Hal yelled a warning once more.

Though most men were quick to crouch down, John Cheverell was too slow and spun around, struck by a bolt through the arm.

"Get him into the hall!" ordered John, hammering at Sir Walter's axe with his sword. The knight leaped back for a moment but then, regrouping his men, launched himself forward once more. Such was the force of his attack that even John was pushed backwards but Sir Walter could not drive home his advantage. Instead he cried: "Cease!" and, with surprising suddenness, pulled back. With practised skill, his crossbowmen switched their attention to the rebel right and another of the Bretons was hurled back onto the cobbles.

Even so, Sir Walter seemed content not to press too hard, exerting just enough pressure to cause losses with the least risk. There was something almost admirable, John thought, about how skilfully he marshalled his forces – and

he had barely used the Poole men at all. He would know –
as John did – that if the assault carried on unchecked for
much longer, the gate way would be cleared and the castle
must be taken.

Sensing the importance of the moment, John roared up
to his two archers: "Hal! Alain! Now's the time! Make it
count!"

But he was not the only one bellowing. Only a few
yards away across the barricade, his rival rallied his men:
"On me! A Nevil! A Nevil!"

Abandoning their bows, the crossbowmen drew their
swords and joined the rest of the men at arms surging
behind Sir Walter. Taking up his battle cry, they finally
forced a path through the heap of lumber and rubble.
Scanning his ragged line of shaken defenders, John saw one
or two already on their knees; only Conal and Will were
keeping the line intact. Through the chaos, another voice
seized his attention: George Palmer was gesticulating again
by the chapel. Knowing that if he left the defensive line at
that moment, it would crumble, John was forced to ignore
the warning.

Using their remaining arrows to deadly effect, Hal and
Alain were able to strike down two of the better-harnessed
knights, earning a brief respite for the buckling line. Then,
as was often the way in battle, several incidents occurred so
close together that no-one afterwards could remember
which had happened first.

Hal's final arrow sliced into Sir Walter's neck and he
dropped to his knees. His sudden fall spread dismay
through the ranks of his men at arms and they hurried to
drag him away out of the gate before John's men could fall
upon him. If there was a shout of triumph from any of his
own men, John never heard it, for all other sounds were
blotted out by an explosive blast from behind him. And, of
course, he knew at once exactly what it was. He had hoped

that Sir Walter possessed no black powder, but he was wrong.

Though he stared across at the chapel, a pall of smoke obscured his view. Calling out Palmer's name several times, he could discern no movement at all in the shroud of dust and debris.

"Stay at the gate!" he told the rest of his men, before stumbling across the cobbled yard, strewn now with razor sharp flints.

"Palmer!" he yelled. "Are you there, man?"

Fearing the worst, he headed for the space between the chapel and the outer wall where he had last seen Palmer. The only good thing was that, so far at least, there had been no sudden rush of Sir Walter's men through any gap in the wall. Until the smoke began to drift away on the sea breeze, he had no idea how badly the wall had been breached. Then he saw that the wall opposite the chapel had not been breached; it had been obliterated. It was gone completely - and not just the wall, but the ground beneath it, for the blast seemed to have removed the entire section of cliff upon which the wall had once stood. He wasted no time looking around for the perpetrators of the blast for he expected that he, or they, might be in the same place as both the wall and the cliff face – far below on the rocky shore.

"That's buggered us," grumbled a voice nearby.

"Palmer?" cried John, turning to see the fellow staggering towards him.

Though his face and clothes were black from the smoke, Palmer seemed to have survived relatively unscathed.

"Thank God you're alive!" said John, clasping an arm around the man as he stumbled forward.

But with an agonised scream, Palmer broke away from him and fell down upon his chest. John saw that the brave servant had not fared so well after all. Lacerated by countless fragments of flint, Palmer's shredded back was red with blood. If there was a blessing, it was the ugly black shard mortally embedded in the back of his neck. Unable to offer any solace for the man, John could only crouch beside him, hearing his screaming agony gradually wane to a deathly whimper. He stayed with the dying Palmer, to deliver a rudimentary blessing of sorts – for, even in their dire circumstances, the poor fellow was owed that much. Then, with a long sigh, John stood up and trudged back to the gate.

The enemy, disconcerted by their leader's wound, had fallen back. But now that the castle's west wall ended by the chapel, their retreat would be short-lived. It might be a risk for those who entered by that route but, once several did so, neither the gate, nor the yard itself could possibly be defended. They had done all they could… better to draw back now while they could.

"Fall back to the keep!" ordered John. "Take whatever weapons you can carry."

By God! It had been even worse than he had imagined. Hoping the gate might be held for a day or two, it was galling to concede it after only a few hours of stubborn resistance. In doing so, they gave up their best chance of survival. Now, they must wait it out in the keep and rely upon Henry Tudor, who would not even know that they were in trouble.

53

6ᵗʰ November in the evening, aboard the Margaret, in Studland Bay

Two days and two nights cramped aboard the ship had dampened Eleanor's utter joy at being reunited with her daughter. Unable to dispel the oppressive fears that now festered around her, Eleanor paced the deck with relentless disquiet. Nor was she alone in her dark mood. Not much was said all evening and the few who did make idle conversation did not dare speak to Eleanor – for which she was grateful.

Of course she was pleased that Kate was safe – a miracle for which she offered silent thanks almost hourly to the Holy Mary – but too many others were not safe. Earlier, around midday, they had all witnessed the fireball from the far side of the point and Eleanor wondered what the thunderous blast meant for her son and nephew at the castle. She might never see them again and all in the name of some trifling Welsh earl who sought to make himself a king. A man she neither knew nor trusted – aye, and a man for whom she cared nothing - had wagered his fortunes upon the lives of her family.

As the night wore on, she continued to traverse the Margaret's deck, not caring that she made others nervous by doing so. Let them be nervous – because they ought to be! When she reached the bow yet again, a small voice moaned at her from the gloom.

"Please aunt, must you?"

Cloaked in darkness, she allowed her grim face to soften, for Meg was hurting with an agony that was all too familiar to Eleanor. Thomas Skirett, Meg's Thomas - a youth shat out the bleak arse of London – was dead. Another one butchered by courage, thought Eleanor… sweet Virgin, God liked His martyrs young, didn't He?

Meg sat alone and Eleanor was surprised that Alice, or Isabel - or whatever the hell she was called now - was not consoling her cousin. She owed her that, surely; except, of course, she was a lass facing demons of her own.

"Will you sit with me, aunt?" asked Meg.

Never able to refuse Meg, Eleanor sat down on the bare deck boards beside her niece and took her hand. What though could she say to salve Meg's grief? Only what folk always said…

"The pain will ease," she murmured, "as time passes."

"He'll still be sodding dead though, won't he?"

"Aye, he will," conceded Eleanor, fighting back the tears that threatened to engulf her. For, in an instant, Meg's blunt reply had rekindled the raw, bewildering anger she felt at the first sight of Grave's lifeless corpse. Grief compelled you to abandon the usual courtesies… and rightly so.

No woman wanted a dead hero; they wanted a living, breathing man – brave and gentle, if possible – but alive. Being alive was surely a basic requirement for any man you loved; yet men seemed to find so many ways to die...

Since the bond between them required no words, Eleanor wasted no more of them and merely remained with her niece. Everyone else, it seemed, had finally found a place to sleep and, since Emma had seized possession of Finch's cabin, for everyone else that meant somewhere on deck, swaddled in a blanket - if they were fortunate enough to find one. Most would be huddled together on the stern deck, hence Meg's retreat to the bow, where she and her aunt now gazed out across the bay towards Handfast Point. The rest of the ship's company gradually embraced slumber, which was as well, Eleanor thought, for there was much healing to be done.

Listening to the calm sea gently lapping at the ship's timbers, Eleanor and Meg sat together awake until, after a few hours with only the stars to watch, the pair dozed fitfully in each other's arms.

Yet, as ever, Eleanor found sleep elusive; for how could she rest at ease when so many daggers of concern prodded at her? Meg's grief and the fate of those at the castle were only a part of her concern. There was also the presence aboard of the murderous Bess Fisher – and, aye, that circumstance would very soon need to be addressed…

It was that hour close to dawn when the starlit sky was fading and the heavens seemed somehow lighter, though it was not yet light. That was when Eleanor noticed the claw hanging over the ship's rail in front of her. She wondered idly how long it had been there. Had it just appeared? And how did it get there? Aboard the Catherine, she had heard many seafarers' tales about creatures of the sea, but were there such beasts in this bay and so close to the shore? She thought about asking James Finch, or his son, but weariness dictated otherwise. Since the claw had not moved, she ignored it; it would wait till after dawn. Perhaps, if she ignored it for long enough, it would just fall off the rail.

It didn't; instead another claw joined it. So, there were now two claws, side by side; but as Eleanor came fully awake, she saw that they were not claws, but hands – gnarled and bony hands. Easing herself upright, she leaned forward to look closer, and felt Meg stir beside her. Strong fingers clutching at hers told her that Meg too was wide awake.

She could smell him then – not some creature of the sea at all, but a breathing, sweating man. Slowly, careful not to make a sound, Eleanor reached under her kirtle to ease out the blade that resided there. Meg too, she was pleased to see, had retrieved her knife in silence. When a second pair of hands gripped the rail, Eleanor cast around in the darkness for a more potent weapon, but the only item within reach was a shaped length of wood lying on the deck. What it was actually for, she had no idea, but its size and weight were perfect for her purpose. By the time she had bent down to retrieve it, yet another hand had appeared on the rail.

"Go!" she breathed to Meg. "Go and rouse the ship!"

The instant Meg pattered off across the deck, Eleanor lifted up her makeshift club and smashed it down on each hand in turn, rewarded in each case by a howl of pain from below. But by then Meg was already screaming an alarm and Eleanor cried out: "To arms, to arms!"

When a head appeared above the rail, she hammered it hard with her length of wood. After that, men swarmed over the rail so fast, she could do no more. Running towards the stern, she passed several crewmen already hurrying to meet the attack. The light was still far from good and, as a mêlée began to spread across the ship's deck, it was hard to distinguish friend from foe.

◠◠◠◠◠◠

Isabel, woken by desperate cries from above deck, flung open the cabin door. Dashing out, she promptly tripped over Sarah and Peter who lay entwined just outside. With a groan, she picked herself up and shook them awake. But the two Londoners had not been the same since learning of Thomas Skirett's death and now they shrank away from her into the darkness below deck. As her mother followed her out, Meg raced past them both, climbing up to the stern deck and shouting: "To arms, to arms!"

But Isabel had no weapon, and even less idea of how to use one. Then she gasped, as she saw the dark, struggling figures clustered around the main mast. Another cry from

Meg warned her that several more were clambering over the stern rail onto the small, raised section of deck.

"Get back inside!" screamed Lady Radcliffe, but it was already too late.

Before Isabel could move, a stocky seaman wrapped a strong arm around her waist and lifted her clean off her feet. Screeching at him, Lady Radcliffe wrenched at his arm, only to be knocked aside with a single blow of his fist.

Seeing her mother slam into the gunwale, Isabel screamed. Meg was suddenly there, darting in close, to stab Isabel's captor under the arm. The wound must have been deep for in a moment he was wheezing and coughing up blood, allowing Isabel to break free from his grasp. In a daze, she backed away, unable to tear her eyes from him as he dropped to his knees, choking on his own blood.

A warning shout from Meg broke the spell and Isabel hurried to her half-conscious mother; only to see another assailant capture Kate and drag her towards the rail.

"Get 'er in the boat!" ordered a third man, before turning to go after Meg.

Eva, crouching on the deck by Meg, stuck out a foot and tripped him so that he was already falling when he reached Meg. But though she scratched and shrieked at him like a wildcat, he managed to get up onto his haunches in time to dash the knife from her hand. Taking her in a firm hold, he hauled her along the deck to join Kate.

"Isabel!" Meg shrieked at her, "You have to fight!"

But Isabel sat rigid, frozen by fear, with Lady Radcliffe beside her. A yard away, Eva cowered too, terrified. Her cousins were fighting, thought Isabel – scrapping for their very lives - but they were losing! And though the lionhearted Meg still snarled at her captors, Kate had already been hoisted up onto the rail and was only awaiting someone to lower her over the side. They could not win; so, what was the point of resisting?

"Isabel!" yelled Meg, in despair. "Help us!"

When Isabel met Meg's eyes, her cousin fixed her with a glare that seemed to pierce right through her. "Fight, coz, fight!" Meg was bawling, as she struggled to free herself.

But Isabel had never fought, even last summer, in the depths of her despair in London, she had succumbed. How could any girl hope to resist such brutes who could snap her in half with a single blow?

"Fight!" Meg screamed at her. "Fight, Izzy - or we all die!"

Isabel gave a start as a voice close by shouted: "I'm coming, lady! I'm coming!"

Harry, one of the younger crewmen from the Catherine, pushed past her making for the ship's side where two men were manhandling Kate and Meg up over the side. When they heard Harry coming to their aid, the two girls redoubled their efforts, fighting and spitting at their captors, clutching at every spar and every scrap of rigging to prevent being tumbled over the rail.

Bowing her head in shame, Isabel saw, at her feet, the man stabbed by Meg lying in a pool of slowly-congealing blood. At his side lay a discarded cudgel, but Isabel could only stare at it, until another cry from Harry made her look up again. The youth's club pounded at the shoulder of Meg's captor allowing her to pull away a few yards, only to be seized again and slapped hard across the face.

Seeing a screaming Meg, cap torn off, being dragged away by the hair, shocked Isabel to her core. Plucking up the bloody cudgel from the deck, she ran with trembling steps and swung it as hard as she could at Meg's tormentor. The moment she struck the man's head, it made such fearful crack that she dropped her weapon in alarm. As her victim crumpled to the deck, she hauled Meg into her arms.

A cry of "Lady Kate!" made her look up again to find Kate still clinging to the ship's rail. One arm was still held by her captor until Harry aimed a blow at him. With an angry yell, the fellow at last released his hold upon Kate to plunge his long blade into Harry's belly. At the moment of her release, Kate was still trying to pull free and thus fell down to the deck to land beside her saviour, whose midriff was now a gaping, mortal wound.

"Hurry, Kate!" screamed Meg and Isabel, as one, but Kate remained on her knees on the deck.

"What's she waiting for?" cried Isabel. "Kate! Run to us!"

"She must be hurt," said Meg, "or she'd have run."

"No," murmured Isabel, tears stinging her eyes, "she… she doesn't want to leave him so…"

Retrieving her knife, Meg sprang to her feet. "Pick up your weapon!" she told Isabel.

After only a moment's hesitation, Isabel snatched up the cudgel. Feeling a reassuring squeeze from Meg's hand, she gulped in a deep breath and the two girls ran to help their cousin, who now stood, bereft, over Harry's still body.

Only when Harry's killer reached out to recover her, did Kate attempt to scramble away towards Isabel and Meg. Easily, he blocked her path, so instead she skirted around the stern deck to pull herself up by the rigging until she could rest her boots on a low spar.

Edging closer to his frightened quarry, her pursuer thrust out a hand to seize her leg, but she kicked out at him and slid her feet along the spar. By the time her cousins attacked him, he had hold of Kate's boot. Though Isabel clubbed him on the back of the head and Meg made savage, repeated stabs at his back, he managed to tug Kate's foot off the spar. As he went down under the welter of blows, she lost her balance and, with a shriek of terror, grabbed for a rope beside her.

Just as Isabel was raising her cudgel to hit the fellow again, she glimpsed Kate falling. Hands clawing at the dawn air, her cousin seemed to stop in mid-air - but then she was gone, plummeting down from the ship's stern.

Rushing to the rail, Isabel and Meg scoured the black surface of the water below, screaming her name over and over again.

54

7th November just before dawn, aboard the Margaret, in Studland Bay

Hearing the shrieks of the lasses, Eleanor made for the stern. She had to get to the girls - to Kate! But it was a struggle trying to weave a path through the brawling men. By the time she forced her way to the stern deck, it was strewn with bodies, among them her sister, Emma, and Will's lass, Eva, but both, mercifully, were still moving.

Isabel and Meg rushed to her, seeking the comfort of her embrace. Though she noticed a ribbon of blood seeping through Meg's hair, the pair seemed otherwise only bruised by the assault. While the two cousins wrapped their arms around her and wept, Eleanor stood stiff and unmoving. In an instant, she had scoured the deck with a mother's eye, studied the bodies littering it, and discovered that her daughter was not among them.

"Kate?" she cried at her two nieces, still holding tightly to her. Their voices shrieked at her, one after the other, until she wanted to hear no more.

"Harry tried to save her!" cried Isabel.

"But she went over!" moaned Meg.

"And we couldn't save her," wept Isabel.

Standing there on the deck, Eleanor felt all the breath leave her body, all the blood drain from her face as such a chill swept through her, as she had not known since the loss of her dear brother Ned…

"Aye, I see," she whispered, releasing Isabel. "Go, my dear. See to your mother and Eva…"

But Meg's hand she gripped ever more tightly, murmuring: "Show me, lass..."

As Meg led her to the ship's side, Eleanor stopped and bent down to stroke Harry's pale face with her hand. "Poor lad," she whispered, "he saved her once..."

"Aye," said Meg, drawing her aunt to the ship's side. "If she'd fallen in the water, aunt, but..."

Eleanor looked down.

Below them, a small boat, no doubt tethered there by Slade's men, swayed with the movement of the waves. It was empty, save for Kate, who lay unmoving, her beautiful neck bent at an ungodly angle.

Slapping the ship's rail, Eleanor was lost... For Slade had found a way to steal her daughter after all.

"Sweet Virgin," she muttered, "what more do you want from me?"

"Aunt," wept Meg, beside her, "I tried my best...but I couldn't..."

Facing her, Eleanor cradled Meg's face in both hands. "Never blame yourself for this!" she cried, "for the fault lies elsewhere..."

Releasing her niece, she picked up a bloody cudgel from the deck and walked away, with Meg crying after her: "Aunt! Come back! Where are you going?"

How was it that her daughter lay dead and the knife in her own hand was as yet unbloodied? Well, she would soon change that. Lurching past two combatants locked together, she came face to face with a grim spectre.

Pale as a wraith, with dark shadows of dried blood over her clothing, Bess Fisher cut a haggard, desperate figure.

"Give me a weapon!" she demanded, thrusting her bound hands into Eleanor's face.

At that moment, Eleanor wanted only to split Bess's head open from crown to chin for what she had done to Simon, but she did not. She faced Bess and said nothing.

"Let me fight!" begged Bess.

"Aye, but who for?" scorned Eleanor, above the din.

"You, damn you!" croaked Bess. "I saved your daughter, didn't I? By Christ, that must earn me something!"

"Aye, but much good it did her!"

"She's?"

"Aye, dead - as you soon will be!"

But, though she laid her blade at Bess Fisher's neck, Eleanor stopped. Revenge could wait a little longer because, if there was even a small chance that the Fisher woman would fight with her against Slade then she had to seize that chance.

"Let me help you avenge her," pleaded Bess. "I risked my life to free that girl!"

Slicing her knife through the ropes that bound Bess, Eleanor held up her weapons. "Knife, or club?" she growled.

"Oh, knife, always," said Bess, snatching Eleanor's blade.

"You stay close to me," warned Eleanor, "or I'll crack your skull myself!"

"Two bitches together, eh?" spat Bess and the two women exchanged a brief, dour stare: no respect, no bond, just a raw understanding.

Several men, who must have climbed aboard amidships, now blocked their path forward. Eleanor and Bess, fearless, ran straight at them. If their opponents had attacked at once, the pair would have died there. But, as Eleanor had discovered many times before, when men were faced by armed and determined women, they tended to hesitate. After all, how much harm could two women do?

In that ruinous moment of doubt, the seamen learned precisely what Eleanor Elder and Bess Fisher could do. Since neither woman expected quarter, they never once considered giving any. Striking hard and fast, Eleanor clubbed her first adversary so that he stumbled to one side and distracted his comrade who Bess then stabbed in the neck. A glancing blow from a third man's cudgel caught Bess upon the shoulder and she fell to the deck, panting to recover her breath. But Eleanor, driving her own club into his midriff, winded him and sent him sprawling on all fours with another clout.

"You're down there!" she snarled at Bess. "Finish him!"

Though Bess and her opponent rose up at the same moment, her strike was so fast he could scarcely blink before her blade speared into his eye. While Eleanor was watching Bess, her own adversary recovered his wits and charged at her like a bull. A strangled oath burst from her when his heavy frame punched her back against a gunwale board. She knew she could never match his strength, but watched, transfixed, as a small hand wrapped itself around his mouth. Head pulled back by the nose, his chin lifted a little and a large, blade appeared to saw across his throat. His blood sprayed out over Eleanor until Bess let her second victim fall. Eleanor groaned, for the worst had happened: she owed Bess Fisher another life.

Holding out Eleanor's knife, hilt first, Bess gave a grimace of distain.

"I found a bigger one," she said, with obvious delight.

Before the two could go any further, two more seamen leapt in front of them. Seeing their dead comrades at the feet of the two blood-soaked women, they wasted no time with warnings and came at them hard. Knife in one hand and cudgel in the other, Eleanor took a gamble and cracked her adversary somewhere around the kneecap. When he yelped with pain, she stabbed at him, but he dodged her blade. Narrowly evading his answering thrust, Eleanor caught him under the chin with the end of her club.

Hearing his jaw snap back as he slumped against the ship's rail, she was about to leave him when he made a last desperate lunge at her, so she cracked her weapon against his head once more. Kate was dead; there would be no quarter and no remorse…

Turning on her heel, she found Bess standing triumphant over her bloodied opponent.

"What are you waiting for?" snapped Eleanor.

"You told me to stay with you!" rejoined Bess.

Raking her eyes across the main deck, Eleanor saw a bitter struggle being waged in the harsh dawn light – and, as far as she could tell, it was almost lost.

"You hurt?" she asked Bess.

"Not yet!"

"Pity!" retorted Eleanor.

"That all you can throw at me, lady?" sneered Bess.

"God damn you!" said Eleanor.

"Oh, He has, my dear; he has! So stop whining - just move," yelled Bess, "or some brute will stick us where we stand!"

Eleanor gave a sharp nod but then seized Bess by the arm. "Just watch where you put that knife… dear!"

"If I come at you, lady, I'll be coming from the front!" promised Bess.

With a toss of her head, Eleanor turned away to peer at the seething, roaring mass of men. Catching a glimpse of Master Finch in the heart of the fighting, she decided there were worse places to be, when you were grieving and hurting, than with James Finch. But then she saw his opponent and swore aloud.

"What?" yelled Bess, above the clamour.

"Slade!" growled Eleanor; setting off so fast that even Bess was left trailing behind her.

Here was a golden chance to kill the man who had wrought all her misery – and she was not going to miss it!

With Slade dead, Kate would be avenged and the whole struggle aboard the Margaret could be brought to a swift end.

Even as she hurried to join Finch, she could see that he was struggling, for Slade was a formidable swordsman. She was two yards away when Slade thrust his sword clean through the chest of the ship's master. Finch, who had kept her alive when the Catherine sank beneath them, was dying; and though she might rend the skies with her screams, she could not save him. The brave seafarer staggered towards her, his lifeblood pouring out onto the deck. As he sank to his knees, gasping out his last breath, she yelled his name in despair.

Slade knew it was her at once and swivelled to meet her. Eleanor threw herself at him, knife flashing. With contemptuous ease, he blocked the furious slash of her knife and cracked the hilt of his sword into her temple.

Seeing her collapse, stunned, to the floor, he loomed over her with sword raised.

"God's blood! How long have I waited for this moment?" he cried.

"Too long, you pissing fool; you waited too long!" shrieked Bess Fisher, stabbing Slade through the side with her long knife.

With an angry grunt of pain, he swung his sword arm around, to carve across Bess's breast and she fell to the deck.

Eleanor, head spinning, struggled to stay conscious, the vision from her one good eye clouded. Slade swayed above her, clearly hurt, but still alive and roundly cursing both women. When her sight cleared a little, she saw only the grimace on his face as he lifted his sword to drive it down into her.

Blind rage forced her up onto her knees, probing with her blade for a mortal wound. Though he towered over her, with sword raised, he seemed powerless to strike. Stabbing him twice in the thigh, she stared in triumph at the crimson cascade spilling down his leg. As she slumped back to the deck, she didn't care that he would impale her upon his sword; because she knew that, whatever he did to her now, he would still bleed to death.

Slade stood, as if spellbound, watching the blood pump from his leg at an ever-increasing rate. Lying there helpless beneath him, Eleanor witnessed every twitch and shudder, every last spasm of his dying body until finally, he sank down on his haunches and slid, lifeless, onto the bloody deck.

Head pounding, Eleanor crawled across to Bess who, despite her terrible wounds, appeared to be alive. Flopping down beside her, Eleanor whispered: "By the Virgin, what does it take to kill you?"

"You owe me another life now, lady," breathed Bess. "I've earned my freedom… that's certain…"

But the tremor in her voice betrayed her; and in the depths of those dark brown eyes, Eleanor read her fate.

"Stay with me," Bess pleaded, in a hoarse whisper. "I pray you, let me not die alone."

Though Eleanor had no reason to care, God help her, she could not leave Bess. Gripping the young woman's hand in hers, she held it tightly while all around them the battle for the ship passed into its death throes. Only when Bess breathed no more, did Eleanor release her hand, for she knew in her soul that they were both hewn from the same heartwood. Alone, without the patient love of her family, Eleanor Elder might so easily have lived the life of Bess Fisher. When Bess died, she died a little too.

Part Seven: A Royal Landing

55

7th November 1483 in the morning, at Handfast Castle

It was a gloomy morning but it matched their predicament well enough. They had only two choices: surrender and be hanged, or fight to the death – so, no choice at all really…

"How long do you think can we last?" asked Will.

"As long as that great door lasts!" said Hooper.

"That won't be long then!" scoffed Will.

"And it'll get bloody after that!" agreed Hal.

"Caught like eels in a sodding trap!" grumbled Conal.

John let them talk. Though it would change nothing, it was better to let them work their fears out in the open. It always helped him too to hear the thoughts of his most trusted men.

"Assume they'll break through that rotten excuse for a door," he told them. "What then?"

"We cut the legs off the bastards, one by one, until there are none left," declared Conal.

"What if they take the doorway and get into the hall?" asked John.

"Then we fall back to the tower," said Will. "They'll have trouble crossing that narrow bridge! It's rotten as hell."

"But they've crossbows," said Hal. "Once they're at the top of the keep they can pick us off at their pleasure."

"Alright, so we fall back to the top of the keep then," said Will. "Only one spiral stair to defend – we could hold out for days!"

Hal was about to respond but John held up his hand to end the discussion.

"I think what Hal was about to say was: 'What are we holding out for? What might occur, in a few days, that hasn't happened yet?'"

"Well, obviously, Henry of Richmond should arrive," declared Will. "That is why we're here at all, coz, isn't it? We hold out for Henry Tudor's landing."

"But what if he doesn't come?" asked John.

"Well, he's supposed to, isn't he?" said Will.

"Aye, but the noble Duke of Buckingham was supposed to bring his retainers from the west to join us," groaned Hooper, "and now his head's struck off!"

"Let's say that Henry does come," said John. "Why would he come up here?"

Seeing that his question confused them, he added: "Henry Tudor doesn't know about this place at all – he doesn't even know that we hold it, let alone that we're in trouble."

"So what will he do?" asked Will.

"If he comes at all," said John, "he'll wait. He'll be waiting for us to tell him how things stand in the town. He most certainly won't risk a landing unless he knows how strong the king's forces are and where they'll be. And, since we're stopped up in here, we can't tell him what he needs to know…"

"What about a signal beacon from the top of the keep?" suggested Hal.

"Aye, but would Henry see that as a greeting, or a warning?" asked John.

"Well, what about those on the Margaret," said Will. "They could tell him, coz."

"Aye, they could, Will, except they don't whether we still hold the castle or not. All they can tell Henry is that they don't know who holds the castle. So what does he do then? Send men up here? As things are, they would be easily cut down by Walter Nevil, I think."

"If he still lives, lord," said Hal.

"Oh, you can be sure that wound didn't kill Sir Walter," said John. "He has a neck like an ox!"

"I still think we could retreat across the foot bridge to the tower and destroy the bridge," said Will. "He could never take the tower; he'd have to starve us out."

"Or he could simply burn the bridge himself and leave us here to rot," said John. "Not a happy ending, Will…"

"So let's just open the door and go out fighting!" snarled Conal.

"And when you say 'go out', you mean die," said Will.

"I'd rather die with a bloody scian in my hand than starve to death!" grumbled the Irishman.

"I'd rather not die at all!" retorted Hal.

"You're gonna die anyway," argued Conal.

"Conal has a point," said Will. "If we could make a run to the stables, we'd have a chance at least. Walter's men had a few horses, didn't they?"

"A small chance, coz," said John. "There wouldn't be enough mounts for all of us – and anyone on foot would be hunted down more easily in the open.

"Then we're all dead men," replied Conal.

"Lord!" cried Alain, who was on watch outside on the tower rampart. "Ships!"

John stood up and moved out onto the wooden platform, a sudden hope kindled in his heart. The others shuffled out with him as every man was eager to cram into the small space.

"Hal! You've sharp eyes," said John. "Whose ships are they?"

Hal eased forward to the parapet and squinted at the vessels approaching from the west.

"The lead ship flies the flag of the Duke of Brittany," said Hal. "And its fellow flies a banner with the... royal arms and a red dragon upon it!"

"It's him then!" cried Will.

"Aye, but two ships..." breathed John, unable to disguise his disappointment. "Only two ships... out of an entire fleet? In God's name, where are the rest of them?"

"Shit," muttered Conal. "We're buggered then..."

Hal's keen eyes were still on the two vessels now entering Studland Bay. "Storm damage, lord, I'd say."

"Where?" asked John.

"Look! A broken foremast on the first ship," said Hal. "You see? And a torn sail on the other."

"Aye, I suppose that might explain what's happened to the rest of the fleet. By Christ, we know all about storms at sea, don't we?"

They waited without another word as the ships sailed slowly to a halt in Studland Bay.

"I'm certain Finch will take the Margaret over to the king's ship as soon as he can," said John. "At least then they'll know where we are."

"Lord..."

"What, Hal?" said John.

"I'm just looking at the Margaret ..."

"And?"

"There are some small boats alongside her."

"Doesn't the Margaret only have one boat?" asked John.

"Yes, lord," said Hal, a tremor in his voice. "And those weren't there yesterday."

For a long moment no-one spoke until Will voiced the question in all their minds. "Could the Margaret have been boarded, do you think?"

"I suppose," said John softly, not even wanting to contemplate the thought. "Can you make out what's happening on deck?"

"It's too far to see, lord," said Hal, a harsh tone revealing that his own dark thoughts echoed those of his master. "But, if it's been boarded…"

"Did anyone see Elias Slade yesterday?" asked John. "Conal? Alain? Will?"

But all those who would have known Slade by sight shook their heads. During the whole of the previous day's struggle, John could not recall even a glimpse of Elias Slade. Roger Cayne had been there in the background, but not Slade. In the fire of battle, he had not even thought about it, but now it seemed most odd. And aboard the Margaret were all of their women folk…

"We have to get to the Margaret, lord!" cried Hal.

With a sigh, John replied: "Aye, but as we've all just agreed, Hal, we'd never even get to the beach…"

"Lord!" cried Alain. "Sir Walter Nevil is gathering his men in the yard…"

"Aye, he's coming in, lads."

"So," asked Hooper, "where do we make our stand?"

56

7th November 1483 in the morning, on the Margaret, in Studland Bay

Watching the crewmen sluice down the deck forced Eleanor to relive every moment of the struggle. They could wash away the blood right enough, but not the memories. Having taken one long, final look at her daughter, laid out with the other victims of the dawn assault, she stood up to gaze along the line of corpses.

She had insisted on wrapping the lass in sailcloth herself. It was an act of love, but also guilt - the last penance of a mother who had failed her child in too many ways to count. She hoped the bodies could be buried at St Nicholas on Studland so that Kate would be forever close to Grave, who had loved her so well. Now she tried to look ahead, for despite all their loss, the Elders were not yet finished. Up on the point, another struggle would be raging – one which would decide the fate of them all.

"Look! Ships!" cried Meg.

"By the Virgin, not more of the devils!" groaned Eleanor, dragging herself to the ship's rail.

"Not little boats, aunt!" said Meg. "Ships!"

"God's blood, Meg!" cried Eleanor. "What do I care about a couple of ships?"

"Aye, but I think one's flying a green and white banner with a dragon upon it! It must be King Henry!"

"And what do I care for that man either?"

"But… surely, the reason we came here at all was for Henry Tudor, wasn't it?" said Meg.

"That was your brother's purpose," said Eleanor. By God though, it was never hers! All she ever wanted was to return to England, but even the cost of that had proven too high – far too high…

"If that bastard Henry had stayed in Brittany, my daughter would still be alive!" raged Eleanor. "Sweet Virgin, Grave would still be alive too! Aye, as would your Thomas, Meg!"

Meg, stern-faced, took the barb head on. "But none of them are alive, aunt! Nor ever will be! They're with God now!"

"Then God is a good deal better off than we are!"

"But, if it's Henry…" Even Meg faltered in the face of Eleanor's cold stare.

"Speak to me no more about that man!" barked Eleanor, turning her head away to gaze instead at Handfast Castle perched high upon the point. "All I care about now is up at the castle: my son, your brother, Hal and all the others…"

"But we can't just ignore Henry!" protested Meg. "We have to tell him what's happened!"

"I don't! Ask your Aunt Emma – she's his… friend, isn't she?"

While Meg marched off along the deck, presumably to find a more amenable aunt, Eleanor focussed her good eye upon the two ships - two ships only… All this sacrifice for two ships! Wasn't the hero, Henry, supposed to be bringing a whole invasion fleet? Another disaster, she supposed; good Christ, the man was doomed to fail!

Turning away to study the castle again, she grew ever more frustrated that she could not discern what was happening up there. The sight of Meg bringing along Emma and Isabel did nothing to raise her spirits. She couldn't help it: whenever she saw Isabel or Meg, she could only think of Kate. Though they were in no way to blame, their presence was a constant reminder of what she now lacked.

"We should send a boat over to Henry," said Lady Radcliffe. "So that he knows we're here."

"You can do as you please," grumbled Eleanor. "But I don't give a damn whether Henry Tudor is here, or not! We've barely finished shrouding our dead and binding up our wounded! And look at what's left of the crew – they're exhausted!"

"I understand," said Lady Radcliffe, "and you know I do, sister for have I not lost a son and a husband?"

Eleanor could hardly argue with that. "Aye, you have..."

To her astonishment, Emma took her in a warm embrace.

"I understand," she whispered. "At first, I blamed everyone: John, you, everyone... but, Ellie, I have learned to think about the living, not the dead. There are still so many that we love both here and at the castle. Whatever we do now, we must keep those folk safe."

For the first time in many years, Eleanor felt as if she had, once again, the love of an older sister. They would never see the world through the same eyes but perhaps, even after so many years, they could truly be sisters once more.

She released Emma, but continued to grip her hand. "Sisters again, Em?" she murmured.

"Aye, sisters again," agreed Lady Radcliffe.

Squinting, Eleanor fixed her eye once more upon the two ships.

"They're not doing much, are they?" she observed.

"But they don't even know where John is, do they?" declared Lady Radcliffe. "They don't know where anyone is – friend or foe! And Studland is swarming with Mayor Cayne's soldiers – King Richard's supporters... But if

Henry knew what was happening, he might be able to help. Even with two ships, he must have quite a number of fighting men…"

"Aye, we have to tell King Henry," said Meg.

Eleanor bit back a sour remark about 'King' Henry. Her sister was right: all that mattered now was helping those at the castle and, if Henry had the means to do so, then perhaps she must go to him.

"If only we knew what was happening up there," she groaned, flexing her legs which had become stiff and cold whilst she stood at the rail. "I'll speak to Master Finch and see what he thinks."

On her way to find Matthew Finch, she passed by the line of corpses again, all laid out along the length of one side of the vessel. Several men were still finishing swabbing down the decks with sea water. Weapons of all sorts had been piled up in a great heap and for a moment she paused, overwhelmed by the sheer number of weapons.

"Sweet Virgin," she murmured, "how did we ever survive the night?"

"By God's will, my lady," answered Matthew, who had moved to join her. "By God's will - and a great measure of courage!"

"Your father, Matthew… I'm so sorry…"

"If he had to die this morning, my lady, I know he'd have been pleased to die protecting those he loved. I'm just sorry we could not save your Kate."

She nodded. "Be glad of what you did do, Matthew. But how do the living fare?"

"Well, my lady, I've eight fit crewmen but they will struggle to sail the ship between them. Of the rest, a few are wounded and like to recover, but at least five others will die before nightfall."

"By Christ! It's even worse than I thought," replied Eleanor, with a shudder, "and what I thought was bad enough..."

Matthew looked across the bay. "He's arrived then," he murmured, "but with only two ships..."

"Aye," she agreed, understanding his bitter tone. "Hardly enough for an invasion, is it? But perhaps enough to rescue John and the others."

She glanced at his crew, some of whom were resting for the first time in many hours.

"If we can, Matthew..."

"We can sail across to Henry's ship," said Matthew, "but I won't ask my crew to do any more. They've shed more than enough blood here."

"Thank you," said Eleanor, pressing his hand.

By the time she returned to the others, Matthew was giving orders and the ship was soon moving with the wind which Eleanor thought seemed to be to their advantage. When they were close enough, Matthew hailed Henry's ship for permission to come alongside.

"Who's going to tell him?" asked Eleanor.

"Since his grace entrusted me with this venture," said Lady Radcliffe, "it should be me."

"Aye, a fair point, sister - and you're better at being tactful... and respectful," agreed Eleanor. "But then again, we are in haste; and I'm better at haste than you are..."

As soon as a gangplank was safely secured and before anyone could stop her, Eleanor strode across and jumped down onto the other ship. The moment she set foot upon the deck, several men converged to intercept her.

"I need to see Henry of Richmond at once!" she announced.

"Who are you to make such demands?" asked an older man, who spoke in a gruff Welsh voice.

Eleanor paused mid-stride. He was right: an introduction was the least he deserved. "I am Lady Eleanor Elder! Now, who are you?"

"I am Jasper Tudor, Earl of Pembroke!" he replied stiffly. "And you look to me like a common whore!"

"Do you know a lot of common whores then?" enquired Eleanor.

Ignoring the jibe, he replied: "You don't look like a lady to me."

"Aye, that's been said before," grumbled Eleanor. "Yet, I am – and I am a lady in a hurry!"

"And how do I know that you are who you say?" Pembroke pressed her.

"My brother, Ned Elder, crushed you at Mortimer's Cross," she growled. "Perhaps you remember him?"

Though he did not react to her taunt, he said: "I look at you – all plastered in blood and filth and I do not see a lady!"

"Does the sight of blood offend you, my lord?"

"On a woman, it most certainly does!"

"As for the state of my dress," snarled Eleanor, "if you cast your eye over our deck you'll see our dead! Because, while you were sleeping, we were fighting, bleeding and dying! So I want to see Henry now, because – now that he's finally arrived - we need him to actually do something!"

"You make no sense, woman! His grace is not to be disturbed – he is exhausted after the storms we've endured."

"Storms? For the love of Christ!" blazed Eleanor. "Don't talk to me of storms! Now get him up – or I shall! Because if he does nothing, John Elder and his men, on Handfast Point over there, will soon be dead!"

"I don't believe you," replied Pembroke.

"Well, you should do, my lord," interrupted another voice. "She's my sister and every word she says is true."

"Lady Radcliffe?" Pembroke muttered.

"Let her speak," said Lady Radcliffe, smiling across at her sister.

Pembroke, though he looked far from happy, turned back to Eleanor.

"What then is the danger, my lady?" he enquired.

"King Richard's men, of course! And the longer we stand around talking, the sooner our men will start dying. You need to send men to relieve the castle - now!"

Staring up at the castle on the point, Pembroke said: "I shall not be sending men ashore at all – especially if our enemies hold the beach!"

"If you don't help them, those at the castle will die!" cried Eleanor. How could the fool not grasp that her son was in mortal danger? And all she had left was her son...

"What matters most is keeping King Henry safe," declared Pembroke.

"Well, he's not King Henry yet!" retorted Eleanor, "And he never will be, if he chooses to abandon those who are fighting for him!"

A murmur around the deck told her that her words had found a degree of favour with some at least.

"Our men are trapped in the castle," continued Eleanor, gritting her teeth. "That's where King Richard's men are!"

But a glance at Pembroke's face told her that the earl remained unconvinced.

"For the love of Christ," she snarled at him, "just give me some men and I'll lead them myself - I know the place well enough!"

The earl's response was to laugh in her face.

"Oh, don't," murmured Lady Radcliffe.

But Eleanor, torn apart by the events of the morning, had heard enough and her fist was already swinging at

Pembroke when a strong hand seized it from behind and returned it firmly, but gently, to her side.

"Not a wise move, lady," murmured a deep voice, close behind her.

Whirling around to see who dared to restrain her, Eleanor stopped open-mouthed, and speechless.

"If the lady's right," said the newcomer, "then we have to support Lord Elder."

Eleanor was staring at the figure standing before her. "René de Merckes," she said softly, unable to drag her eyes from him.

"I'm flattered you remember me," he replied, "after such a… brief meeting."

"Brief, but memorable," murmured Eleanor.

By then Pembroke had hastily roused Henry from his cabin and he joined the others staring up at the point.

"We sent Lord Elder into this, uncle," said Henry. "We cannot simply abandon him!"

"My boat is already in the water, your grace," offered De Merckes.

"By whose authority?" demanded Pembroke.

"Well, Lord Pembroke, it is my boat!" said René.

"Very well, de Merckes," said Henry. "Uncle, prepare to send more men."

"I'll send one of my most trusted captains, your grace," said Pembroke.

"With your grace's permission," said René, "I'll join my men?"

Henry waved him away, but then noticed the dishevelled Eleanor. "Who is that?" he asked.

"I am Lady Eleanor Elder - a member of the Elder family that you've not yet met, my lord."

"Your grace…" warned Pembroke.

Eleanor pointed at De Merckes. "And I'm going with him."

"No!" cried everyone, save one.

"She knows the land and where the enemy will be," explained De Merckes, holding out his hand to her. "And I've fought with her before…"

Though most folk upon deck were horrified, none dared gainsay De Merckes. And his reasoning made sense; without some local knowledge, his men might well blunder into trouble.

Gripping her hand, René dragged Eleanor away before Henry decided to stop them. The crowd of lords and crewmen parted to allow them to cross the deck and clamber over the side down into the waiting longboat.

"Fought together?" she hissed at De Merckes. "As I recall, we almost fought each other!"

"I thought you needed saving!" he told her. "You looked just angry enough to slap the king!"

"I am!"

Her bitter response brought a frown to René's face. "What's happened?" he asked.

"Too much," was all she permitted herself to say; for she had to hold herself in check if she wanted to see her son rescued.

De Merckes dropped down into the boat first and then lifted Eleanor down - much to the amazement of his men.

"Don't worry," he told Eleanor, "you can tell me all you know on the way over to the shore and then just stay in the boat."

"I shan't be staying in the boat," she growled, "and I'll need a sword – something light… because I'm out of practice…"

For a moment, René hesitated but then, perhaps reading the anguish in her face, he called out: "Make haste, my friends - and someone find the lady a weapon!"

57

7th November 1483 in the morning, at Handfast Castle

Still the axes pounded against the door – and it could not hold much longer. Not for the first time that morning, John lamented the absence of a portcullis. Once, in the castle's golden years – if it ever had any – there would have been a portcullis, but not now. The sound of the axe blows was changing, as more of the timber was splintered away. Soon their enemies would be amongst them and his plan, such as it was, would be put to the test. The wounded had been helped or carried up the stair to the second floor where they could rest in the two bed chambers – indeed it might be their final place of rest. Water and food was stored up there too, in the care of the local men: Audley, Cheverly and Twynho.

Clasping hands with each of his trusted men who remained by the door, John gave them a nod of respect. For a few moments there was silence as each man prepared himself for what was to come. When a great shard of oak spun out of the door and flew at the opposite wall, their lord gave a grim smile.

"To your places, lads," he said. "You know what to do; but only upon my signal…"

They scattered to their posts until only he and Conal remained. "Ready, old friend?" he asked.

"Always ready for a bit of a scrap, lord," grinned the Irishmen.

As the door was finally hacked apart the pair withdrew up the stair, where they would make their stand. The first floor doorway was simply too broad to defend so, from the start, John decided to cede the whole floor, including the hall, to Sir Walter. They would try to defend only the one stair leading to the top storey of the keep. Of course, with a plentiful supply of arrows, it would all have been different; but God had willed otherwise.

Great pieces of the door were smashed aside as the attackers crashed through. Sir Walter Nevil, showing that he was not a man to let others take the lead, was first into the keep. Many others followed but John did not see them for he was already waiting at the top of the spiral stair.

It was a narrow stair and, in places, the stone treads were worn enough to make any man take care, unless of course he was being assaulted by a crazed Irishman and his lord. After their initial surge up the steps ended in blood the besiegers fell back to the landing to nurse their wounds. A great deal of shouting followed, but no further clash of arms. Since John had ordered the removal of several planks from the foot bridge, Sir Walter would not be able to reach the tower unless he replaced them. Thus he could not shower the defenders with crossbow bolts from the tower. Reckoning that Sir Walter was not a very patient man, John did not expect him to wait long enough to starve them into submission.

If the knight wanted to capture his rebels, he would have to fight his way up the stair to get to them. He would expect a swift outcome because he had the men to achieve it. By sending fresh men up every few minutes, he could sustain his assault for hours, whilst John had only a handful capable of defending his position – and those few would eventually tire. Only by inflicting the heaviest possible casualties upon their opponents, could they even dream of surviving. It would be bloody...

When the onslaught began again, the attackers thrust pollaxes before them, prodding and stabbing. But, hampered by the narrowness of the stair, they could be kept at bay by two men working together. At first John, Conal and Hooper shared the defence between them but, since John's ribs were still sore from his earlier wound, he was forced to rely upon Conal to take the lead. With the ferocity of the attack continuing unabated, others were also required to take their turn. By midday, after almost two hours of relentless fighting, Sir Walter broke off the attack. Though several of John's men at arms had suffered wounds, he still held the stair.

"We've blunted his axe!" laughed Conal.

"It's just a respite, that's all," said John.

"Aye, but he's lost a few of his best men," said Hooper.

"Perhaps," said John, "but not enough… and we're tiring too fast. You both know how it goes from here… we start to make mistakes and then we start to die…"

"You are one miserable captain, John Elder!" scoffed Hooper, with a weary laugh.

But John, staring at the top of the steps, made a sudden motion for him to be quiet. Had he heard the scrape of a boot on stone? Hooper and Conal regarded him in puzzled silence.

With a sigh, John relaxed again, but the next moment, there was a great roar as three men charged to the top of the stair, one after another. Their sole aim would be to gain a few feet of space on the landing. If they could but hold out for a few moments, the others would ascend behind them. Then, as a unit, they would surge out into the passage, forcing back John's valiant men at arms and the defence of the keep would be over.

"Hold them!" bellowed John. "In God's name, hold them!"

But it was no good – and he knew it: there were now too many pressing forward against them.

"Is it time, lord?" cried Conal.

"We can only do this once!" barked John, battering the man before him and feeling his ribs tighten with pain.

"If we don't do it soon," replied Hooper, "it'll be too damned late!"

Looking across to Alain, who had been waiting at the far end of the passageway throughout the fight, John bellowed: "Now, Alain! The signal, now! Give the signal!"

Seeing Alain disappear up the steps to the battlements, John turned back to the fray, where one of his Breton mercenaries was down on his knees. While Hooper dragged the man back, Conal tried to fill the gap, but to no avail. Very soon their position would be overcome. Sir Walter himself had joined his vanguard to force home the attack in one brutal push. The belligerent knight was scarcely a yard from John when a cry of alarm brought a grimace of doubt to his bloodstained face. For the first time that day, Sir Walter's resolve faltered, as he and his men were distracted by raucous cries from below them.

"An Elder! An Elder!" John too heard the shouts ring out as the royal soldiers began to fall back down the stair — some slipping on the bloodied steps.

"Get after them, lads!" roared John, leading the pursuit.

Battering his way down to the landing by the hall, he found a mass of heaving, blood-soaked bodies. Whilst Sir Walter's men at arms had been pre-occupied with storming the stairwell, Will, Hal and several others – upon Alain's signal - had replaced the missing boards on the bridge and hurried across it to attack the besiegers in the rear. Thus Sir Walter's men were now trapped between Will's small band and John's cohort descending the stair. Several were killed in the first shock of the attack and now they were hard-pressed from two sides.

"Retreat!" bellowed Sir Walter, his wrath echoing around the walls of the keep.

Pleased though John was to see the royal men at arms beginning to flee, he knew they could not be allowed to retreat in good order. Still greatly outnumbered, he must inflict as much damage as possible upon his harassed enemies. Above the deafening clamour in the enclosed passage, he could only shout his orders in the hope that his men could hear.

"Will, Conal! On me! Drive them out! Drive them out!"

The three men, all seasoned mercenaries, pressed forward. Wielding his pollaxe without mercy, John punched at a knight who tried to turn and face him. Blow fell upon savage blow until his doughty opponent was hammered backwards and John leapt forward over him. In his left hand was a long knife which he used to gouge or gut any opponent who did not succumb to his axe. In moments they were pressing through the shattered doorway to the keep, and once outside, they harried the king's men back down the steps. One or two slid off and fell into the cobbled yard.

As his men fell back in disarray, Sir Walter was cursing to the heavens as he tried to rally them. The suddenness of Will's ambush and the force of John's assault had weakened Sir Walter's force but not destroyed it. Thus, John's first, swift assessment of the bloody mêlée before him gave him little encouragement.

"Keep close order!" bellowed John for, if they did not, their enemy's superior numbers would swiftly defeat them. From the door of the keep they forced their opponents back halfway across the yard, but as soon as the battle was joined at close quarters, their progress slowed. And, in the open yard, the numbers against them soon began to tell.

Glancing around him, he found Conal protecting his left side and Will his right, while Hooper was fighting a stern rear guard with Hal and two of the Breton mercenaries. The Dorset men, Twynho, Audley and others were somewhere in their midst with Alain and the remaining Bretons. His men were doing well and keeping together as a tight fighting unit, but for how much longer?

"Will," he shouted. "Have you seen Mayor Cayne? Is he killed, do you know?"

"He wasn't there when we came at their backs, coz!" replied Will.

"I've not seen him either, lord," said Conal, as he thrust his scian at a new adversary.

But John soon lost all interest in the fate of Poole's mayor, because his men were now coming under attack from three sides. As he had feared, they had failed to inflict enough carnage upon their opponents to destroy their will to resist. Gradually, they were being encircled there in the yard. Even so, Walter must have known that John would not surrender. He might defeat John's men in combat but he would pay the highest possible price in blood to do so. His next shouted command boomed out around the walled yard.

"Cut them down like the rebel chaff they are! Drive the beggars into the sea!"

So that was to be their fate; Sir Walter was no longer trying to defeat them, only to drive them back past the keep towards the ruined chapel. John had no need to remind his comrades what lay beyond the chapel. Nothing lay there, save a sheer, crumbling cliff and a plummet to certain death.

"We're sore pressed, lord!" cried Conal.

"You got somewhere else to be?"

"No!" retorted the Irishman, "but I hope you've got a-" He broke off to parry a blow with his thin blade, aiming a wild slash at his adversary to force him back.

"I was hoping you had another plan!" he gasped.

Hacking two men aside with a succession of savage blows from his pollaxe, John still found himself almost surrounded. Conal, staying close beside him, darted forward to deliver a mortal blow with his scian already bright with blood.

"Hah! I only had one plan!" shouted John, "And we're living it right now!"

58

7ᵗʰ November 1483, on the shore at Studland Bay

The moment the boat grazed the stony shore, René leapt out, with Eleanor following close behind. Watching René's men cross the open beach, she was oddly impressed. This was no untrained rabble; alert and watchful, they moved as one, not a pack of lone warriors. René de Merckes clearly knew what he was about.

"We can wait for the others among the trees," she told him, gazing back into the bay at the second craft, which was still some distance offshore.

Shepherding his comrades into the cover of a thick hazel grove beyond the beach, René sent several men to watch the nearby track. On the boat Eleanor had told him all she could recall about the castle and the approaches to it.

"So, if the castle is not taken," he said, "we can attack the besiegers; but we'll need some help, I think, from those within…"

"If John Elder still lives, he will come to your aid," she said.

"You seem very sure of your nephew, lady?"

"As sure as I am of myself," said Eleanor, "and my son is there too – neither man will let you down."

"And if the castle is already breached?" asked René. "Have you thought about that?"

"Aye, I thought of little else while your men were straining at their oars!" murmured Eleanor.

"So you know perhaps, it may be that… nothing can be done?"

"There's always something to be done, René – if you have the will…"

Leaving her remark unchallenged, he asked: "What about the track up to the castle – is it safe?"

"No, it isn't! You should prepare for an ambush before we even reach the castle," she told him. "Don't forget: the king's men too will have seen your ships. They may be expecting us."

René nodded. "And their best chance of stopping us, is before we get anywhere near the castle."

"Aye, and there are many places that could happen," she added, "for the track cuts right through the forest. Many of the trees are thin and wiry, but sometimes closely packed."

He nodded with a smile.

"I amuse you?" growled Eleanor.

"No, I am just surprised, my lady, that you see the world through the eyes of a soldier."

"Not the eyes of a pirate, at least!" she scoffed.

"What is so wrong with being a pirate?" he asked. "Who is not a pirate these days?"

"Aye, Master Finch told me that any man could be a pirate…" she said and the memory of Finch's death brought back all her bitterness.

"Of course, it's true," he agreed. "Was not your own great Earl of Warwick the very best of pirates?"

"Warwick!" Eleanor spat out the word with distaste. "The Warwick I remember was many things, but not great… I lost a husband because of him. Virgin's blood, he did his best to destroy the whole Elder family!"

Only with difficulty, did she rein in her fury. "But still… some of us still live, while Warwick slowly rots away in his grave…"

"I'm very glad you are on my side, my lady," said René, his eyes meeting hers.

Finding herself staring at him a little too long, she turned away, irritated that she had revealed so private a moment to a stranger.

"Aye, today we fight together," she said. "But then today you're not a pirate, are you? Just a mercenary – a man for hire... Is being a soldier for hire, I wonder, any better than being a pirate?"

"Both earn me some coin, my lady," he said shortly. "And don't tell me you're here because you believe Henry of Richmond is your true king!"

She noted his raised voice and slightly sharper tone. "No," she conceded. "I don't care a shit for Richmond! I'm here for my family - only that."

"Yet, whatever our reasons, as I said, we are on the same side."

"Aye, but you and I, René, could never be allies for long."

"God's breath!" he exclaimed. "Must you challenge every word? What do you want from me, lady?"

But of course, she didn't know that. Since the day she was born, Eleanor had been ruled by raw, often conflicting, emotions. Kate's death had rocked her to the core, yet it was not grief that troubled her now. Encountering René de Merckes again had thrown her heart into turmoil. The spark - kindled at her first sight of him when he leapt onto the deck of the Catherine - could not, it seemed, be so easily extinguished. Even the grim fingers of death, though they pursued her like a plague, could not snuff out the flame.

When the Breton's hand touched her arm, she gave a start. "What?" she snapped.

Confounded by her reaction, he simply pointed. Looking up, she found that while she had been searching her soul, the other boat had landed on the shore.

"Aye, I see it," she told him, curt and dismissive.

"My lady, you should stay here," he said at once. His tone was more formal now; he was saying the words his men expected to hear.

"I didn't come here to stand about and wring my hands!" she retorted.

"I must insist, my lady!"

"Insist away," snarled Eleanor. "It'll make no difference to what I do!"

"I could bind you to a tree!" he cried.

"You could try!" she blazed back at him, borrowed sword clenched in her hand.

Their fiery altercation was interrupted by the arrival of the Earl of Pembroke's captain.

Waving him into the trees, René told Eleanor: "This is Cradoc. He's Welsh, but Pembroke likes him."

Cradoc laughed. "You must be Lady Eleanor!" he cried.

Eleanor winced. Why did the man have to shout so?

"You've a nasty wound on your forehead, lady," said the Welshman. "Are you in pain?"

"Aye, all the time," grumbled Eleanor.

"The lady is rather impatient," René confided to Cradoc.

"The lady is furious!" declared Eleanor.

"Promise me, at least, that you will stay close to me at all times," pleaded René.

"She can't come with us," said Cradoc.

"Don't you start!" cried Eleanor.

"Lord Pembroke was most definite about that."

"Well, Master Cradoc, you may serve the Earl of Pembroke, but I don't," said Eleanor. "Now, are we going or not?"

What did they expect her to do? Sit under the trees and think of nothing but the cold, betrayed body of her daughter?

René took her gently by the arm and pulled her to one side. "Promise me," he said.

"Sweet Virgin! I promise!" she barked at him and stormed off towards the track.

Of course neither René nor Cradoc could allow her to take the lead – nor did she wish to – but at least she had them on the move. And she did stay with René, partly because she felt safer with him… but also because, well… because…

They made swift progress up the track, reckoning that it was as good a way as any of reducing the impact of any ambush. There were about two score of them – enough, Eleanor hoped, to make a difference. Since Slade and Clynt were both dead, only Mayor Cayne remained to be defeated; and, from what John had told her, the mayor would be a far less dangerous opponent than either of the others. There was every reason for hope and the further they advanced up the track without incident, the more confident she became. Though Henry Tudor might not make a successful landing here, his men could at least ensure the safety of what remained of her family.

It took only a single crossbow bolt to cause her newly-acquired belief to evaporate. Its victim, one of René's men, was hurled into her with such force that she too was knocked clean off her feet. Screaming with rage, she rolled onto her knees but stayed there as chaos unfolded along the track. Cradoc and René were both bellowing orders as assailants raced out of the trees from both sides of the track. Wielding clubs and knives, the attackers cried out for King Richard and St George, as they set about their victims. A further crossbow bolt plucked aside another man – and, in response, her comrades scattered into the trees where a brutal, disjointed mêlée ensued.

Getting warily to her feet, she drew out her knife and gripped it in her left hand with the sword already clutched in her right. Glancing down at the narrow-bladed sword, she frowned. It was so long since she had even lifted such a weapon. Did she still have the strength, or the speed, to use it? Or even the will? For without that, she would not last very long…

A hand seized her by the shoulder and, thinking it was René, she hesitated. As soon as she looked up, she saw that it was not René. Breaking free, she swung her sword wildly at her assailant, but drew from him only a guffaw in response as the weapon flew from her hand and disappeared into the trees. As he swung his cudgel, she groaned with frustration and only evaded the blow because she was still off balance.

The momentum of her mighty, if ineffectual, swing took her a yard away from him. Wasting no time, she ran off the track and tried to lose herself in the woodland. The trees nearby were mainly hazel – unmanaged in Simon's time and allowed to run wild. Here they were so numerous, they encroached upon the track and, in some places, formed an almost impenetrable barrier. Because many of the trunks were so spindly, a woman could squeeze between them with ease. Her pursuer, however, broad-shouldered and tall, found it more difficult. In the open, his great cudgel was a deadly weapon, but it would not serve him so well in the close confines of the forest.

Wandering some distance from the path, Eleanor headed for the most densely packed stand of trees she could see. Even she struggled to force her way between the trunks, but if she hoped to discourage him, she was soon disappointed. Perhaps he had decided there was more to be gained from pursuing a defenceless woman than returning to an uncertain outcome at the skirmish. Even so, she reasoned, there was no chance that he could get to her – not without an axe at least.

With a groan, she watched him take the axe from his belt... a small forester's tool – handy in a brawl, but even more useful in his present situation. Scrambling further back, deep within the hazel thicket, she stood motionless, hoping he would lose sight of her amid the phalanx of grey-green trunks. But then she heard the rhythmic, determined beat of steel upon young wood, as he began to clear a path towards her. So, where should she confront her adversary?

Though she caught only an occasional glimpse of him through the scantily-clad autumn branches, she could always tell his position by the dull, repetitive thud of the axe. Her movement was critical now; she must let him come to her; yard by yard, step by step, she must bring him to a place of her choosing. He might view her as a timid, terrified woman, but she was now the stalker and he, the unwitting prey.

Squeezing between saplings which would snag a man's clothing and weapons, she continued to watch him. The closer she could lure him back towards the track, the more chance there was that her comrades would find her. Every time he hammered his axe into wood, Eleanor took a step, matching her pattern of movement to his. Behind her, in her right hand, she gripped the hilt of her knife ever more tightly, as she continued to slip through gaps too narrow for him. But he was nearer now - near enough to see clearly; near enough to smell. Studying his clothing, she was relieved to see that he wore no breastplate, just a thick, leather jerkin. Mind you, even that, if sufficiently padded beneath, would most likely stop her short-bladed knife.

By God, she would have to get in close; but how close would he let her get? She would have almost no time to strike... Beads of sweat rolled down her forehead: one stung her good eye, another dropped from her chin onto a brown, curling leaf below. Only for a moment was she distracted, but it was enough. She mouthed a silent curse when she found him only a yard away. Nerves frayed, she held her breath, waiting for his next move. Either he would take a pace to his right to chop through another hazel sapling, or he would try to strike her with the axe from where he stood.

Eleanor unsure whether to curse or pray, did a little of both…

"Aye, there's courage for you!" she raged at him. "Take your blade to a mere slip of a half-blind lass, would you, you turd-faced, lice-ridden excuse for a man? And may sweet Mary, the Holy Virgin, keep me from being struck down by that fucking axe!"

Wild-eyed, he lifted his weapon to hack at another trunk and Eleanor breathed again. Of course, he should have killed her; because the moment his axe was embedded in the hazel, Eleanor let out a scream and stepped forward to bring her knife up in a blur of movement. Lunging with all her strength, she drove the blade under his raised arm. Lancing through flesh, ribs and lung, it was the perfect, mortal thrust; except that she could not pull it out.

Face contorted with pain and rage, her opponent levered out the axe blade and swung it back at her head. Abandoning her knife, Eleanor dived down into the bracken, praying the axe would miss her head. It didn't.

As she went down, the blade of the axe scored across her crown and sliced through her shoulder. Pain engulfed her and she almost passed out. When she tried to rise up, she felt warm, wet blood dribbling down her forehead. Swaying like a drunkard, her vision began to blur as she peered through the trees and moaned, for another man was only three or four yards away.

Legs buckling under her, she fell down into the bracken again.

"May the Virgin save me from going blind again," she mumbled. "Holy Mary, hear me, I beg you: I'd rather die!"

59

7th November 1483, early afternoon, at Handfast Castle on Studland

While his battered and bloodied line retreated, step by agonising step, John crouched, with Conal, alongside the blackened chapel wall.

"Fifteen more paces, lord!" cried Conal, darting a worried look behind them, "If we fall back any more, they'll have us over that edge!"

"Aye," said John. "I see that!"

Staring beyond the mass of Sir Walter's men at arms, he studied the open gateway and an implausible idea began to take root in his head. The gateway, though almost impossible to defend, would surely give them a better chance than being driven off a cliff! It would take some doing though – and a helping hand from the Lord, he reckoned. But, in a strange way, perhaps their dire position might just give his men the strength to do it; for nothing moved a man quite like the threat of imminent death.

"Pass the word!" said John, "our right flank falls back, while we press forward on our left to the stables. From there we make for the gate."

"The gate, lord?" hissed the Irishman. "But, in the open… outside the walls, they'll cut us to pieces!"

"Not if we stay at the gate and hold them there," John argued, stooping to snatch up a discarded pollaxe from the ground.

"But we can't defend the gate from the outside, lord!" cried Conal, aghast. "Christ knows we can't defend it at all!"

411

John's reply was savage. "You wanted a plan! Well, that's it - unless you'd rather be pushed off the damned cliff!"

Conal puffed out his cheeks and then, after only a moment's hesitation, he gave a shrug and scuttled away, moving swiftly from man to man behind their line. Whilst his comrade passed the word, John contemplated how their objective could be achieved. If they could force a path keeping the stables at their back, they might just be able to fight their way to the gate. But, if their intention was too obvious, Sir Walter had only to despatch half a dozen of his best men to defend the open gateway and thwart them in one simple step. The drive towards the stable must seem like an end in itself, as if they were making for the horses. The race for the gate must come as a shock tactic - aye, and one which could only be executed at the very last moment.

He glanced across to the right flank where Hooper, Will and Hal led what would become their rear guard as they pivoted across to the stables. The moment he and Conal launched their attack on the left, that would be the signal for Will and his fellows to fall back on the right. Encouraging the royal men at arms to advance on that flank was an essential step in turning Sir Walter's force. Yet, the rear guard was at grave risk of being cut off from the rest and killed; his cousin and the others would thus be in mortal peril.

Muttering a silent prayer for them all, John gulped in several lungfuls of salty air and took a tighter grip upon his weapons – a pollaxe now held in each hand. As soon as Conal returned to his side, they eased past two Bretons ahead of them and began their onslaught. Chopping down the first man he faced with a blow to an exposed neck, John pressed forward, careless of flesh and bone crushed beneath his boots.

Seeing the space open up to John's left, Conal carved a path to the stable doors. Slicing his scian hither and thither, he caused panic amongst many of those who were less well-harnessed. Never before would they have encountered such murderous precision with a length of steel. Most recoiled and sheered away in terror, leaving only one man wielding a heavy mace. But one was not enough to halt the dread Irishman's progress. Though he swung his mace with grim intent, his resistance ended in a bitter scream when Conal's scian half-severed his hand at the wrist. Wresting the mace from his victim's trembling fingers, the Irish warrior charged on.

Breathing deep, John went with him, bringing his axe down hard upon his next opponent. Glaring at the fellow as he staggered backwards, John pursued him, with shocking, mortal blows that no man's body was made to withstand. Either side of him, he knew that Conal and the Bretons would be doing the same. Killing was a brutal, Godless trade.

An anxious glance behind reassured him that Will and Hooper were managing their part well. Then, clear as a hawk's cry, he heard Sir Walter's voice yell out: "They're making for the stables!"

Too late, thought John; Sir Walter was far too late, for their merciless advance had already driven as far as the stable doors and now it was time for the last gambit. Exchanging a look with Conal, he clasped the Irishman's hand once more, lest it should be the very last time. Both knew it was not a moment for caution, or half-measures; if their next push made no impact, there would not be another.

"You ready?" cried John.

"I'd sooner be in a stew somewhere!" yelled Conal.

"Stop complaining, you mad Irish bastard!" he roared, as he launched a fresh attack, pounding his axes against breastplate and helm.

Hearing his battle cry: "An Elder, an Elder!" being taken up by his comrades, he strode forward again with renewed vigour, legs pumping and arms swinging. The two warriors now bludgeoned a path away from the stable building and into the main press of Sir Walter's men at arms. No plan, no method and no finesse – just eyes fixed firmly on the gate.

John always thought himself to be a good man, but sometimes, he had found, for a good man to prevail, he must discover the dark monster within him. This was such a time… Every man who stood in his path would be hacked into oblivion – until he had no more breath, or strength, to continue.

Using all the barbarous skills they had acquired as mercenaries, the two men gouged at eyes, ripped at bellies and bowels, or cracked skulls in their merciless attempt to tear a bloody gash in the enemy ranks. Relentless and pitiless, the two men cared not whether the broken line reformed or not, as long as they were able to burst through it, dragging the rest of their comrades with them. In the face of such savagery, Sir Walter's men were compelled to give ground.

Yet blood was spilled and flesh torn on both sides for one of the Bretons had fallen, bleeding heavily from a head wound; another fought on, despite a deep gash on his leg. Though the carnage wrought in the enemy ranks was far greater, John knew that their disarray would not last for long. He prayed it would last long enough to allow John's exhausted men to reach the gate.

Though they had scattered many before them, he saw that a ring of men had formed up around Sir Walter. Such men would be a different prospect altogether: at ease upon the battlefield, they would have no fear at all when faced by a couple of armed men, however strong or skilled. Nevertheless, when he saw them gathered around their leader, John almost laughed with joy. Sir Walter clearly believed that John was attempting to resolve the battle at a stroke by taking on the knight himself - which suited John very well.

Instead of continuing towards Sir Walter, he suddenly skirted around the powerful knot of men and carried on past them to the gateway with Conal. A sudden cry of alarm from Sir Walter told John when his rival realised his error. For the first time, John heard a note of desperation in the knight's voice as he bellowed: "To the gateway!"

By then, of course, John and Conal had already reached their goal and were taking up a position in front of the shattered gates, to allow their surviving men to join them. As they reformed into a line two deep, John was relieved to see the last two, Will and Hooper, join the rest. The gateway was not wide; and there was some hope at least in trying to hold such a narrow gap.

Sir Walter, perhaps assuming that the rebels would simply flee though the open gates, was taken by surprise for a second time. Gradually though, it must have dawned upon him that John intended to try to hold the gate. Abruptly he withdrew his men further back into the yard and, John, for an awful moment, feared that crossbows would be brought up. If that happened, all their blood and effort would have been in vain. When no crossbows appeared, John, despite his initial relief, began to wonder why.

Nevertheless, he was glad of the respite, which meant that several of his wounded men could bind up their wounds outside the gate in the shelter of the wall. Though they were all dog-tired, he reckoned that Walter's men must be too – especially since their casualties had undoubtedly been heavier. No-one could fight so hard and so long without a break. He could only pray that few of the royal soldiers would be keen to make an attempt on the gate that afternoon.

Moving to stand beside Will, he murmured: "You alright, coz?"

Will grinned back at him, holding up a cut and bleeding left hand.

"Well, get it seen to then!" urged John.

"Thought I'd wait till I had a matching one on my right hand," said Will. "What now then?"

"When they've had a little rest, they may try to force us back through the gateway…"

"And that won't work because…"

"We won't let them," said John. "But, if we can't hold them, Conal and I will go after Sir Walter…"

"What are we doing here, John?" asked Will.

"We've come to put a new king on the throne, Will."

"We're not going to though, are we?"

"No, coz, we're not - not this time."

"But Henry's here now – he could still lead the revolt."

"With only two ships" said John. "There'll be no revolt here…"

"So what are we going to do?"

"I thought we might take back this castle…"

"How? You do know we're still outnumbered… we could still make a run for it though, down to the shore…."

"You know better, coz," said John, "we'd never get there."

"Lord Elder!" said Hooper, but his warning was hardly necessary. It seemed that Sir Walter's men were more resilient that he expected, for they were charging across the cobbled yard, voices snarling and boots snapping upon the stone. Attacking with enormous force, Sir Walter put his best men in the vanguard, seeking to shatter John's line with a single, overwhelming thrust.

It should have been a brief, unequal struggle: Sir Walter's well-harnessed, battle-hardened knights against a smaller number of lightly-armoured men. But because of the narrowness of the old gateway, Sir Walter could not bring his greater numbers to bear. By arraying his strongest, most experienced men across the gateway, John hoped that they had at least a small chance of matching their opponents.

In the first few bloody moments of impact, John was rocked back, desperately parrying each blow. Death stared down on him when a pollaxe deflected off one of his own and thudded into his breastplate. But the deflection proved vital, lessening the blow. Seizing upon the reprieve, John battered his opponent's helmeted head until his two axes knocked the man off his feet. The vicious-looking pollaxe blade might cut or maim, but it was the hammer blows that splintered bone and crushed a man's vital organs. Thus paralysed, no man could fight back.

In such a cramped space where men fought shoulder to shoulder, swords could only be wielded as clubs. Axe and mace brought men to their knees and any man who fell became yet another obstacle for the tiring combatants to overcome. As long as his own key men stayed on their feet, John reckoned their ragged line might hold. The longer they absorbed the royal assaults, the more likely it was that they could force Sir Walter to fall back. On the other hand, it might take only one man at arms to be badly wounded for John's entire line to fold. But in the end, it wasn't just one man who suffered a grievous wound.

Hearing a sudden cry of alarm from Hal to his right, John stabbed a glance beyond Hooper, where his cousin Will should have been but wasn't. Will was down and crawling on the bloody ground on all fours. Trapped at the opposite end of the line, John was powerless to help, but saw Hal thrust up a sword to block an axe aimed at Will's head. Though his swift action saved Will, the axe slid off Hal's sword and bit deep into his left arm. Crying out in agony, Hal too went down.

"Hooper!" roared John, desperation in his voice.

But Lady Radcliffe's ever-dependable man at arms had already seen that the whole right flank was crumbling and stepped across to intervene. "On me!" he yelled. "For King Harry! On me!"

With Hooper, stood the steadfast archer, Alain, until a blow from a mace smashed into his helm and felled him too. John blinked in disbelief: three of his most loyal men, including his cousin, badly wounded – or worse! From the start their task had been near impossible but now, stripped of several of their best men, John knew they were doomed.

Conal, who had toiled at John's side all day, darted away to help Hooper bolster their failing right flank and, backed up bravely by Will Twynho and Tom Audley, they actually succeeded in pushing the king's men back a yard or two, allowing two of the Bretons to drag the wounded men out from under everyone's boots.

For a moment, it seemed, both sides took a step back, pausing to take breath, but John knew their positon at the gate was now hopeless. Sir Walter's men would launch one more assault – and it would only take one. His bold endeavour was all but over.

60

7th November 1483, in the forest below Handfast Castle on Studland

The shadowy figure steadily hacked a path towards Eleanor through the hazel, and she knew she was in no condition to make a fight of it. She had no weapon and her much abused head was still weeping blood. Praying her Breton pirate might be nearby, Eleanor did the unthinkable: she screamed for help – or at least she tried to.

"René…"

By Christ, was that all she could muster? A pathetic whimper that a child could have bettered! When she cried out his name a second time, it only served to encourage the pursuing man at arms and he was almost upon her now. As she tried to move away, she muttered prayers to the Holy Virgin, knowing her pleas would fall upon deaf ears. She stopped rubbing her good eye and found, to her great relief, that her vision began to clear. Quickening her pace, she dared to hope again, but the bracken tugged and tore at her kirtle. Hearing him closer behind her, she knew there would be no escape this time.

"Why call my name when you keep running away from me?" shouted René.

Eleanor stopped, her heart suddenly pounding in her breast. She looked back at him and promptly fell over.

A muscled arm reached down to offer a hand and pull her to her feet. Coming up too fast, she felt faint, but René held her. She leaned against him, feeling his chest against hers, as she took several slow, deep and soothing breaths.

"It was you," she murmured. "Why didn't you say something, you fool?"

"You seemed frightened enough as it was…" he replied, gently wiping the blood from her face.

"I wasn't frightened," she told him, though that, of course, was a lie.

"Come," he said, "I'll take you back to the track."

Though she wanted to protest, she was too exhausted to care and instead allowed him to lift her up and carry her. Back to the track, back to the world of blood…

"What's happened?" she asked. "Did you get Roger Cayne?"

"No, he got away with two or three others," said René.

"I seem to have lost my weapon," she said, with a sigh.

"Probably safer without one!" he scolded, but then, relenting, he pressed the knife into her hand. "Try not to leave it behind next time…"

"Thank you," she said, praying there would not be a next time.

When he let her down onto the track where his men waited, their glum, impatient faces left her in no doubt about their feelings towards her. But she just scowled at them, for it wasn't the first time Eleanor was obliged to brazen out her behaviour amid a crowd of men.

"I think he's somewhere in the trees!" announced Cradoc.

"Then we should head straight to the castle!" urged Eleanor. "What are you waiting for?"

"We were waiting for René, lady," grumbled Cradoc. "Who was busy looking for you…"

"Aye, well he found me," said Eleanor, "so we can go!"

"Not you, my lady!" said René.

"Aye, me!" she snarled at him.

"You're still half-blind and a bit dazed!"

"I'll never be better than half-blind," retorted Eleanor, her eyes welling with bitter tears, "so it'll have to do, won't it?"

"But lady…"

He looked so distraught, she took his hand. "I've already lost a daughter, René. My boys are up there - they may already be dead, but I'll be damned if I won't try to help them! Stop worrying about me; if I fall, I fall. Now, move on!"

Cradoc and René exchanged a look of resignation and then led their men up the track as fast as they could. Eleanor, despite her desperation, was obliged to go more slowly. If she did not, she feared she might faint away. Her head still ached, and though the bleeding seemed to have stopped, it felt as if her whole scalp was on fire.

Even before they reached the edge of the forest, she could hear the familiar sounds of battle. It was not over then and, if her boys were still fighting, then the reinforcements might yet make a difference.

"Come on, lads!" urged Cradoc.

Watching René and Cradoc deploy their men as they passed through the ruined outer wall of Handfast Castle, she caught a glimpse of others, moving along the edge of the trees. She stopped in the lee of the wall to scan more carefully the fringes of the woodland. At first, she could see no-one. Had her lone eye misled her?

Hearing Cradoc and the rest cry out for King Harry, Eleanor was tempted to laugh, but instead she continued to survey the treeline. Only when the man moved, did she notice him and, by then, it was too late. The crossbowman loosed a bolt and she heard the cry of alarm almost at once. She searched in vain in case there was another but, remembering the ambush, she decided there might only be one of them. Further along the line of trees, she saw two more men emerge from the forest, but without crossbows.

The pair moved with caution but, even from distance, Eleanor recognised Roger Cayne. These fellows then were the sorry remnant of the mayor's locally-raised force.

Retrieving her knife from its sheath, she was about to move towards them when the crossbow was used again and another man cried out. Not René, she thought. Thank the Virgin! The callous thought hurtled into her mind before she could stop it. Though she was desperate to pursue Roger Cayne, she knew that, in all conscience, she must try to thwart the crossbowman first.

Looking across to the castle, she could see that there was a struggle in the gateway and bodies lying outside it, even she could not tell friend from foe. She hoped that René and his comrades could. But if René and Cradoc were forced to stop and search for the assassin with the bow, they could not go to her son's aid. The thought drove her forward, through the crumbling wall, which she used to shield her from the bowman's view, until she was opposite his position in the trees. He must still be reloading, she decided, so haste was paramount if she was to stop him before he loosed another deadly projectile.

Crouching beside the fallen stones, she paused, seeing him clearly now, concentrating on ratcheting his bow. Risking another glance behind her to the gate, she gave a sudden gasp. A cold hand pressed against her heart, as she saw Will propped against the wall outside the gate with several others – and none of them was moving. Shivering, she turned back to the crossbowman to discover that he was now only five yards away and raising his weapon once again.

"No!" she screamed, leaping up.

Desperate to stop him killing another man, she ran straight at him and could only watch as he, in panic, adjusted his aim to make her his target. But her course was set and, blade clenched in her hand, she would either gut him, or his bolt would hurl her back, stone dead, against the wall.

61

7th November 1483, in the afternoon before Handfast Castle

Facing the band of men massed around the towering figure of Sir Walter Nevil, John saw only the gleam of triumph in their eyes. Donning their helms once more and gripping their weapons more tightly, they were determined to put every last ounce of effort into their next assault, for they expected it to be their last.

John could see only one forlorn hope: if he could somehow kill the giant of a knight who commanded them, then perhaps he could break the resolve of the rest. If…

Glancing across at Conal and Hooper, he gave a shake of the head and the Irishman, at least, knew very well what his gesture meant. After a few short words with Hooper, Conal left him and made his way back to John's side.

"You won't even get to him!" he snarled at John.

"It's all I have left," murmured John.

"Could be worse, I suppose," said the Irishman.

"No, it couldn't!" said John, watching their opponents prepare to advance.

"It could!" insisted Conal. "At least we're not charging uphill! Because you always have us going up the sodding slope, never down."

"I'm sure that's not true…" said John, eyes fixed upon Sir Walter who, since he was by far the tallest man of them all, was hard to miss.

"It pissing is!" said Conal. "But then I like a good moan…"

"Aye, that's something I won't miss!"

The fiery Conal transferred his attention to the men who were advancing once more upon the gate. "You're grinning now, lads!" he cried out, pouring all his scorn upon them, "but soon you'll be crying out for your mothers!"

"If I don't make it," said John, "try to get Will to the ship, to his mother… any way you can…"

"Save your breath, lord," grumbled Conal. "If you go down, God knows, I'll already be dead!"

John focussed all his attention upon Sir Walter. How would this knight of undoubted power fare in the messy, bloody sort of combat in which both he and Conal excelled?

When the royal force struck, the thin line of defenders folded almost at once. With a final, anguished glance back in Hooper's direction, John allowed several attackers to sweep on by him. Then, with Conal protecting his right side, he concentrated his power ahead and to his left, where his target stood. Summoning up all his strength, he brandished both axes to devastating effect. Arms aching with the sheer muscle-tearing effort of it all, he delivered fearsome blows with every short pace he took, until he found himself facing two of Walter's knights, both armed with swords. In such a broken melee, a sword could once more be a lethal weapon, so he moved in close, forcing them to club at him with their sword hilts.

Slamming one of his heavy axes into the nearer of the two opponents, before the man was even down, he had to turn his attention to the other. Conal, anxious to support his lord, stabbed his thin blade through a narrow gap under his adversary's armpit. But then Conal, in turn, was caught off-guard and swore horribly as he took a deep cut to his left shoulder. Even so, such was the Irish warrior's mettle that he managed to skewer the offending assailant before dropping to his knees.

Having cracked the skull of his wounded opponent with a terrible blow from his pollaxe, John looked around for Sir Walter. The knight was close by and he was not alone. Even John's unyielding spirit wavered when he saw that he must face not only Sir Walter, but three more of his henchmen.

On the ground, a yard away, lay Conal, whose groans told him that there would be no help from that quarter. With a sigh, he stood tall to face his enemies, when he was astonished to hear, from outside the gate, several shouts of "King Harry! King Harry!" And, for the first time that day, he saw Sir Walter's knights hesitate.

Henry's men sounded close, John reckoned, though perhaps not close enough to save either him, or his comrades. All the same, their very presence put doubt in the minds of his opponents – and a scrap of doubt was all he needed. Arms running with blood, he bellowed at the ring of men who faced him.

"That's King Henry come to destroy you! If you yield now, you might yet save yourselves!"

In response, several of the knights lowered their weapons slightly, but Sir Walter did not.

As John took a step towards the doubtful knights, a wounded man at his feet lunged up with his sword towards John's groin. Though he turned the thrust aside with an axe, the blade sliced into his calf and, in a sudden rage, he plunged the pollaxe spike down through the man's skull.

Glowering at the rest of them, he yelled again: "Yield! Yield now, or, by God, I'll kill you all!"

Sir Walter glared back at him and, perhaps gaining confidence from the fact that none of Henry's men had yet appeared, decided to settle matters before they arrived. Hurling himself at John, he delivered several shuddering blows one after the other. Though he managed to block each one, John could feel the strength draining from him. A glance down at his leg told him that, though the wound would not kill him, it would severely hamper his movement against such a formidable opponent.

"Lord, if you hear this miserable sinner," murmured John. Then he broke off as Sir Walter charged at him again like a wild boar. "Oh, never mind, Lord…"

62

7th November 1483, early afternoon, before Handfast Castle

Eleanor's left shoulder was burning so hot that, when she looked at it, she expected to see flame searing her flesh. But what she saw was a great bloody hole in her flesh where the crossbow bolt had torn clean through her. The pain swept over her in waves.

Opposite her, still near the trees, stood the owner of the weapon which had punctured her shoulder – the same damned shoulder that one of his sodding comrades had already sliced through! To her surprise, he had not yet started to reload his bow and seemed somehow, downcast – beaten almost; yet she had never gotten close enough to even touch him.

Seeing her staring at him, he took a pace forward; at once, she scrabbled around in the long grass for her knife but could not locate it with the fingers of her right hand. Just moving caused further torment in her shoulder, but he kept coming towards her until he was only a yard away.

"I'm sorry, my lady," he said softly. "I didn't answer the call to arms to hurt a woman." Bending forward, he said: "I beg you to forgive me, if you please; I shall see that your wound is attended to."

Though her wound shrieked at her, Eleanor said nothing. She was moved by his plea, for this was no callow youth, but an older man – perhaps with a wife, or a daughter, here in Dorset.

"Eleanor!" roared a Breton voice from behind her. "Eleanor!"

The crossbowman, suddenly realising how vulnerable he was, began to back away.

"I forgive you!" cried Eleanor, though she knew it was too late for him.

The man's regret killed him, for René de Merckes swept past Eleanor and chopped his sword down upon the bowman. Wearing only a leather jerkin, the poor man was carved apart, through neck and chest, reduced to a quivering, bloody shape. There was no place for regret on the field of battle, thought Eleanor, only blood.

When René knelt down beside her to examine her wound, she was still looking at the fallen bowman, whose blood was steadily soaking into the grass. A sudden pain lanced through her shoulder as René's probing fingers brushed against the wound.

Seizing his hand, she pulled it away. "Don't ever be a surgeon!" she told him. "You have the touch of a bear!"

"You'll live!" he said.

"He was asking my forgiveness," she said, "the bowman…"

"He should have thought about that before he wounded you," was René's gruff response. "And killed two of my men!"

"Shouldn't you be somewhere else?" she cried "Helping my son and nephew?"

"Cradoc's there – and you needed my help."

"No, I didn't!"

"You're losing a lot of blood now," said René.

"Am I?" murmured Eleanor, struggling to concentrate on what René was saying.

Blood was a bitch, she thought. It really was. Since she turned fifteen, she had been condemned to walk along the banks of a long, unending river of blood. She feared for her very soul and, sitting there upon the bloody grass, she just wanted it all to stop.

When René picked her up, she smiled at him – at least she thought she did - unless she was dreaming. He was still talking to her, but she did not take in his words. Then René cursed and dropped her. Landing awkwardly on the grass, Eleanor was brought wide awake by the screaming torture in her left shoulder which had borne the impact of her fall.

"René!" she cried, outraged. "What are you-"

But René was lying beside her, blood seeping from a raw wound across his back.

Above them both stood Roger Cayne, his sword wet with blood.

"You didn't wait long to find another lover, did you?" he taunted her.

Turning to René, her eyes found his. He did not look dead yet, she thought, but she had no weapon, having carelessly tossed hers away when the crossbow bolt found her. She rolled over to take a closer look at him, only to cry out in agony as she crushed her ruined shoulder. Taking short breaths, she leant over René.

"You've killed him!" she cried. "You've killed him!"

"Good," replied Cayne. "One less mercenary to hang then!"

Examining her pirate's wound; she winced at the flesh laid bare to the bone.

"Your touch is better than mine," breathed René, his hand finding hers and drawing it to his belt.

Leaving him, Eleanor tried to get up on all fours but dizziness engulfed her and she was forced to give up. Instead she sat down, facing Roger Cayne.

"God damn you!" she bawled at him. "Help me up at least!"

"Help you up?" said Cayne. "I doubt you could even walk."

"I can walk if you give me your hand to get to my feet," she argued, "or are you just going to butcher a defenceless woman here where others might see?"

"Defenceless? I doubt that! Where is your knife, lady? I know you possess one."

"Somewhere over there, by your friend with the crossbow," she muttered.

So little did he trust her that he actually went across to recover the knife. Then for good measure he asked her to show him her hands, which she did.

"You're not very trusting, Master Mayor, are you?"

With a shrug, he extended his hand. "Life has taught me not to trust anyone – man or woman – and least of all, you!"

"Very wise, I'm sure," she agreed.

As he grasped her good arm, her left hand reached under the skirt where she had been sitting.

"But even if I did have a knife," she said, "I'd have to stab you with my poor, bloodied left hand, though I feel certain that all the agony would be worth it."

He didn't see it coming, but she hoped that he felt every last scrap of her rage and grief when she plunged René's long knife into him. He cried out, but her scream was far louder, as he tried to wrestle away her arm. She pushed the point of the blade as deep as she could, whilst he, in wild despair, wrapped his hands about her throat. Though she was choking, she still doggedly held the weapon there, thinking of Grave, of Simon… and René, as finally she felt her spirit ebb away and the pair of them fell locked in a deadly embrace.

63

7th November 1483, afternoon, at Handfast Castle on Studland

When faced by impossible odds, John's philosophy was always the same: attack. Though Sir Walter's initial onslaught had driven him back, he still held in his hands two great lumps of hardened steel. And, if it was God's will that he was to perish, then before he did, he would inflict as much damage to his adversary as he possibly could.

Hammering an axe at the knight's shoulder, he followed it with several ringing blows to his head and chest. Though his manoeuvre was a great success, John forgot to take account of his wounded leg. When he turned abruptly, he found himself unable to drive off his right leg. Off-balance, he lurched sideways and Sir Walter's powerful sword thrust only missed him by inches. Helpful though that happy accident was he knew that Sir Walter could not continue to be so unlucky.

What was worse, one or two other men, witnessing the tall knight's stubborn belligerence, were edging forward and looked set to re-join the fight. Unable to put his full weight on his wounded leg, John gave a great sigh and tore off his battered helm. Sir Walter, perhaps deciding to encourage his comrades with one final effort, raised his sword, holding it aloft with both hands in a high guard. John nodded, accepting the unspoken challenge, and staggered forward until he stood almost toe to toe with the great knight.

All his adversary had to do was crash his sword down upon John's bare head, but first he would have to withstand John's last desperate assault. With both axes whirling like the hammers of a demented blacksmith, John laid into Sir Walter before he could bring down his sword. Unable to evade the punishing pollaxes, Sir Walter dropped the sword as he was pounded down onto one knee. Though the knight's formidable armour was finely crafted, the sheer force of the blows was simply too great.

"By God!" he croaked, so crushed he seemed almost incapable of speech.

John too, could barely stand, utterly spent from the barrage of blows he had delivered. But renewed shouts of: "A Harry, a Harry! An Elder, an Elder!" echoed all around them – louder and closer this time. Men closed in to surround the remaining combatants, led by the indefatigable Hooper and many others that John did not recognise. Walter's comrades exchanged a few glances and then scattered. Some hurled down their weapons onto the cobbles, while others tried – but failed - to flee through the now crowded gateway.

Wheezing for breath as he tried to speak, John ordered Sir Walter to remove his helm. When he did, clearly devastated by the punishment he had absorbed, he saw the carnage among his knights and seemed to lose all appetite for the fight. Thus he remained upon his knees, shocked by the sudden reversal of his fortunes.

Bending down to Conal, John was relieved to find his friend still alive.

"You'll not shake me off that easily, lord," growled the Irishman.

"Lord Elder!" cried a man close by with a broad Welsh accent. "I'm Cradoc! A captain of the Earl of Pembroke! And there are more Bretons here too under René de Merckes. You are Lord Elder, I suppose?"

"Aye," nodded John, clasping the fellow's hand. "By Christ, we're glad to see you! I don't suppose you're the scouts for a landing?"

"Scouts? No, by God!" replied Cradoc. "We're the only landing there'll be here, my lord."

It was no surprise, for John already suspected as much.

"God's blood!" roared the Welsh captain, surveying the yard and gateway littered with so many bodies of both living and dead. "And I was told we'd land among friends!"

"Aye, me too," said John bitterly, looking down at the battered knight who had caused him so much trouble. "Sir Walter?"

The knight lifted his weary, disconsolate head. "Lord Elder…"

"Do you yield to me and give me your word, as a knight, not to try to escape?"

"I do," conceded Sir Walter, for there was no longer any fire in his eyes.

"Very well, then your wounds will be treated - as will those of your men."

Sir Walter nodded his assent and kept his head bowed.

"Lord Pembroke will demand any prisoners," declared Cradoc.

"What Lord Pembroke will demand does not matter, captain," said John, cutting him short, "because I command here. I'm obliged to you for your help, but the terms of Sir Walter's captivity are mine to decide – mine alone."

"Terms?" cried Cradoc, aghast.

"Aye, terms," affirmed John.

"But he's an enemy of the king!"

"Somehow, I don't think he would agree with you about that. Now, go and make your report to Lord Pembroke and King Henry. I've other matters to attend to."

Though Cradoc grunted in disgust, he argued no further.

John helped Conal to the gateway where Hooper and the other survivors were tending to the wounded.

"Where's Hal?" he asked Hooper.

"Gone off somewhere," replied Hooper.

"Gone off?" cried John. "I thought he was dying!"

"His arm will never be the same again, but he's alive," said Hooper.

"Well, in God's name, where would he go?"

"He seemed quite excited about something," said Hooper vaguely, "but I had others to see to…"

"Will?"

"He'll be walking crooked for a while, but you can see him for yourself. He's been asking after you."

John gave Hooper a grateful nod, clapping him on the shoulder. "Without you, we'd all be dead now…"

"Aye, well someone's got to keep an eye on you young fools."

John grinned back at him and went to find his cousin. Hal would no doubt turn up in his own good time.

64

8th November 1483, outside Handfast Castle

It was René's men, searching for their captain, who found Lady Eleanor. Hal, having his ruptured arm dressed, just happened to be the first of John's men they passed when they carried in their unconscious leader. When they told Hal that the lady was dead, the news came as a hammer blow. He refused to believe them; surely they must be mistaken, for how could they even know of Lady Eleanor when she was still aboard ship? After a moment's thought though, he recalled that earlier, when he was lying wounded, he imagined he heard a woman scream. If there was a chance, even the smallest chance, that it was truly her...

In halting English, the Bretons told him where to find her body. For a moment he considered fetching Will first, but then remembered that Lady Eleanor's son was barely able to walk. So, instead, Hal went alone and found her not very far away at all – lying on the far side of the ruined outer wall and thus obscured from sight at the gate.

It was a shock to find her lying in the arms of Mayor Cayne – not a place she would want to be, dead, or alive, he thought. Staring down at the pair, he noticed with a fierce pride that her bloody hand was still fastened upon the hilt of the knife which had gutted the mayor. By God, though, she looked terrible: one shoulder badly cut and with a black, ragged chasm punched through it; and her beautiful hair... matted with blood where her scalp had been sliced into. But, by Christ, it had taken a lot to kill his Lady Eleanor.

"You've surpassed yourself at the end, dear lady…" he murmured, choking back the tears. "But, by Christ, what will I tell Mary?"

"Tell her… to get her… fat arse up here," croaked Lady Eleanor. "Because I think I'm going to need her…"

"My lady!" cried Hal. "You're alive!"

Lady Eleanor opened her good eye and stared at the patch of blood on the ground beside her. "Where's René?" she gasped.

Hal responded with only a blank look. "Rene?"

"The Breton!" rasped Eleanor.

"Ah, yes; his men took him away."

"Alive, or dead?"

"I'm not rightly sure, my lady…"

He saw Lady Eleanor wince as she tried to extricate herself from the grasp of Roger Cayne and at once he rushed to help, trying to protect her ravaged shoulder as he did so. Raising his lady up, he was obliged to catch her as pain forced her back into unconsciousness. Though the raw wound in his arm opened up again, he lifted her up and carried her. And he would carry her until he dropped, for she was Lady Eleanor Elder, whom he loved like a sister.

65

9th November 1483 in the morning, at Handfast Castle

Since the previous afternoon, much had been revealed and much resolved. Wounded men had been helped as far as anyone was able. Some had returned to their various ships; others, such as John's own household men were recovering at the castle. Cradoc had reported to Henry of Richmond what had happened and the other captain, the badly injured René de Merckes, had been returned to his own ship.

When folk came up from Matthew's ship late in the afternoon they brought with them such devastating news that it was hard for John to take it all in. Despite his efforts to shield the women of the Elder household from danger, it seemed that all he had done was draw them further into the path of the storm.

That evening, and even now in the middle of the following morning, a sense of gloom lingered in the air. They had won at Handfast Castle, but it was the hollowest of victories and it could not mask their failure, nor the heavy price they had paid for it. After the hours of bloody struggle, he'd had hardly any time to reflect upon what he must do next. But, as with many other matters, he was finally learning to make the hard decisions… to be the leader his father would have wanted him to be.

The Dorset landing, of course, had been thwarted before it began, but the news from beyond Poole was also far from encouraging. The rebellion elsewhere - so dependent it seemed on the far from dependable Duke of

Buckingham - had faltered after his execution. John received the grave news with a good measure of stoicism. Perhaps, deep down, he had been expecting such an outcome. He had a feeling that perhaps Henry's cause might be all the stronger without Buckingham allied to it. The pact with Buckingham had, after all, been only a means to an end – an end which would now have to wait. Though he had not said as much to Isabel, John had to acknowledge that Henry might never achieve the kingdom he so coveted. If so, then John would not be returning to England for a very long time.

Henry, he gathered, was now worried that the king's fleet would trap him at Poole when news spread of his arrival and was desperate to set sail at once. Though he considered continuing along the south coast to Exeter, another centre of the revolt, his advisers dissuaded him. With only two ships and a handful of men, his attempt at invasion and conquest was over.

The remaining Dorset rebels, Twynho and the others, had left soon after peace was restored to the castle, anxious to protect themselves from the pursuit that would inevitably follow. There would be retribution against all those who had taken up arms against their king. Someone would have seen Tom Audley, John Cheverly and their friends at the castle; someone would tell the authorities for a fee – someone always did...

Then there had been the thorny problem of Sir Walter. Since all the others who had conspired to destroy John's family – Bess Fisher, Roger Cayne, Diggory Clynt and Elias Slade - were all dead, only Sir Walter remained. Cradoc told him that Henry of Richmond insisted that the knight be brought to his ship, but John risked his master's wrath by refusing. Henry was not pleased - and it seemed that the Earl of Pembroke was incandescent - but what could either of them do about it? In John's mind, since Henry was not actually king, Sir Walter was his prisoner and therefore his to dispose of however he pleased.

During the evening he sat down beside his captive in the tower chamber that looked out over the sea. Sir Walter greeted him with a puzzled look.

"What?" groaned John.

"I'm not sure where to start," murmured Sir Walter. "I still have a dagger in my belt, so I could just draw it out and kill you here."

"Aye," said John, "you could try, I suppose…"

"You think you're strong enough to stop me?" asked Sir Walter.

"Just now, probably not," admitted John, "but you won't do it anyway."

"Why not? You're a traitor to my king…"

"But you, Sir Walter Nevil, have given me your word. Like me, you'll fight like a street rat if you must, but you respect more than just the blade of a sword."

Sir Walter shrugged. "My damned head's still sore from the thrashing you gave it; I'm not sure I could even lift a dagger. So, what are to be your terms then?"

"The late Mayor of Poole was a base and dishonest fellow, but my aunt killed him, so I can demand little more penance from him. Elias Slade too has been slain – also, it seems, by my aunt."

"A formidable woman, your aunt," observed Sir Walter.

"Aye, it's been said," muttered John, "and rather too many times for my liking…"

"So, your terms?" prompted Sir Walter.

"I'll keep you here till I leave then you'll be released."

"Released? Truly?" Sir Walter looked astonished. "But why?"

"I can't keep you prisoner. Either I hand you over to Pembroke, execute you, or let you go. I'm not executing anyone – enough good men have died here already. I don't much care for Lord Pembroke, so he's not having you. So, as I said, when I go, you go. In return you will give me your word that you will not pursue my aunt, nor those other female relatives of mine who now seek to remain in England at peace."

"Even though I might respect such a promise, you know I cannot speak for Master Catesby," said Sir Walter.

"I know, but you could help persuade him that these women have suffered more than enough loss, Sir Walter. It was I who brought this treason about, not my relatives."

Sir Walter inclined his head. "Very well," he agreed. "I shall repay your honour to me with a solemn promise that I will do whatever I can for your family."

◠◠◠◠◠◠

It was approaching midday and, within the next hour, the dead would be taken into Studland village for burial and the preparations for departure would begin in earnest. Very soon, the would-be king would sail away and John had no choice but to leave with him; all that remained to be resolved was who would be sailing with him. And, of course, there was his Aunt Eleanor…

Head and shoulder bound up, she had insisted upon getting out of her bed to accompany him in a slow and careful walk around the cobbled yard. Clinging onto his arm, she seemed a frail thing to him at that moment and he wondered if she would ever be the force she once had been.

"You look terrible, aunt!" he told her, when at last he persuaded her to sit down on a bench in the castle yard.

Pulling a face, she growled: "So do you! We are a pair, aren't we, John? I sometimes think we're both cursed… We have both lost so many who were dear to us. I thought - after your father - that would be it; that the family could look forward to years of peace. But the wheel has turned and the loss just seems to go on and on…"

441

"Evil men, aunt, caused all those deaths, not a curse..."

Gazing across the yard, she lowered her voice, almost to a whisper. "All the same, John, I want no more blood upon my hands. I've had enough and I've made a promise to myself: no more bloodshed..."

"Was that before, or after, you killed Mayor Cayne?" asked John.

Her answer was a determined glare and somehow, even though she was at such a low ebb, she seemed, just for an instant, as fierce and full of life as ever. Her cap, disguising the carnage on her head, was set just above her bruised face and the grubby brown leather patch still covered one eye, but the other bright, green gemstone sparkled back at him with all its customary fire. How could he have doubted her?

"I shall take the lasses to Ludlow," she told him, "but, until your position is settled, I think it would be best if you kept well away from there, don't you?"

"Aye, aunt, I understand... though Meg's my sister-"

"Half-sister," corrected Eleanor, "and by God, she's the better half too – and better off away from you!"

"Perhaps, but-"

"It's no good, John," she said. "This family must see no more of its women die – God's breath, my Kate must be the last of them... you must see that!"

"Aye, aunt," he conceded, "of course I do."

"And Isabel must come with us," said Eleanor.

The thought of losing her wounded him beyond words. In vain, he sought an argument to keep her with him, but could find none - save love.

"Aye, I know that too, aunt," he said. "A rebel camp in Brittany is no place for her."

"Good," she said. "Then it's agreed. Matthew Finch will take us to Bristol and we'll make our way thence to

Ludlow. Pray God we can all find some peace there. Now help me up."

66

9th November 1483 in the early afternoon, at Handfast Castle

All was quiet now in the castle yard and in the adjacent keep. For a few more hours, the ravaged castle had been busy… noisy with the sounds of anxious voices. Men came and went. Carts came and went. Sir Walter Nevil too had been despatched on his way and now it was time for the rest of them to leave for other men would come, as word spread. The king's men would come to seek out the guilty.

John, his leg newly-dressed and bound with clean cloth, sat with Isabel in the chamber where Sir Simon Cayne had breathed his last.

"Everyone said our love was doomed," she said, "from the start. What hope is there now for us, if we can't even live in the same land?"

"You cannot go where I'm going! There's nothing certain about the life I'll have now."

"But God knows we've already spoken the words to each other! We're as married as any pair in all Christendom!"

"Perhaps, but you can't wander with me from one place to the next, never knowing if it will be your last resting place. And a good wife obeys her husband…"

"But-"

He shook his head. "No, Isabel, no! You can't come with me, nor can you go with your mother – for I doubt even she knows where she's going next! You will go with Aunt Eleanor and know that, when this madness is over, I will come for you. I may have sworn an oath to Henry

444

Tudor, but I swear another here… now… to you. I swear that I will come back… and we shall be together. I swear it, Isabel, I swear it!"

Fingers intertwined and eyes locked upon each other, they kissed in a long farewell embrace. Neither wanted it to end, but John pulled away from her, took her hand and pressed his lips to it.

"Stay safe with my aunt and my sister in Ludlow."

"It will seem like forever…" she murmured.

"Aye, it will seem so – but it will not be… forever. Now, go and prepare yourself for the journey - your mother and Aunt Ellie are waiting to see me."

Watching her go tore him apart, but it had to be thus. He had tried a different path before and it did not end well for anyone. He would not make the same mistake again.

When his aunts came into the chamber, he told them what he had agreed with Sir Walter.

"You've let him go?" hissed Lady Radcliffe, "Who knows what he may have overheard in the castle?"

"He'll know where the Margaret is sailing to – and who will be aboard," said John.

"Aye," murmured Eleanor, "but he knows that those of us sailing on the Margaret have broken no laws – we were merely shipwrecked and then mistreated by the Mayor of Poole."

"But if Sir Walter is Catesby's man," said Lady Radcliffe, "he'll report everything to his master."

"Since I was always going back to Ludlow, sister," said Eleanor, "it was never going to be a secret, was it? If Catesby wanted to, he could find me there easily enough."

"Aye," said John, "and Sir Walter is now in my debt."

"Perhaps he is, but he may decide that you can't be in debt to an outlaw," Lady Radcliffe pointed out.

"He'll not make war upon the women of this household," John assured them. "Catesby will act as he pleases, but I believe Sir Walter will do all he can to protect you in Ludlow. And, if I stay away, then Catesby will find no grounds to act against you."

"That may work for those in Ludlow," said Lady Radcliffe, "but it won't protect me. Catesby will hunt me down."

"Then lie low!" urged John. "You don't need to be involved anymore."

"I assure you that I shall be very much involved – doing all I can to help Henry Tudor take the throne of England!" declared Lady Radcliffe. "Because when he does, I shall see Master Catesby fall. Then at least, it won't seem as if my husband and son died for nothing!"

"Then you are a brave lady, Aunt Emma," he said.

"Not brave, John, just persistent. But you're certain that Sir Walter didn't learn of my involvement?"

"He did not, aunt, I assure you," replied John. "He knows nothing about you; he's never even seen you. You are quite safe… as long as you are still under Lady Stanley's protection…"

"If I am not, then I doubt I shall be seeing either of you again! If Catesby has any evidence of my involvement here, he will drag me away whether Lady Stanley protests about it, or not. After this disaster, her protection might well be limited. She may be Lord Thomas Stanley's wife, but I suspect the king will be ordering Lord Stanley to keep his wife under much closer control in future!"

There was a knock at the door and Hal came in.

"How's the arm?" asked John.

"Very good, lord – unless of course I wanted to be an archer."

Though his reply was accompanied by a smile, it fooled none of them. Hal's torn arm muscles would never again draw a bow and the life for which he had trained with John's father was gone forever.

"Well, you won't need your bow in Ludlow, Hal," said Eleanor. "You're going to have a new wife to care for — and, by God, you'd better care for her!"

"Yeh, lady. That's more than enough change for any man to cope with…"

"But I shall be right glad to have you with me again, Hal," said Eleanor.

"I came to tell you, lord that Master Finch needs to sail very soon," reported Hal, "and Master Hooper awaits Lady Radcliffe - when she's ready. Oh, and the Earl of Pembroke threatens to sail without you!"

"Very well," said John, firmly clasping his loyal man's undamaged hand. "I've no idea how I'll survive without you, Hal, but I can think of no other man in all Christendom to whom I'd rather entrust the safety of the ladies of this house."

"I'll keep them safe for you, lord, though half of me would sooner be with you…"

"Aye, but half a man would do me no good - and they need you."

When Hal went out John thought there might have been a tear in the man's eye; they had shared much: he and Hal.

As his aunts embraced in farewell, it struck him that something had changed there too: a tenderness had grown up between them that he had never before witnessed.

Lady Radcliffe gave him a swift kiss upon the cheek and walked out with the rather ominous words: "I expect you'll see me again soon enough, nephew…"

Gently embracing his Aunt Eleanor, he said: "You'll need to rest on the ship, but you have the lasses to look after you…"

"By the Virgin, it's more likely that Meg will be looking after all of us, though it appears I've lost one of them already. That Flemish lass, Eva has, it seems, decided to go with Will to Brittany – to tend his leg she said, though I suspect her duties will extend a little further."

"One less girl can only help your sanity, aunt!" grinned John.

Eleanor looked him in the eye. "First: do not get my son killed," she told him. "And second: do not get yourself killed. Oh, and since I now owe René de Merckes a life, you'd better look out for him too…"

"Does René know where you're going?" he asked.

"He may do," she murmured, "though I doubt we'll ever meet again - and what is he to me, in any case? Just some rough pirate…"

Having planted a final kiss on his cheek, Eleanor walked out of the chamber without a backward look.

67

11ᵗʰ November 1483, in Catesby's chambers in London

Catesby observed Walter Nevil as he shifted uncomfortably under the lawyer's stare.

"Hardly a great success…" said Catesby.

"No, Master Catesby."

"Much blood spilled, to little purpose."

"Indeed."

"Perhaps you did not play your part well enough?" suggested Catesby.

"I did all that you asked – and more."

Catesby found it embarrassing to watch the large man whining his excuses.

"So you claim. How is it then that the very man you were there to support, the Mayor of Poole – a loyal subject of his grace – was butchered to death? And you had Lord Elder at your mercy, yet somehow, he managed to defeat you!"

"Master Catesby, if he had been at my mercy," replied Walter, "he would now be dead."

"Yes, but he isn't dead, is he? By God, man, by your own admission, you had him bottled up in the castle and still he managed to escape!"

"He is a formidable opponent," pleaded Walter.

"And what of the greater prize? The Earl of Richmond was there but you didn't even get close to him!"

"He never landed there himself – just sent his dogs of war…"

"So, despite the considerable cost to the crown of outfitting your men - and paying for some of their weapons and horses – it seems we have gained nothing! God only knows why the young bastard let you go! He could have spared me the trouble of having to pick through the bones of this sorry carcass with you!"

Catesby gave a mighty groan of frustration. "And what of Lady Eleanor Elder?"

"It seems she was merely shipwrecked on the Dorset coast," said Walter.

"Yes, Walter, but shipwrecked on her way to meet her traitorous nephew!" declared Catesby.

"I don't think Lady Eleanor had anything to do with the revolt. Afterwards she vowed that she did not want to see her nephew again."

"And why would I believe a word that foul woman says?"

"It seemed genuine to me."

"Of course it did, Walter, but then you are fool; I'm not. Do you know where Lady Eleanor is going?"

"Yes sir, I do: Ludlow, by way of Bristol."

"Ludlow? Are you sure?" Catesby was surprised because Ludlow was not a surprise at all.

"Certain," affirmed Walter.

"There are only a handful of places I might look if I wanted to find Lady Eleanor," mused Catesby, "but one of the first would certainly be Ludlow. So, why would she go there?"

"I got the feeling that the women just wanted to go home."

"Oh, did you, Walter? Well, spare me your feelings! I didn't send you to Dorset to piss about and tell me about your sodding feelings! Your task was to bring me John Elder in chains, or in pieces! Instead you feed me a load of horse shit about feelings! By God, at least I knew where I was with Bess Fisher!"

"Hah!" cried Walter. "Bess Fisher was one reason I failed – she killed one of the loyal captains herself!"

"Loyal?" Catesby gave a bitter laugh. "The only thing those pirates and thieves are loyal to is profit. They certainly don't care a toss who rules the land!"

"Master Catesby, does this mean I will lose... my knighthood?" he asked.

"Hah! In order for you to lose it, Walter, it would have to have been conferred on you in the first place," replied Catesby. "You never had a knighthood, you dolt, just a letter that told Mayor Cayne that you had one!"

"But you told me I did!"

"I'm a lawyer, Walter. I told you a pack of lies. Never mind a knighthood; you're lucky to still have your head! I work for my master, the king, not you. Now get out and don't come back! "

"But-"

"If you value your life, get out now!" shouted Catesby.

He waited for the heavy door to close behind the departing Walter and then heaved a sigh. The Elders still contrived to get under his skin. Always they were there, within his grasp, only to slip away and that's what gnawed at him. But next time he would be certain and, one by one, he would destroy them all for their traitorous meddling. Let Lady Eleanor and the others scuttle away to Ludlow, for he would have a man watching; and when that vile woman revealed her true cause, he would bury her with it.

But first he must pursue Lady Radcliffe, who had proved far more elusive. The whispers that she had been spirited out of London by Lady Stanley had never been confirmed, but it smelt right – one traitor does ever beget other traitors. Well, now she must be hunted down, for when John Elder returned to England – as Catesby was certain he would – he must have no allies left. None at all.

○○○○○○ ○○○○○○ ○○○○○○

Historical Notes

PLACES:

Poole

In the fifteenth century, the town of Poole was gradually taking over from nearby Wareham as the principal port of the area. Poole's large natural harbour not only provided a safe anchorage for merchant ships but also became a haven for an increasing number of pirates and smugglers. By 1483, Poole was a growing town in danger of outstripping its boundaries and its prosperity was further boosted by a major annual fair held in the week following All Souls Day.

The shape of the modern town is much altered from the 1480s – so much so, that any attempt at mapping or reconstructing what it might have looked can only be achieved by guesswork based on the few, rather sketchy maps from centuries ago. After much land reclamation, it is very difficult to imagine the town almost completely surrounded by water.

You can still see the King's Wool House which now serves as the town's museum – and is well worth a visit! Close by, is a house called Scaplen's Court – open to the public in August. In the book, I have used a fifteenth century version of this building as the house of the fictional Mayor Cayne.

The church of St James in the 1480s was located on the same plot of land where the present building stands, but it was a much smaller, possibly wooden, building and very likely in a poor state of repair.

The area still known as Baiter was, in the 1480s, a rather unpleasant, swamp-infested area – as described in the book. It was a dumping ground and burial ground which lay outside the town ditch and was accessible by water only at high tide. It would have attracted the criminals and the unfortunates in equal measure.

There was a quay in the 1480s, though much, much smaller than the one there today. Wooden jetties would have thrust out into the harbour to the west and east of the quay to provide places to offload smaller boats when the tide was lower. At very low tide, many parts of the shoreline would simply be mud.

Handfast Point

Handfast Point is a headland on the Isle of Purbeck in Dorset known nowadays as Old Harry Rocks. Centuries of erosion have reduced the land area of the headland and that process still continues today. Caves were sculpted into the chalk at times and one of these is used in the book. In medieval times it seems certain there was a castle of some sort on the point which most likely fell into disrepair during the fourteenth and fifteenth centuries. It was replaced in the Tudor period by a new structure but the castle which provides a key setting for this story in 1483 is the original decaying, early medieval castle.

Studland Bay

Studland Bay, near the entrance to Poole Harbour, was a safe anchorage for ships and provided some protection from the strong south-westerly winds. The village of Studland and its church of St Nicholas existed in the 1480s but the shoreline of the bay would have been very different from today. Along the coast the shallow waters were ideal for salt pans and the area of enclosed water known as the Little Sea was simply part of the coastline in those days.

There was very little in the way of extensive sand spits and the sand bars which we see today. Ships were wrecked from time to time on the Dorset coast and the conditions described in the book – storms, rocks, shallows, tides, races, etc are as accurate as I could make them.

Sluys

Sluys [now Sluis] lies just across the present day Dutch border from Belgium. It is a delightful town but has suffered from its position, being heavily destroyed in both World Wars - not to mention in previous centuries. During the fifteenth century Sluys became the port on the River Zwin through which trade from the Flemish city of Bruges passed. But by the 1480s Sluys was already in decline as the River Zwin continued to silt up. The Black Ship is a fictional tavern but there would have been similar places in the narrow streets amid crowded housing wedged against the warehouses and boatyards of the port.

Chateau L'Hermine in Vannes

Henry Tudor lived in a number of places whilst in exile under the protection of Duke Francis of Brittany. On the eve of his attempt to take the English throne in the autumn of 1483, he was staying in the Chateau L'Hermine in Vannes.

PEOPLE:

Richard, Duke of Gloucester

Though Richard does not actually appear in this book, I feel he needs a mention since much is done in his name! It is difficult to find any English historical figure who has divided opinion as much as Richard III. This is not the place to explore the arguments which are well rehearsed – repeatedly – elsewhere. However, it is only fair to spell out to the reader, in case I have left any doubt, how I regard Richard.

I see Richard as a confident man who believed in his abilities and proved himself time and time again during the reign of his elder brother. This self-belief, I would suggest, lay at the root of both his undoubted achievements and his fatal flaws.

When Edward IV died, Richard saw himself as the man to lead the country through the coming minority of his nephew, Edward. Many others agreed for he was clearly the most powerful nobleman and he commanded respect from the majority of his peers. He envisaged, I think, an awkward period in the first few months of the new reign. This was not because he had any personal animosity towards Queen Elizabeth because – contrary to what is said far too frequently - there is little evidence that he did!

Richard, however, had doubts about the extent to which he would be able to shape the new king's views. So, rather like his father, he decided to take bold action and he may well have been influenced in his approach by the rather panicky letters of Lord Hastings – who did have a personal axe to grind against at least one of the queen's family.

I don't buy the idea that Richard was some monster who intended from the outset to seize the throne. Nevertheless, unable to control the young king's will, Richard decided he had no choice but to take the throne himself. The rumours which circulated in England and elsewhere in the summer of 1483 that Edward IV's two sons were dead hurt Richard's regime and provided some support – though limited and fragmented - for Henry Tudor.

Henry Tudor, Earl of Richmond

It would be difficult to describe Henry as a popular figure in history for he is often portrayed as a pretty miserable individual. Yet, given the difficult experiences of his childhood, it is perhaps not that surprising that he grew into a man who found it hard to trust anyone. In this story, Henry has been in exile for some years and it was never really expected by anyone – including, I suspect, even his loyal mother – that he would ever become king. The peculiar circumstances of 1483 gave him a chance of doing so, but the revolts of that year did not put him on the throne and it seemed that his one chance had gone.

Lady Margaret Stanley

As the wife of the influential Lord Thomas Stanley, Margaret (née Beaufort) was very much at the centre of politics in 1483. Despite the fact that her exiled son, Henry Tudor, possessed the last vestige of a Lancastrian claim to the throne, she managed to keep her powder as dry as dust. Because of her position and her links with just about everyone who mattered in 1483, she is often seen as some spider-like mastermind quietly making everything happen as she wanted.

In reality, I believe, she wanted what most mothers did: to see her son again. To achieve that end she had spent hours trying to persuade Edward IV to allow Henry to return – and it may well have happened. Of course, the death of Edward IV and the subsequent removal of his sons changed the whole political landscape of England and Margaret was well-placed to exploit that change. Hence, she began to communicate with those who were unhappy with the new king.

Jasper Tudor, Earl of Pembroke

Jasper Tudor was a Lancastrian die-hard. He was Henry's uncle who had been a faithful servant of the House of Lancaster and was fiercely loyal to young Henry. Without Jasper's determination to protect his nephew, I doubt the boy would have survived. Jasper himself had been heavily defeated by Edward IV at Mortimer's Cross in 1461 after which his father, Owen, had been executed. If he had a somewhat blinkered view of anyone who might be a Yorkist, it is perhaps quite understandable.

William Catesby

William Catesby was a lawyer who rose to prominence under Richard III and became very closely associated with Richard's government. In this book, he is very much one of the villains - presented as ambitious and ruthless. This is, I believe, a pretty accurate assessment for he certainly amassed a great deal of reward for his support of Richard's bid for power and achieved a lofty status during the ill-fated reign. One could argue that he was no more acquisitive than the likes of Buckingham or Stanley, but I see him as less scrupulous than even those two nimble nobles. Whilst he is thwarted in this story, the reader has not yet heard the last of William Catesby, for he will return!

The rebels of 1483

What I hoped to convey was an atmosphere in the autumn of 1483 that was full of doubt, suspicion and fear. In that context, most folk – even those close to the centre of power – were not sure what was happening or why, especially during the autumn revolts.

The man, whose name is most often associated with these abortive revolts in the autumn of 1483, is Henry Stafford, Duke of Buckingham. Buckingham had supported Richard III's seizure of the throne, but by September – for reasons which are not very clear – he decided to rebel against Richard. His part in the revolt was dogged by bad luck, bad weather and incompetence. Other revolts in Kent and Exeter gathered a little more support, but I have chosen to focus on one of the less prominent areas: Dorset.

There were rebels in Dorset and I have named four of those listed in the original sources: **Richard Morton, Thomas Audley, John Cheverell & William Twynho**. Placing them where I have – on Studland – is entirely my own invention – as are the Cayne brothers, of course. Though Poole was certainly a possible landing place for Henry's invasion, it appears from the limited evidence we have, that there was little enthusiasm for him there. Henry Tudor did sail to Poole and there is some suggestion of an abortive landing there, but the rest of my story is fiction.

Derek Birks
May 2019

Author's Note

Thank you for reading **Echoes of Treason** and I hope you enjoyed it.

How accurately does it represent life in the period of the Wars of the Roses?

John Elder is not entirely typical of his class and time, because while most of his peers would have been trying to build up their family by astute marriages and the acquisition of lands, John always rather hoped to break away from his inheritance. As always though, I've tried to present him as the head of more than just a family. His affinity embraces the servants in his household, the archers and men at arms who fight and sometimes die for him. Such ties held fifteenth century society together in a way that is difficult to comprehend today.

The relationship between John's young half-sister, Meg and the London guttersnipe, Thomas Skirett, is introduced in the previous book, **The Blood of Princes**, and highlights the problems of a gulf in social class. For the modern reader it also raises another issue – Meg's young age. Though child betrothals and even marriages were common enough in the later Middle Ages, they were rarely consummated until the individuals were mature enough to do so. There were notable exceptions – such as Margaret Beaufort herself – but it was unusual. The argument put forward by Meg herself is that her experience and maturity proved she was indeed old enough.

In a similar – though also radically different – way, John's liaison with his first cousin, Isabel [formerly known as Alice Radcliffe] causes some outrage in the family. The church forbade such relationships – unless of course you could afford to pay for a dispensation from the Pope to allow it! In practice, and especially for ordinary folk, few cases were brought to church courts for this particular 'crime' and often when someone had an ulterior motive for preventing the marriage. The Elders have always bucked the social trends and part of their attraction is – I hope – their willingness to take a risk!

So at the end of this story we leave the Elders apart again, but perhaps with a little more certainty in their lives. John will follow Henry Tudor back to Brittany in the hope of a return to England, while Eleanor will go to Ludlow and be a mother hen to the younger members of the family. Her sister, Emma Radcliffe, will continue to assist her mentor, Lady Margaret Beaufort, in an attempt to oust Richard III – and William Catesby will do everything in his power to thwart them all.

Will John and Isabel end up together again? What chaos will Meg cause in Ludlow? Will Eleanor and Emma ever find some peace?

Whatever does happen, you can be sure that the Elders will be in the thick of the action and intrigue.

If you have enjoyed my work then you might like to give it a favourable mention either in the shape of an **Amazon** or **Goodreads** review.

As an independent writer, I must market my own work and one thing that helps me enormously is the response from readers. Please feel free to get in touch by using the contact form on my website and sign up to my newsletter to find out what I am up to.

Many thanks.

Derek Birks
May 2019

About the Author

Derek was born in Hampshire in England but spent his teenage years in Auckland, New Zealand, where he still has strong family ties.

For many years he taught history in a secondary school in Berkshire but took early retirement several years ago to concentrate on his writing. Apart from writing, he spends his time gardening, travelling, walking and taking part in archaeological digs.

Derek is interested in a wide range of historical themes but his particular favourite is the late medieval period. He writes action-packed fiction which is rooted in accurate history.

His debut historical novel, **Feud,** is set in the period of the Wars of the Roses and is the first of a series entitled **Rebels & Brothers** which follows the fortunes of the fictional Elder family.

To find out more about his books, or to contact him, you can go to his website: www.derekbirks.com. You can also follow him on Twitter **as** @Feud_writer and on Instagram. His author page on Facebook is: www.facebook.com/feudwriter.

Derek has also produced a series of short non-fiction podcasts for those who are interested in the period of the Wars of the Roses. These can be accessed from his website or from other podcast providers such as i-Tunes.

Rebels and Brothers

If you have not already done so, you might like to take a look at the previous series, ***Rebels and Brothers***. These four books, starting with ***Feud,*** tell the story of John's father, Ned, and his sisters, Eleanor and Emma. Their story begins at the start of the Wars of the Roses in 1459 and the series finishes just after the victory of the Yorkist King, Edward IV, in May 1471 at Tewkesbury.

It is 1459. England stands on the brink of chaos and as the Wars of the Roses begin, the rule of law breaks down...

Whilst York and Lancaster go to war for the throne, in the heart of Yorkshire the Radcliffe family have an old score to settle with their neighbours, the Elders.

When the feud breaks out Ned Elder is a young, untried knight. With his father executed, his older brother butchered and his two sisters roughly abducted, it seems that Ned is the family's last hope of survival. Yet he barely escapes with his life and is pursued across the land with only a few loyal companions. To defeat the Lancastrian Radcliffes, Ned must join the civil war on the side of York, but victory seems a long way off.

Imprisoned in a remote nunnery, his wild and rebellious sister, Eleanor, has not given up - but can she find the strength to fight back? The fate of the Elders will hang as much upon the courage of Ned's sisters as his own skill with a sword.

As the civil war rages across the snow-covered battlefield of Towton, the Elders fight for survival and the bitter feud is played out to its bloody conclusion.

'From the eye-catching cover to the last page, Feud is an exciting story of survival through personal upheaval during a vicious war, where the outcome is not always certain.'

Historical Novel Society

Find **Feud** on:
Amazon UK: https://amzn.to/2Qtpjda
Amazon US: https://amzn.to/2Us6A3X

9 781910 944332